Torian Tales Series

Heart of the Siren
(Book 1 of A Siren's Tale)

The Head, the Heart, and the Heir Series

The Spare Who Became the Heir and Other Stories
The Head, the Heart, and the Heir
Broken Sons
The Heir Rises
The Last True Heirs
Revenge of the Forbidden Lands
Fight of the Fury
The Last Spell

Extended Omnibus Books
Volume 1
Volume 2
Volume 3

Heart of the Siren

A Siren's Tale

Alice Hanov

Gryphon
Press

Heart of the Siren

**Gryphon
Press**

Published by Gryphon Press
Waterloo, Ontario

Copyright © 2025 by Alice Hanov

All rights reserved. No part of this book may be reproduced, scanned, or distributed in any printed or electronic form without the prior written permission of the copyright owner. To request permission, visit alicehanov.com.

Ebook: 978-1-998835-36-2
Amazon Paperback: 978-1-998835-47-8
Paperback: 978-1-998835-37-9
Hardcover: 978-1-998835-38-6

Edited by Grim House Publishing LLC, Jasmine McKie (@Faye_Reads), and Jahmayla Nichole Pointer.
Cover design by Blue Raven Cover Design.

Dedicated to all the readers who wondered why the prince always saves the girl.

Torian
N
Nordlic Sea
Oreean Sea
Forbidden Lands
Anginfill Territory
Zverm Forest
Kingdom of Betruger
Moorloc's Castle
Ogre Mountains
Verlassen Castle
Kingdom of Datten
Dark Forest
Dark Forest
Kingdom of Warren
Nordlic Sea
Black River
Huestur Territory
Oreean Sea
Sigil Territory
Tacita's Peaks
Crimson Mountains
Hessen
Darren
Konvern Territory
Orcane
Southern Kingdoms
Forest of Endilaus
Fans
Madras
Bearen
Sieden Sea
Kingdom of Tyndorf
Sieden Sea

N
Nordlic Sea
Nordlic Sea
Sieden Sea
Tori
Anginfill Territory
Zverm Forest
Bloot River
Huestur Territory
Sigil Territory
Konvern Territory
Crimson Mountains
Forest of Endilaus
Kingdom of Tyndorf
Sieden

ian
Forbidden Lands
Oreean Sea
Kingdom of Betruger
Moorloc's Castle
Ogre Mountains
Verlassen Castle
Kingdom of Datten
Dark Forest
Dark Forest
Kingdom of Warren
Oreean Sea
Tacita's Peaks
Hessen
Darren
Oreane
Southern Kingdoms
Fans
Madras
Bearen
Sea

Author's Note

Welcome to the first book of my new Torian Tales saga. I adore each and every one of my readers, and want you all to be safe. Below is a list of potential trigger issues that will be in this book. This list does not include all of them, but it has those I could think to include. If you think there should be additional things on this list after you read the book please reach out to me and I will add them to the list on my website, at AliceHanov.com

- Abusive parent
- SA in past and on page
- Dubious consent
- Violence and Murder
- Mutilation of Men
- Cliffhanger
- HEA comes in book 2 not 1

Chapter 1

Elva

His calloused hands roamed along my chest, proving he did not know what breasts were for. How was my sense of smell so off lately? For the fifth time, I grabbed his hand and guided him back to my nipple, but he bypassed them and grabbed my hair instead. *What the hell?* "You know, for a man who was oozing bravado at the bar, you're acting as inexperienced as a maiden on her wedding night."

"You feel like heaven," he slurred, not even listening to me.

I rolled my eyes. In a bar of willing men, how did I end up with this drunk, bumbling idiot? *That's the last time I listen to Leifur.* I could've used my song and made him do what I wanted, but I'd vowed never to use that power to get a man into bed. Not after what was done to me.

A sharp hiss escaped me as the oaf pulled my hair. The last thing I need is for him to notice a flash of color in the dim lighting, see my blue and green streaks, and fall into a drunken panic. I'm not ashamed of being half-Siren, half-Selkie, but hiding my colored tresses in a braid is just good sense. While selkies are mysterious, everyone on this side of Torian knows exactly what sirens are capable of.

"Sorry," he grunted, and went back to failing miserably at his task of doing something to arouse me.

If he didn't figure out how to get my shirt off in the next minute, I'd let my siren take over and deal with him. It has been nearly three weeks, and all I wanted tonight was a quick, rough ride before we head out of town.

Out of patience, I grabbed his hair and brought his mouth back to mine. Taking control, I pulled him off the wall and walked him toward the bed. As he tried to protest, I turned my face from the kiss. "Hold your tongue and take off your pants."

The man unbuckled his pants so recklessly that he tripped over the corner of the bed I'd been leading him to. Groaning, I rubbed my forehead, just as the door flew open.

"Elva, we have to go. Now!"

I glared at my brother-in-law. "Leifur, get out. I'm busy."

Leifur's claws extended from his fingertips as he gripped the doorframe. "No, Elva. You have to come. It's Sindri."

"Poseidon, help me," I groaned. "What has my brother done now?"

I left the useless man still sprawled on the floor with his pants around his ankles, grabbed my bag from the table, and chased Leifur down the rickety stairs of the inn and out the back door. Immediately, I heard shouting—a commotion coming from the town square.

"What did he do?"

Liefer's blue-grayish skin glistened with sweat. "He ... uh ... he picked the mayor's mother."

"Idiot. How many times have we told him if he's going to seduce an old widow, it needs to be someone nobody cares about?"

"It doesn't matter right now! We need to help him."

I quickened my pace with Leifur a step behind me. At the edge of the alley, I slowed and peeked around the corner of the inn. Sindri was standing in the open town square holding his hands up in front of his chest in a semblance of surrender. My brother's wickedly charismatic smirk was plastered across his face, but when his mismatched blue and green eyes locked on mine, I knew he was in over his head.

I've always been the strong one—a warrior siren to my twin's sultry siren. He could win over any woman with little more than a smile, but men were another story. Despite preferring the company of men, his siren abilities only worked on women, so he used his charms to convince the wealthiest widows in each town to lavish us with gifts—everything from jewels and clothes, to food and rooms at the inn, and occasionally something larger, like a horse. His skills kept us fed and comfortable on our travels.

Leifur elbowed me and nodded toward the stallion standing behind my brother. "Seems we should have taken his threat seriously. But I never expected him to actually find a horse, so he wouldn't have to walk anymore."

I rolled my eyes and went back to sizing up the men who had it in for my foolish brother. There were ten of them, just over the limit of what my siren could handle. Warrior sirens were made to fight, and our powers of seduction weakened quickly when more than two or three men were involved.

"I know you don't like using your siren song, Elva, but—"

"It's fine. I'll create a distraction to draw them away. You just get Sindri out."

Leifur nodded and tugged at the ends of my braid. Once loosened, my hair cascaded around my shoulders. "Distractions work better when they know what they're dealing with," he said.

I inhaled sharply and, before I could change my mind, I ran into the square, unleashing my siren. I felt my eyes shift to black, and my teeth extend into fangs. Once the mob spotted my green and blue streaks, they turned their rage toward me. It had gone beyond shouts and threats now. They had drawn their weapons, and they were aimed in my direction. Taking in a deep breath, I filled my lungs and let out my song. The force of it shook my frame as the sound reverberated through the square, and every man facing me dropped their weapons. By the time I'd emptied my lungs, they stood like statues—blank-eyed and slack-jawed.

Sindri hurried to my side and slapped me on the back. "Thanks, Elva. I was getting a little nervous."

I shoved my twin hard enough that he stumbled into Leifur. "Get your things. We need to go. Now. It's been three weeks, and Leifur interrupted me, so I'm not as strong as I should be."

Sindri kissed Leifur's cheek before wrapping his arms over his husband's shoulders. "You interrupted my sister getting *refreshed,* and you lived to tell the tale? Impressive, love."

"By the looks of that male, I did her a favor. I don't think he could tell a breast from an ass."

I growled at my two siren companions. "Get your things or I'm leaving without you."

"Someone's in a mood," Leifur teased, but took my bag and tied it to the saddle of the brown horse behind Sindri.

"She always is when she has to use her song and hasn't gotten any dick in a while," Sindri added, earning himself a murderous look from me.

Chapter 2

Elva

Our trio traveled swiftly on the path before veering into the woods to hide from any of the Raunheim people we expected would pursue us. We walked a suitable distance, weaving the horses through the old growth bushes and birch trees, deeper into the Forest of Endilaus, until we found a secluded clearing where we could settle down for the night. I set up our cloth tents while Leifur disappeared into the woods to gather firewood. Sindri finished preparing the horses for the night before he slunk over to me.

"I'm sorry," he said quietly.

"For what?" I asked, driving the final tent stake into the ground with a rock.

"That you weren't able to take care of things before I got into trouble. I know it's been three weeks—"

"Not three weeks," I said sharply, tossing the rock aside. "Twenty-four days, Sindri. I haven't been with a man in twenty-four days." I crossed my arms, glaring at him. "Do you remember the last time I went twenty-nine days and my siren came out to take care of the situation?"

"Yes, Elva, of course I—"

"Because you are acting like you don't. I killed those men."

"They were robbers."

"They were still people! They didn't deserve to be ripped apart by my siren because I failed to find a man to bed in time."

Sindri raised his hands in surrender and stepped closer. "I understand it's frustrating for you." I opened my mouth to reply, but Sindri put his finger to my lips to shush me. "I understand the things you need to do to keep your siren in check. It's much harder for you than it is for me and Leifur. It may not be fair, but we can't change it. We'll just have to find you someone in the next town."

I pushed his hand away and dropped to the ground to set up the fire pit. "Honestly, you probably did me a favor."

"How so?"

Branches snapped behind us as Leifur arrived carrying a massive armload of wood. "Because that fool she found was as green as your right eye," he said. "He was in there for ten minutes with her, and they were still fully clothed."

Sindri burst into laughter as he took the wood from Leifur, and they worked to start a fire.

"Did you at least find any information from the others at the bar?" my brother asked.

I sighed and shook my head, pulling out our rations. "We're two days away from Tyndorf Castle. When we get there, we'll stop at one of the rougher looking inns near the edge of town. Hopefully, I'll find someone to take care of my needs there, and then we'll get some information to help me hunt down that asshole who turned me into this monster. Preferably someone who knows what they're doing."

Sindri smirked at Leifur. "My sister likes it rough."

Leifur chuckled, poking at the wood as the fire crackled to

life. "I'm well aware, both from experience and sleeping in rooms next to hers   ."

"We can't all be delicate flowers like you, Sindri," I teased, and threw his bread rations over the fire at him. Leifur chuckled and went back to tending the fire. My handsome brother-in-law had been assigned to me when I turned twenty-three and hadn't produced a child yet. While I was his first failure at producing an offspring with a female siren, I was the first one who truly cared about him as more than a donor. Our friendship blossomed so quickly that even when it was clear he wouldn't be able to help me produce the child that was required for me to stay in the Siren territory, he refused to abandon me. And once he met my brother, I knew Leifur would never leave us. He had craved a loving family, only to have the sirens he was assigned to leave the moment they were pregnant, but it was then that he found his perfect family in a pair of unwanted low-born siren twins. So if humans came, I would deal with them however I had to. But the idea that the sirens might come to take them back kept me up at night.

Sindri turned the bread over in his fingers, sniffed it, and made a face as if he'd gag before tossing it behind him.

"Sindri." Leifur shoved his shoulder.

The siren just laughed, pulled three fresh loaves from his bag, and tossed them to us. "Fresh bread and dried boar, courtesy of the widow." He grinned and took a large bite.

"As much as I hate the situations you get us into," I said. "I won't complain about what your siren charms get us."

"That's the advantage of having a sultry siren brother, my dear warrior sister. You protect us, and I provide for us. And my husband—he just looks handsome with all those muscles from working so hard."

I giggled as Leifur pulled up his sleeve and flexed his bulky biceps. His grayish-hued skin that would camouflage in the water went iridescent in the firelight, and his blue hair and eyes sparkled with the light.

"Thank you for coming with me," I said softly.

"Stop thanking us." Leifur directed, tossing an apple at me. "You were only exiled because you turned twenty-four and couldn't become pregnant, as if our only value as a siren is our ability to procreate." He opened a bottle of ale and took a swig.

"That's because it is," I said, grabbing his ale and taking a swig. "Your prowess is why you were so treasured. You didn't have to come with me."

"If they exiled you, that included me." Sindri grabbed the bottle from my grasp. "With so few of us males, and my refusal to ever touch a female siren, I was useless to them. And then I corrupted Leifur, too. Clearly, I was a menace!"

"Being half selkie certainly didn't help things," Leifur said.

"You love my selkie half," Sindri said and kissed his husband.

"Of course I do. Both of you." He winked at me and ran his hand through his blue locks. "I love your luscious blue and green hair, and that you have an eye of each color. You're both beautiful."

"I am, aren't I?" Sindri smirked. "Though I think it's unfair that our little warrior got the gorgeous scales during her cycle while I got the gills. Why do I need gills? Sirens can breathe underwater without them."

I raised my eyebrow at my brother and pursed my lips. "I'd rather have the gills than have scales appear at random times. I know you think they're beautiful, but at least your gills have a use."

"The scales track how close you are to losing control and letting your monster out."

"That makes it worse, Sindri."

"Your scales are part of who you are, Elva," Leifur said. "They made all the other sirens jealous of you."

I glared at my overly kind brother-in-law. "They also helped to get me exiled." I looked down at my side for the telltale glistening against my white, iridescent skin. "Can you see them yet?"

"Not yet," Sindri said. "Even if today was a monumental failure with your little drunk friend, it seems to have silenced the siren for the moment."

"Thank Poseidon!"

"When we arrive at Tyndorf, mask your hair," Leifur said. "I know you hate doing it, but it makes things easier for you."

"I only hate doing it because it won't last. We spend hours coloring it with walnut shells only to have it be blue and green again in the morning."

"That's why I shave my head," Sindri said.

I laughed. "You know that doesn't work for me either."

"I know," he said. "But it's not my fault your hair grows back overnight."

"We should get some sleep," Leifur interjected before Sindri and I could get into a proper argument. "I know Elva's going to want to leave before the sun comes up so we can put more distance between us and Raunheim."

"How well you know me." I smiled at them. Leifur stood and held his hand out to Sindri, and helped him up. The two men walked around the fire and leaned down to kiss me on the cheek, heading to their tent.

Watching the fire crackle, I pulled both knees up to my chin. *I'll find the last of the ones who broke me. Kill him, and then we'll find a home away from it all. There has to be a town somewhere in Torian that isn't terrified of the Sirens and will let us stay there. We just want a place to live out our lives in peace.*

Chapter 3

Elva

The putrid smell of the bubbling, thick brown sludge overpowered even the flowers surrounding our camp. We rode hard the entire day yesterday, so that we could make it to Tyndorf by nightfall tonight. Along the way, we'd collected as many walnuts as possible, and once we'd filled the bag, we stopped to make the dye we needed for my and Leifur's hair. Sindri was happy to assist in applying the mixture, but always avoided helping make it, so Leifur and I had done all the dirty work. Using our siren claws, we shredded the thick green walnut husks and filled our pot to the brim before adding water to cook everything.

I disliked releasing my claws, but they made quick work of the husks. With the adrenaline rush of a battle, I never noticed the stinging when my fingertips grew out into thick talons that could cut through tree branches or bone. But any other time, it stung like being stabbed.

After the sludge was cool, I covered Leifur's hair with enough to take his bright blue down to a darker shade. Then, with my knees pulled up to my chin, I sat while my brother and brother-in-law applied the paste to my hair and bottled up the remainder. The paste would dry on my head and fall off as we rode. Then, for the rest of the day and into tomorrow, my blue and green tresses would be dark walnut brown, and I could blend in with the other women in Tyndorf. Leifur's color would last longer since his hair wasn't tied to his powers the way mine was.

"Have you ever traveled to Tyndorf before?" Leifur asked as we neared the city walls. Unlike the smaller towns that built their ramparts out of tree logs, Tyndorf's city wall was constructed from stone.

"Once, when I was young and traveling with the siren warriors, back when they still allowed me to train."

"What's it like?" Sindri asked.

"It's like the other towns and villages we've been through, but much larger," I replied. "The king was already insane when we came back then, so I don't think he'll be any better now. But his children are only half-human, so I'm hoping he'll let us buy some land and hide here."

"You think he'll have sympathy for us?" Leifur asked.

"Probably not, but we might be of value to him in some other way. Rather than finding one wife to marry like most humans, he spent a year traveling around and mated with every female of various species he could find. He ended up with a collection of children who are all half-something non-human."

"I remember those rumors." Sindri rode the stallion up beside me, eager to hear the tale. "Do you know what they are?"

"If I recall, his oldest son is half-werewolf, and his oldest daughter is half-sorceress. Another was something like a centaur or satyr, and the rest I can't remember."

"A half-werewolf?" Leifur snickered. "Do you think he got her pregnant while she was in wolf form to help him get the werewolf son?"

Sindri and I laughed before he added, "If he did, I hope she clawed him viciously."

"It would have served him right," I continued. "I remember the older warriors saying how horribly he treated the women and how at least one woman and child died. He wanted a siren too, but never managed to capture one."

"Naturally. Sirens, dire wolves, and gryphons are the scariest creatures, after the dragons," Sindri said, hissing softly as he let his siren fangs slip free, sharp and glinting in the dim light.

Leifur nodded. "I'd add minotaurs to that list. They don't look scary, but their extreme strength and bad tempers make them terrifying in my book."

I cocked my head to the side and examined my brother-in-law. "I'll accept that addition."

The boys chucked, but I turned my gaze back toward the rampart and inhaled deeply. The faintest hint of walnut lingered in the air amid the scent of the forest. Spring in the Forest of Endilaus was always full of floral scents mixed with some musty smells from the fresh earth, and depending on where you were, occasional hints of animal territorial markings. And now, salt.

"Remember, we're nearing the Sieden sea," Leifur said. "That means we're back in kelpie territory. I know they prefer to go after humans, but they won't hesitate to trick us if they get the chance."

Sindri rolled his eyes. "I'm not going to be tricked by a stupid water horse. We all learned as younglings to never get on the back of any wild horse we run across."

Leifur tightened his hold on Sindri, pulling him closer and pressing a quick kiss to his neck.

"I'm glad to hear it," I said. "I would have half expected you to think you could charm one."

Sindri smirked. "My charms don't work on any other creatures, but I've always wondered if your song could."

"I have no intention of ever finding out."

"You spoil all my fun."

I veered my horse toward Sindri and punched him squarely in the leg. He moved to retaliate, but Leifur's grip on him was firm.

"Enough, children." Leifur teased.

"You need to learn to respect your elders," Sindri snapped.

"You're six minutes older. I'm not respecting you for that."

"It's at least an hour, and you know it."

"How much money do we have?" Leifur asked, clearly trying to break up the childish bickering that my twin and I were known for.

"I have some silver coins, a bit of copper, and a few of the pearls from what we brought," I replied, adjusting my hands on the reins.

Sindri snickered, waving a small velvet pouch in the air. "I've got gold and gems, thanks to my new friend."

"That should get us some rooms at an inn close to the castle —" Leifur started.

"No," I said. "We should stay close to the rampart. I know you want to stay somewhere nicer, but we need to keep a low profile. Their royals may be half-human, but that doesn't tell us how the people will react to sirens. I'm not taking any risks until we get a feel for the place."

"Leifur's hair will give us away even if yours doesn't," Sindri said. From the tone of his voice, he wasn't thrilled with my insisting we stay at the cheaper inns.

"No one cares about a male siren, and you know it," I snapped. "Mortal men aren't worried about you having control over women. What they fear is losing control of themselves."

"Admit it," Sindri said. "You're hoping to find information on Aamon, and you'll only be able to if we stay with the thieves and lowlifes. There's nothing wrong with trying to enjoy ourselves once in a while."

My glare could have frozen fire, but Sindri was already pushing his horse away from me. "It worked before," I muttered to myself.

"Elva, look at this," Leifur called from up the road. He was standing with a small group of peasants, examining a poster nailed to a wooden board. It announced a royal tournament in Tyndorf to celebrate the princess' wedding.

Sindri read aloud as we approached: "There will be generous prizes of gold, jewels, knighthoods, and other titles."

Leifur and I shared a look of excitement. His blacksmithing skills were unmatched, even in the Siren Kingdom. And I remembered from my trip to the mortal kingdoms years ago that human knights fought differently from siren warriors. I hoped it would give me an edge if there was a dagger contest.

Sindri chuckled. "Regardless of whether you win, there'll be a lot of wealthy noble women for me to woo."

"Just don't make a mess of it this time," I warned.

"Same for you, dear sister," Sindri said, smirking. He leaned closer to me as another wagon passed us. "After you fumbled your last male, you better pick one who can get the job done at the inn tonight."

"You can stop counting my cycle, Sindri."

"No, I can't. You're on day twenty-six, and that last time you hit day thirty, it took you and Leifur a month to look at each other again."

I shot him a warning glance, but he continued, elbowing his husband. "Right, Leifur? Didn't you say you had to tie her down to keep her from clawing your face off?"

"Enough!" Leifur barked, his patience fraying.

Sindri crossed his arms, sulking. "It's been a boring month for me."

"That won't be a problem now. With a tournament happening," Leifur said, "Elva will have her pick of men, and maybe even non-mortals. They're always up for a good time."

I tuned out their relaxed teasing and focused on the city walls as we approached. They were built from the rocks that littered the shores of the Sieden Sea. The limestone was pale and weathered, cloaked in moss and ivy that crawled so high I had to crane my neck to see their tops.

When we rounded the road that led towards the gate, we saw a group of guards interrogating everyone who sought entry. My brother noticed them too, and when he glanced at me, I gave him a reassuring nod, while biting my lip so hard I almost drew blood. Sindri may be the older twin, but I was the stronger one. I'd insisted we prepare for this moment earlier, but nerves still gnawed at me. *Please don't let him mess this up.*

Leifur slid off his horse and climbed behind me. Since Sindri always dressed the best of the three of us, he would play the role of the Lord, giving us a chance we'd get in without being searched or harassed.

Making my horse trot slowly, I studied the three guards. Each wore the traditional black Tyndorf armor, with a broad chest plate, and interconnected bits of metal attached to the sleeves all the way from the shoulder to the wrists. But as they moved, the slips of metal rattled, betraying the fact that the shirts were obviously too large for them. They weren't very important or of high rank. *Typical mortal men, using their position to bully the poor peasants trying to enter the city.*

The smallest guard was shouting at an older man on the wagon ahead of us when the larger man turned our way. A wicked grin spread across his face as he slapped his companion on the shoulder. Their eyes lingered on me as the third guard waved the wagon through dismissively.

"Let me handle this," Sindri whispered and urged his stallion forward. "Good day, knights of Tyndorf. We've come to witness your tournament. We've heard of it from the Nordlic Sea and couldn't possibly miss it. Tell me, what events will you be taking part in?"

The lowly guards puffed out their chests and strutted up to Sindri. They leaned in and whispered something that made Sindri laugh much louder than was necessary. The largest guard kept glancing at me.

"Not him," I murmured through gritted teeth. Leifur wrapped his arm around my waist, pulling me close as he shot the man a warning glare. The guard grunted and returned his attention to my brother and his elaborate story.

We were only stopped for around a minute, but it felt more like an hour. After their laughter faded, Sindri pressed a gold coin into each guard's hand, and they waved us through. Still, I could feel their eyes linger on us until we were through the gate and out of sight.

Once safe, Leifur guided his horse beside Sindri. "What did you say to them?"

"I asked if women could compete, and told them my sister here is quite good with a sword."

My hands tightened on the reins, pulling them away from Leifur. "So that's funny to you?"

"Not to me, but it amused them. They've never seen a warrior of your caliber. And it bodes well for us. If the others in town feel the same, then betting on you to win should pay out extremely well, assuming they have an event with daggers."

"Are you ever not plotting?" I asked.

"Nope, never!. And that's what you both love about me. The big oaf said the best inn to find some fun is just down these two smaller roads. It's called the Pirate's Booty."

Chapter 4

Elva

Horses secured in the inn's stable, Sindri, Leifur, and I slipped into the Pirate's Booty through the back door. Despite the sun still being out, the tavern was packed. Serving wenches darted between tables, their trays loaded with steaming meat pies and frothy mugs of ale. Most of them were barely dressed—skirts so short that they flashed their backsides when they leaned over, and their tops barely contained their breasts.

"Classy," Leifur muttered under his breath.

"We can't spend all our money on the first day," I said. "This will do fine for tonight." I was already scoping out the men clustered at the bar. None of them caught my interest—or the siren's. Frustrated, I switched tactics and took a deep breath through my nose, letting my siren senses flare to life. The air was thick with sweat, ale, and the faint tang of manure from the stable, but then, there it was: a scent like leather and musk that made something in me perk up. *Interesting.*

"Grab any seats you can, loves!" a redheaded server called out to us over the bar.

"I'll grab the drinks," I said to Sindri and Leifur. "You two find us a spot."

I slipped around the tables full of men, who were laughing and shouting boisterously, trying to discover where that smell had come from. But as I moved, the smell faded under the stench of sweat and ale. My siren stirred restlessly, annoyed by the lack of progress.

By the time I reached the bar and ordered our drinks, the place had grown even more crowded. As I waited, I spotted Sindri and Leifur in a booth at the back corner and set off across the room. I had to squeeze between chairs, and more than once, roaming hands found their way onto my body. The first time it happened, I bit my tongue, but the second time, I felt a rage bubbling inside me, and I had to remind my siren we couldn't afford to cause a scene. Instead, I used my other skills—the ones my instructors had tried to break me of. When they touched me, I touched back. They were too drunk to feel it, and it was too loud to hear the coins jingling. By the time I arrived at our table, I had five satchels to drop in front of Leifur, and he pocketed them before anyone could see. While waiting for our meat pies, we took turns sizing up the room. The patrons were mostly farmers and day laborers, dressed in threadbare tunics and boots caked with dirt. A few wore the Tyndorf crest—a snake coiled around a sword being held aloft by a dragon. They were likely guards who lived on the outskirts of the town. Some had women beside them or on their arm, likely their wives, which narrowed the pool for me.

Sindri elbowed me. "Smell anyone you like yet?"

I shot him a dirty look.

"Don't be mad, we know what stage you're at. It's our job." Sindri grabbed his mug and took a long swig.

"That glare means no," Leifur said. He clicked his tongue while he glanced around the room and stopped short. "What about that one? The blond in the guard uniform. I would wager an ale he catches your eye."

"Not this month," Sindri said before I could open my mouth. "He's too young to know what to do with her. Maybe another time, when she's not this far into the cycle and the siren has more patience."

Leifur snorted. "The scruffy-haired one? Really?"

"Big muscles, older," Sindri said with a shrug. "More likely to know how to handle her. I'll take your ale and raise you a meat pie."

"Would you two stop betting on my sex life?" I demanded.

Leifur and Sindri turned to me, both of them smirking like fools. "No." They replied in unison before Sindri added, "We've been married for two years now. We need something to entertain ourselves."

I groaned and tried to take a large gulp of my drink, only to find the mug empty. "Time for another round. I'll grab it." I stood and slipped past my brother's chair, snagging one of the coin purses Leifur had tucked into his bag.

"You're just using that as an excuse to get away from us, aren't you?" Leifur asked.

"Precisely."

I took in the men before me and planned my route carefully to avoid the worst offenders from earlier, and to get me nearer to any men I hadn't passed on the first trip. As I neared the bar, the scent grew stronger, teasing my siren and making her stir restlessly beneath my skin.

When I reached the bar, I waited for our drinks. Now that it was dark outside, the place had filled up more, and I knew if I went back to the table, our drinks would take forever while they handled the orders from everyone crowding the bar. Mugs in hand, I was about to return to my brothers when a man collided with me. Ale sloshed and soaked my shirt and splashed up to my chin.

"I'm so sorry. I didn't see you there." The overly apologetic man grabbed a rag from the barkeep and tried to dry my chest, but I grabbed his wrist and gave him a look that could freeze blood. "I'm more than capable of drying myself."

He opened his mouth to argue, but then he went pale as his eyes darted past me. A low, gravelly voice spoke up behind me, sending tingles down my spine. "The lady clearly doesn't need your help, Sven, so keep your hands off."

"Apologies, sir. And you too, lady." Sven handed the barkeep a gold coin and hurried back to the seat on the opposite side of the room.

"No need to thank me," the man said.

I turned to face the stranger, and the scent of worn leather hit me like a punch to the gut. He stood at least a head taller than me, dressed in black guard slacks and a snug red tunic that showed off arms that would make even Leifur look thin. His hair was a mix of black and gray, but his face was youthful, framed by sharp cheekbones.

But it was the smile that got under my skin. It was the kind of smile that said he knew exactly how good he looked and wasn't afraid to use it. Combined with that heady leather scent, it was nearly too much. My siren surged forward, demanding I take him, claim him, right here in the middle of this crowded tavern.

"Why would I thank you?" I asked, gazing at the coarse stubble on his face. "I didn't need your help, and am perfectly capable of taking care of myself."

"I'm sure there is something I could help you take care of."

I couldn't stop my snort and laughed at him. "Does that actually work on the women here?"

His smirk faltered for a moment before he recovered. His eyes narrowed, as if trying to figure me out. I leaned over the bar to grab my new ales, pressing my breasts together just enough to make sure he noticed. When I glanced back, he was staring at them, and I knew I had him.

Ales in hand, I caught his eye and shrugged. "You'll need to try harder if you want to help me take care of myself tonight."

The smirk returned, wider this time, and he took a step closer. "Tell me what you need. I'll do it."

"Where's the fun in that?" I smiled and started toward our table.

"I would offer to fight your brother, but I don't think you want him harmed."

His words stopped me cold. I scanned him for any sort of weapon, but he was unarmed. If necessary, I could toss my ale on him and get my dagger from my hip before he could make it to me. "What makes you think he's my brother?"

He shrugged and stepped closer. "If he weren't, I would hope he'd be the one fetching the drinks."

My mind was racing. *How does he know?* I could feel my siren rising, edging into my voice as I spoke. "Maybe he's just an asshole."

The stranger's voice dropped lower, sending more tingles down my spine. "No. You wouldn't tolerate that."

"You have no idea what I would tolerate."

"Oh, but I'd like to find out."

He was leaning in so close I could feel the heat of him against me. And that scent was all I could think about. My mind went blank as something in me shifted. *Go away, siren.* But it was no use. She'd fixated on him. She wanted him, and if I didn't give in, then my siren would take matters into her own hands, which almost always ended bloody.

He seemed to know exactly what I was thinking. His eyes locked onto mine, and there was no mistaking the intent behind them. "When you're done delivering your brother's drink, I have a room upstairs. I'd love to continue our conversation there, in private."

I glanced over at Sindri and Leifur. They were making rude gestures at me and pointing at the stranger. I scowled, plunked their ales back onto the bar, and grabbed his hand.

"Let's go," I said, pulling him toward the stairs before I could change my mind—or before the siren could take control completely.

He took the lead, and I followed him up the creaky stairs to the third floor. The wooden beams groaned under our feet, echoing through the quiet hallway. The walls were bare, except for knots in the boards. At the end of the hall, we reached a door marked with a metal number one. The man took a key out of his pocket and unlocked it, holding the door open for me.

As I stepped inside, I was taken aback by the elegance of the room. The rest of the inn was sparsely decorated, but this room was exquisite. Besides a desk and a wardrobe, there was a cupboard with an ornate ceramic pitcher of water and several mugs. The bed was a work of art. Each of the four-post beds was intricately carved with ivy leaves that appeared to grow up and around the bed. I walked over and touched the blanket. It was softer than any material I'd ever felt. "Do you get such nice accommodations for all your conquests?"

"These are my quarters. If I entertain a lady, this is where I bring her."

There was a slight thump behind me. He'd taken a large coin purse out of his pocket and dropped it beside the water. A gold dagger followed.

"What is it that you do that can pay for such a glamorous private room?" I asked, my eyes lingering on the dagger. "Are you a warrior of some kind?"

He crossed his arms and leaned against the table, smirking. "I don't even know your name, and you're asking about my work."

"Why wouldn't I?" I countered.

"I suppose we could skip the formalities," he said, raising an eyebrow. "Would you prefer we not use our real names?"

"Why would you ask that?"

"You seem like the secretive type."

"You're right. Real names and life details won't be necessary." I couldn't stop looking at his speckled hair and intense green eyes. They seemed to change shade as he moved his head to study me. "I'll call you ... Malachite."

"The gemstone."

"Your eyes remind me of it."

"Alright." He took a few steps toward me and stopped, seeming to take me in slowly. His gaze lingered on my face and hair. "I'll call you Pearl then. Since you seem to sparkle like one."

My favorite gem. Heat spread through me—a dangerous sign this late in the cycle. My siren stirred restlessly, drawn to something about him that felt different. His scent was intoxicating, richer and more alluring than anything I'd ever encountered. It was as though he'd been made for me.

I tilted my head to the side and stepped closer to him. He didn't pull away. Instead, his brilliant green eyes locked onto mine. Staring into them, I gripped the bottom of his shirt, untucking it slowly from his pants. He tugged his shirt from my grip and pulled it over his head, revealing a tattoo of a fox and wolf on his biceps. The ink seemed to shimmer in the dim light, as though alive.

He dropped his shirt to the floor, then reached for me, backing me against the doorframe. My breath hitched, pulse racing. I'd been with so many men that I assumed nothing would surprise me anymore, but the tattoos on his chest looked so realistic I found myself tracing them with my fingers without realizing it.

Malachite leaned down to my ear and whispered. "I promise

not to hurt you, little Pearl. Pick a safe word, and if I become too much for you, say it and we'll be finished."

I turned my face to him and stared, still unable to figure out what it was about him that drew me in so fiercely. "I don't need one. I'm more than capable of handling whatever you do to me."

His smirk returned. "I knew you'd be different from the other women I've brought here."

When I opened my mouth to reply, his lips slammed into mine. I shifted and barely got my arms around his neck before he pressed his full weight against me, pinning me to the door. His body was a wall of solid muscle, and his scent made my head spin. His lips consumed mine, stealing all the breath from my lungs until they ached for relief. A rough hand fisted my hair, yanking my head back as his teeth sank into my lower lip hard enough to draw blood.

I winced at the sharp sting, fighting to keep my siren in check. My hands moved on their own, tearing off my shirt so quickly he barely got his hand out of my hair in time.

He caged me between him and the door, and stared down at my heaving chest. "Need to catch your breath, little Pearl?"

I playfully batted my eyes at him as I dragged my nails down his chest hard enough to leave faint marks. "If that's all it takes for you to need a break," I purred, "then I'm going to be very disappointed tonight."

A feral growl rumbled from him, and in one swift motion, he turned me around and pushed my chest against the wall. My hands slammed into the wall beside my head, trying to keep my face from scraping the rough wood paneled wall as he reached around and feverishly cupped my breast. His fingers pinched my nipple with a hint of pain that made me gasp.

His lips found my shoulder, tracing a fiery path up to my neck. I arched my back and pressed my rear into his groin, and he responded by sinking his teeth into my skin.

The moan that escaped me was deep and needy. I tried to move, but he held me firm, his teeth digging deeper into my neck. A warm trickle ran down my chest, and I gasped when he kissed the wound; a jolt of pleasure shot straight to my core.

I sucked in a breath and waited. Siren blood had one of two effects on males of other species: either he'd become insatiably aroused, ensuring he gave me what I needed, or he'd die a quick and painful death. The toxins in my blood were there to kill weaker males. I could feel his body tense against mine as the blood took hold.

A sharp breath left him, and he squeezed my breast harder and ground himself against me. I squeaked in surprise as his free hand loosened the drawstring on my pants. His hand was blazing hot as he dipped his fingers into my pants. He moved with agonizing slowness down my waist, as though savoring every inch.

He chuckled low in his throat when my legs instinctively parted to give him easier access, as if my body had betrayed me and now belonged to him. In a way, it had.

"I'm curious to see if you're all talk or if you're—" His words cut off and became a guttural moan when his fingers found me ready for him. Sirens were naturally wet and slick most of the time, but his rough touches would have sent me into heat if I'd been another species. His chest vibrated into my back from the sound of his moan as I pushed myself harder against him, desperate for him to continue. Instead, he pulled his fingers back. A small whine escaped me.

"Don't worry, little Pearl, we're just getting started."

He flipped me back to face him, and I grabbed his belt, unclasping it and ripping it from him in one motion. His eyebrows raised, and he fisted my hair, pulling me into a rough, demanding kiss. I struggled to match the intensity of the kiss while getting his pants undone, but I finally freed him. I moaned when I felt how hard he already was, so different from other men I'd been with.

I gripped him tightly, still trying to feel out which part of me was in control. He was thick enough that my fingers couldn't reach around his girth, but not so much that the siren was needed to keep me from being injured. I stroked him firmly, and he growled, releasing my hair. I heard fabric rip as he tore my pants in half.

He grabbed my thighs, lifting me, and I let out a startled yelp as he slammed into me, pressing me against the wall again, this time with my legs spread wide. It only took a few pumps for me to adjust to his thickness, and then I wrapped both arms around his neck and met his thrusts by slamming myself onto him.

He slapped his hand beside my head and grunted as he pounded into me. Heat surged through me as every stroke of his cock sent a rush of tremors straight to my clit. Gasping for breath, I felt the pressure climbing until it overwhelmed me. I didn't care who heard me, and I screamed when I fell over the edge with waves of pleasure crashing over me, so intense I thought I might black out.

But Malachite didn't stop. "Regretting your lack of safe word, Pearl?" he taunted, his hot breath brushing against my neck. I moaned loudly, digging my nails into his back. "Harder," I pleaded, struggling to keep my siren at bay. I had to make sure he finished so it would satisfy the monster for another cycle.

Chapter 5

Njall

Something was different about my little Pearl, and I don't mean her right green eye and left blue eye. I'd been with a hundred women before. The experienced ones would moan and scream at my touch. The noble ladies I talked into my bed never had a clue what to do, and would just lie there like a dead fish. But this one? She was a storm, just as insatiable as I was. When I bit her lip and tasted her blood, something feral stirred in me. And when she screamed loud enough to rattle the rafters, I brought her to my bed where I made her finish a second time. That time, she came so hard that I thought she might tear my cock off.

But even then, she wasn't done. She straddled me, her hands clawing at my chest like she wanted to carve her name into it. When she was riding me, I fisted one hand in her hair, yanking her head back so she had no choice but to meet my gaze. Her plump lips parted slightly, soft and inviting, and I couldn't help myself.

Ferflucs.

I slammed my lips against hers, as her hands drew blood from my chest. Seems fair after I drew hers. By the time I'd shoved my tongue into her mouth, she'd started riding my cock faster, and I moaned into her mouth. I felt a smirk spread across her lips, and she bounced on my lap, a vulnerable position I rarely let a woman put me into.

Wicked little temptress.

I let her have control for all of two breaths before I'd had enough. Gripping her hips, I flipped her on her side and pulled her ass into the air before I slammed into her from behind, sending her forward almost onto her face. Her hands clawed the sheets as I pounded into her. And then I saw them—small, shimmering scales scattered across her hips, one trail running down her leg, and another curling up her side. They caught the light like jewels, and something primal in me surged to the surface. I grabbed on hard, letting myself lose control in a way I rarely could.

My position in Tyndorf was high enough that I could never allow myself to finish with a woman I brought to my bed, but this one muddled every thought racing through my mind, and before I knew what was happening, I was on the edge of finishing. When I tried to pull away from her, I couldn't. It was as if she'd locked me inside her. She slammed back on me so hard; I couldn't have stopped myself for anything in the world, and I came inside the strange woman beneath me.

The satisfied moan she let out was like nothing I'd ever heard in my life. *What are you?* She collapsed on the bed, her chest heaving, and I finally managed to pull free. A thin layer of sweat glistened on her skin, catching the light and making her shimmer like some creature born of water and moonlight. She had dozens of healed over knife marks scattered across her back and legs, with a rather deep-looking X scar on her left hip. I dared to touch one on her back, and she twisted around, glaring daggers at me.

"You had a hair on your back," I lied, and her expression softened.

"So, are you ready to concede?" She sat up and gently traced my tattoo again with her finger.

"Concede? Oh no, Pearl. I'm not finished with you yet."

"Tsk tsk. I need actions, not words, Malachite."

Chuckling, I cupped her face and kissed her, before laying her back down on my bed.

The moon still hung in the sky when I dressed in fresh clothes and laced up my boots. Pearl lay on her side in the bed, clutching a pillow to her breast. She'd been asleep for ages. She'd looked so beautiful that I refused to wake her, making her the only woman I'd ever let sleep in my bed. The others, I would have thrown out as soon as I was finished with them.

"There's something different about you." I dropped some fresh pants on the bed from the stash of women's items I kept in my room. My little Pearl stirred at the sound, releasing the pillow and rolling over. Now, in the light, I spotted something. Leaning closer, I brushed aside a lock of her nutty brown hair to reveal hidden blue streaks underneath.

A siren. We hadn't had one in Tyndorf for at least a decade. My mind raced with the implications. She was dangerous, and I knew I should wake her, drag her to my father. She'd lied when she said she didn't know who I was. *You sought me out.*

I marched to the door and grabbed its handle, but couldn't bring myself to open it. *It has been many years. Perhaps she doesn't know who I am.* It was strange. She was in disguise and traveling with two males. That was not how her kind attacks.

Still, duty called. If I didn't report this and my father found out, I would face the consequences, and I wasn't going to let some pretty face land me in the dungeon again. One last look at her, and I ripped the door open, determined to find the general.

Chapter 6

Elva

It was like I was lying in a cloud. I wanted to snuggle in and never leave, but the sound of a closing door brought me back to reality. We couldn't afford such finery. I pushed myself up and rolled over. The room was even more charming in the early morning light. The walls were paneled with black pine, and instead of the scent of stale ale that inns usually had, the air was rich with that intoxicating leather aroma. It was strange that I could still smell it after I'd taken care of things.

I spotted my shirt and an unfamiliar pair of pants nearby. When I reached for them, my cheeks heated at the memory of last night. I never stay in a man's room after I'm done with him. Then again, I never came that hard in my life. Not only had I spent the night here, but he'd given me new clothes to replace the pants we'd damaged. That a man who wasn't my brother could be kind was unnerving. *Is this what affection feels like? Genuine affection that leads to love?* Sirens weren't supposed to feel love—lust, yes, but not love. It was against our nature. Yet Sindri and Leifur had shattered that belief. Not only did they love each other dearly, but they loved me just as fiercely.

Trying to be quiet, I slipped out of bed, and my feet sank into a thick rug. *How does this room keep getting better?* Stretching, I glanced around. He was gone. The coin purse and knife were gone from the table. Just to be sure, I sprang across the room and flung open the wardrobe doors. Only clothes remained. Nothing under the bed, either.

"Okay, he's gone," I muttered. Confused by what was going on inside my head, I felt a desperate need to get out before he came back. I pulled my shirt over my head and the pants up my legs, yanking the drawstring as tight as it would go. Digging through his wardrobe, I found several expensive-looking garments that would fit Sindri perfectly. I threw them over my arm and left.

The stairs led down to my brother's room. "Sindri, open this door!"

It took my brother frustratingly long to open the door. When he did, he looked hungover. "There you are." He grinned when he saw my oversized pants. "I wondered if you'd run off with him."

"Haha." I pushed past him into their room, which was far more modest than the one I'd just left—two worn beds that they'd shoved together, old, stained bedding, no wardrobe, a single chair against a rickety table.

Leifur greeted me with a hug. "We were worried. You usually end up in our bed after a few hours."

"His room was better," I admitted, and held up my arm with the clothes.

"Mine!" Sindri's eyes lit up as he grabbed the top four pieces and tossed them onto the bed to decide what to try on first. I handed the simple tunic and pants to Leifur.

"Everything go alright?" he asked, brushing my hair aside to look at what was likely a nasty bite mark on my neck.

"He didn't die, if that's what you mean."

"Elva—"

"We're good for another month."

"Thank Poseidon. The last thing we need is your scales showing up today. We have a hard enough time hiding your hair."

My hands instinctively flew to my thigh. Scales were always the last warning before she took over.

"Speaking of," Leifur said, gathering my hair in his hands. "We need to touch up the brown. Some blue is showing through."

"Already? It should have lasted until tonight."

He shrugged. "We either missed a spot or didn't use enough. Relax, Elva. That's why you made a large batch. Sit." He gestured to the chair and headed for my travel bag on the floor.

Sindri now sported the sapphire blue shirt and twirled to face me. I picked that one because it would bring out his eyes and was as soft as a newborn chick. "So, you slept there? He must have been *very* good."

I was ready to tell him off, but Leifur stepped in before I could say anything. "Leave her alone, Sindri." My brother crossed his arms, looking like a sulky child, while a sly grin spread across Leifur's face. "Judging by all those bruises and scratches on her arms and neck, she'll be pretty sore today."

"Fine, he knew what he was doing," I said. "Happy now?"

"More details, please," Sindri said, as Leifur opened the jar and used a leather glove to spread the dye mixture in my hair.

I raised an eyebrow at my brother. I'd noticed mortals were usually private about their conquests, but sirens could be down-right competitive when it came to sex. Sindri always needed to know where his husband ranked on my list, to make sure his choice to marry didn't cause him to miss out on anything exciting. "He's in my top," I said finally.

"Top what?" Leifur asked. "Ten? Five?"

"Three?" Sindri's eyes grew wide, and his mouth dropped open.

"I passed out afterwards, and when I woke up, he was gone."

"So you robbed him?" Sindri teased. "I'm rubbing off on you, dear sister. I'll fetch the water for your hair so you don't stink all day." He slipped out the door, leaving Leifur and me alone.

Leifur leaned closer, his voice softening. "Are you alright?"

"Just a little tender," I said, rubbing the bite mark on my neck. "He was as aggressive as I am."

"Hopefully, one of us can win something at the tournament and convince them to let us stay. That way, I don't have to keep bedding you every time we end up in the middle of nowhere for some time."

"You bedded me first."

"It was my job," he said. "If we stay long enough, maybe you can try to have an actual relationship."

"Always the romantic," I teased, but Leifur grabbed my hand and tugged until I met his gaze.

"I understand," he said gently. "Most sirens don't believe we can feel things for another, but your brother is all I need. I love him."

I squeezed his hand. "I know, but you fell in love with every siren you were with before. All those siren females that left you once you'd gotten them pregnant—every one of them broke your heart. Until me, and then you met my brother, and he charmed you off your feet."

"He did. The queen was furious when I refused to take another lover."

I smiled. "At least you know my brother won't leave you because of a pregnancy."

Leifur leaned down and hugged me. "I'm the luckiest siren ever. I not only have my husband, whom I adore, but his gorgeous sister too."

I kissed him on the cheek, and he smiled. "Don't be afraid of wanting more, Elva. You deserve it."

"Deserving it doesn't mean it'll happen."

The door slammed shut, and we both turned to see Sindri standing there with a mischievous grin. "It does if we're talking about sex, and I would know," he said.

Leifur shot me a look, and I couldn't help but chuckle. I swear my brother-in-law is the most patient siren in Torian to put up with Sindri. My brother was a sultry siren from birth and could talk any female creature into anything, but Leifur and I had to work for our skills. If he hadn't been half-selkie, my brother would have risen to the highest rank possible for males—king of the sirens. But our father was unworthy, so we were too. We were mutts who should never have been.

A loud snap drew my attention to the fingers before my nose. "Where did you go, Elva?" Leifur asked.

"Dreaming about your friend's cock?" Sindri snickered as he moved behind me to rinse the dye from my hair with a small bowl of water.

"No," I said, pulling my favorite dagger from its sheath and pointing it at him. "I'm trying to decide how many daggers to take when we sign up for the tournament."

Chapter 7

Elva

The morning air was crisp as we shoved our way through the crowded marketplace, trying to figure out where to sign up for the tournament. Wooden stalls lined the square-shaped market, and vendors shouted over the crowd to hawk their wares, while locals haggled over every coin. The locals' clothing sparkled, covered in more gold and jewels than any other place we'd visited so far. Tyndorf had a large, affluent population, and that was wonderful news for us, considering Leifur was an expert swordsmith. If he didn't win the tournament outright, he'd surely land a job offer. His work was exquisite; my daggers were a prime example of his crafts-manship. All we needed now was enough money to buy some undesired land in the woods outside the rampart. Mortals didn't like the woods, so we figured our plan would work, provided Sindri didn't charm the wrong widow, and I kept my temper in check.

Sindri shouted our names, and we ducked into a small alleyway to let him catch up. He'd found a merchant woman selling food and was cradling three steaming stuffed buns. I bit into one eagerly, burning my tongue, but the moment I tasted the honey and soft cheese, I moaned, "Sindri, this is delicious."

"Only the best for the loves of my life," he replied.

Leifur was blowing on his breakfast and reading a sign that listed the tournament events. "This is quite the affair. Three days long. What is it celebrating?"

An older woman dressed in a lavish gown, adorned with gold and jewels, overheard us and chuckled. "Why, the wedding of the Princess to the General, of course. We were wondering if that girl would ever settle down. It seems sorcerers live longer than we, so she was in no rush, but her father finally put his foot down."

"How old is she?" I asked.

"Twenty-seven, but she still looks eighteen."

"And the esteemed general?" Sindri asked.

"Thirty-seven. Been serving the king for years," the woman replied. She smiled at Sindri and accepted his arm the instant he offered it to her.

"Do you know where we sign up for the events?" Leifur asked.

"There'll be a booth on the road leading to the castle and tournament field."

Sindri whispered something to her, and she giggled like a girl before the two of them headed in the opposite direction.

Leifur adjusted his satchel and shrugged at me. "Know what you're competing in?"

"Daggers, and maybe swords, but the mortals here are so huge, their reach will probably do me in."

"Your aim is deadly with those daggers," Leifur replied.

"Thank you. I spent a decade mastering it."

"Oh, I know," he said, offering me his arm. "All the younglings knew to hide when you got to try weapons."

We pushed our way through the crowd until we left the

market square behind, following the road toward the tournament field. By now, it seemed half the town was awake and on the path with us, because we could barely move through the sea of people. Normally, all these people would make me anxious, but if they're celebrating a royal wedding, it makes sense. I pulled my satchel a little tighter and pressed on.

Leifur held his finger up and then vanished for a moment, returning with two more buns. My mouth watered at the sight, and I didn't wait for him to offer one before I ripped it from his hand.

"I knew that would make you feel better."

"Ank t," I mumbled over the mouthful I had already taken.

"Welcome."

Leifur squeezed my shoulder, and we continued with the crowd toward the fields. Attempting to blend in, we both put on huge smiles and allowed ourselves to point out the beautiful decorations strung up in the town. The wooden houses were decked out in ribbons, streamers, lanterns, and dragon's breath flowers in every color of the rainbow. Dragon's breath was rare in the siren territory, but in the south, we'd seen it growing along the road, and it made everything feel safer somehow. Bouquets of them, bound with twine, hung on doors and window sills.

"I think I might know the princess' favorite flower," Leifur whispered to me. I snorted in response, and he playfully pinched my elbow. The air was buzzing with excitement, as I grabbed Leifur's arm and hugged him. I heard delighted laughter. The surrounding townspeople were now being funneled into a pair of lines to enter the castle grounds. The enormous wooden doors were wide open, and the people heading left were mostly families, while those heading right appeared to consist primarily of strong young men.

"I think we go right," I told Leifur, and he nodded and followed me. Glancing around at the men who would likely be our competition, I found myself underwhelmed. A few here and there would give my commander, the siren general, a run for her money, but most wouldn't hold a candle to her prowess. Leifur's smug grin told me he felt the same. We waited our turn, trying not to draw attention to ourselves, when a boar of a man came up behind us and slapped my ass.

"What are you doing here, little lady? This is the line for the men."

Leifur's expression darkened, but I only had to raise my eyebrows and purse my lips, and my brother-in-law stood down. "He's not worth it," I muttered through clenched teeth.

As our line inched forward, the oaf behind us grabbed my arm. "I'm talking to you, girlie," he growled, yanking me back. "You wouldn't want—"

He never got to finish his comment because a muscular arm struck him in the face, sending him sprawling to the ground. I pushed Leifur behind me and turned back to find a satyr looking at me. I'd never seen one in real life and froze in surprise. Part man, part goat, he was more handsome than most of the men we'd met in our travels. His head was covered by thick, luscious brown hair, the shade of which perfectly matched the fur on his bare, muscular goat's legs. His face, torso and arms were that of a man, while his legs and the curved black horns protruding from his head were from a goat. I couldn't help but stare. He wore a loose leather vest that hung open, showing off his chiseled torso, but nothing more than a loincloth on his lower half. I had to swallow to hold back my siren as she was determined to learn more about this creature before us.

The satyr leaned closer to me, heating the air between us. "He didn't hurt you, did he? I'd hate for a guest in our kingdom to judge us all because of one ignorant thug." He grabbed hold of my hand and kissed it, but I barely noticed, as his horns still mesmerized me. They almost seemed to sparkle in the sunlight. *The things I could do with those.*

Leifur reached his arm out toward the satyr. "I'm Leifur, and this is my sister-in-law, Elva."

The satyr looked at his outstretched hand before grabbing it and giving it a good shake. "Baldr." After releasing Leifur's hand, he returned his gaze to me. "Elva ... that's an unusual name for southern Torian. You must be from the middle—siren and selkie territory, or perhaps Sigil Territory? Good thing you have your brother here to protect you."

Leifur snorted. "If anyone is protecting anyone, Elva is taking care of me."

"Beautiful and a fighter? You're sounding more and more like my type by the minute. Perhaps I could show you around Tyndorf. Give you my tour."

A heat surged through me as Baldr's eyes swept across my body. "I'll consider it." I wrapped my fingers around the end of my braid and met his gaze with a playful smile.

Something brushed against my leg. I glanced down, and my breath caught in my throat.

"Apologies," Baldr said with a charming grin. "My tail has a mind of its own when it comes to beautiful women."

I crossed my arms, trying to appear nonchalant despite the flush rising to my cheeks. Leifur, noticing my reaction, pushed me gently toward the satyr. "If I were to take you up on your offer, where might I find you?" I asked.

"I keep a room at the King's Path Inn. I'll leave a key for you with the barman."

"I'll have to see if I'm feeling up to it," I teased. "It was a long journey to get here."

"Well, I can promise you it will be a tour you'll never forget." Baldr took my hand once more and kissed it, before turning and heading off into the crowd.

Leifur leaned in close as soon as Baldr was out of earshot. "Tell me you're going to bed him. Because if you don't, I'll have to. A satyr is on both my and Sindri's list."

I playfully shoved my brother-in-law, pretending to be embarrassed by his teasing. "What list?"

Leifur grinned mischievously. "The list of creatures we want to bed before we die. I have a satyr, a royal, a werewolf, and a northern human on my list. Your brother has—"

"I'm well aware of what's on Sindri's list," I groaned, shaking my head.

"He does like to remind us, doesn't he?"

I blinked my eyes at him and smiled slyly. "I think he's a little jealous you bedded me before he got to you."

"That was for work," Leifur replied, trying to hide the slight shade of pink that crept across his pale cheeks.

"You seemed to enjoy yourself a little too much for it to just be *work*."

Leifur sighed. "What can I say? You have great tits."

I smiled and pressed my breasts together. "I do, don't I?"

"Next!"

We turned to see an overweight, old guard sitting at a table next to a sign that read 'Swords, Daggers and Axes'.

"You're up." Leifur pushed me forward.

Chapter 8

Njall

Telling General Magni about the siren had been a mistake. The man couldn't keep anything from my father, outside of bedding my sister for years before properly asking for her hand. My father was incensed to learn that a siren was in Tyndorf. While he enjoyed bedding every creature he could find, that one was walking our streets who could potentially control him was unacceptable. After he was finished screaming, threatening, and throwing things at us, he ordered the general to bring extra guards to the castle to ensure no one was trying to infiltrate the royal family—which meant him, Ingvar, and Hulda. My father couldn't care less about me, and Baldr was only useful to him as entertainment.

Unlike the other kingdoms, where birth order decided who took the throne, my father had come up with a unique way of doing things. When we were five, he ranked us based on the powers we'd inherited from our mothers. Ingvar, with his werewolf strength, came first; Hulda, with her sorcery, second, and Baldr was third. Despite being firstborn, I was ranked last, after even our mermaid sister who died in infancy. As a child, I craved my father's approval, but I soon learned it was futile. Despite having loved my selkie mother, he wanted nothing to do with me after her death, as if his betrayal and her broken heart were somehow my fault.

In the meantime, I could do nothing except wait for Ingvar to take the throne, in the hopes that he'd release me from my royal obligations so I could finally make a life for myself somewhere.

At least I'd been smart enough to keep quiet about where I'd seen the siren. Mentioning the Pirate's Booty was enough. That she'd been in my bed would only have made things worse.

After the extra guards arrived, the king dismissed us. Ingvar and Hulda each left with at least three men following them, while Baldr and I were sent on our way with a warning to stay out of trouble. The general and the king would devise a plan themselves to capture the siren—a task that was apparently beyond Baldr's and my abilities.

When the door to our father's office slammed shut, Baldr clapped me on the back. "Well, I'm off."

"Where exactly?" I asked.

"We didn't have plans today, did we?" he asked.

"No. I just assume at some point our father will want to know where we are."

"Ah. I've got plans with a stunning maiden I ran into at the market today."

"One of your famous tours?"

"Only the best for our guests." He grinned. "But really, this one's gorgeous. If she's as much fun as I suspect she is, I'll see if she's interested in having you join us."

"I can find *my own* bed partners," I snapped.

"Of course you can," Baldr said with a wink. "I just think it's fun to share, and the ladies never complain." When I didn't return his grin, he groaned, rolling his eyes. "Njall, stop being such a controlling older brother."

"It's easy for you to say," I snapped. "You're not the one that keeps getting punished whenever one of us doesn't do what Father wants."

Baldr threw his hands up in surrender. "Fair enough. I promise to keep out of trouble and stay away from any wicked sirens who may cross my path. Now may I go out and play?"

I groaned. "You're worse than a child."

Baldr laughed. "Benefits of being the youngest." Then he turned and dashed off on whatever conquest he had planned for the night. I watched him go, hoping he'd at least paid attention to General Magni's description of the siren.

Turning away, I walked through the endless corridors lined with polished marble floors and filled with more gold trinkets and paintings of long dead royals than anyone should ever own. In my suite, I stripped off the shirt that still smelled faintly of Pearl and tossed it on the floor before I pulled a fresh one from my wardrobe. My mind wandered back to our night together, before I knew what she was, and I tried to figure out when she could have influenced me.

She must have done something to me. Her touch, her scent—it all felt extraordinary. Her skin was smoother than any I'd ever felt in my life. I'd heard stories about sirens. She'd likely been with hundreds of men, so it made sense that she'd been so incredible in bed. But the idea that she could read minds, know exactly what I wanted—that seemed far-fetched.

I poured myself a large glass of ale and sat by the fire. I pulled my mother's beach glass pendant off my neck and stared into its depths. The pale blue glass glinted in the firelight. I couldn't remember her ever mentioning sirens—or anything that might help me now. Yet here I was, enchanted by one of them.

I downed the ale in a single, long swig, determined to never let it happen again.

Chapter 9

Elva

"Where are you going to put your daggers?" Leifur asked as I tugged on the strings to tighten the corset I'd chosen.

"Nowhere. I'm not taking them."

"What about your sword?"

"No." I turned and glared at him. Leifur sat cross-legged on his bed. "Stupid second brother," I muttered under my breath.

"What was that?"

"Nothing, you annoying trout."

Leifur stood and crossed his arms as he stared down at me. I ignored him and continued preparing myself in the mirror. We'd switched to a new inn to make sure the man I'd bedded and robbed couldn't find me too easily, and in the process I'd given in to my twin's request for a nicer establishment.

"Sindri would ask the same."

I let my siren surface just enough for my eyes to shift to black, the first sign she was coming. By the time my incisors grew to twice their length, he backed off.

" I forgot how much easier warrior sirens can shift into a

vicious killing beast. I know you can take care of yourself, but I'm allowed to worry."

I sighed, letting the siren recede as I finished pulling my hair out of the braid. My locks, now a dull brown, cascaded around my shoulders. "Thank you, but I'm more than capable of handling myself, especially where one male is concerned."

Leifur spun his finger in the air, and I turned obligingly for him. "I like the new corset. The color suits you."

Sticking my tongue at Leifur, I thrust my hand into the corset and adjusted my tits to position them in the most flattering way. After that, I was ready.

"I would wish you luck, but I know you won't need it," he said.

"Don't wait up," I said, heading for the door. The walk to the center of town was a lot faster this late in the day, as most people were likely at dinner or preparing for the celebrations. Our inn was in the poorer part of town, but it was at least cleaner than the Pirate's Booty.

The closer I got to the castle, the more elaborate the decorations and houses became. Plain windows gave way to ornate flower boxes and shutters, and the sizes of the houses doubled and then tripled. Laughter and fiddle music drifted toward me before I even rounded the last bend.

The King's Path inn stood against the wall that separated the castle grounds from the proper part of town. The building was larger than I'd expected, and the walls were made from carved and polished stones that glistened in the setting sun. A man emerged from a side street, lighting the torches lining the road. The tall poles were crafted from stone and held huge oil lanterns that cast a soft light, their warm glow spilling over the cobblestones as the scent of roasting venison and fresh bread wafted through the air.

I waited until he disappeared down the main street before

adjusting my corset a final time and stepping inside. Laughter and music filled the crowded inn. The bar was beautifully carved from stone and stretched the length of the room. An older man and woman were scrambling to serve the patrons drinks. Fiddlers were set up in a corner, surrounded by a group of young guests drinking ales and singing along to the music much too loudly. Every table was occupied with locals and tournament participants; the latter being easy to spot by their non-Tyndorf colors. A pair of young ale maids was carrying trays of food and drink through the crowd. I tried not to disturb their work as I crossed the room to the bar.

The older man took a lascivious look at me and nodded. "You're the one I've been waiting for."

"Excuse me?"

"You're here to see Baldr—the satyr. He has a type, and you fit it to perfection." He slurred the last word and ogled my chest.

I crossed my arms and glared at him, waiting for him to provide me with further information.

"The satyr's room is on the top floor," the woman behind the bar said. She tossed me a large brass key. "The stairs are at the back, and if things get out of hand ... the girls are on the second floor."

A wicked grin slowly spread across my lips. "Don't worry, I'll try not to hurt him." I winked at the man's startled expression and headed to the stairs. Unlike our inn, everything here was new and smelled of cedar and vanilla. The fiddle music faded behind me as I gripped the iron rail and climbed the stairs.

The second-floor hallway was long and lined with doors, each inscribed with a name rather than a number. *Oh, it's a brothel.* A satyr living in a brothel made sense, but it made me wonder about the women he would usually be with. I continued to the top floor, where a single door awaited, secured with a brass lock. I slipped the key out of my pocket and bounced it gently in my hand. The door was solid wood with bronze fixtures and a huge lock and handle, but the knocker drew my attention. It was a goat's head with a ring in its mouth. Its horns curled upward, just like Baldr's, and its sapphire eyes gleamed invitingly. I resisted the urge to pocket them and instead slid my key into the lock, twisted it, and pushed the door open.

Chapter 10

Elva

I stepped inside a pristine foyer, leading into a short hallway, where an expensive hand-woven rug stretched across the floor. The walls were adorned with oil paintings of the sea and surrounding forests and glistened in the torchlight. I closed the door behind me with a gentle click and proceeded toward the arc at the end of the hallway. It opened into a giant sitting room. Intricately carved couches faced an immense fireplace made of sparkling sea stones. The fabric covering the couches was the most intricate I had ever seen outside of the Siren Queen's chambers. I cautiously tread into the room. The fire sputtered and crackled, and I heard a door open behind me.

Baldr was standing beside a table, pouring himself a drink. "I thought I heard the door open." He finished pouring his beverage and held a glass out to me.

Without speaking, I crossed the room and accepted his glass, my eyes roving over him. He'd changed clothes from earlier and now wore only a pair of loose, flowing pants. They hung precariously low on his hips, just enough to tease, and covered the top half of his legs, until they bent at the knee. Curiosity had me shift just enough to see his tail coming out of an opening at the back of his trousers. The rest of him was fully on display, and I couldn't help but admire him with an intensity I tried to mask. His brown hair hung loosely across his face, and his muscles were sharply defined across both his chest and arms.

He held his glass out to me, and I gently tapped mine to his before taking a sip. The ale was richly smoky and bit my tongue before igniting a slow burn as I swallowed. I pulled back the glass and looked at it, expecting to see some smoke coming off it. When I looked back at Baldr he had already closed the distance between us, with a slight smirk on his face. "I have it shipped from the north," he said.

"Must be nice to be rich," I replied, taking another gulp of the ale. I never needed courage to be around a man, but something about Baldr felt different—it felt dangerous, and I couldn't sort out why.

His fingers grazed mine as he took the glass from me and placed it back on the table. I turned my gaze up at him, and he ran his fingers through my locks.

"I remember something about a tour," I said in the most sultry voice my non-siren self could muster.

"I offered, didn't I?" He smiled as his hand moved behind my neck and gripped my hair, sending a wave of heat through my core.

He leaned down so his lips were almost touching my ear. "You have three options to start with: a tour of the town, of the inn, or my bedroom. Which would you prefer?"

I pressed my siren down as hard as I could, fighting the urge to let her rise to the surface. My hand drifted up his chest, tracing the lines of muscle beneath his skin. The satyr was mine tonight. Biting my lower lip, I turned to face him. The scent of earth and leather overwhelmed me as he gripped my hair harder so I'd have to meet his gaze.

"Well?"

I smiled before I pressed my lips to his, and he used his free hand to pull me flush against him. He was a solid wall of muscle, and using all the force I could muster, being pinned against him, I slid my hands up his chest and wrapped them around his neck. An animalistic moan left him, and he gripped my thighs to hoist me up, allowing me to wrap my legs around his waist. Without breaking our kiss, he kicked open the bedroom door and threw me onto his giant bed. I only caught a quick glimpse of the space before he was at the edge of his bed, watching me. His pants hung lower now and were only being held up by his erection.

Realizing how large he was made my insides heat with anticipation. I'd learned about satyrs in my seduction lessons, and they were said to be one of the most well-endowed creatures in our world, but I never expected to bed one.

Baldr chuckled. He likely noticed me staring and climbed onto the bed. His weight made the mattress lean to the side as he crawled toward me. I eyed him as he got closer, playing with the leather straps on my corset. When I moved to unlace myself, his hand shot out and grabbed my wrist, pinning it above my head.

"Not just yet." His voice dropped an octave as he spoke.

A wicked grin spread across my lips as he stared at me. As he leaned in, his eyes seemed to change color. He growled as he sniffed my neck, and my insides turned to mush. The surrounding air smelled of earth and rain, and I realized how satyrs got their reputation for seduction—pheromones. Only the sultry sirens could use that trick to lure in their lovers. The rest of us had to work for our conquests and make do with our songs. Knowing what I knew about males, I had a choice here: to stop things and call him out on this whole setup, or to give in and enjoy the ride.

I grabbed the back of his head with my free hand and pulled his mouth down to mine to kiss him. He tasted of spicy smoke leftover from the ale, and it sent tremors of anticipation through me. As I expected, he didn't need any encouragement. Baldr's kisses were rough and demanding. His stubble scratched my chin as he pushed his tongue into my mouth. When he released my wrist, I let out a desperate moan. Laughing, he moved his kisses to my neck and used his free hand to make quick work of my corset ribbon. Of all the men I have been with, none had ever undressed me that swiftly. He pulled the leather from beneath me and threw it across the room.

The room had a slight chill, making my nipples pebble instantly and my body shiver. Perhaps his chilly room was intentional. Baldr abandoned my neck, and his mouth latched onto my right breast. As his tongue gently flicked my nipple, his free hand found my other breast and pinched the nipple. The combination of pain and pleasure made me buck beneath him, and earned me a suck and pinch. My hands snaked through his hair until I found the base of his horns. The curious side of me wondered if they were sensitive, so I stroked the shaft of one, and a guttural moan vibrated against my breast. I bit back my giggle and grasped both his horns.

A deep growl left him. Continuing to work, his eyes turned up and glanced at me. Their intensity fueled me, and I clutched his horns and pulled him off my breast. His mouth found mine again, and I kissed him back with the same enthusiasm he gave me. Releasing my breast, his hand found my waistband, and without hesitation, slipped into my pants.

Fingers flitted over my clit like drops of rain, there for a moment and then gone. I released a breathy sigh, and his kisses became rougher. Running my fingers down his muscled chest, I tugged the string of his pants, sending them sliding down his thighs so he could kick them off with ease. Reaching for his cock, I gasped when I gripped it, and realized it curved toward his stomach, and had a much larger bulge on the head than I'd ever seen. Glancing down, I couldn't help but turn my head to the side a little to take in the entire thing.

"Don't worry, you can handle it," Baldr whispered, as he slid his hand out of my pants and pushed them down my legs before throwing them off the bed.

Sitting back against the pillows, he watched as I carefully examined his cock. Not only was it impressively large, but it seemed to be ribbed along the shaft. Locking my eyes on his, I leaned down and swirled my tongue over the tip, making his head drop back as he moaned. Enjoying his response, I gripped his dick with both hands and stroked him as I took the entire tip into my mouth. Animalistic grunts of pleasure burst from him, the harder I sucked as I took him deeper with each bob of my head. Finally, I popped out his cock and straddled his lap. Baldr grabbed himself and lined up with my pussy as I slowly lowered myself onto him. The stretch to take him was unlike anything I'd ever felt. For a moment, I was nervous I couldn't take him, but as if he'd read my mind, the satyr moved his hand to stroke my clit, sending a rush of wetness to aid his entry.

Inch by glorious inch, I worked my way down on him until I was flush with his pelvis, and his entire cock was buried inside me. Taking a moment to catch my breath, he moved up to fist my hair with one hand and slap my ass with the other. I jerked at the sharpness of the slap, and my entire pussy was set off. I rocked back and forth on the satyr until I adjusted to the size, and then I grabbed his horns for support and bounced myself up and down on his cock while he worked my clit mercilessly. As I felt my orgasm build, he moved his free hand to tweak and roll my nipples, adding a bit of pain to the pleasure that was threatening to tear me in two.

When I was on the verge of coming, he grabbed my hips and threw me down on the bed. He tossed my leg over his shoulder and grabbed my wrists again to lock them above my head. Pulling his cock out of me for a moment, he smirked down at me before he slammed himself back into me, pushing me up the bed from the force of it. I screamed as he continued to pound into me like a bull charging a target. By the time he was spent, and filling me with his cum, I'd orgasmed at least three times, and couldn't speak because of how hoarse my throat was.

Baldr lay beside me, panting loudly enough to wake the dead. I enjoy it when I manage to wear a man out during sex, and the satyr did not disappoint. After we both got a hold of our breath, I stood from the bed and gathered my things.

The floor behind me clacked as hooves hit it. "Time for that tour."

I was about to lace up my pants, but stopped and looked up, "Tour?"

He grinned at me like a child with a new toy. "I promised you a tour and I'm a satyr of my word."

I looked him over, and he did not indicate deception. His movements were fluid as he stood and moved toward the wardrobe, this time opting for pants rather than a loincloth. "It gets chilly at night this time of year. If you didn't bring a cloak, I'll provide you with one."

I glanced into the wardrobe to see at least two dozen items in various colors, fabrics, and lengths. "Left behind from your conquests?" I slipped my corset on and did up the front ribbon. Baldr snickered. "No. I just like having options." I heard him rifling through fabric across the room as I focused on the ribbons, a job I usually left for Leifur or Sindri.

"This one matches your eyes."

I looked up, and Baldr was holding a beautiful cloak that seemed to change color from sea blue to hunter green as he turned it in the light.

"It's gorgeous," I said as he held it out to me. The fabric was the softest I'd ever felt. Instinct told me it was too much, and that he must have an ulterior motive, but I couldn't stop touching it. If Sindri could accept all his treasures, why shouldn't I? I draped the cloak over my bare shoulders, marveling at how it seemed to glow against my skin.

Baldr looped the metal fastener across the cloak and stepped back. "I knew it would suit you," he said, and offered his arm with a flourish. "Shall we?"

Chapter 11

Njall

Ashriek drew me from my frustration, and a group of women came stumbling out of a tavern. I sheathed my sword when I recognized a few of them as regulars in Baldr's endless list of conquests. *Hopefully, he's in his room so I can drag him home to our father and go back to bed.*

The door slammed behind me as I entered the tavern. It was even more crowded than my place was, but with the advantage that nobody would rob my brother here. He overpaid for his room, and having him around meant the knights not only let the brothel run upstairs without issue, but they also used the ladies' services themselves.

Looking around at the very drunk patrons, I almost turned around and left. I didn't want to deal with their fake congratulations anymore. No one cared that my sister was getting married. All they cared about was that the wedding meant three days of food, entertainment, and gold flowing from the castle into the town. That the groom was the general was good for the people. If Magni was in a good mood, so were his knights, and that meant peace in the town and fewer brawls and demands for bribes.

A path opened in the crowd, and I dove in and made a beeline for the bar. Ragnar took one look at me and hurried to the back. The old man always hated me, but Gertrud saw and moved to the end where I was headed.

"He's not here," she said.

"This is his favorite time of day," I replied, confused. "Where is he?"

"Left an hour ago with some pretty young thing."

I groaned and rubbed my forehead. Of all the nights for my brother to leave with his latest whore, it had to be tonight. "You don't know where they were headed, do you?"

"Sorry, love," Gertrud said, giving me a sympathetic smile. "I overheard him joking about a tour, but I can't say I'm surprised. There was something different about this one."

I leaned in closer to the bar. "Different how?"

"She's got sass to her, and a way about her. She could handle anyone."

I swallowed hard. "What did she look like?"

"Well, her eyes were different colors."

Ferflucs.

I debated coercing some knights to help me find my brother, but it wasn't worth the hassle. I was a prince of Tyndorf, but I wasn't the crown prince like Ingvar was, and Baldr was known for his wild nights of drinking, gambling, and womanizing. No one would believe that a woman could be a danger to him. But I knew it had to be Pearl. I could understand her happening upon one of us, but two princes in one night? Here was my proof that she was up to no good. I needed to find my brother and make sure she wasn't doing anything to him. She may have hidden her siren locks, but I knew what she was, and I'd make sure everyone else did too.

Turning to shove my way past the drunkards, I managed to get out of the bar and into the cool evening air, grateful to be away from the stench of ale and body odor. I took a shortcut down an alley behind a brothel to get to Baldr's favorite tavern when I heard a high-pitched shriek of laughter. *Hulda*. I stopped walking and listened for which direction it was coming from, then turned around. I looked around at the houses and realized what part of town I was in. My brother liked the wealthy part, I liked the seedy part, and my sister liked the part where the entire kingdom came to act on their carnal urges.

I'm too old to be collecting my stupid siblings.

Speeding up, I walked past two brothels, one pleasure dungeon, and three smoking parlors until I reached the most expensive establishment in town. A pair of former knights stood guard at the door. I recognized them both as men Magni had to remove from the ranks because they were too aggressive. They looked me up and down and then opened the gold-covered doors of the Dragon's Keep without a sound. As I stepped inside, it was like I'd been transported to another world—a dragon's lair, to be exact. The walls looked like the jagged stones of a cave, with gold and silver gems of all types and sizes protruding from them. Even the floor was laid with gold coins, as though you were walking on the dragon's treasure. Inside, the madam stood dressed all in gold, with a tiara that would rival any in our treasure hold perched atop her silver hair.

"Evening, Your Highness," she said with a slight bow, her movements as graceful as a deer but as dangerous as a dire wolf. "Are you here for pleasure, pain, or to forget the world outside?" She extended her bejeweled hand, and I kissed it, my eyes lingering on the rings adorning each finger. One of them, I was certain, had been in our treasure room a few months before. It seemed my sister wasn't the only one visiting this establishment.

"Neither, Madam. I have come at the request of my father to retrieve my sister. We need her for fittings and whatnot."

She nodded, as though this were the most ordinary request.

"Of course. We mustn't keep the king waiting. I'll take you to her."

I followed her deeper into the cave. The doors we passed through became more extravagant until we reached one made from gold and decorated with gems that spelled out the words, 'Royalty only'.

"Your Highness and her guests can meet in here," she said, bowing before leaving me alone outside the door. It no longer surprised me that people showed my sister so much more respect than they did me. She was the second-ranked sibling, after all. I decided against knocking and stepped inside.

I should have knocked.

The room reeked of dragon's thistle, my sister's favorite hallucinogenic herb. Its effects were more potent on sorcerers than mortals, so she could indulge while ensuring that her lovers remained attentive to her. The space was as elaborate as I'd expect from Hulda. Gems, carved statues, and exotic flowers decorated the place, and there was a nature motif that reflected her lineage. The sorceress side of her was from the Tiere line, the sorcerers who could control animals and had a strong connection with nature. In the middle of the room was a bed so large that they must have built the room around it, because it wouldn't have fit through the door.

On the bed lay a high-ranking nobleman's son, naked, with my sister straddling him. Beside them stood his friend, one hand gripping her hair, and the other guiding his cock down her throat.

I stood at the door with my palms pressed against my eyes, and my face turned toward the ceiling, waiting for Hulda to finally notice me. Likely, she had and couldn't be bothered to acknowledge me. Their moans grated on my patience until I finally snapped, "Hulda, you've been summoned."

I heard a loud pop, likely her pulling her mouth off the noble's cock, and a rustle of fabric. Risking a glance, I found her standing in a silk robe with her usual wicked smile. "Hello, brother. I didn't see you there."

"How could you, with a lowly noble's cock down your throat? Is this how you spend the night before your wedding?"

"Of course not, silly. This is how I spend my weekends."

"And how does your betrothed feel about this?"

"I'm sure he's busy sowing his wild oats. Now, what do you want? As you can see, I have my hands full at the moment." She smacked the ass of the noble who was just in her mouth and playfully pushed him onto the bed. Both men watched her every move like puppies awaiting their next command. They were high.

Tying her robe, Hulda tousled her hair.

"Maybe if you stopped telling everyone how full your hands are." I said, "You wouldn't be forced to marry." My sister had never been ashamed of her sexuality, but in recent years, she'd been taking it to extremes and flaunting her exploits even more than our brothers. Father disapproved of it in his most prized heir.

Her taunting smile dropped, and she narrowed her eyes. "You of all people shouldn't be judging me for who I bed."

"What's that supposed to mean?"

"I'm not stupid like the men in our family. You didn't magically find a siren. You bedded her and made up a lie about finding her to cover your tracks. We haven't seen one in over a decade, but you somehow run into her even though she's in disguise? Please, you had sex with her." She pushed my shoulder with an accusing finger. "How do I know you aren't under her control now?"

"Because I'm not. You know Ingvar and I are not easily influenced."

She sighed and looked me up and down. "Fine. You're not under a spell. Then what do you want? If you're looking for a recommendation, Heidi in the silver cavern is a delight. She looks sweet and innocent, but screams like a banshee when she comes. And she'll let you take her anyway you want." Before I could tell her to stop talking, she finished. "She's a favorite of Magni and me. Unlike you, my betrothed understands that sorceresses have desires far stronger than any maiden. He's happy to share me with anyone I want, male or female, since I let him play too."

"Hulda, enough," I growled, but she just cackled.

"I knew that would make you angry. It's all true, though. If you didn't want to learn about my sex habits, you shouldn't have interrupted me."

"Well, that conversation with Magni is why I'm here. Father wants us in the castle until after the wedding. He's worried Anginfill may have convinced the sirens to join their cause and attack."

She glanced back at the naked nobles. "Fine. Let me finish and go back with you."

"You have five minutes."

Thirty minutes later, my sister stepped out of her room. She was dressed, but her favorite violet gown barely covered her. She was fluffing her brown curls and stuck out her tongue at me.

I stood and marched over to her. "So, you can no longer tell time?"

"I would not rush my pleasure for you or our father."

"We have to find Baldr, too. I checked his place, but he wasn't there."

"Of course not," Hulda replied. "He'll be out chasing one of the women he met today at the tournament registration. He spent most of the day there, and it certainly wasn't helpful."

"Figures."

"He usually comes home after he's done with them. It's the only place with a tub large enough for him. We should check the castle." Hulda went to the door and whispered to the madam before she headed onto the street. I rushed to follow her, but the madam stepped before me and held out her hand. Sighing, I dropped my satchel of gold into her hand and wrenched the door open to follow my sister.

I spun in a quick circle, looking for Hulda. Every shadow looked like a crouching figure now. Were there other sirens? I spotted my sister at the end of the road. She was waving at someone, and to my astonishment, Baldr rounded the corner.

"I found him," Hulda smiled smugly as I hurried to catch up. She had always been ridiculously lucky, even as a child. At first, I thought she cheated at all our games, but as I got older, I figured her luck must be tied to her sorceress half. As I came up to them, Hulda was complaining to Baldr about how I'd interrupted her fun.

"You know better than to not knock, Njall," Baldr snickered. "You complain that I'm too open with my body and sexuality, but our dear sister is far more so than I."

"I'm very aware of that, thank you." I had no time for their jibes—my mind was elsewhere. If Anginfill had sirens on their side, they were planning something, and it would be soon. The wedding would be the next day, but I couldn't help feeling that the town was on the edge of a storm, and I had no idea when it would break.

Chapter 12

Elva

Both of my brothers were still awake when I returned. Leifur had told Sindri about the satyr, and they wouldn't let me go to sleep until I recounted every juicy detail of the night, not once, but twice. Leifur used the time to touch up my hair paste, and I was relieved to learn the man I'd robbed hadn't come looking for me. After my brothers heard enough about my evening, Sindri handed me a key. His new widowed friend had given him enough gold that we could afford two rooms, and they'd already moved my things into the smaller one. I hugged him goodnight and headed to my room across the hall.

The lock stuck a little, but once I wiggled it just right, I got into the room. It was furnished with a desk, a bed, and a fireplace, and I was grateful that my brothers had lit the fire for me. My bag was sitting on the chair by the table, and my blades were laid out on the bed. I unsheathed one and inspected it. These daggers were a gift from my instructor after I'd finished my warrior siren training. We were each given a weapon as a parting gift, and it was usually the one that suited our skills the best.

I replaced the dagger in its spot and reached for the last one in my set. Smaller and worn, it was the first blade I'd ever been given—the day my siren came in. I locked my hand around the handle and pressed it to my chest, remembering that day. Sindri had sobbed when he realized we were different —me a warrior, and he sultry. It broke his heart, and honestly, it would have broken mine too, if it hadn't already been shattered.

That very day, we were separated. He went to learn how to wield his gifts, while I was sent for physical training. That is, after I finished my rehabilitation with the elder sirens. A siren who was terrified of men was useless, they'd said. My hands were shaking from the haunting memories of that time, and the dagger clattered onto the floor. I had been weak then, and others took advantage of my innocence. But that weakness is gone now. Once my brothers were safe, I would hunt Aamon to the ends of the world if need be.

Leifur had cleaned my blades for me, but he knew not to touch this last one. The dried blood served as a reminder of how far I'd come and how much work I had left to do. "One more," I whispered, wrapping my daggers in their leather case. "When I find him, I'll add his blood to my blade and put an end to the pain I've carried all these years."

I placed the daggers next to the sword on my desk and got to work untying my corset. I tossed it on the chair, and my pants quickly followed. Slipping into the bed, I sighed in contentment. I loved my brothers dearly, but having my own room at an inn was the best feeling. We shared a tent every night we traveled, especially when it was cold, so being alone in a bed with a full belly was a luxury I'd nearly forgotten. I turned to my side and watched the fire crackle, its golden light dancing across the room as I drifted off to sleep.

Years of getting up before the sun to train meant that I was naturally an early riser. I dressed and headed downstairs to the main floor. The tavern was empty except for a woman polishing mugs behind the bar. I ordered breakfast to be sent up to my brother's room and went back upstairs with a jug of spiced cider and three mugs. It took several rounds of knocking before my brother finally yanked the door open, muttering threats under his breath.

"Good morning to you, too," I said brightly, pecking him on the cheek, and he grumbled even more.

Leifur was by the washbasin, splashing water on his face when he spotted the jug in my hands. His eyes lit up, and he was across the room in a blink to retrieve one for himself. "You are a treasure, Elva."

"A treasure that bites and wakes you up," Sindri muttered. He flopped back onto the bed, pulling the blanket over his head.

I ignored his dramatics. "The food should be up shortly."

Leifur cradled the mug in his hands, took a gulp, and let out a satisfied moan. "I love southern cider."

Sindri's head popped out of the blanket. "Hey! Don't you dare make sounds like that for anything that isn't me!"

Leifur and I giggled. "I don't know what spices they use down here," Leifur said, "but—"

"Euphoric?" I suggested, and Leifur nodded and drank again.

"Fine, give me some of your life-changing cider." Sindri scooted to the foot of the bed, still wrapped in the blanket, as he took the mug I passed his way. He sniffed it, shrugged, and took a swig. His eyes widened almost immediately, and he stared at us in mock disbelief.

"Told you," Leifur said.

A knock interrupted us. "That'll be breakfast," I said, and let them in with our food.

We ate quickly, and once we were full of bread, soft cheese, dried goat, and berry spread, Leifur and I dressed in our leathers for the day's events, while Sindri went all out, draping himself in the finest clothes we had. He was meeting his new widowed friend so he could escort her to spend the day watching the events.

When we reached the main road, we were sucked into the river of people flowing toward the castle. It felt as if the entire kingdom had turned out for the celebration. Many of the stands were closed and taken down from the road, leaving only the bakeries and taverns open, and even those were standing room only. Tyndorf certainly knows how to throw a celebration.

Leifur had signed up for both blacksmithing competitions—the skill-based challenge and the artistic one. In the skills competition, he would be given something to reproduce and a time limit. The winner would be the person who crafted the most identical items in the given time. The artistic challenge is more open-ended. Competitors can create whatever they like, provided it serves as a wedding gift for the bride or groom. The winners will be chosen based on which gifts the royal couple preferred.

As for me, the dagger competition will be that morning, and swords in the afternoon. I would have preferred it the other way, so I could go into daggers with everyone underestimating me, but luck hasn't been on my side lately.

The crowd surged around us, and a group of children bumped us, trying to squeeze their way through the crowd. I tightened my scabbard to make sure my daggers wouldn't shift. It wasn't until we reached the castle grounds that I could move freely again.

Sindri quickly spotted his widow across the field. He kissed Leifur and me on the cheek and dashed off. We watched him bow to her before offering his arm and leading her off towards the competitions.

"It's unfair," I said, shaking my head.

"What is?" Leifur asked.

"How easily Sindri slips in and out of his siren persona. I feel like mine fights me every time I need to put her away."

"It makes sense," Leifur said. "He is so much like his siren. The only difference between them is that his siren can only woo women, while he can steal the hearts of men, too."

I couldn't help but snicker at the truth of his observation.

Leifur continued, "But yours—you two are at war. Your siren wants to burn the world to the ground and murder every male in sight, as a punishment for what those men did to you. That is, after she's had her wicked way with them. You want that too, just without as much of the murdering part."

I snorted, which made Leifur laugh, so I playfully shoved him. He lost his footing and stumbled into someone.

When the man turned, and I saw the royal crest on his shirt, my blood ran cold. Leifur had stumbled right into a prince. My brother had biceps larger than my thighs from working as a blacksmith, but this prince, while shorter, was muscular everywhere. His hair was a bushy white and gray, and his yellow eyes were fixed intently on my brother.

"Who do you think you are to touch a prince of Tyndorf?" the prince demanded.

"Apologies," I said, grabbing Leifur's arm. "We'll be on our way and won't trouble you any further."

I knew I had said the wrong thing immediately. A growl rumbled from the prince as he seized Leifur's arm and pulled him closer to examine Leifur's scalp. "Blue hair ... you must be that siren my general and brother are all worried about."

Leifur shot me a wild-eyed glance. "I'm only here to compete in the blacksmith compe ... compe ... competition." Leifur only stuttered when he was scared, and hearing it sent me into a rage. "We apologized. Now let us go." My voice was rising. I knew I had to calm down or things would go badly for us quickly.

The prince turned his attention to me. "You need to leave, young lady. This siren has you under his spell. I accept your gratitude for freeing you. Now be gone."

"Elva, just go," Leifur whispered through clenched teeth, but his eyes told me he knew I wouldn't be doing that.

I hesitated, weighing my options: draw my daggers or try to reason with him. Before I could decide, a familiar voice called out from behind me.

"Ingvar, come on," Baldr shouted, and the crowd parted for him. Today, he was wearing a traditional shirt with the same crest as the princes. "If I have to listen to Hulda complain one more time about how bright it is out here, I might have to lock her in a tower. And while Njall may think that's a great idea, I'm sure Father and Magni would disagree."

A pit opened up in my stomach, and all my air left me. *No, it can't be.* The satyr smiled when his eyes landed on me. "Hello again, Elva. A pleasure to run into you so soon." His eyes narrowed as he took in the scene before us, particularly Ingvar's grip on Leifur's arm. "What is going on here?"

"I caught the siren. Now be helpful or get lost."

"Siren?" Baldr looked from me to Leifur. "But he's male. Aren't all sirens female?"

"And that's why you're not crown prince," came another voice from behind us.

No. Please no.

I turned and saw the man from our first inn marching through the crowd. The man I had bedded and then robbed was wearing the same crest as Ingvar and Baldr. *A prince? Malachite and Baldr, both princes. I'm going to be sick.* I swallowed back the nausea rising in my throat.

"Did you pay attention to any of our lessons?" Malachite asked.

"Only the anatomy ones," Baldr replied smugly.

Malachite had dark bags under his eyes. He must have been tired or frustrated. When he spotted me, he stopped in his tracks and his lips twisted into a snarl. "You!"

Baldr stepped between me and Malachite. "What business do you have with Elva?"

"Is that the name she gave you? She gave me Pearl."

"You picked Pearl!" I shouted back.

"Sorry if I'm unused to choosing names for the women I sleep with. That's my brother's territory."

"I don't need to pick names," Baldr said. "They give me their real ones."

"Wait—she gave you her name. Did you bed her?"

"Of course. Look at her—she's gorgeous."

I rolled my eyes. This was going downhill, fast. "It isn't what it looks like!"

"So you didn't sleep with two of the princes of Tyndorf in the last two nights?"

All four men turned to me at once, and despite being used to men's attention, their harsh scrutiny made me feel exposed, and my cheeks burned. "Who I sleep with is none of your business," I managed after I came to my senses.

"It *is* our business if you did it to gather information from us." Malachite shoved Baldr aside and lunged at me. I wasn't expecting it and couldn't move fast enough. He grabbed my shoulder and yanked me away from Leifur. "Who are you working for? It's the Anginfill king, isn't it?"

"I'm not working for anyone!" I screamed back as I clawed at his hand to get him to release me. "I'm traveling with my brothers, and we came for the competition. Now unhand me!" I tried to slap him, but missed. Thankfully, I'd managed to keep my claws retracted.

"I don't believe you," Malachite spat, his grip tightening. "You're coming with us. Let our father decide what to do with you."

"No, please," Leifur begged, trying to pull away from his captor. Ingvar waved a few knights over, and soon he was being led away by two other men.

"Do you really think she's a spy?" Baldr asked as Njall dragged me forward, following Leifur.

"Whores have been used as spies for centuries," Ingvar replied, grabbing my other arm. "If she'd have run into me, I'd have let her into my bed."

"Where are you taking them?" Sindri shouted as he pushed his way through the gathering crowd.

"Sindri, go!" I yelled back.

"Silence, whore," Ingvar growled, his fingers digging deeper into my arm.

Baldr turned to Sindri, confusion plastered on his face. "Who are you?"

"I'm her brother, and I demand to know where you're taking my sister and my husband."

"Guards!" Njall barked, and they pounced on Sindri, restraining him.

"Let him go! He has nothing to do with this." I was struggling to focus my breathing and keep my heart, anxiety, and siren all under control.

"If he's your brother, that makes all three of you sirens," Njall said.

I went cold and thought I might be sick. A slight smirk appeared on Njall's face. "You're wondering how we figured you out," he said.

I stared at him defiantly.

"You missed some hair when you dyed it," Njall said.

"We'll come with you, but let us walk. You don't need to drag us," Leifur pleaded.

I could feel Leifur's eyes on me, and I suddenly knew why I was losing control. He'd realized it even before I had. He always did. My stomach clenched as Ingvar tightened his grip on my arm, and the memory of another man holding my arm tried to break free.

"We're not letting you go," one guard sneered, laughing. "We're not stupid."

"D-Drag me then, but let my sister walk," Leifur stammered.

Baldr turned to me, smirking. Sweat was making my hair stick to my neck. I knew I couldn't hold her back much longer, so I took a deep breath and released her.

Chapter 13

Elva

Screams surrounded us as a song erupted from my throat. The viciousness of my siren's song was enough to send people fleeing, even with no additional magic from me. Baldr, Ingvar, and Njall all leaped away from me at once, finally giving me the air to breathe.

"I warned you," Leifur said. One guard holding him moved to punch him, but I roared in his direction, and the man went white.

I turned toward the princes, and all three stiffened. My loose hair fell in my face, and I brushed it back with a taloned hand. The dull, brown dye that Leifur had worked so hard to put on it was gone, and the vibrant hues of blue and green were back. Somehow, my siren form had removed all attempts to hide her. My eyes were black now, even if I couldn't feel that change; the slightly darker way I saw the world now told me. The other shifts, I could feel. The fangs that sprouted in my mouth were enough to strike fear into the surrounding men. It seems this part of Torian had never learned that sirens were more than seductresses. We could also be monsters that kill without mercy. I was terrifying enough that even my kind had feared me.

"Keep your hands to yourselves," I hissed. "And I won't have to hurt you. My brothers and I can walk ourselves to wherever you're taking us."

The guard closest to me swallowed hard, and I felt a smirk spread across my lips. I closed my eyes, breathed in, and pictured the Sieden Sea. The slower my heartbeat, the calmer I felt, and soon all the rage rushing through me was gone. When I opened my eyes, Leifur and Sindri stood at my side, and the guards were inching away cautiously.

"Ready?" Sindri asked so softly I doubted anyone besides me heard him. I nodded, and he slung an arm around my shoulders and led me after the guards who were now giving us a wide, wary berth.

We walked past gawking citizens who were waiting for the festivities to start. I wondered if our discovery would delay the events of the day. Once we entered the inner walls of the castle grounds, the crowds thinned, and the group of guards escorting us grew larger. Ahead, the pale stone of the castle gleamed in the sunlight. Immediately, I thought of the limestone that made up the Siren Island in the Konvern Territory. But if humans had ripped this from the seafloor and brought it up here, that left me with more questions than answers.

Ingvar was arguing with the lead guard marching beside him. Baldr seemed in good spirits, but from what I'd heard about Satyrs, it took a lot to upset them. I caught Njall staring at me. It was hard to read his expression, and he turned away from me before I could try to decipher it. The idiot probably thought I orchestrated this whole mess, as if I'd known he was a prince after meeting him in a run-down tavern bar.

We entered the castle from one side, through narrow, unobtrusive metal doors. The cramped entranceway opened into a beautifully decorated hall, whose walls were draped in tapestries and paintings that told stories of battles won and lost. My fingers twitched as I stopped to study one depiction of the sea. The intricate stitching made it seem to come to life. I reached my hand out to touch it, but Leifur tugged me away, steering me toward a pair of ornately carved wooden doors at the far end of the hall. Their fasteners and nails were made of a gold alloy, so they sparkled in the light, and the polished wood reflected our images like a mirror. The guards parted, leaving the princes, Leifur, and me in front of the doors.

Ingvar pounded his fist three times on the door and waited. When a deep voice responded with *enter,* two tall guards reached around Baldr and Njall and pulled the doors open. Leifur and I followed the princes into the room.

If the hall tapestries had been beautiful, they didn't hold a candle to the ones in the throne room. Gigantic stone columns stretched from the floor to the arched ceiling. Our footsteps echoed, and I heard a grunt beside me. It was Njall. He was watching Leifur like a wolf eyeing prey. I grabbed my brother-in-law's arm and pulled him to my other side as they ushered us toward the back of the room. A large, empty throne rested on a raised dais.

Leifur leaned toward me. "What are we doing here? There's no one here."

Before I could respond, a vicious bang echoed through the entire space, startling him. From an entrance behind the throne, a giant of a man stalked toward us. When he got closer, I saw the glint of his crown and realized it was King Hilmir. I grabbed Leifur's hand, and he must have realized too, because he squeezed it back.

Despite his advanced years, the king was still muscular, especially compared to the other royals of Torian. His head was covered with thick and lush, gray and black hair that matched his beard. He was dressed resplendently for his only daughter's wedding. The teal velvet made his brown eyes seem darker, and the accents of coral made me think of home.

"What is the meaning of this, Ingvar?" the king barked, his voice echoing off the stone walls. "You dare to interrupt your sister's wedding celebrations? And for what, some petty thieves? Chop their hands off. Throw them in the dungeon. I don't care what you do, but be done with it."

"They aren't thieves," Baldr replied. I flinched when his hand brushed my shoulder. "Well, she isn't."

"She is," Njall replied. He followed Ingvar toward their father. "She robbed me after we slept together."

Baldr leaned closer to me. "You robbed my brother? Impressive." He left us behind as he followed his brothers.

"Robbed you? I still don't understand why you brought them here—" King Hilmir stopped abruptly, and I felt his eyes on me. I knew that look he had—a scowl on his lips, slightly widened eyes, and a darkening of his cheeks signaled disgust, surprise, and lust. These were the three emotions my kind were known for bringing out in people.

"A siren," Hilmir muttered, as if the word explained everything.

"They all are," Njall said, pointing at Leifur and Sindri as though they were specimens on display.

"Male sirens? I thought they were a myth," the king said, his voice barely above a whisper as he patted Ingvar on the shoulder. "All the accounts I've collected over the years tell of them being vicious monsters. But these ... they could pass for humans."

"We are not in our siren form," Leifur said.

"He's right," Ingvar said, following his father as he circled us. "In the market, she certainly became a monster."

I snarled at him, and his eyes flashed. He growled back with an intensity that made even me step back. Leifur went white as a ghost.

Hilmir rubbed his hands together and came closer to us. I could smell the ale and pickled eggs on his breath, and I couldn't help but step back.

"What to do with a group of thieves who are known monsters?" he mused aloud.

"We aren't monsters," Leifur snapped. "We're sirens, and we can't help what we are any more than your sons can."

The king's eyes narrowed at my brother, and I moved forward to grab Leifur's hand, but the king backhanded me across the face. Before I could stop myself, I lunged for him, fangs and claws out. Ingvar and the general had me in seconds and pinned me to the ground.

Blood trickled down the king's cheek from where I'd managed to nick him, and one of his sleeves had been slashed to ribbons. The general pressed his knee into my back, making it hard to breathe, and I winced as pain shot through me. My cheek was pressed against the cold stone floor, bits of grit digging into my flesh. I couldn't turn to face the king, but his boots clunked against the ground and then entered my field of vision. He squatted and stared at me as I struggled against the general's hold. I wanted more than anything to free myself and show him exactly what I was made of.

The king laughed, a deep and ominous sound that sent a chill down my spine. "I've been searching for a siren for decades, and you just come walking into my kingdom. How fortunate for me." He looked away from me and shouted triumphantly, "Lock her in the dungeon. The bitch will need to be taught some manners, but she'll be useful to me, eventually."

The implication that I would be trained like some pet filled me with rage and ignited a fierce determination. I fought against the general's hold, ignoring the pain.

The king laughed again. "Use the cell with the chains. I don't trust her not to escape before I have the time to play with her. And gag her—just as a precaution."

Behind me, a scuffle broke out. Sindri's snarl was unmistakable, and I suspected my brother was doing something stupid. Leifur cried out, and the sound of two bodies hitting the ground made my stomach twist with worry. Ropes ripped at my flesh as my hands were bound behind me, and I was pulled to my feet as a cloth was forced into my mouth. Leifur and Sindri were on their knees. The guards were binding their hands behind their backs. The general shoved me at Ingvar and went to deal with my brothers. Ingvar backhanded me across the face before turning me to face the chaos happening around us. I found Baldr and tried to plead my case to him with my eyes, but he was too focused on Njall. They were having their silent conversation across that room with each other, so I turned my focus on my brothers.

"What do you want me to do with them?" the general asked as he tied them.

"Throw them in the dungeon, too. We'll find something to do with them."

"We didn't come here to hurt anyone," Leifur shouted.

"You call robbing my brother innocent?" Ingvar snapped, digging his fingers into my arm hard enough that I tried to shake him off me. "And now, this one attacked my father!"

"We only take what we need to survive," Sindri retorted. "We came here to earn money and find a home, to live in peace."

"So, you expect us to believe that you came here with no ill will and simply wanted a quiet life?" Njall asked. He turned to look at me for a second before turning his gaze to Baldr.

"Don't let prejudices against our kind cloud your judgment," Leifur said. "You all know what it's like to be different."

The king's voice boomed through the hall. "My children are

powerful! I hand selected each of their mothers to ensure they'd have gifts beyond human capabilities!"

"Couldn't find a siren, though," Sindri snapped. His words hung in the air as the king's eyes widened in rage. Hilmir raised his hand to strike, but before he could, a deafening bang echoed through the hall, and the entire castle shook.

Chapter 14

Elva

Ingvar released me to balance himself, and I fell backwards on my hip. The force was enough to knock my gag loose. The princes and guards all struggled to stay upright while my brothers stayed on their knees. After the castle stopped shaking, there was silence, and we waited for what came next. When another bang, louder this time, echoed through the room, I scrambled across the floor toward my brothers. The vibrations were enough to send some of the ancient artwork crashing down from the walls, nearly hitting some of the guards. The tremors subsided as quickly as they had begun.

"Ingvar! Magni! Find out what's going on," the king ordered. Ingvar nodded, and we heard the awful sound of ripping flesh and fabric as he transformed into a huge, ash-gray wolf. My heart nearly stopped as the beast stalked toward me, but he leaped over me and bolted for the door, the general close behind.

"I know these might be our last minutes alive," Sindri whispered. "But that was hot."

A force wrenched me from the floor onto my feet, and I

found Njall staring at me. "Don't even think of running," he snapped, as if he'd read my mind.

Before I could respond, the back door of the hall flew open, and the general rushed back in.

"What is it?" Hilmir shouted.

"The *ferflucsing* Anginfills have allied with the Huesturs. We're under attack from both kingdoms."

"Worthless heathens," the king bellowed, and I felt Njall tense at his father's rage.

"We need your orders, Your Royal Highness," the general said. "Which do we go after first?"

"Bring the nobles inside. Protect the castle against whoever tries to enter, regardless of the kingdom."

"What of your people?" Leifur asked, and the king and general's heads jerked back to us. They seemed to have forgotten we were there.

"Peasants can easily be replaced, but nobility cannot," Hilmir said coldly.

"Where is Hulda?" Baldr asked. "Is she inside, or at the celebrations?"

"She was supposed to be outside with the people this morning," the guard who had almost been hit by the falling artwork replied.

"Someone needs to go find her," the king snapped.

"I'll go, the general said, and was heading toward the door before he finished his sentence.

"Baldr. Njall. Take a handful of guards and bring our prisoners to the dungeon. Then go find your brother and make sure he gets inside. If Hulda and Ingvar aren't back safe and sound, it's on your heads."

King Hilmir stormed across the room and sat heavily on his throne. "And someone get my bodyguards."

Njall gripped my shoulder, his fingers digging into my flesh as he shoved me forward. "Move faster." Guards and knights kept slamming into me as we pushed through the crowded halls. Baldr had handed my brothers over to two burly guards, and they were letting them walk without shoving them into every obstacle in our path. When we reached the stairwell, it was mercifully empty, so we could walk down ourselves, with the guards leading us while Njall and Baldr kept whispering to each other behind us.

"Are you going to sing?" Sindri whispered to me as we reached the bottom of the stairs.

I opened my mouth to reply when a hand clamped over it, muffling my voice. Another hand grabbed my waist, holding me in place. I watched in shock as Njall snatched an unlit torch from the wall and struck both the guards in the head, knocking them unconscious.

"What are you doing?" Leifur asked as Njall turned back to him, holding one of my daggers.

"Turn around," Njall ordered.

Sindri went pale white and backed into the corner of the stairs, while Leifur looked frantically for a way to escape. Baldr's grip on me tightened as Njall grabbed Leifur, spun him around, and cut his ropes. Then turned to my brother in the corner and freed him as well. Baldr spun me around, and the ropes that had been chafing my wrists fell away.

Njall pointed down the dimly lit hallway. "Go down there and take the left tunnel. Follow it until you find a black door. Take that and you'll arrive at the edge of town."

"You're letting us go?" I asked as Baldr handed me my daggers and Leifur's sword.

"We've seen what becomes of our father's *pets* when he's done with them," Baldr added.

"No one deserves that," Njall said softly. "Especially not someone as beautiful as you, little selkie."

The princes turned and went back up the stairs, and Leifur grabbed my arm to lead us into the tunnel, but I hesitated. "Njall?" I called out.

The prince stopped and turned back, meeting my gaze for a moment.

"Thank you," I said.

He nodded and was gone, and I followed my brothers. By the time we found our way out of the castle and into the town, it was nearly deserted. With how the general had spoken of the other kingdoms, I'd expected chaos, but it seemed they were concentrating their attacks elsewhere. We crept across the marketplace looking for signs of how to get out of Tyndorf without getting mixed up with this whole mess.

The marketplace was eerily silent except for the sound of our boots scraping against the cobblestones. I removed a pair of my daggers and clenched them in my hands. The commotion was coming from the east—a clash of steel on steel, shouts, and the thunder of boots. A group of Tyndorf guards was fighting with a group of soldiers. The Huestur men wore green and brown uniforms. Their territory was on the edge of the Zverm Forest, and their colors were chosen to hide them.

An arm grabbed me and pulled me out of view. I tried to scream, but a hand covered my mouth.

"It's just me," Sindri whispered.

We listened to the sound of blade on blade, as the two sets of soldiers fought in the yard. Sindri nodded toward an alley, and we moved swiftly, trying to avoid the pockets of fighting soldiers and guards. We headed roughly in the direction of our inn, because the people there knew how to take care of themselves, and it was on the edge of town, far from the chaos. When we made it out of another small alley, I froze.

"Elva, let's go." Sindri tugged my arm, but I pulled it back.

"I hear someone," I whispered, straining to listen.

"We can't stick around here," Leifur said, but I covered his mouth and leaned in, trying to pinpoint the sound.

Then I heard it—a faint rustling followed by muffled voices. Without waiting for my brothers, I turned and hurried down another road. I knew they'd follow. The streets were a maze, and after several sharp turns, I peeked around a corner and saw her.

"Is that the princess?" Leifur whispered.

She was unconscious, slung over a man's shoulder like a sack of grain. He wore the formal clothes of a high-ranking officer, possibly a general or noble. They were in a group of at least forty soldiers—far more than I could handle on my own.

"Which kingdom's colors are maroon and gray?" Sindri asked.

I swallowed. "Anginfill." They were known throughout the entire world for their viciousness. Leifur pulled us back into the shadows so they couldn't see us, but we could still hear them.

"We'll get her to my ship," one of the soldiers said. "After we set sail, order your men to retreat. We have what we came for."

"What about the other one?" another voice asked.

"The prince? Give him to the Huesturs; they'll take him on their ship. The king can't bring his entire fleet after both of them, so he'll have to choose."

The wicked laughter that followed made my blood run cold. I'd heard men laugh about me like that, and it made me want to retch. I grabbed Sindri's hand and squeezed it tightly as we hid in the shadows, hoping the men wouldn't walk by this road and see us.

But my brother seemed to have inherited luck for both of us, and the men headed away from us.

"We have to go back to the castle," I whispered urgently.

"Not yet," Leifur said. "Let them all leave first. Then we tell them."

I shook my head. "But what if it's too late then? Who knows what unspeakable things the Anginfills will do to the princess before then? We go now. I couldn't live with myself if they do to her what Aamon did to me."

"Elva—" Sindri whispered.

I stood and made my way back toward the castle and the chaos that surrounded it. The groan my brother let out was loud enough that I heard it halfway up the road, but he still came after me. We moved through the shadows and hid in alleyways, behind decorations, and nearly collided with a waste bin as we hurried around a corner. Our trip from the castle had taken seconds, but the way back seemed to take an eternity.

When we finally approached the outer walls, I ran to the first guard we spotted. "We need to see the king."

He sneered, eyeing me up and down. "Get lost, wench. No one needs a whore right now."

"I am not a whore," I hissed through clenched teeth. My siren was already stirring in me, but Leifur put his hand on my shoulder, and I remembered that killing the guard who was just doing his job wouldn't solve our problem.

"Fine, then," Sindri said in his smooth and calming voice. "If you don't want the king to know which kingdom just abducted his daughter from your pier, we'll be on our way." His hand slid on my lower back, and he turned me toward the street.

Footsteps behind us made me turn, expecting a guard, but Baldr appeared instead. "You saw who took Hulda?"

"And who took Njall," Sindri said.

"Come with me," Baldr ordered and shoved the guard out of his way. We rushed down a marble hallway lined with endless portraits, making two lefts and a right before stopping at maple doors. On them was carved the kingdom's crest—a man sized hammer and spear, crisscrossed beside a rock being smashed by the hammer. It was the crest of a kingdom founded on hard work that was now overshadowed by the king's ruthlessness.

Baldr pushed the first door open, and we entered a sitting room. I glanced around the room, and judging by the amount of pants thrown around and no shirts, it was probably Baldr's. He dropped onto a massive green couch and motioned for us to join him. "Tell me everything you saw. Now."

I let Sindri explain what we'd seen and heard. Out of the three of us, he is always the best with words, and I will always be a bit jealous of him for it.

"So Anginfill took Hulda, and Huestur took Njall?" Baldr asked.

"Yes," I answered, looking back at him.

Baldr rubbed his thick thighs and exhaled heavily. "My father can't know Njall and I freed you. I'll have to tell him what you saw and say it was me who saw it."

"And then he'll send men to get them back, right?" Leifur asked.

Baldr's fingers scratched his legs. "He'll choose Hulda. Our father tolerates me, but he hates Njall. He'll send the army to get Hulda and leave my brother to rot in the Huestur dungeon."

"And I thought sirens were terrible parents," Sindri said.

Baldr stood and moved to his desk. He pulled out a drawer and flipped it over. The entire underside was covered with gold bars, as if they'd been glued there. Using a letter opener, he pried one loose and held it out to me. "This one up front, and the rest when you bring him back."

I took the gold and ran my thumb over it. I'd never seen such pure gold in my life.

Sindri snatched it from me. "Bring who back?" he asked.

"Njall," Leifur said. "You want us to rescue your brother?"

Baldr nodded. "My father won't send anyone. The Huesturs

breached our wall and part of the castle with a cannon. Every man in this kingdom will be devoted to retrieving Hulda or repairing the castle." He paused, tapping his fingers on the chair, deep in thought. "Even if my father isn't willing to pay for my sister's rescue, the general most certainly will. His marriage to Hulda is the only thing that will keep him in power once he hits forty. My father is already looking at replacements for him."

"What if we fail?" I asked. Getting into Huestur would be dangerous, but that gold could buy us the life we always wanted. And there was no guarantee we'd succeed. If we only ever got one bar, it would be hardly worth such a risk.

"I'll pay you half if you can prove you tried, or that he's dead."

"Deal," Sindri said, before Leifur and I could say anything. He handed the bar back. "But we'll need this in coins. A bar won't help us in the small towns. Plus, we'll need horses and supplies."

"Sindri," I hissed. "Shouldn't we talk about this?"

"No," he said flatly. "You're always talking about wanting a home. This is our chance."

I stared at my twin in shock.

"And gold gets people to talk," Leifur said, pulling his lips into a weak smile.

"Do you know anything about the Huestur kingdom?" I asked Baldr.

"Not much, but I have journals from our knights that might help."

"Alright. It's a deal," I said.

Chapter 15

Elva

"What are you thinking about, Elva?" Leifur asked. I hadn't realized my horse, Acorn, had slowed, allowing my brothers to catch up.

"I was thinking how thankful I am to not be human," I replied, adjusting my grip on the reins.

"That's the truth," Sindri added. "Could you imagine being a dullard and having nothing exceptional about you? How sad for them."

Leifur glanced ahead toward the forest we were riding toward. "This road is eerily quiet."

"I assumed it was because of the celebration," I said. "But maybe the humans are finally learning to steer clear of the creatures in the woods."

Leifur guided his horse, Slate, back and grabbed our mule that was loaded up with the rest of our supplies. "Better keep her close. Just to be safe."

"The Forest of Endilaus doesn't have that many vicious beasts," I said.

"How can you say that?" Sindri was glancing around as if the trees would reach out and bite him. "Harpies are vicious—"

"Scorned women," I interrupted.

He scoffed. "Unicorns have daggers on their heads."

"They're called *horns*," I corrected. "And they need them to protect themselves from poachers who seek to steal their magic, especially since their blood is said to have healing powers."

"What about Kelpies, then?" Sindri asked. "Wicked beasts, they trick you into riding them and then try to drown you!"

"Which is why you don't ride them," Leifur said.

I sighed heavily. Since we'd entered the forest four days ago, Sindri had been a pain in my ass. If he wasn't complaining about how sore his delicate rear was from riding on the horse, he was complaining about the temperature, bugs, or being bored. More than once, I hit the end of my rope, and if Leifur hadn't intervened, I might have left these woods an only child. But this crunching wasn't coming from Sindri.

A stick snapped from behind us. I turned my head, but both brothers were still on the path. Leifur stiffened and searched the woods that ran along the path. Sindri was too busy rummaging through his satchel to notice our concern. I watched Leifur cock his head to the side, and I knew what we had to do.

I tugged our mule's reins closer to Acorn's and led them into the dense underbrush on the side of the path. She could tell something was off and fought me the whole way. Leifur somehow got my brother's attention, and they both slipped into the woods on the other side with the mule. I stroked my horse softly to soothe him.

Then, a group of knights on horseback rounded the corner. Dressed from head to toe in green and chestnut brown, they were Huestur men. They carried oversized shields painted with their kingdom's emblem of a sailboat with swords crossed behind it.

Sirens often joked that they carried big shields to make up for the size of their dicks. I held my breath, hoping the horses wouldn't give us away, but the men were young and luckily for us, they weren't in the mood to be careful.

"Pay up," the man at the back shouted. "I told you no one would come for the prince. They're too busy saving that beautiful sorceress."

Another man dug into his satchel and flicked some coins at the first man. He caught them and made obscene gestures in response. I rolled my eyes. These weren't skilled warriors—they were barely men.

The oldest of the bunch was in the front, riding the largest horse. His black hair was sprinkled with flecks of white and gray, matching his horse's mane. "Enough," he said. "If anyone were coming, they'd hear you from the villages and steer clear."

"Even Tyndorf men are smart enough not to leave the path in the Endilaus Forest," someone replied, earning a chorus of chuckles.

The smallest of them looked confused at his comrades. "But women are always going into the forest." His voice rose a little as he spoke.

He can't be over fifteen, I thought. They're starting younger and younger. *No wonder the boys think they own the world by the time they turn eighteen.*

"Of course *they* can," the leader replied, tossing his heavy green cape back. "The forest is overrun with harpies, kelpies, and unicorns. Young maidens can charm these creatures, or so the stories go."

"What about the mermaids and sirens?" the youngster asked. "Aren't they on the other side of the forest, too?"

The men all laughed together. "Idiot boy," one of the older men scoffed.

"Mermaids and sirens are water creatures. They don't come onto land except to breed," the man who won the bet stated confidently. "If I ever ran into one, I'd show them what a real man can do. Then they'd never want to go back to the sea."

I rolled my eyes again and could swear my mule snorted at his comment.

"You're even stupider than you are ugly," the captain said, smacking the man upside the head. He had a full head of thick brown hair, but his beard was so thin he looked more dirty than manly. "Mermaids only come out of the water to find food. They'd gut you and drag you into the water before you got your pants open."

I couldn't help but hang on to their leader's words. Out of all of them, he seemed to be the only one who had an idea what he was talking about, and frankly, he was handsome enough that even my siren noticed and approved. Keeping her back was more challenging now. If she got out, we'd all be in trouble.

"Now, as for the sirens, they'll let you breed them if they think you're worthy. Their entire goal is to produce more sirens. But if you're not worthy, they'll gut you and leave you to die while they rob you blind."

"And selkies?" the younger knight asked.

"Selkie females stick to their kind. Males will have dalliances, but the females only breed with their males. Only a handful of records exist where a human male bred with a female selkie, and those all ended badly for the selkie. Either the human man didn't live up to her thoughts of him, or she became so homesick she withered and died."

"Have we gone far enough yet, captain?" the first man asked.

The captain dismounted his horse and pulled its reins tight. Wrapping them around his hand, he stared down the path me and my brothers had just come from. "No one is coming for the prince," he replied. "The rumors of the lowest-`ranked being expendable weren't exaggerations."

"Let's go back, captain," the first man said, bringing his horse closer. "If we hurry, we can make it to the tavern in time for an ale before we're expected back. We only have a few more days to stay around here, and then we can head home."

The more skilled man glanced around them slowly. I leaned closer to my mare, hoping to hide in the brush. The knight seemed to look in my direction for far too long. He narrowed his eyes, and I held my breath.

"Captain? Do you see something?" The youngest man dismounted and walked over to him. I waited, perfectly still, heart pounding, willing them to turn away when something spooked the young knight's horse. It reared back, drawing every-one's attention.

"Landon, you idiot," the other knight shouted and dashed to grab the reins before the horse bolted.

In seconds, the captain was back on his horse. "Let's head back, before the boy loses his horse and we spend the next three hours searching the forest for it."

I couldn't help but pity the youngster as he turned beet red and took the reins from the older man. In less than a minute, they were all on their horses, heading back toward the villages that led to the kingdom of Huestur. When they were out of our sight, we stayed hidden for a while longer, and finally, I exhaled loudly and looked at my mule. "Ready?" I whispered and pulled her out of the bush.

We cautiously crossed the dirt road and found Leifur and Sindri emerging from the bush.

"I think we should leave the main trail," Leifur said. "If any others are out looking, we could be in trouble."

"Did you hit your head when my back was turned?" Sindri

asked. "We cannot go into the forest. That's where the harpies are."

I studied my brother's face and asked, "Why are you so afraid of them?"

"Because they are wicked and mean."

"You're traveling with me. The harpies in this forest only go after men who are vicious to women. If one comes after you, then you deserve it."

"I most certainly would not," he shot back.

I glanced at Leifur, but he just shrugged at me. He was also unaware of whatever my brother had done to earn the ire of the winged version of a warrior siren.

I relented. "Fine. We'll stay on this trail for now, but only because we can travel faster. If we run into another group of soldiers, we are going into the woods. And we're avoiding inns for a while, too."

Before Sindri could ask, Leifur answered. "We don't know how many groups of guards the Huesturs left to watch for anyone trying to rescue the prince. We need to avoid all of them."

My brother nodded in agreement, and we got onto our horses to continue our journey through the woods. We didn't run into anyone else for the rest of the day.

When the sun began its descent, the crimson mountains lit up in a barrage of red hues, making the forest around us glow as if it were on fire. Taking it as a sign, we veered off the trail and trekked deeper into the trees to set up camp for the night.

Our journey to retrieve the prince would take us through the Forest of Endilaus, skirting the base of the Crimson Mountains. The alternative would be to abandon our horses and travel by water, but I had no intention of setting foot into the sea, even if I suspected that's how the knights got Njall to their kingdom. That section of water belonged to the mermaids, and we knew better than to mess with them. Beyond the mountains, we'd face the Sigil Territory, which was mostly bogs and marshlands, and then the Huestur Territory, with its dense forest and a massive fortress perched on the water's edge, if the journals Baldr had given us as part of our supplies were to be believed. I desperately hoped the fortress had underwater tunnels, like the sleek underground aqueducts of our Siren castle. If it did, I had my way in; if not, I'd have no choice but to rely on my song and daggers.

Chapter 16

Njall

The last door slammed shut, the sound echoing down the tunnel. I sank to the ground and rested my head against the cold stone wall behind me. *They're gone.* The water that had gathered on the ceiling dripped onto my arm again, and I flicked it off. It had been two weeks since I'd been taken prisoner, and like clockwork, the general and king of Huestur would visit to taunt me on their way to supper.

I could do nothing but laugh at how little my father thought of me. Regardless of his feelings for me, or rather lack thereof, I knew he couldn't leave his son to rot in an enemy's cell. It would make him look weak, and weakness was something my father despised more than anything.

But tonight, they'd let slip a detail that lingered in my mind. Hulda had been abducted, too. If she had been kidnapped, my father would certainly put all his resources and energy into getting her back. After all, she was his second-ranked child. And that would leave few, or even no men to come and find me, at least not until she was safe, and who knows how long that would take.

My only hope now rested with Baldr. While my fun-loving brother wasn't the most reliable in all aspects of life, he had a big heart, and he wouldn't be able to leave me to suffer forever. My hopes for a speedy rescue had been quashed tonight, but I had to hold onto the belief that he would come for me, eventually.

Leaning on the wall, I tried to picture my father's expression when he discovered we'd let Elva go. He'd be furious, hopefully enough that the giant vein on his neck would burst and we'd finally be rid of him. In my twenty-seven years of life, he'd gone through too many *pets*, and each female had been used and discarded when he grew bored with her. They would start as his alone, but when they failed to please him, he'd send them off with whichever group of men were leaving for the front lines, leaving them to be used as the soldiers saw fit. None of the women had ever returned.

Gripping the pendant from my mother, I thought of her kind face and her striking green eyes. The same green as Elva's right eye. I'd been too quick to judge her, to use her to get in my father's good graces for once. I'd thought a siren could handle herself against him, maybe even put an end to him for me, but then she'd been arrested, and I'd seen a flash of her green hair. Sirens were rarely fully siren. They were always mixed with something, and I'd almost destroyed the only other selkie I'd ever met. The only other selkie I was ever likely to meet, since my father had forbidden me to ever tell anyone what my mother had been.

Everything made sense now. The moment Elva stepped into the bar, I'd felt her, sensed her. It's why I approached her, something I conveniently forgot when having her arrested. At first, I'd thought she bewitched me with her siren powers, but now I wasn't so sure. When she'd sung at the guards to make them release her, it felt nothing like the connection we had when we were in bed together.

I pushed myself off the ground and tried to brush the dirt from my pants, but it did little good. After weeks of being down here, my wool pants were stiff from the layers of grime on them. My tunic was just as filthy. The cotton was wearing thin in places, and spots were ripping, letting the cold through when I would try to sleep. I picked up my empty dinner plate and tapped it idly on the ground, noticing how easily the sandy earth shifted.

I needed something—anything—to occupy my mind while here, or I'd lose myself to thoughts of Elva and the desperate hope that she'd managed to escape the chaos.

Chapter 17

Elva

I woke up stiff, sore, and shivering. During the night, I'd rolled out of the blanket I was sharing with Sindri, or more likely, my blanket-hog of a twin stole it and left me to freeze. Grumbling, I stepped out of our tent and shuffled toward the fire pit, trying to shake off the morning dew and icy chill in the air. Thankfully, it still had a few glowing embers. Tossing progressively larger sticks into the pit, I watched the tiny flames spark to life, and sighed happily.

As the fire grew, I grabbed the bits of remaining wood to put on a pot of water and sat beside the flames to warm myself and prepare breakfast. We'd been traveling for four days and hadn't encountered any more knights or guards. The handful of peasants we had seen showed no interest in engaging with us and often hurried past as quickly as they could.

Sindri may have complained about his encounters with local harpies and kelpies, but in truth, he knew little of the wild and truly dangerous creatures of Torian. Sultry sirens were meant to stay within the safety of our kingdom, luring in partners to strengthen our numbers. It was the warrior sirens who ventured far and wide, learning about the creatures that roamed beyond our borders and ensuring we could defend ourselves if needed. I knew what lurked in the coming lands and had the scars to prove they were not to be toyed with.

Today, we'd leave the Forest of Endilaus, and to avoid getting too close to the mermaid's territory, we'd be hugging the base of the Crimson Mountain. The blood red mountains we'd seen in the distance now loomed over us, only a few stone throws away. I turned my back toward them and looked to the west. Somewhere, beyond those peaks, and far past the mermaid territory, was our home—the Konvern Territory. But it was also the place that had cast us out.

A pang of guilt twisted in my chest as I thought about why we'd been exiled. A siren who couldn't bear a child was useless. And so, I'd been discarded. Sindri and Leifur had given up everything to stand by me, even when the rest of our kind turned their backs. I vowed to make it right. For them, I'd do anything. My only fear was that one day, the siren queen would change her mind about them, decide that two male sirens were too valuable to lose, and come after us.

In the north, I could see the sea. Our journey to retrieve Njall from the Huestur Territory was also my chance to give us a better life. We'd save him, get him back to Tyndorf, and find a plot of land. Leifur could open a small blacksmith shop, and he'd make money for us to live on. People hated sirens, but my brother was a very talented blacksmith, and if living on the road had taught me anything, it was that people would tolerate you if you could provide them with something they wanted. We'd get animals and plant a garden. Despite his love of finer things, my twin was an exceptional gardener. He'd grow the food, I'd take care of the house and animals, and Leifur could provide us with anything we couldn't make ourselves.

I still didn't understand what made Njall disobey his father and let us go. When I let my mind wander there, my plans became muddled. My life goal was simple—set up a peaceful life for my brothers and exact revenge on the human who'd helped turn me into a monster. That was it. No feelings, no princes who changed their mind about getting me arrested, and no mind-blowing sex that was better than anything I'd ever experienced in my life. I didn't need that.

We'd left the main road and were now on the seldom-used paths that ran along the base of the mountain. We needed to be more diligent about overgrown roots and falling rocks, but on the bright side, we'd only seen two people in the days we'd been traveling these paths. Minerals from the mountain runoff had stained the earth here a deep red. In several places, it seemed as if we were walking down a river of blood.

"We're running low on food," Leifur said as the sun rose higher in the sky.

I looked up to let it warm my face while weighing our options —fishing or finding a town to replenish our supplies. "We'll find a river to water the horses and catch a few fish," I replied. "Then we'll look for a village to restock."

"Works for me. I love fish," Sindri said. He led the way, and we soon found ourselves at a small offshoot of the Bloot River. We hadn't even finished tying up our horses before we heard a loud splash.

"You picked the right stream," I said, and set about feeding the horses while my brothers retrieved the fishing gear. Once the horses were settled, I joined them at the water's edge. Sindri was sitting at the riverbank. His hair was a mess, and his shirt askew, but I decided against teasing him today. Instead, I sat down beside him and rested my head on his shoulder. The shore on this side of the river was mostly made of piles of red rust colored fist-sized rocks with weeds and grass growing around them. The water was moving slowly, its ruddy hue deepest in the middle where fish stirred the sludge. Downstream, some saplings were growing from around the rocks, and I strolled over to tie my lines to them, in case we hooked a larger fish while I was busy in another section.

By the time I returned, my brothers had already managed to catch five fish the length of my forearm. We roasted them over the fire, and they flaked perfectly, tasting better than anything we'd eaten since the last town we'd visited. When we lived in Konvern with the other sirens, nearly three-quarters of our diet was seafood. Living on the sea and being in it every day, we developed a craving that was tough to satisfy during our travels on land. It's one reason I hoped we'd be able to settle in Tyndorf. Not only was it on the edge of the Sieden Sea, but a century ago, the Crimson Mountains had split into a strait. We'd have access to water and seafood from both sides.

With our bellies full and food replenished, we cleaned up and were loading the horses when I heard a low growl.

"Leifur." I gripped my brother's arm, and he froze to listen, but it had stopped.

"What's wrong?" Sindri asked, bringing the last of our cooking supplies.

"I heard a growl."

Leifur's eyes snapped to mine. "What kind?"

"Big. Dangerous."

Leifur grabbed the supplies from Sindri's arms and began stuffing them wherever they'd fit.

"Get on your horse," I ordered, and for once, Sindri didn't need to be told twice. He swung onto his gray horse and motioned for me to follow. At that moment, I heard it again, and this time they did too.

"That was a wolf," I whispered. Leifur scanned the woods. Keeping his eyes glued to the tree line, he gathered a few rocks. Heart pounding in my chest, I did the same, but handed him the stones. With his brute strength, honed from a lifetime of blacksmithing, he could turn any solid object he could into a weapon. Sweat trickled down my back as I slid along the side of Acorn and grabbed the reins of our mule. As if reading my thoughts, Sindri took them from me and gripped them tightly. If things went badly, he would get two horses out of here fast.

I cursed under my breath. After seeing no one for two days, I'd grown lax. My daggers were stowed with my clothes. Reaching into my boot, I pulled the one backup blade I kept for emergencies, and watched the tree lines.

This time, multiple growls echoed back.

Chapter 18

Elva

The next few minutes of our lives were a blur. Three wolves streamed out of the woods at once. They were matted and lanky and desperate for food. Sindri dashed off with the two horses. One wolf gave chase, but Leifur hurled a rock at it. Being the animal lover he was, he hit the wolf in the leg, and it went down with a sharp yelp.

I would not have been so gentle.

As the other two came racing toward my horse, Leifur pushed past his mount and flanked me, clenching a heavy stone in each hand. "Take the one on the left," I told him. I threw better with my right arm, and he could throw with both.

"One. Two. Th—" Before he could finish counting, both wolves lunged for us. Leifur's first rock missed, but when the second thudded against the wolf's head, it dropped to the ground and didn't move. I threw my dagger and hit my mark, striking the other right in the eye. It howled and cried as it swung its head back and forth, as if trying to dislodge the blade. Leifur grabbed another rock and, with one swing, put the creature out of its misery.

Chest heaving from my adrenaline-fueled breaths, I turned to him. "No more camping until we are through the mountains?"

He nodded. "Agreed."

We rode away from the woods as fast as the horses would go until the road forked west toward a more populated path. Unlike the mountain trail, this one was dark brown and worn smooth from all the carts that had been dragged down it. It wasn't long before we encountered a local farmer hauling a wagonload of animal feed back to his homestead. When I dismounted Acorn and approached him, he stopped. Sindri made a face and pinched his nose, but I smiled sweetly at the man. Despite his dirty appearance, we learned his farm was a prosperous one, and he was happy to point us toward a nearby village with an affordable inn. I ran my hand down the man's arm, and when he left us, I was attaching a sack of bread and cheese and a bottle of ale to my horse. I wanted my brother to see that he wasn't the only one who could acquire us provisions.

Music filled the forest as we neared the village. Something exciting was happening. Leifur handed me my scarf, and I was thankful for the chill in the air, so I could wrap up my hair with no one asking questions. After another few turns, we saw the wooden walls the farmer had told us about—massive structures that reminded me of the ever-growing coral beneath the siren castle. As we rode closer, I realized they weren't only tall, but the trees they'd been made of were wider than my body. Leifur whistled in awe, and even Sindri seemed to finally pay attention to what was ahead.

"Are we sure this is the town we want to sleep in? I can hear the ruckus from here," Sindri said.

"The farmer said this was the only one we could reach tonight," I reminded him. "Do you want to sleep outside again after our visit this morning?"

"Not particularly," Sindri said.

"Good," I replied. "Because packs of Crimson Mountain wolves don't travel in threes. They hunt in packs of ten, and they'll stalk their prey for days."

Sindri spurred his horse to hurry ahead of us.

The walls of Eldenwood were green from the years of moss growing on them. It reassured me that these walls had lasted quite some time with no evidence of recent invasions. By the time I arrived at the gate, Sindri and Leifur had dismounted and were talking to the guard on duty. He was middle-aged, but the sword that hung from his scabbard was so hefty, I was unsure I could wield it. His head was full of thick blond hair, and his beard was messy but clean. *If he shows up at the inn later, I will have to find him.*

The guard explained that the noise was because the town was celebrating. Their Lord had finally found a wife, and the union promised a prosperous future for the village. He winked at me as he gave us directions to the inn and promised he'd stop by for a drink after his shift ended.

We led our horses through the gate and through the crowd of people who were drinking in the streets. I took the mare's reins from Sindri and pushed through the throng while Leifur followed close behind. My brother is just as likely to stay with them as he is to follow me, but Leifur wanted to settle in before they joined in the festivities. The houses in town are small and simple, seeing it made me long for this kind of life even more.

One day we'll have this too.

We passed by the butcher and then a bakery. I was thrilled to know we could restock our dried meats and bread before we left tomorrow. The streets led us to the town square, where the townspeople were singing, and a group of children were dancing around the large fountain that stood in the middle of the market. At its center stood carved stone wolves, their statues guarding the heart of Eldenwood.

"A little too on the nose for the area, don't you think?" Sindri whispered.

I shushed my twin, but couldn't stop the grin that crossed my lips. A small girl who'd been dancing with her friends skipped to us. Her braids bounced as she stopped and held out a yellow wildflower to me.

"Welcome to Eldenwood," was all she said. The moment I took the buttercup from her, she giggled and hurried off.

"Interesting custom," Leifur said, taking the flower from my fingers and tucking it behind my ear.

"Come on. Let's get our room."

The Eldenwood Inn was just across the market square, built from the same dark logs as the town wall; this inn appeared to be three stories high, towering over the adjacent structures. Leifur noticed an open barn door on the side and paid the young stable hand to take care of our horses. Then, satchels split between us, we headed into the inn's tavern.

Inside were a few worn tables and chairs, a large window took up the entirety of one wall, and a bar with stools set up on the other. The stairs in the back corner probably led to the rooms. Despite the ruckus outside, the inn was empty except for a woman behind the bar.

"Don't you worry about how empty we are," she said as the three of us glanced around. "Everyone's out celebrating. They'll be back for dinner after dark, and then the place will be more packed than my sister's bra."

Sindri snorted, clearly entertained. "I like you," he said, handing his bags to Leifur and hopping up onto a barstool. "We need two rooms," he said, smiling coquettishly at the woman. "Or a large room with two beds."

She fetched an oversized brass key from a row of hooks behind her. Sindri thrust his hand out toward me and snapped his fingers. Rolling my eyes, I pulled out a pair of brass coins and placed them on the bar.

"Here's your key," Oudette said, handing it to Sindri. "Third floor, room on the left."

"Thank you dear. Now, could you tell what time dinner will be served?"

"Six o'clock, handsome. I'll save you the best cuts."

"You've been most helpful." Sindri winked at her. She was blushing as she turned around and resumed cleaning the stack of ale mugs.

"Couldn't help yourself," I muttered as we climbed the creaky steps to the third floor.

"As long as there are no wolves, I'm happy," Sindri said as we arrived on the floor and unlocked our room.

"I'll just be happy to have my blanket, and not having to smell you two is a bonus," I said, giving my brother a pointed glare. He grabbed a pillow off the bed and tossed it at me. I caught it and dropped it on my bed.

Later that evening, as the bathwater warmed my skin, I felt a rare moment of peace. Sirens had no problem with cold, as long as it was water. An icy river or sea didn't bother me, but cold air and snow on my skin felt brutal. After two weeks of bathing in frigid rivers, the hot water that was sent up feels amazing. I know I'll have better chances of finding a man for tonight, now that I don't smell like our horses. My siren is going a bit stir crazy, and I am thankful to get some of this pent-up frustration out.

Dressed and ready, I headed downstairs to meet Sindri and

Leifur in the tavern. Boisterous voices filled the hallway as I left our room and locked the door. Oudette hadn't been lying when she said the bar would be crowded. Before my feet even left the stairs, I could feel the heat from the mass of bodies crowded around the bar, all shouting for drinks. Perched on the last step, I scanned the room for my brothers and found them at a table by the door with some locals. Sindri was being his usual flirtatious and touchy self, wooing the ladies who had joined them. Leifur just watched from his side with a cocky grin, letting my twin enjoy himself.

But when I caught his eye, he dropped his smile and jerked his head toward the back of the room. Normally, I could read Leifur like a book, so this startled me. Searching the crowd, I saw only locals, until a woman dressed in leather caught my attention. As she looked over at me, her blue eyes practically screamed across the room at me.

Coral!

By the time I was at her table, my old friend was already on her feet, embracing me.

"How I've missed you, my vicious little sea dragon," she muttered as we clung to one another.

"And I missed you, my adorable little otter pup."

At this, she pulled away from me and narrowed her eyes, trying to look frightening.

"There's my otter." I pinched her cheek, and she swatted at my hand playfully.

"Do you have to join your brothers, or can you sit with me and catch up?" she asked.

"The boys will be fine," I said and plopped into the chair beside her. "Tell me everything! Are you here alone or with others? Why are you here? How are the girls? Does the general miss me?"

"There isn't that much to tell," she said, pouring me a glass of ale from her jug. "I'm on patrol with a small group of warriors. We're all checking different small towns. The sisters back home are all well, and yes, General Maer speaks of you often."

I took a swig of the ale and waited. "And? What aren't you telling me?"

She shook her head and leaned toward me, lowering her voice. "We've had a few sirens not return, so we're trying to see if their disappearances are connected. We're to meet back at the edge of the Endilaus Forest in a week."

"Missing? How many sirens?"

"Four. That's enough that it could be a coincidence, but it could also be something else."

"Are you thinking humans, beasts, or selkies?"

"Still unsure. We're just being cautious."

"I'm sure no one in Konvern wants to hear from me, but if I see anything suspicious, I'll send word."

"I'd appreciate that," Coral replied, finally taking a sip of her ale. "A single siren is always an easier target."

"I'm not alone." I barely got the words out before I laughed.

"Oh, please! I'm sure Leifur spends all his time keeping Sindri out of trouble."

"Not all of it."

We both giggled as Leifur turned toward us, having heard his name. Coral just waved at him and blew him a kiss. He rolled his eyes and turned back to his table.

"Is he still bitter?" she asked.

"You broke his heart, Coral," I said.

The siren groaned loudly and took a large swig of her ale. "Me, and every siren he ever mated with."

"Not me," I said, pouring her another ale.

"That's because you didn't have a baby." Coral's eyes went wide. "Elva, I didn't mean it."

"I know," I said, swallowing how much the comment had

hurt me, and patted her leg. "Besides, he couldn't have fallen in love with me because he was falling in love with my brother. And Sindri won't leave him like the other sirens did."

"Poor Leifur. He was the most prolific male siren." Coral wrapped her arm around my shoulder and squeezed, but I could tell from her quick breaths and her efforts to control them that she was nervous.

"Whatever it is, just say it," I finally said. "We'll both be leaving tomorrow, so we don't have time for stupid games."

"The queen's upset."

"When isn't she?"

"I mean about Leifur."

"Ah," I replied, staring at my brothers over my glass. "And Sindri?"

"They knew he would likely leave with you. Honestly, after he refused to ever mate with a female siren when he became a sultry siren, no one cared."

"But Leifur was useful."

"He was."

"And what does our top fish plan to do?" I asked.

Coral's eyes darted to the window, then back to me. "I don't know. I'm not high enough to be privy to that information, but you need to be careful."

"We are. All I want is a little spot of land where we can live in peace. Is that so much to ask?"

"No, of course not!" Coral clinked her mug to mine just as the door opened and the handsome blond guard appeared in the doorway. I immediately sat up and adjusted my hair scarf and breasts.

"Ohh. On the prowl, are we?" Coral teased, looking around. "The blond in the uniform?"

"Yes."

"Excellent choice. Go have fun," she said, taking my mug. "I'll still be here when you're done."

"Are you sure?"

"He looks like he knows what he's doing. You'll be back, and then we'll color your hair with the tonic I have. The one made for warriors always lasts longer."

Chapter 19

Njall

moan escaped me as Elva's nails scratched down my back. Her soft body was pinned between me and the bed, her legs wrapped around mine as I thrust my cock into her. My name tumbled from her lips, a desperate whisper, as I kissed her hard, one hand gripping her bottom—

"Wake up!"

I jolted upright and fell off the cot. I watched dazed as a plate hit the ground near my head. A pair of buns rolled off of it onto the dirt, as the iron door to my cell clanged shut.

I walked to the iron bars, gripping the cold metal as I peered down the tunnel. The guard who brought my food was gone, and the area was deserted, as usual. Only one tiny torch provided a sliver of light to illuminate the pittance of food they'd left for me. It was two stale, slightly burned buns, a single mug of warm ale, and a mystery meat sausage that would either be so bland it had no taste, or so tough I wouldn't feed it to a dog.

In the corner was a small wooden slat bed with an old wool blanket on it. The other far-off corner had a bucket of water for occasional cleaning, and a rusted old bucket for waste. I'd only seen a handful of rats so far. In my father's castle, this would have been a luxurious cell, considering that I was its only occupant. They even emptied the bucket twice a week. I couldn't believe that this is where I've been living for the past few weeks.

I kicked the dirt wall and heard a rip.

"*Ferflucs!*" A piece of my tunic was caught on the iron bars. I reached around and discovered the tear extended down my back. This is why I hated my royal clothes. The fabric could be as soft as it wanted, but if it couldn't stay together, it was useless. Sighing, I grabbed the food and went over to the bed to sit. I sniffed the sausage and squeezed it between my fingers. Today was a good day—it had some softness, so although it would be bland, at least it was edible. I took a large bite and chewed slowly, trying to trick my body into thinking I was eating much more than I was.

After polishing off my food, I flipped the plate around, examining it from every angle. There was one area that seemed to be thinner, so I scraped it against a stone in the wall until the edge was thinned out like a blade. Making sure I was still alone, I shoved my bed aside to reveal the tunnel I had started a few days ago. I knew it would take weeks, if not months, to get out of here, but if my father's army was going after my sister, I would have plenty of time.

Chapter 20

Elva

After I finished with the guard, Coral and I took our ale to the room to exchange stories of our travels with these prudish humans while my brothers continued to enjoy drinks in the bar. It seemed Oudette liked Sindri enough to pay for their drinks, so they stayed out late to indulge. Coral applied the siren's tonic to my hair. Because of my mixed heritage, I will still have two shades, but now my blue and green locks have changed to dark crimson and brown. I'll be able to keep my hair down and slip into Huestur territory without being spotted so quickly or maybe at all if all their guards are as oblivious as the ones we had come across in the forest.

The next morning, we set off again, much later than I would have liked. Even after riding for hours, I can't get Coral's warning out of my head. I am terrified because the siren queen might come after us to take my brothers back. They are all I have left in this world. Worse, I know if she tried to take them, they'd refuse. *What if they got hurt because of me? How would I live with myself?*

As usual, Leifur noticed something was off. He let Sindri ride ahead, singing to himself, and slowed down to match my pace at the rear.

"So what did you and Starfish talk about?"

I rolled my eyes at his disdain for my friend. "*Coral* and I talked about many things before she helped me hide my hair, and ..." I groaned. "She relayed a warning."

"What sort of warning?" he whispered.

"The queen is unhappy you left."

"We expected as much. We knew two male sirens leaving with a barren female siren was never going to sit well."

I flinched at his use of barren. He didn't mean it to hurt me, but I knew it was my failure that caused all of this. "Expecting and knowing are different. We know they might come after us to get you and Sindri back."

"They can try, but we won't be separated. They take us all or none of us."

"Leifur–"

"No." My brother-in-law was rarely forceful, preferring to live his life as happily as possible while remaining realistic. But now, his eyes darkened to black, and his fangs sprouted of their own volition, and I could see his marvelous sea foam scales peeking through his hairline. The idea that I'd let them leave me behind was not one that he would consider. "Sirens don't have family because we are all supposed to be one family," he said in a throaty whisper as he reined his siren in. "But I never felt like anyone cared about me until you and Sindri came into my life. He showed me what I'd been missing."

I reached over and squeezed his hand. Leifur had been an exceptional male siren in that he impregnated every female siren he'd ever been with, except me. The problem he had was that he'd fallen in love with every one of them, and no sooner than they'd become pregnant, they'd leave, and he'd be heartbroken. Not that they were cruel; it was in a female's nature to take what they needed from any male and then leave. But when he was assigned to me, I could tell he was different. He was kind, and I saw in him the love and devotion I'd experienced when I came back broken and needed to be put back together by someone who cared more than my so-called sisters. I understood that day why wounded and assaulted sirens were sent to the males to be healed. They showed the compassion and kindness very few of the females possessed.

"You are and always will be my family," I said. "Just as much as Sindri is. You are my brother until the end."

Leifur's shoulders dropped as he let out a heavy breath. "I'm glad to hear that. I was worried you'd consider sending us back for our good or some such nonsense."

"I'm far too selfish to do that. Besides, I know you wouldn't listen even if I tried."

Leifur just grinned like that day he'd first met my brother. "We should come up with some sort of plan for what we'll do if our *sisters* decide to come for us."

"I already have," I said, urging my horse forward. "And it's not going to be a pretty reunion."

Chapter 21

Njall

Blood poured from my nose as the guard pulled back his fist again and sent a right hook toward my face. I moved to dodge, but again, I was too slow and took another blow to the face. I stumbled back but caught myself before I went down. After two weeks, the king had grown bored of simply taunting and starving me, and began to pit me against his favorite men, or younger guards, as a punishment. The outcome was never in doubt; the amount of armor each man wore into the cell made it clear who was meant to win.

Standing safely outside the bars, the group of nobles jeered and placed bets, their voices echoing off the damp walls. I wiped the blood from my lip with the back of my hand, and I tried to drown out the ruckus while focusing on the guard. He was larger than the last two, and though he stood shorter than Baldr, he knew how to throw a punch. I was already feeling dizzy after so many knocks to the head in the last few days. My vision blurred as I raised my hands to shield my face.

I realized he was leaning a little to the right. When he came at me again, I swung my left hook with every ounce of strength I had, feeling the satisfying crack of his jaw beneath my knuckles.

The nobles booed as the guard staggered, clutching his face. When I drove another punch into his gut, it sent him crashing into the far wall. He slid down, gasping for breath. I stepped carefully around the puddle of blood that was spreading, thankful that they'd moved me to a different cell for the fights. My head spun as I shifted my weight, trying to stay light on my heels despite the exhaustion pulling at my body. The guard finally recovered, pushed himself off the wall, and accepted a mug from one of the nobles. He chugged the contents, then slammed to the ground and roared, pounding his chest like some feral beast.

I swallowed hard and readied myself for the next attack. When he charged again, his fists were relentless. Despite blocking several of his throws, one punch caught me square in the gut, driving the air from my lungs, and another snapped my head sideways. I hit the ground hard.

The nobles cheered, but I stayed down, spitting a mouthful of blood onto the dirt floor. There was no point in getting up again. I already knew how this would end.

Chapter 22

Elva

Figuring out where Njall is being kept in the castle would be my biggest challenge, since I know nothing of its layout. As I watched the fire sputter and crackle during my night watch, I tried to recall the things I knew for certain about the Huestur Castle and lands.

The Huestur Territories were smaller than the lands controlled by Tyndorf, but the forests here are thick and over-grown. The trees here are fewer in variety, growing so close together that they formed a suffocating canopy, blocking out most of the sunlight even at midday. The wagon trail we used would have been tended to in any other forest kingdom, but here it was overrun with roots, vines, and holes left from years of wear. We took a break here to get out our warmer clothes since the lack of sunlight made the forest feel frigid.

I'd only seen the castle once, when I was training to be a warrior. We had to practice letting our siren side take control so we could swim longer distances, so we would travel to the Huestur castle and then back to Konvern. It had been one of my favorite training excursions. I thrived in the water, unlike some sirens whose other half was a land creature. My ability to breathe in both forms gave me an edge, and for me, the water was a peaceful place. I felt safer there than anywhere on the ground.

Most castles on the water used tunnels to move supplies between the ships and the palace. I was pretty sure that I could get in, but once inside, the challenge would be to find Njall. I figured I could use my siren gifts to coax the information out of someone. If not, I could always beat it out of them.

I used the rest of my watch practicing with the new daggers Baldr had given me. They were heavier than I was used to, and made of a different metal that wouldn't fly as far as my usual ones.

"We'll need to find fresh water today," Leifur announced as I threw my last dagger at the makeshift target I'd set up. "Preferably this morning."

"Agreed," Sindri said, walking over to inspect my handiwork. He was dressed in a beautiful sapphire blue tunic with buttons carved from mother-of-pearl. "You're getting better. Now you just need a bath, so the guards can't smell you coming."

Leifur coughed to hide his laugh as I pulled the daggers out of the tree. Sindri was already strutting back to camp and called back over his shoulder, "Don't shoot the messenger!"

Leifur's sense of direction was by far the best, so I let him lead us toward the river. With the thick forest canopy, endless shadows, and glowing eyes that seemed to follow us as we weaved through the thickets. After spotting yet another pair of red eyes that vanished in a blink, Sindri became anxious, and his horse, Cobble, sensed it. I tried to keep my composure so the other horses would stay calm, but the more we traveled, the more densely packed the trees became, and it was a struggle to navigate through them. Sindri expressed his concerns louder than I'd have liked for a group trying to sneak up on a castle. Leifur had to shush him, and even I was beginning to regret bringing him along.

When I heard the gurgle of a rushing river, I let out an anxious breath and flashed a forced smile at Sindri. "See?"

My brother rolled his eyes and hurried his horse after Leifur, leaving me alone in the thicket.

My nerves had been getting the best of me for the last few days, so I allowed myself a few deep breaths before I pushed after them. Fear that Njall was being tortured to death, and we'd have nothing left to save, was bubbling to the surface as the closer we got to the castle, and since we'd run into Coral, the nightmare that the sirens could be coming to take back my brothers at any moment had been invading my sleep every night.

The trees near the river were the thickest we'd come across, but the bank on the other side was eerily bare.

"I'd heard it was red, but never quite believed it," Sindri said as I stepped out of the forest. Indeed, the river was red as blood.

"It's the runoff from the Crimson mountains," I explained, sliding off my horse.

Sindri leaned over the rocks and sniffed the rushing water below. "Is it safe to drink?"

"Perfectly." Leifur patted his horse as she took a long drink. "The crimson mountains are filled with iron. It's where my ore comes from and also what turns the water red."

Sindri grimaced and turned away.

"You'll live, sweetie," Leifur said. Sindri grudgingly handed over his water flask. Leifur filled all our flasks, and once the horses had their fill, we slipped back into the woods, thankful that no one had spotted us.

We swerved to the south to sneak around the towns that bordered the river. The path was narrow, forcing us to move in a single file. Keeping quiet was a challenge until we heard passersby ahead. At the sound of voices, Sindri smartened up, and we tightened our bags to prevent any noise. The day wore on as we persevered through the thick undergrowth.

Soon, the surrounding darkness was from the sun heading low in the sky and no longer the canopy above us. When we finally emerged from the forest, we found ourselves on a beach, and we could see the castle in the distance, further down the shore. Its silhouette was stark against the fading light.

"How close do you want to go?" Leifur asked.

"I don't think we should get any closer," Sindri replied. "We can travel much faster through water. Besides, if we leave the horses here, they're less likely to be spotted."

I looked at my twin in surprise. "You aren't the only one with good ideas, you know," he said, crossing his arms defensively.

"Of course she's not, love," Leifur said and pulled him in for a quick kiss.

"We can travel by water, but what about Njall?" I asked. "No one we talked to knew what his mother was. He could be fine in the water, or he could drown in a minute."

Sindri grinned and held up a tiny vial filled with silvery liquid. "That's why I convinced Coral to give me this."

Leifur grabbed the vial. "When did you talk to Coral?" he questioned, narrowing his eyes.

"It was when I went to take a leak. I saw her on the stairs. I knew she'd have tonic on her, and I wanted to get some just in case."

"How much did it cost you?" I asked, sliding down from my horse.

"Six gold coins."

"Six!" Leifur hissed as he handed me the bottle. "That shouldn't have cost over three."

"She knows Sindri," I replied. "He's always squirreling away gold in case he sees something pretty."

"Or shiny," Sindri added. He grabbed my fingers and closed

them around the tiny vial. "Six pieces of gold is a small price to pay if it gets us our home."

I pressed the vial to my chest. "Thank you." He pulled me into a hug and kissed my forehead.

"I got you the tool," he said as he stepped back. "Now you go get the prize pig."

Chapter 23

Elva

Despite Sindri's insistence that I sleep first, since I was the one who'd be heading into the castle, I couldn't shake my restless thoughts. When I woke, I was greeted with a hearty fish meal, but I had no appetite, so I picked at the food while my brothers settled in for their rest. Soon, the sky was so dark I couldn't see where it ended and the Nordlic Sea began. The castle was lit up in a brilliant orange glow from all the fires and torches that burned through the night. I couldn't help but admire the beauty of it, as I waited for the guards and people inside to go to bed.

Leifur appeared beside me, wearing a pair of water pants. All sirens owned them. They fit snuggly to prevent drag, and only went to our calves, so those of us who shifted more in the water had the space to allow free movement. Out of the three of us, I shifted the most.

My brother and I could both breathe underwater better than other sirens. As children, we'd been told it was because selkies and sirens could both breathe underwater. Along with that, I could swim at a speed previously unknown to sirens. My skills probably came from my father. I found I could summon my selkie side the way our sisters could summon their siren side. Whenever I did, scales ran from my forehead down the side of my body reaching my feet, overtaking the siren ones that appeared when I waited too long to find a man in my cycle. But what gave me the largest boost of speed was the webbing that grew out between my fingers and between my toes. They expanded to give me a pair of fins closer to a mermaid's tail than a siren's feet.

Leifur also possessed some of the webbing when underwater. Sindri's feet didn't change, but he could still swim much faster than average.

"Do you hear music?" Leifur asked, gazing at the castle.

"I suspect they're celebrating something," I said, tucking my tightest tunic into my water pants. "It might be smart to sneak in while everyone's distracted."

"Hair down or braided?" he asked.

"Braided, please."

Leifur took a few minutes to tuck my wild locks into a braid so tight, I was sure I would get a headache if I had to wear it on land all day.

We heard rustling, and Sindri emerged, dressed in his own water pants and swimming tunic.

"Are you two thinking of coming too?" I asked, looking him over slowly.

"Only if you need us," he said. "I'm well aware you are more than capable of handling most things, but it never hurts to be prepared." He nodded to the small beeswax covered leather satchel that I'd fastened around my waist. Inside it was the tiny vile he'd purchased from Coral.

Leifur finished with my hair, so I stepped to Sindri and gave him a big hug. "We've gone as far down the beach as we can. You two need to keep the fire going, so I can find my way back here once I have Njall."

"Are you sure you can handle all his dead weight?" Leifur asked.

"I'm more worried he'll be too full of hot air to sink," Sindri said, and I laughed with them as we walked down the beach a little further. I would not tell them that I was scared he was dead. Our horses were asleep, so we didn't want to wander too far and stopped when we could hear jubilant shouts joining the music coming from the castle.

"Remember," Leifur whispered. "In and out. No funny business."

"I know. Don't worry, I have no intention of taking any additional prisoners."

"Good. If anyone gets in your way—"

"I take care of them." I patted the lone sheath on my chest that held my favorite dagger.

"Then off you go." Sindri kissed my cheek for luck, and I dashed across the shore and slipped into the water.

On nights like this one, I was thankful to be a siren, because the water was freezing as I waded into it, but within a few heartbeats, my body had adjusted. I moved swiftly into the waves, feeling the water move steadily up my legs until my entire waist and chest were submerged. The waves pulled at me as if desperate to bring me back to the depths where I was born— where I belonged. Taking a few deep breaths, I drove into the next wave and released my siren. My eyes shifted to black, and I could immediately see underwater, even at night. It was a talent I wished I could use on land, too. I dove, kicking my feet clumsily while I waited to reach the depth that would allow my feet and arms to morph into the fins I needed to get to the castle.

The water cooled as the surrounding pressure grew, and a calm settled over me. I felt my feet and hands web, and then I kicked powerfully to surge forward and down through the dark depths. I maneuvered around glistening schools of fish, underwater rock mounds, and thickets of various sea grass. Soon, the natural landscape gave way. Large stone slabs, likely having fallen from ships in bad weather, replaced the rough rocks that littered the sea floor. Instead of the scales of colorful sea life, the sparkles were from gems and gold lost by humans. Soon, even the taste of the water changed. Swimming up to the surface, I raised only my eyes out of the water and saw I was much closer than I'd expected.

My memory had failed me. I had thought that most of the castle was built on the land, but either I'd been wrong or they'd done some architectural marvels in the last decade. The entire back of the castle stood over the water, with a colossal arch that opened to the sea, large enough for a ship to pass through. Somehow, the Huestur kingdom had made it possible to not only keep their knights and horses within their walls but also their most prized warships. The sheer size of it overwhelmed me for a moment before I got a hold of myself.

If the ships can hide inside, there must be another entrance for smaller boats to escape in case of attack.

I dove back down and took large gulps of seawater. I could taste the oils and animal hair that had come off ships coming from one direction, and ale and blood from another. I turned toward the ale, knowing that where there was ale mixed with blood, there would likely be waste. Humans had such a disdain for bodily functions that this way would likely be less protected. The way a woman's monthly bleeding horrified the men was something all the sirens laughed at. It was as if the men somehow believed they didn't all begin as this lining of blood inside a woman.

My hands sliced through the water as I pulled myself forward, the taste of humanity strengthening with each kick. When I came upon a patch of light shining into the water, I cautiously surfaced my head. I had arrived in a small littoral cave of sorts. From inside the rock formation, I couldn't tell if it was built as part of the castle or if they had built the castle above it. Several small boats were tied up along a dirt landing, bobbing gently on the small waves. I swam silently toward them and slipped between them to get a better look. Four torches flickered on the landing, casting shadows that danced across the walls. Beyond them, a dark hallway stretched into the rock. From the water, I couldn't tell what direction it went, but I hoped it would go down, since most castles hid their dungeons deep in the bowels of the place.

I shook my hands and feet and pushed back my siren. By the time I emerged from the water, she was contained once again. A soft breeze hit me, but there wasn't a soul in sight. Instinctively, I moved to wring out my braid but stopped myself and instead let the water run down my drenched back. I checked that my dagger and the siren tonic Sindri had procured were still with me. My confidence rose when I spotted a barrel of small torches against the wall. I lit one from the mounted torch near the boats and crept toward the hallway I had spotted.

Now closer, I could see that it was a stairwell heading up. With a last glance behind me, I tiptoed up the steps to the first landing and peeked around the edge of the wall. It was well-lit, but empty, so I continued until I reached a dark hallway. I was still trying to decide whether to try the hall or continue up the stairs when I heard giggles from above.

Cursing the puddles I'd left behind me, I hurried around the corner. The giggles grew louder, and when I braved a quick peek, I spotted two young maids carrying empty jugs. They were so focused on their conversation, they didn't notice me or my puddles as they headed down the stairs I'd just ascended. For a moment, I considered following them, thinking that if they were heading down with empty jugs, I must have missed some path that would lead to the ale room. But then a cool breeze hit me, and the air smelled foul, like piss and stale sweat. I remembered it from the crowded sleeping quarters of the warriors when we traveled around learning our skills. That putrid, unwashed stench was hard to forget. I resisted the urge to plug my nose and hurried down the dark hall.

The narrow stone path was a maze of twists, turns, and offshoots, but I had no problem following the odor. My eyes were burning when I heard chatter from men, and I slowed my movements. The scattered torches provided shadows between them, and I dashed from one dark spot to another until the path opened into a large room. Squatting low to the ground, I crept along the wall and glanced inside. It was a prison. Cells of various sizes housed all manner of men. Some were wearing the uniforms of Tyndorf, likely those captured during the attack, but others wore normal clothes, and one even appeared to be dressed as a court jester.

Careful not to reveal myself, I tried to look further down in the cells down the path, but it was no use. Hearing footsteps, I slunk back to make myself as small as possible in the dark hall and extinguished my torch. A group of three men came from the right and walked toward me, a heavy door slamming behind them. I held my breath, and just as they were close enough to be able to spot me, a scream bounced off the stone walls. The three guards immediately raced past me, and when I braved a look, they were shouting at someone in a cell a good distance down the cell block. The other prisoners cheered as the guards fumbled with their keys, trying to get into the cell that was causing the commotion.

This was my only chance. I clambered to my feet, and with a glance to make sure everyone was distracted, I dashed toward the door from where they'd entered. With a rough pull, it opened, and I slipped inside.

Chapter 24

Elva

I held the door so it would close quietly, hissing at the gash in my side where I'd cut myself on the rusted edge as I slipped through. I was at the top of a steep stairwell. Torches flickered as I reached the bottom. Here, it was much colder, and the air felt moist. I rested my hand against the wall and felt the drops of water running down the stone. I must have been below the waterline. Letting out a slow breath, I craned my neck around the corner to see another dark hallway and silently groaned. With how many dark tunnels there were, I wasn't sure I'd be able to get out of here even if I found Njall. Part of me wanted to give up, sneak back out, and try again another night, but I knew I had one chance to do this, and it was now.

The torches on the wall were smaller. Standing up on my toes, I tugged at one and wrenched it from the stone. I looked around to see if there was anything I could use to extinguish the others, but found nothing. Biting back a groan, I lay my torch down and used my dagger to cut the bottom half of my shirt off. Then I wrung my hair out onto the fabric to make it as wet as possible. After twisting it together, I cracked it like a whip at the torch on the wall, and the flame vanished to make sure no one would see me coming.

"Well done," I whispered to myself and continued down the stone path, extinguishing torches until the whole path was dark outside of the torch I held in my hand. At the end of the path was another door, identical to the one I'd seen on the floor above. Dousing the final torch, I grabbed the icy iron door handle and pushed it open.

"What are you doing here?" A deep baritone voice barked as the door closed behind me. I spun and saw a single guard. He was tall with a full head of hair, and his arms were like those of the chiseled statues that decorated the siren halls. Considering what I had planned for him, it was a shame, since he was rather handsome. He eyed me with a mixture of suspicion and lechery, his gaze lingering on my body rather than the dagger in my hand.

Pouting my lips seductively, I stepped toward him, and he didn't even flinch as I grabbed the top of his chest plate with one hand and my dagger hilt with the other. I pulled him toward my mouth and kissed him for a moment before I rammed my dagger into the side of his throat. I sucked his scream and final breath into my lungs before he pushed away from me and crumpled into a heap on the ground at my feet. I pushed his arm off his waist and found the key ring I had hoped would be there. Seconds later, I was on my way down the hall again. With luck, he'd be the only one in this part of the dungeon.

I listened for any signs of other men as I picked up my pace to check each cell in this area. I'd already been inside the castle too long, and I was worried Sindri would lose patience and do something stupid like try to come after me. After passing thirteen cells, I was feeling as if this entire thing was hopeless when I heard a cough. I stopped walking and tried to place the sound, and when I heard it again, I dashed past another three cells. Njall was on his hands and knees behind what looked like a pile of hay and boards. He looked like he was digging, but that made no sense when this entire level was underwater.

Silently, I crossed the path and pressed my elbows against the iron bars. "Trying to end it by drowning doesn't seem very regal."

Njall flinched and dropped his makeshift shovel. It took a moment for him to recognize my voice, but when he did, he slowly turned his head to face me.

"What are you doing here?" His question came out more like a growl than a man, but I didn't let that bother me.

I held out the key ring and spun it on the end of my finger. "Saving your spoiled ass, so get up." The compilation of confusion, fear, and indignation on his face was enough to make me laugh. His expression morphed into rage. "Oh come now, Your Highness. You should thank me."

Njall stood slowly like a wolf stalking prey, and lunged toward the bars, but I wrenched the keys from his grasp and wagged a finger at him as if he were a child.

"Uh uh," I scolded. "Only good boys get released."

He glared at me with more fear than I'd ever seen from anyone in my life, outside of the men my siren had murdered. "And what exactly do I have to do to be *good*?"

I couldn't help the grin that spread across my face as I leaned closer to the bars. "For starters, you could apologize for getting me and my brothers arrested."

"Just that?" He grinned wickedly at me. "Not for bedding you better than anyone else ever has and then just leaving?"

A heat spread through my core at the memory of our night together, but I couldn't let it show on my face or confirm his suspicions about how it was for me. "Was that you? Must not have been that memorable." He opened his mouth to reply, but I snapped back. "Your satyr brother, on the other hand ... that was a night I'll always remember."

Njall's eyes narrowed at me, and his jaw clenched so hard I worried he might break a tooth.

He's not jealous, is he? I stood taller.

"As much as I enjoy seeing a man who wronged me behind bars, we should get going. I'd prefer not to kill anyone else tonight if I can avoid it." I spun the keys in my fingers, searching for the one that would match the lock on his door.

"How many men did you bring with you?" He looked down the hall before fixing his gaze on me.

I paused and took a moment to really take him in. He was filthy and smelled worse than Sindri when he was transitioning from boy to man. I stood there clean, rested, and ready to kill to get him out of here. And yet he assumed I had help. "No one," I snapped as quietly as possible. "Because no one else is coming, *Your Highness*. They're all saving your sister, so you'll need to get off your high horse and let a lowly little siren save you. Or else you'll stay in this cell until the Huestur king tires of you and has you killed for sport. I've heard he enjoys letting prisoners go free in the forest to feed the dire wolves."

Njall's face went ashen at the mention of the beasts that even my kind knew to avoid.

"Then why are you here?"

"To rescue you."

"Because?"

"Baldr sent me."

"Ah," he whispered. "So you're being paid."

"Of course. I don't work for free. He offered me all the gold I wanted if I brought you home." I found the key I suspected was the right one, thrust it into the lock, and wiggled it. When I heard the click, I shoved the door open. He leaped back just in time to avoid being hit, but still grabbed it before it could slam against the bars and potentially give us away.

"The way I see it, Your Highness, you have two choices." I

nodded toward the corner where he'd been when I arrived. "You can stay here and keep doing whatever that is, and probably die here waiting for your father to send his men. Or you can come with me, and I'll get you out of here alive."

He grunted at me, and before he even took a step forward, I had my dagger out and under his chin. "I was promised gold even if I confirm you're dead."

His Adam's apple bobbed as he swallowed hard, trying to avoid the blade.

"Do we have an understanding?" I asked, letting my siren side surface for the briefest moment. I wanted to remind him that my dagger was the least dangerous thing about me.

He gulped softly. "Yes."

I held my dagger there a moment longer before I sheathed it, then stepped aside. Once he was out, I took one last look at his cell and felt a pang of pity. I wouldn't want to stay here, and he'd endured weeks.

I turned toward him, but he had his back to the cell and was trying to figure out which direction to go. "Left," I said, and the two of us took off toward the door.

Njall shot me a curious glance as we stepped over the body of the dead guard. "He was in the way," I said, and focused on retracing my steps toward the water. When we reached the door that led to the regular cells, I held my hand out to slow him.

"What?" he whispered.

"These are the normal cells. They were actually guarded, unlike the rest of the path to the sea."

"The sea?"

"Yes, how else would a siren get in here?"

"We're leaving through the water?"

"Stop asking asinine questions." I opened my satchel and pulled out Sindri's vial. "Drink this."

"What is it?"

I barely held back my snort. "A tonic sirens use to bring prisoners of war back to our castle. Now drink it." I pressed my ear to the door trying to listen, but the wood was too thick. "We'll just have to go in."

"And if there are guards?"

"We handle them." I held my dagger out to him and pushed my talons out of my fingers, hissing slightly at the sting.

"Can you subdue them without them raising the alarm?"

A smirk spread across my lips as I pushed down on the door's handle. "Yes. I'll do it the way I always handle men. Just wait and see ."

I threw the door open, and sure enough, the three guards from earlier were leaning against the wall together, passing around a silver flask. The moment they saw me, they stood at attention, and I acted. As soon as my siren song filled the space, the three men froze and stared up at me, openmouthed. I took the silver flask from the first, a slightly older man, and quickly surveyed the other two. Seeing a bulge, I snagged a coin purse from one's pocket and fastened it to my hip.

"What are you going to do with them?" Njall asked, coming up behind me.

"Aww, are you concerned for your enemies?" I teased.

"No. I want to make sure they have no idea how I escaped."

"Then you have nothing to worry about." I held up my talons and drove them into the first man's neck until they hit the wall. Njall watched as blood squirted everywhere. The rage on his face told me these men had a history with him, so I handed him my dagger. He sliced the younger man's neck before driving the dagger into the older guard's eye and then his neck, before holding it out to me.

"You keep it. You might need it." I reached up and grabbed a torch from the wall before we headed into the darkest part of the path.

My patience was tested almost to the limit as we hid in a dark corner and waited for guards and servants to leave the stairwell that led to our exit. Before, I'd only seen the two young maids, but now the party was in full swing. We watched at least nine servants make their way down the stairs and return with various jugs of ale. Two guards even came back with a barrel between them.

"Did they feed you that well?" I asked Njall while we waited for the guards' footsteps to leave the stairs.

"Hardly. I was lucky to get food that I could chew without breaking a tooth."

I realized part of the reason his clothes had looked so bad on him was likely because he'd lost some weight from not being fed. My brothers and I were used to only eating a meal or two when things got busy, but I was sure a prince, even if his father hated him, would still be fed enough to keep him fit. I shook away the sympathy for him that was creeping into my mind and reminded myself that if he hadn't had that change of heart, I'd have been in his father's dungeon, where we'd be starved and put through unthinkable acts as his *pet*.

"I think the coast is clear, let's go," I spoke too soon. Shouts came from far above us. Metal clanked as men streamed into the stairwell. I grabbed Njall's arm to pull him back into the darkness. The guards were getting closer. Trying to decide which way to go, Njall grabbed my face and kissed me.

Heat rushed through me as he stepped closer. The instant his skin touched mine, a needy moan left my lips, and he kissed me harder. His hands roamed across my ass and back until he squeezed my thighs and lifted me off the ground before shoving me into the stone wall behind us. As he ground his groin into me, I couldn't help the breathy moans that left me as he moved his kisses to my neck, hitting the exact spot he'd bitten me weeks before.

Footsteps pounded behind us as the guards rushed past, oblivious to the two guests going at it in the corner. Njall paused, still holding me against the wall as we listened for the footsteps to fade into the distance. Then, he dropped me so suddenly that I barely caught myself before I hit the ground. "Let's go," was all he said, as he hurried to the stairs.

I growled through my teeth as I caught up to him. I need to make sure that he didn't get us lost in these tunnels. We only took one wrong turn as we raced toward the small dock I'd arrived on. But once we got closer, I could hear shouting again.

Ferflucs, I cursed under my breath. The echoes in the tunnel made it impossible to tell if the sounds were coming from behind us, ahead of us, or both.

"What if they found your boat?" he asked as we rounded another corner and heard the lapping of waves.

"Who said I came by boat?"

"I thought you said you came by the sea!" Njall said as we emerged into the sea cave.

"You can swim, can't you?" I asked. I was relieved to hear the sounds were behind us.

Njall's eyes went wild. "I don't swim!"

The shouting was getting louder, and I would not stand around and argue with him. I grabbed a torch off the ground and extinguished it against the wall before turning toward the stubborn prince.

"Then it's a good thing that sirens and selkies are exceptional swimmers." Before he could reply, I slammed the torch against his temple, and he fell into the water with a loud splash.

Hopefully, he drank the tonic.

Chapter 25

Elva

Njall sank quickly, and I struggled to get to him while I was still in my human form. But by the time I'd made it to the bottom, I'd morphed, and my control was better. He'd come to rest on a pile of ale barrels. I grabbed under his arms and held onto him while I used my feet fins to propel us. With the commotion we'd set off, I couldn't risk going to the surface for a long while yet. Small bubbles escaped Njall's mouth and nose, and when they finally stopped, I watched closely. He was still, and in the darkness I couldn't tell if he was blue or not.

Suddenly, his chest heaved as he took a breath of water, and then another. Relieved he'd been smart enough to take the tonic, I pulled him along the seafloor, looking for the natural waypoints I remembered when I first entered the water down the beach. When I found the round mound that reminded me of the ones in Konvern, I knew I'd made it far enough down the shoreline. Clutching Njall tightly, I swam to the surface and popped my head out of the water.

My brothers' fire was just up the beach. I pulled Njall to the surface of the water, and he coughed and sputtered before he breathed air again. As I swam toward the shore, I called for Leifur and Sindri. My brother-in-law ran out to me and slid his arm around Njall's back, taking his weight from me. Once all of us were back on the shore, we placed Njall on his side near the fire.

"We knew you'd found him when everything suddenly lit up," Sindri said, gesturing toward the castle.

"It appears they lit every torch and fire in the castle, and then the shouting got so loud we could hear it down here," Leifur added.

"How many did you have to kill?" My twin asked me, eyeing my ripped and bloodied shirt.

"Only four."

"Not bad. I expected at least eight," Leifur said.

"I came across more than a dozen in there, but they didn't bother to light the servants' passages, so staying in the shadows was easy."

"When do we leave?" Sindri asked.

"As soon as we can," I replied. "Pack up the fish and get His Highness to wake up. Then once we're all changed, we'll move deeper into the forest. We'll skip the fire this evening to avoid being seen."

"We should travel as far as possible tonight and hide out during the day," Leifur suggested. I nodded without looking away from the castle. "I'll go start packing up."

Sindri waited for his husband to be out of earshot before leaning toward me. "Are you okay?"

"I'm fine," I snapped.

He seemed like he wanted to question me further, but he let it go. Sindri knew my tells and when not to push me. He just patted my shoulder and headed toward our camp, leaving me to my thoughts.

Something felt off, and I couldn't place it. It wasn't fear or anxiety or even excitement at achieving what we'd traveled so far to do.

A shout from Sindri made me turn toward the fire. My brothers were fighting with a disoriented Njall, and I rushed across the sand toward them.

"We won't hurt you," Leifur said, holding out his hands to calm the prince.

Njall was waving the dagger I'd given him, along with one of the large pronged iron forks we'd been using to cook the fish.

"They won't, but I will if you don't stop threatening my brother," I said.

"You!" Njall turned the fork toward me. "You knocked me unconscious in the castle."

"I did," I admitted, before I leaped at him and ripped the fork from his grasp. I grabbed his wrist to stop him from trying to stab me. Disarming him had been too easy, so he was still out of sorts. "I needed you to listen and not argue, a skill you are clearly lacking. It seemed like the best plan."

"You could have just asked."

"Yes," I said, smiling sweetly at him. "But that would have taken time, which we didn't have. We're lucky the guard didn't question us when we were in the hallway. I didn't want to press our luck."

"Why wouldn't the guards question you?" Leifur asked.

Sindri looked at me suspiciously, and before I could stop myself, my cheeks flushed, and my twin snickered. "Because Elva's exceptional at causing distractions," he said.

I rolled my eyes and ignored him. "The other reason is that humans struggle when we bring you to the sea depths. I didn't have the time to deal with that either. Just be thankful we got you out."

"I'm thrilled, now you can let me go."

Sindri laughed. "Sorry, Your Highness. You're our meal ticket. You're not going anywhere."

Njall made a move as if he intended to go for my brother, but my knock on the head had taken more out of him than he realized, and he stumbled for a moment. Leifur grabbed his shoulder to steady him and helped him down to the ground.

I crossed the camp and grabbed my skin of fresh water. "Here, have a drink and eat something. If we want to evade the Huestur army tonight, we need you to have enough strength to stay on your horse."

Sindri grabbed the other forks with fish on them. "No funny business. My sister is lethal when necessary. Especially if she can't sing her way out of a predicament."

Njall took the skin and had a small sip, swishing the water in his mouth to test it.

"Oh, for goodness' sake." I grabbed my skin and took a large swig. "It's fine." When I dropped this skin in Njall's lap, he immediately took a long drink from it.

"I'll ready the horses," I whispered to Leifur. "Make sure he eats and drinks. They weren't feeding him in there, and we'll run into problems if he can't stay on his horse."

"Understood." He pulled a small loaf of bread out of the supply bag.

I fed the horses, and then dug dry clothes out for Leifur and myself from our supplies, and found where we'd hidden Njall's clothes. I knew if Sindri had seen them, we'd never get them back from him, so Leifur had buried them below my underclothes. It was the one place Sindri would never check. I suspected our guest wouldn't want to ride our mule, so I moved my bag to her, allowing him to take the horse his brother had provided us.

Once I'd secured the loads evenly across our horses, I set about changing out of my ripped clothes. My pants were rung out and tied to my satchel, but the shirt was not worth keeping, so I grabbed the bottom to pull it off. As I did, a hot pain shot through my left side. I tossed the shirt into the woods and looked down to see a deep cut on my side, from when I got caught on the rusty door earlier. I groaned at myself for getting injured and exchanged the shirt I'd chosen for a darker one. The last thing I needed was one of my brothers seeing blood on my shirt and getting themselves worked up.

By the time I returned to the fire, all the food had been eaten. I tossed Leifur the clothes for Njall and made my brother leave him so he could get dressed in peace.

"Why do I have to go help with the horses?" Sindri whined as we packed up the last of the cooking supplies.

I just ignored my brother's pouts and made sure everything on the horses was secure, as Leifur and Njall made their way to us.

"Feeling better?" Sindri asked when Leifur came with Njall in tow.

Njall nodded. "My head still hurts, but having a full belly is a pleasant change." He looked up in surprise. "These are my horses."

"Baldr gave them to us," I explained. "He wanted to make sure we'd make it out here. I assumed you'd want Acorn, so I moved my things to our mule."

Njall didn't even acknowledge me, but went to each of his horses, stroking them and addressing them by name.

"We've taken good care of them," I assured him, as we each grabbed a rein and made our way into the forest, leaving behind the beach.

"So what's the plan?" Njall asked as he climbed into Acorn's saddle. "I assume we aren't just going to wander in the forest until we get caught."

"You didn't see the woods when you arrived because you were taken by boat—"

"How did you know I was taken by boat?"

"We saw them take you," Sindri replied. "We're the ones who informed them of your and your lovely sister's abductions."

"You didn't bother to help?"

"There were only three of us, and a lot more Huestur and Anginfill men," I explained. "But we saw which kingdom took you, and we went back to the castle to make sure the right people knew."

"Baldr?"

My brothers nodded, and I expected Njall to ask more, such as who was sent after his sister, but he didn't. He simply looked ahead and waited for Leifur to head in a direction. It was just as well. If the Huestur army was out in the woods now, the quieter we were, the better for all of us.

The dense undergrowth muffled our footsteps, but with the thick canopy overhead, it was impossible to see where we were going. At least anyone who tried to pursue us through the forest would face the same issues.

"We should go north," Njall said.

"Why would we go north?" Sindri asked. "Your kingdom is to the south."

"That's exactly why we should go north," Njall replied. "They won't expect it. We won't go far—just enough to bypass their men and get to the Bloot River. Then we can cross and travel along the other side until we get to the mountains."

"It would add days to our journey," Leifur said.

"I'm not in any hurry to get home. It isn't as if anyone would miss me."

I weighed his words carefully. The Zverm Forest on the other side of the river was outside of Huestur territory. The men likely wouldn't expect us to go so far out of our way, and it would put some distance between us.

"The only question is," I mused aloud, "do we head north now, or go deeper into the forest first and then turn?"

"We go now," Njall said firmly. "Their scouts are probably already out. If we move now, we might slip right past them without them even knowing."

"Back to the Bloot River, it is," Sindri said.

Chapter 26

Elva

I thought Leifur had a good sense of direction, but Njall put him to shame. The forest was nearly pitch-black, and my brother-in-law was ready to give up. I even offered to climb a tree to see where the moon was, but Njall had insisted he knew the direction. Sure enough, after a few hours of riding, I could hear a river.

"Are we going to cross tonight or wait for the morning light?" Sindri asked.

Njall chuckled. "I didn't know sirens feared water."

I could sense my brother's annoyance, even though we were on opposite sides of our line. "I'm not afraid of the water," he snapped. "I just don't want to lose anything in the river while it's dark."

"We test the water," I suggested, hoping to stop a fight before it could begin. "If it's shallow enough for the horses to cross safely, we do it now, and if it's deep, we wait and find a safer location in the daylight."

I'd won over the men, and after another hour of walking, we were finally released from the endless trees and found ourselves at the river once again. The moon reflected off the dark water, and I bit my tongue. Although I knew sirens were scarier than most of the creatures we'd come across, after the wolf attack, I couldn't help but feel anxious in the forest where massive were-wolves hunted.

Njall slid off Acorn and scanned the ground. I hopped off my mule and followed. He seemed to find what he's been looking for: an almost comically long stick.

"What are you doing?" I asked, careful to keep my distance in case he was planning revenge for when I'd hit him in the castle.

Ignoring me, he walked to the river's edge and shoved the stick into the water. "If the shore is already deeper than our height, there's no point in anyone getting wet to see, that is, of course, unless the hot-blooded sirens need cooling off."

I rolled my eyes. As a Siren, I wasn't affected by cold water, so the idea of testing the depth would never have occurred to me. But the idea of not being wet while we rode through the chilly air was appealing, though I could have done without the snide remarks.

Njall pulled the stick out of the water, walked a ways down, and tried again, and then a third time. "Some places are deeper, so if we want to go tonight, we'll have to go slowly and use the stick to check for depth."

"That sounds like a great idea," Leifur said. He dismounted and brought his horse up beside me. "Why didn't you think of that?" He playfully elbowed me, and I pushed him back.

"Obviously because she's not afraid to get wet," Njall said.

I narrowed my eyes at the stuck-up, royal pain in front of me. Part of me wanted to shove him into the river. Luckily for him, Leifur knew me too well, and he grabbed my arm, shaking his head.

"Fine," I muttered under my breath and stepped back.

"What was that?" Njall asked, stepping away from the water to shake something off his stick.

"Nothing."

"I want to check a few more dips in the bank to see if they were made from people crossing the river, and then we can pick where we go."

In the end, it was the third last spot Njall checked that we ended up crossing. The water was so shallow that it only came up to my horse's thigh, so they had no problem making it across. Once we were safely on the other side, we swiftly rode into the forest, going only deep enough that we wouldn't be spotted from across the river.

"Now that we're out of harm's way, should we stop and get some rest?" Sindri asked.

"Tired already?" I teased. "Was it stressful sitting on the beach while I snuck into the castle to save the prince?"

"Haha." My brother muttered back sarcastically while I sped up to catch up to Leifur.

"I know what you're going to ask, and I think Sindri's right," Leifur said. "And not just because he's my husband. We've been riding for hours in complete darkness. We all need a break, but the horses especially."

"You're probably right. If one of them gets injured, we'll be in trouble." I pulled my mule's reins tighter and glanced behind me. "But I'm worried our prize might try to run."

Leifur looked back, too. "If he does, it won't be tonight. It's too dark, and he'll need the combined supplies to make it home without being caught."

"I can hear you two," Njall called over.

"Good," I shot back. "Then keep in mind that if you try to run, I'll let my siren chase you, and she loves to play with her food."

I'd worried that having Njall along would be a headache, but for a spoiled prince, he knew his way around a campsite. Leifur handled the horses, and Njall and I gathered the firewood. We'd gone far enough into the woods that we figured it would be safe to have a small fire. I loaded my arms with sticks and branches, while keeping a sharp eye on Njall. He'd said he wouldn't run, but I would not risk it. Even starved, his body was lean and muscular, and I suspected that after how much food we'd given him on the beach, he'd have the energy to outrun me for some time.

"Uh," he cleared his throat, and I looked up to find him staring at me. "Like what you see, little Pearl?" His lips curled up into a wicked little smirk.

"Don't call me that," I snapped, glaring at him.

"What, *Pearl?*"

"No, *little.*"

"And why not?" Njall stepped so close we were almost touching. He was trying to intimidate me, with how much taller than me he was, but I didn't move a muscle until I pulled out my dagger and held it up to his abdomen.

"Because the last man who did found himself smaller in a very tender area."

Njall's face blanched, but he didn't back down. "Do you ever reply to someone without resorting to violence?"

"I do, but rarely once I've gotten to know a man. Most of you are only good for one thing." I said, raking my eyes across his muscled chest.

"Then it's swell that I'm exceptionally good at it."

I used the tip of my dagger to scrape some grime from under a nail before I turned my gaze up at him through my lashes. "It doesn't count if you say it in the mirror."

He leaned down enough that his lips just grazed the top of my ear. "That's not what you said when you were riding my cock."

"How do you know I wasn't faking? I am a siren after all." I pushed past him and strutted toward the first branch I spotted near me.

"You're not that good of a liar."

"And how would you know—" I turned, prepared to throw more insults at him, but he was already standing beside me. I was immediately thankful I'd swam him through the sea as far as I had because he smelled significantly better now than when I'd found him in the cells. The stench of piss and sweat was gone, replaced by sea salt, and the peppermint I'd kept in the bag with his clothes.

He stepped closer to me, his eyes locked onto mine. I swallowed back the nerves and tingling that were spreading as his closeness brought back the memories of the night we'd shared. I'd been with many men, and few were memorable. I knew I'd always remember our night together, even more than the night I'd shared with Baldr.

"Because I've been around liars my whole life. And you, Pearl, are not a liar." He bumped me out of his way and disappeared into the trees to get more wood. In an instant, all my attraction to him vanished.

Jellyfish, I muttered to myself, and headed into a different direction to gather my wood. I intended to make sure my bundle was bigger than his.

When I returned to camp with my firewood, Sindri raised an eyebrow. "Were you two getting naked out there?"

"Catch your tongue," I growled at him, and I moved to smack him, but he caught my wrist before I could.

"Where's the prince?" Leifur asked, feeding the fire with the twigs I'd gathered.

"Getting more wood."

My brothers exchanged a look. "Are you alright?" Sindri asked.

"I'm fine," I snapped, yanking my wrist free. "Where am I sleeping?"

"I'll get your blanket," Sindri said, heading toward the horses.

Leifur added the larger branches to the fire and watched it for a moment before turning to me. "You've been acting strange since you got out of the castle."

I forced a smile at my brother-in-law and poked the ground with a stick. "The conditions they kept him in were ... how do I put it mildly? Inhumane. They starved him and left him to sleep on a pile of hay that stank of piss and vomit. I am aware our kind is known for being violent, but at least we're quick about it. Who knows how long they would have left him there?"

"Sounds like the night you shared with him had quite the effect on you."

"Nonsense." I ignored Leifur and moved dirt around with my shoe. "I've just never seen a species treat its own so poorly."

"Is he, though? Human, I mean. No one knows whether his mother was human or something else like his siblings' mothers," Leifur said.

"He'd be half-human. The siren queen may be a pain in the ass, but at least she treats us with respect. I was banished, not tortured."

Leifur scoffed. "You never should have been. You couldn't provide a child, but you did more to protect the children of others than any of the other sirens who birthed young." His fist clenched around the wood in his hand. I rubbed his shoulder and gave him a reassuring smile. Although Sindri hadn't cared when the queen banished me—he'd simply packed up and followed me

—the entire situation never sat right with my brother-in-law. He'd spent his entire life doing what our kind demanded of him, just like I had, and then, because I couldn't complete one demand, they deemed me worthless, as if all my other accomplishments were erased because I was barren. He'd argued with the general and the queen on my behalf, and for a minute I thought they might listen to him, but in the end their decision had been final.

"Are you thinking of when Sindri threatened to make the queen pay for dishonoring you?" I asked him.

"How'd you know?"

"You get this look on your face. It's an odd mixture of respect, terror, and humor that I never see otherwise."

Sindri joined us at the fire with our mats and blankets. "What's so funny?" he asked.

"Nothing," I replied quickly, as Leifur coughed to cover his laughter.

Sindri pursed his lips as he threw my mat and blanket into the dirt. I rolled my eyes and set up all our sleeping mats, and Njall arrived with a load of firewood and dropped it in front of my brothers.

Sindri had dropped to the ground beside his love. Now he turned to our prisoner. "What side of the bed do you usually sleep on?" he asked.

"Why?" Njall asked, eyeing my brother.

Sindri smiled sweetly. "So we can make room for you. To travel lightly, we only brought two mats and two blankets. You'll have to share with my sister."

Njall's head jerked as he scanned the ground around the fire, letting out a loud gruff of disbelief. Leifur couldn't hold back his laughter any longer. The entire situation was so ridiculous. Never in my wildest dreams would I have imagined I'd have rescued a prince, let alone one from Tyndorf of all places, and would be stuck sleeping beside him or choosing to freeze away from the fire.

"It's fine. I don't need a mat or blanket," I said, moving to the end of the sleeping area, where there was more dirt than wet grass.

Njall's huffs softened. "Don't be ridiculous. There is more than enough room here."

While our mats were not a bed, they were warmer and softer than the ground. But the idea of lying beside him—of his body pressed against mine, made my throat go dry.

"Are you going to stay on your side, or do we have to tie you up?" Sindri asked, smirking at Njall. "Wouldn't want you getting inappropriate with my sister ... again."

Njall's eyes narrowed into slits, and he looked like he was ready to explode.

Leifur diffused the situation. "No one is tying anyone up. The faster we get some sleep, the faster we can keep moving and get as far away from here as possible."

Njall grumbled to himself, but grabbed our blanket and lay down on the mat facing toward the fire. I was going to tell him that was my spot, but Leifur shot me a warning glare. I closed my mouth and lay down on the mat facing away from the fire. I shifted around until my back was flush against his. The heat from his body immediately poured into mine as he draped the blanket over me. Blush crept across my cheeks as his scent filled my nose, bringing back the memories I desperately wanted to block out. It made me thankful to be facing away from my brothers, because Sindri would have noticed and made comments, and the last thing I needed was the memory of Njall's hands on my body being more vivid than they already were with him at my back.

Chapter 27

Njall

branch snapped in the woods, barely audible over the rain landing on our tent. I held my breath, straining to listen for anything else, but the sound of my heart pounding made it nearly impossible. My body had surged into fight mode, coiled and ready to strike if the sound was more than a woodland creature. But it wasn't just the possibility of danger that had my pulse racing. Elva lay beside me, and she'd picked tonight, of all nights, to roll toward me and leave her arm slung across my chest as she slept.

It had been three days since I'd become her prisoner. Sharing a blanket with her in the open campsite had been a challenge, but lying beside her in a small tent, away from her brothers' watchful eyes, was a form of torture that rivaled what I'd gone through at the Huestur castle. Every soft breath she took in reminded me of the night we'd shared before everything fell apart—before I'd made the gravest mistake of my life by turning her in. Back then, I'd seen her as a monster, a siren created to lure and destroy men. But now I knew the truth: Elva was so much more than that.

Another branch snapped, louder this time.

"Elva," I whispered, gently shaking her shoulder.

"What?" she muttered softly before ripping her arm from my chest and pushing herself up off the ground. "Sorry."

"Shhh. Listen," I whispered, my voice barely audible over the rain. For a moment, it picked up, and all we heard was the patter of water against the tent fabric. Then, just as I felt her shift beside me, came another snap. Tension radiated off her, letting me know she'd heard it too. Without a word, she crawled over my legs and moved silently to the back of the tent. My eyes had adjusted enough now that I could see her silhouette moving toward the door flaps. She pulled them aside, and as lightning cracked in the sky, I saw the outline of a knight standing just beyond the trees.

"They found us," Elva whispered as she scrambled back to me. "Grab what you can and get to the horses. I'll get my brothers."

I caught her arm, holding her close so I could whisper. "Where are your daggers? Your sword?"

Elva reached around me, retrieved her dagger sheath from the ground, and slung it across her chest. Then she guided my hand under the mat where she'd been sleeping, and my fingers closed around the hilt of a sword she'd kept hidden from me. I frowned, but said nothing. That was a conversation for later—not now, when every second counted.

Elva crawled to one end of the tent, and I remained at the other. We waited, crouching there. I felt her brush against my shin more than once. When a loud rustle came just outside my end, I pushed her with my foot, and she slipped out silently through the flaps. I grasped the sword, ready to follow, when a shout came from outside.

I leaped out of the tent and spotted two men. They hadn't seen me come out. With surprise on my side, I sliced one's leg, and he dropped with a sharp cry. As the other one turned, I drove my fist into his jaw, sending him sprawling just as quickly.

"Sindri, run!" Leifur bellowed, bursting out of the other tent with a sword in one hand and a hammer in the other.

Lightning flashed as I shouted, "Where's Elva?"

"Forget Elva," Leifur growled when an arrow whizzed past us, striking one of the men on the ground. "She can handle herself. You need to go with Sindri." He shoved me toward his husband, and from the pleading look in his eyes, I knew that I was not to be his prisoner, but his protector. Sindri was scrambling to salvage whatever gear he could from the ground. I hauled him to his feet, and together we sprinted across the campsite toward the horses. A guard lunged at us, knocking Sindri to the ground, but I made a quick time of him with my sword. Its workmanship surprised me—the blade slid through the guard's leather armor and back as if it were cheese.

"Move!" I shouted. When we reached the horses, we fumbled with the saddles as fast as our fingers could manage in the freezing rain.

Shouts came from the camp behind us, followed by Elva's scream. I spun, ready to rush back into the fray, but Sindri grabbed my shoulder. "They've got this," he said, his voice wavering. "Get on your horse, now."

"But—"

"We didn't come this far to lose you now and get nothing out of this trip." He shoved me toward my mount. I was ready to argue, to fight him off and go back for Elva, when her voice cut through the chaos.

"On the horses now!"

Leifur and Elva burst from the camp, their arms full of supplies and both splattered with blood. Sindri was already mounted on his horse, holding the reins of Elva's mule. She swung onto it with surprising agility, and I quickly followed suit, mounting Acorn. We were off at a gallop, the horses' hooves pounding against the sodden earth as fast as we dared.

"Ride faster!" Leifur shouted over the relentless rain lashing against our faces. There was no need for quiet now.

The shouts behind us grew louder, closer, and Elva leaned into her mule's neck, urging it ahead of her brothers. "We need to split up," she yelled back to them. "It's our only chance."

"You get Njall out of here," one of them shouted. I think it was Leifur, but I couldn't be certain at this distance. "We'll lead them away."

"No—" Elva's protest was cut short as an arrow whizzed past her face, leaving a streak of blood in its wake. She let out a sharp shriek, more out of rage than pain.

"Go!" Leifur shoved her toward me, and our horses only just avoided tripping over each other.

"This way," I shouted and veered to the left. A gust of wind had blown back the branches of a tree, revealing a narrow path through a dense grove of pines. It was a foot trail, barely wide enough for our horses. The Huestur men were wearing bulky armor, which gave us an edge.

Elva looked back one last time, then followed me into the dark pine tree path. The air inside was damp and heavy with the scent of wet earth and needles. We pushed the horses further, and when we finally broke through the other side, the only sounds were the soft crunch of our hooves on the forest floor and the patter of rain against the leaves.

Relief washed over me as I turned to look at Elva. She'd dismounted her mule and stood with her arms crossed, watching the trees expectantly.

"They'll be fine," I said, as I slid off Acorn. I reached for her arm, but when she turned back to face me, her eyes had gone black, and her teeth had grown long and pointed.

"'Go north,' you said," she hissed at me, her words dripping with venom. "'No one will come north. They won't look for us there.' You're a useless, spoiled layabout! Why did I listen to you? Have you ever even been in a fight, let alone a battle?"

Her words cut deep. "I have brothers," I shot back, jabbing her shoulder. "What do you think?"

"I don't count fighting with siblings!" she spat, slapping my hand away. "I mean, using an actual weapon. Or do you just run any time things get hard?"

"I didn't ask you to come save me," I bit back.

"And if I'd had any other options to take care of my brothers, I promise you I wouldn't have. If your own family couldn't be bothered, there's something very wrong with you."

My anger flared. "Something's wrong with me? What about you? I've never heard of a siren leaving the Konvern Territory for anything other than breeding. So, what did *you* do?"

For a moment, I thought she might lunge at me. Her eyes darkened even further as she closed the space between us and thrust a dagger toward me, the blade glinting in the dim light. "If I didn't need you alive to get my full pay, I'd make you sorry for that remark."

In an instant, the dagger vanished. She grabbed her mule's reins to lead her further into the underbrush. "You'd better pray to whatever god you stupid humans believe in," she muttered over her shoulder, "because if anything happens to my brothers, I won't have a reason to keep you alive."

I grabbed Acorn's reins and followed her from a safe distance. The horses needed a break after the running we'd put them through. The rain had slowed to a drizzle now, but the air still clung to the scent of wet earth and pine. Watching Elva's movements, I could see the tension in her, the way her shoulders carried the weight of worry for her brothers. It made me uncomfortable.

Ingvar barely tolerated me on his best days. While Baldr was happy to be around me, he was happy to be around anyone, so long as they would drink, smoke, gamble, or womanize with him. And Hulda ... well, I loved my sister, but I don't think she really cared for anyone, not even her soon-to-be husband. Even when we were children, she'd only liked people for what they could give her. But Elva truly loved her brothers. She'd give up everything for them—not just gold, or her freedom, but if it came down to it, she'd give her life for them.

I was so focused on my thoughts that I nearly collided with her. She turned and glared at me.

"We need to find shelter," she said. "It's not good for the horses to stay so wet."

"Agreed." I nodded.

We walked on in silence, keeping our eyes peeled for any sort of shelter that would be big enough to keep us and the horses dry. After an hour of nothing but cold, dark forest, we stumbled across a dilapidated structure. I couldn't tell if it was a shack or a cabin. It looked as if it had been abandoned for years. The yard was overgrown, and even the horse ties were covered in moss and rotting away. Elva and I looked at each other. Her brow furrowed, but after a moment she shrugged, then marched toward the overgrown path that led to the structure.

As we got closer, it became clear that it had been a log cabin. The porch had collapsed, and a tree had fallen and bowed the roof. It had two windows, with one blocked by debris, and a large wooden door. As I took a step on the porch, it cracked, and Elva pulled me back. She tentatively put some of her weight on it, and once she was confident it would support her, she waved me back and crept toward the window. Why she was going so slowly was beyond me, since the pounding rain would drown out her steps.

Elva pulled a hair tie from her back pocket and paused for a moment to tie back her blue and green locks. As she reached behind her head, my eyes darted to her shirt unbidden. A rather large section was stained a deep rust color, and I'd fought with my brothers enough as a boy to recognize that shade.

Blood.

But was it old, or fresh? And how would I find out without her noticing? The last thing we needed was her passing out from blood loss and her brothers coming after me.

A small rock struck me, bringing me out of my thoughts. Elva had reached the window and beckoned me over. I tied our horses to the only post that looked as if it wouldn't fall from the slightest tug and walked over to her, avoiding the broken section this time. Together, we peered into the cabin. It was deserted.

"Let's get inside." I loosened my back and dropped my shoulder before I slammed it into the door, but the thing didn't budge. I took a breath and slammed myself into it a second and third time. I only stopped when I heard Elva groan.

"What now?" I asked.

"You could try the handle first," she said.

"What?"

"The little metal contraption in the middle. If you push or twist it, the door usually opens."

"I know what a handle is," I shot back as I crossed my arms at her ridiculous suggestion. "What I don't understand is why you think someone would leave their door unlo—"

Before I could finish, Elva leaned in front of me. Her breasts brushed the back of my knuckles as a faint scent of water lilies overwhelmed my senses. She pushed down on the handle, and the door swung open. Without a word, she slipped inside.

"So, are you part witch, too?" I asked, following her in.

"No, but when people live this far away from other people, they don't always lock their doors."

The room was dark from the storm outside. I left the door open to help illuminate the place more, but Elva seemed to move around as if she didn't need any light. She was already on the other side of the room, opening and closing the drawers.

She must have seen me staring. "Sirens can see in rather dark spaces," she said. "This is about as dark as I can manage."

My eyes slowly adjusted to the room, and I was thankful my selkie side had a similar dark vision ability to what Elva did. I could finally make out the interior. There was a stone fireplace on the wall and a stack of wood beside it that would last for days. Elva was near a desk, and before I could ask what she was doing, she found some candles and flint. She lit one and handed it to me before walking to explore the other rooms. Not wanting to argue with her, I put the candle down by the fireplace and set about starting a fire to let us dry our clothes.

Once the flames were roaring, I headed out to tend to the horses. I led them to the back of the house, where there was an overhang coming off the roof with a fenced pen under it. "They must have let the smaller poles rot because they had this one," I said to Acorn as I patted him. The gate opened easily, and I unsaddled both horses. I found a rain barrel for them at the side of the house. Once I'd settled our horses, I brought their riding blankets to the main room to dry by the fire.

Elva had transformed the main room. She'd found bedding and set the blankets and a few pillows up on the floor by the fire. She'd draped a mop and broom across the desk to the chair, and her clothes were already hanging by the fire. That she intended to sleep beside me naked sent a bolt of heat straight to my groin. I knew she'd been lying about forgetting our night together, but my pride had taken a hit at the idea that she could so easily dismiss an encounter I'd never forget. I certainly wouldn't mind the opportunity to refresh her memory.

"Well, I hope you like potatoes," Elva's voice drifted from further in the cabin. "Because that's all we have." She came out with a sack, but my eyes went to what she was wearing. It was a soft baby blue dress with delicate bows on the sleeves and an enormous bow on her waist.

"What are you wearing?" I asked, unable to help myself.

"The only thing that would fit. It seems a rather tall person lives here." She pointed toward the chair with a pair of brown pants and a cream-colored linen shirt draped over it. "You should be able to get those to fit you."

I looked from the clothes back to Elva. "Did you find a pot for the potatoes?"

"No." She squatted by the fire and began removing our dinner from the bag.

"Then how do you intend to cook them?" I asked smugly. I may not have known how to cook many foods, but my brothers and I had taken frequent trips out of the castle and into the woods as children, mainly to get away from our father. We'd learn to cook a few things for ourselves so we wouldn't starve. I knew you needed to bury potatoes in a fire's embers when you lacked a pot to boil them in.

"I plan to use these." Elva tossed me a thin chain mail bag. "Leifur made them. We cook all kinds of vegetables in them. We put them beside the fire when we can't let it burn down. Works like a charm." She tossed me another sack. "That's for the horses. If you go feed them, I'll start our supper."

Thunder boomed outside, and the cabin rattled in response. I dropped the metal bag beside her and headed out to tend to the horses. The rain had picked up again and was even worse than before, but lucky for the horses, it was blowing away from their shelter. I fed them and made sure they were comfortable for the night before I ran around the side of the house to the entrance.

Elva was gone again, so I slowly peeled off my wet clothes and grabbed the dry ones she'd found for me. She'd been right about the size—the pants dragged on the floor around my feet, and the shirt made me feel like a child playing dress-up in his father's clothes.

Elva soon returned from the dark room. "Anything interesting in there?" I asked.

"An old kitchen, and two small bedrooms. I got the blankets from them, but this is the only fireplace, so I thought we should ... stick together." She narrowed her eyes at me.

"Or maybe you're just trying to keep an eye on me so I don't run away?" I crossed my arms and glared at her as lightning flashed outside, illuminating the room for a moment.

"You said it, not me."

Thunder rumbled again, and I waited for it to pass. "I could have fled at least a dozen times already and haven't. Why would I now?"

"Who said you'd flee? Maybe you'd just kill me in my sleep now that my brothers aren't here to kill you afterward."

"If you truly believe that, then sleeping beside me is a terrible idea."

"It's absolutely a terrible idea, but I'd rather not freeze tonight."

"That, I can agree with." I motioned for her to take a seat on the blankets. "Ladies first."

She rolled her eyes, but crossed the bedding and took the right side. *Good. I was hoping she'd take that side ... she doesn't remember what side I slept on, does she?* I sat down beside her, but made sure not to touch her again. I didn't want to stir up any more of my feelings from earlier.

I studied the flames, searching for Leifur's creations. Elva saw my gaze and pointed them out in the corners of the fireplace. She was right about them. When the potatoes were fully cooked, they tasted as delicious as anything our chef at the palace could make. With full bellies and dry clothes, we settled in to get some rest, but the thunder and lightning combined with the rain pounding down on the roof made it hard to sleep. At least that's what I told myself. In truth, the faint scent of water lilies surrounding us was driving me mad.

"What if the owners come back?" I asked.

"I think the place is abandoned."

"Even with the potatoes?"

"There was a thick layer of dust on everything," she said. "Even the blankets. And look at that tree sticking through the wall."

"That could be new. It's quite the storm."

"Do you think it'll be gone by morning?" Elva asked, pulling the blanket over herself.

"At this rate? I'm not sure."

Elva sighed.

"They'll be okay," I said.

"Don't pretend you know my family," she snapped, rolling over to face the wall.

"Sorry for trying to comfort you," I muttered, mostly to myself.

Chapter 28

Elva

I'd expected to wake up in a cold room, but the fire was stoked and sent off a heat that made me feel as if my whole body were on fire. Part of me wanted to curl up inside the blankets to escape the nightmare I was living, but instead, I gazed up at the log ceiling. This was the life I was fighting for—a cabin in the woods where my brothers and I could live in peace. Where I could put down my daggers and just live.

A sharp pain shot through my side as I sat up. But before I could deal with that, a scream pierced the air. *Sindri? Or just the wind playing tricks on me?* My heart raced as I hurried to the small window and pushed aside the curtains. The storm was raging outside. Several of the large forest trees had come down during the night, and one had just missed the house while we slept. I strained to see through the weather and glimpsed what looked like a pale face in the trees.

My breath fogged the pane as fear gripped me. Pressing my face against the glass, its features became clearer. It was Aamon. The face of my nightmares was staring at me from the forest outside the cabin. Rage flared within me, overtaking all reason, and I flung open the door and dashed outside.

The rain was coming down sideways and pelted my face hard enough that I suspected it would leave a bruise. Logic screamed that it couldn't be him; if it was, he'd disappear into the underbrush before I got to him, but I couldn't stop myself from screaming his name and pushing myself toward him. In seconds, the rain drenched me, and my whole body shivered. The howling wind drowned out my calls. Suddenly, a violent force pulled me backwards, just as a tree limb crashed down where I'd been standing.

Njall's hand was clamped on my arm, dragging me back to the cabin. He was shouting, but I barely heard the words. I struggled against him, glancing back to search for that face before we crossed the threshold and shut the door.

The door slammed shut behind us, and Njall turned on me, his soaked hair plastered to his head, fury blazing in his eyes. "What was that?" he demanded. He was angry, but there was something else in his expression that I couldn't discern.

I wanted to tell him, but painful memories of the last time I'd opened up to a man who wasn't my brother flooded me. "None of your concern," I said finally, my voice steady despite the turmoil within.

Njall ran his hands through his hair, growling in frustration. "It is my concern if you get yourself killed before we get home."

I crossed my arms and met his gaze steadily. "I thought you'd welcome my demise. Then you wouldn't owe me anything."

"My brother is the one who owes you. Not me." He turned sharply, peeling off his shirt and hanging it on the broom handle by the fire. Sighing, I joined him and stripped out of my wet dress and swapped it for my clothes that were now dry. Even after I changed, I couldn't stop shivering. It was a horrible sensation. I was rarely bothered by feeling wet and cold, but today it seemed I couldn't warm up. Njall grumbled to himself as he squatted down and tossed another log on the fire. The flames crackled, and something inside me snapped.

"I saw him." I hadn't planned to confess it, and so my voice was barely a whisper, but Njall stilled. His eyes fixed on me so intently that it made me uncomfortable, a feeling men rarely inspired. "Who? Your brothers?" he asked.

I pulled my knees up to my chin to warm myself, but didn't respond.

Njall moved to the window, scanning the storm outside. "What did he look like?"

"Like Aamon," I whispered.

"No," he snapped. "I mean, was he too tall or too pale?"

"A little pale, but I couldn't tell his height from here."

"Did you see any salt in the kitchen?"

"A bag. Why?"

"When I was a boy, my father's general told us stories of the creatures that lived in these woods. But these were not the common tales of werewolves or dire wolves or minotaurs, but of demons and witches that dwell near the Bloot River and prey on lost travelers."

I couldn't help but shiver. I'd heard of unnatural beings that lured lonely travelers to their doom, but they'd never been given specific names like demon or witch. Sirens knew there were more things in these woods than what humans had discovered. Some things could hide well. Others left no human behind to tell the tale.

"What were you taught about these creatures?" I asked as Njall hurried into the kitchen.

"It depends on the individual witch or demon," he said as I heard pans clattering. He returned with the bag of salt, then untied it and began pouring a thin line along the door and windows. "Some will keep you alive to use your body in rituals, while others lure travelers into the woods and drink their blood before devouring them."

I had a suspicion he was leaving one use for lonely men off the list. "And?"

He stopped pouring the salt and turned his head to face me. "And some appear as helpless maidens who lure men to their death with the promise of sex."

I couldn't help but smirk at his glare. "That one at least makes sense. I never understood what humans had against playing with their food."

The prince didn't even flinch. "You've never eaten with Ingvar." He resumed pouring the salt line, leaving me to wonder how exactly his half-werewolf brother would play with his food.

Tired of just sitting, I stood and sauntered down the small, narrow hall. Bundles of dried herbs hung in a row among some trinkets on a small shelf: an amethyst stone, a small bowl of acorns, a large dried starfish, a tooth as long as my palm, and other oddities. The hallway led to the first bedroom. This was the smaller of the two. I'd stolen the soft quilt from it the night before, leaving it stripped bare. There was a small shelf beside the bed and a cedar chest where I'd found the dress. I lifted the lid and dug through its contents a little more, thankful when I found an oversized, knitted shirt at the bottom. It was thin in a few places and had a small hole near the bottom, but the green shade reminded me of sea grass, and I was sure it would keep me warm. I pulled off my thin shirt and finally examined the wound on my side. It was red and hot to the touch. We'd need to get out of here soon so I could find Leifur and have him help me with it. I slipped on my fresh shirt, being careful to pull it down to cover my side.

There was a small bookshelf. I spotted a book of legends about the beasts that roamed across Torian, and another of protective charms and spells to keep yourself safe from these monsters. There was a book of medicinal or edible plants. I grabbed the stories and charms books. I wondered what they would say about selkies or

sirens.

When I returned to the main room, Njall was crouched in front of the fire. He seemed to have brought it back to life with gusto. "How long do you think the storm will last?" he asked.

"I've known bad ones to last up to a week in the north, but we won't be staying here that long. I'd need to find my brothers before that."

Njall brushed his hands against his pants as he stood and eyed the books I had in my hands. "Find anything interesting? I'm going a little stir crazy."

I held the books out to him, and he picked the charms one, which honestly surprised me, but I decided not to comment. We settled into our makeshift bed and flipped through the books. I laughed out loud several times. If you believed the stories, sirens were all female and hideous. They only came out of the sea at night to find men to mate with and then ate them before returning to the sea. The author was confused between mermaids and sirens. Mermaids were the ones who came on the beach at night to snatch humans to feast on. It's why their hair is gray, to hide them from the dark water.

When I laughed for the third time, Njall finally asked why. I passed him the book, and he flipped through it, pausing to read a few random pages, most of which made him snicker.

"It's wrong about satyrs," he said.

"What?"

"Right here," he said, holding the book up to me for emphasis. "It says satyrs can't get drunk. But let me tell you, Baldr can. He takes longer, and it takes enough ale to make a bull topple, but when he gets there, it's hilarious."

"What else did you learn?"

"Werewolves are all gray."

"Like their fur?"

"No, their bodies too."

I burst out laughing, and Njall smirked. I assumed we were both picturing his brother Ingvar as a bizarre gray-skinned man. We continued to share entertaining bits from the books as the storm raged on outside. I was grateful for the distraction. Without it, he might get around to asking who Aamon was, and I was already cursing myself for the slip.

It must have been well into the morning by then, and the fire was roaring thanks to the giant woodpile Njall had found outside. It let us cook more potatoes, and after scouring the entire kitchen, we even found a cooking pot and could add some herbs to the water to make potato soup.

Everything was going well until after lunch, when the storm became more intense. The wind made the tree continuously scrape against the house, and the rain beating on the roof made it almost impossible to hear our thoughts. A flash of lightning struck right outside the cabin, and it was so bright it blinded us for a few seconds. The thunder, which came instantly, was as loud as a castle wall crashing down. We ran to the window. Outside, there was a smoking hole in the path we'd used to arrive here. Before I could say anything, we heard another crash. Njall darted to the door and flung it open, just as Acorn bolted in front of the cabin.

"Ferflucs," Njall shouted as he ran into the storm after his horse. I followed him, knowing if we didn't get the horse now, we'd probably never find him, and I had no intention of having to take turns walking beside the mule.

Rain struck my face the instant I stepped outside. While it didn't seem possible, it was worse than this morning. The wind had picked up, forcing me to push against it just to move, and each drop felt like an ice shard being driven into my skin. My side burned with each awkward step, but I pushed down the pain, determined to find Njall and the horse.

"Njall!" I shouted as loud as I could, hoping to be heard over the storm. The forest looked menacing, and the wind rushing through the trees was like screams. The trees swung so far I wondered how they didn't snap from the force of the gale. I called out again and was pushing on toward the tree line when a flash caught the corner of my eye. I shielded myself, turning to face what I expected to be another lightning strike, but there was only the rain. Njall's stories of witches and demons felt unsettlingly real as I shielded my eyes with my hand and stepped into the forest.

Chapter 29

Njall

I may as well have gone swimming with how completely drenched I was, and my face was stinging from getting smacked by branches, but I chased Acorn until he trapped himself for me in a cluster of thick pines. He was the bravest of my horses, and he stopped as soon as he realized who it was behind him. The others would have just kept running. I grabbed his bridle and inspected him. He had no injuries beyond the same scrapes I had. But when I grabbed the rope I'd tied him to, my heart stopped. It was neither frayed nor untied. Something ... someone had cut it.

Ferflucs.

I gripped him tighter and, for several agonizing heartbeats, my eyes scanned the trees—anxiously searching for anyone or anything that might be lurking in the woods. The storm clouds made the forest too dark to see much of anything, and with the howling wind, there was no chance I'd hear anything, either. I couldn't shake the thought that this cabin might be a trap set by one of the creatures said to haunt these woods. As soon as the storm passed, we needed to leave.

I patted Acorn's neck to calm him and led him back toward the cabin as quickly as I could while the storm was fighting my every step. I didn't see Elva and figured she must have given up and gone back inside to warm up. I led Acorn to the back of the house while keeping a wary eye on the woods behind us.

When we arrived, I discovered what had made the loud bang we'd heard. The woodpile was in shambles, strewn across the yard. Most of the logs were still in one piece, but a few had been obliterated. Avoiding the debris, I led Acorn back into the pen with Elva's mule. Miraculously, the horses were unscathed.

Examining the wreckage, I didn't see any burn marks, so it wasn't lightning. And the sound had been too loud for someone to have thrown it piece by piece. There were only two possibilities I could come up with; either the first was that Acorn had gotten spooked and kicked the wood pile, sending it flying, or, more ominously, something in the forest had done it to get us out. *What could they have wanted?* I mulled over some ideas as I checked the gate.

Then it hit me like a punch to the gut. *Elva!*

I ran back to the front door as fast as I could in the storm, threw it open, and shouted for her. No response. My voice wavered when I called her name, but I didn't want to think about it—no time to question it now. I tossed aside the blankets, checked the rooms and kitchen, but there was no sign of her. Panic surged through me as I turned and ran back into the storm.

The wind was blowing as fiercely as before, but I pressed on, moving as if through water around the side of the house where the enormous tree loomed.

She was there. She was lying face down in the overgrown weeds. My breath caught as I kneeled beside her, afraid of what I'd find. Relief washed over me when I saw her chest move slightly.

"You're breathing," I muttered, grabbing hold of her shoulder and shaking her. She didn't stir. Her usually sparkly skin had a cooler gray-blue hue to it, like the sea at dusk. Dark blotches stained her shirt, and a thick stream of blood oozed from the gash on her forehead.

A wicked little voice in my head whispered, *Just leave her here and go home. No one would ever know.*

No one but me, and I wouldn't let another selkie die on my watch.

All the legends about sirens rushed through my mind. *Heartless, seductive monsters who could change their appearance to suit any man and would murder them without guilt once they got what they wanted.* But none of that was true of Elva. She could have killed me after I bedded her and she'd taken my seed, but she hadn't. That she'd stolen some clothing from me didn't surprise me, now that I'd seen how they lived. I'd been taught that sirens were incapable of love, but her devotion to Sindri and Leifur showed me that was a lie. And the only time she'd killed anyone was when we were trying to escape an enemy's castle. If the things I'd been told were true, why were Elva and her brothers so different? It couldn't just be because of their selkie blood, since Leifur didn't have any, and he was the kindest of them all.

"Let's get you inside to warm up," I said, sliding my arms under her shoulders and knees and lifting her off the ground.

Back inside the cabin, I threw extra wood on the fire to warm the room for her, even though I knew our supply of dry wood was dwindling with so much of it sitting soaked and useless out back. The flames roared higher, sending an intense heat into the room as I stripped the soaked clothes from Elva's body and tried to figure out if there were any other injuries besides the gash on her head. Nothing on her legs would explain why she was out cold, but those scars I'd noticed on our night together were more visible in the firelight. The large X-shaped one on her inner thigh was one I particularly wanted to know about, but that would have to wait for another day.

As I removed her shirt, I winced. Her left side was hot to the touch. Turning her toward the firelight, I saw red marks spidering from the wound. My gut twisted at the sight. I knew it was infected.

I tried to remember if any tree limbs had been on the ground near her. *Could this just be an accident from the storm?* The plant book she'd found earlier was under a blanket, and when I grabbed it, my body bumped hers, causing her hand to drop from her waist and leaving behind a smear of blood. I grabbed her hand and examined her wrist. There were two small, round puncture wounds on it, and they didn't look like any I'd seen in my life. They were too small for wolves, too precise for snakes or rodents.

What creatures could want her blood? Not humans, not centaurs. Ferflucs. Sorcerers! The punctures looked like they'd been made with something sharp and deliberate, like a needle. I tossed aside the plant book, grabbed the charms book I'd been reading earlier, and flipped to the ingredients glossary. My stomach sank. *Siren blood* was on the list.

Panic set in as I tried to recall the protections our tutors had taught my siblings and me against my sister's kind when we were children, but nothing came to mind. I glanced back at Elva and examined her face. The sparkle was gone, and she wasn't just pale; she was gray, like the belly of a fish left too long on the shore. It hadn't been a trick of the light outside. I needed to find her some dry clothes soon, or else we could add hypothermia to her list of injuries.

"One problem at a time," I told myself. "Keep her alive, then worry about what did this." I draped a blanket over her to keep her warm and headed down the hall to the herb wall. Thankfully, it was well stocked, and I found every herb except one. I figured this was enough to give it my best shot.

I wasn't a medicine man or an expert in herbs, but years of training with my father's soldiers had taught me the basics. The burly men often liked to show off, which usually led to trouble, and someone had to patch them up. I crafted a tiny bundle of herbs from bits of the thinnest shirt I could find. After the water boiled, I dropped it inside to let it steep. It seemed to be working. I also made a paste to put on the wound itself to help draw out some of the infection. Back home, we'd have used leeches, but I had to make do with what was on hand.

I tied a strip of my shirt around her wrist to stop the puncture wounds from opening again. She couldn't afford to lose any more blood. Once I'd wrapped her in the thicker blanket, I waited. After a while, she stirred just long enough to drink the tea, but she didn't mumble more than a few words before she passed out again. I was relieved she drank the tea. The last thing I needed was her brothers coming after me because something had happened to her.

For most of the night, I stared out the window as the fire crackled, watching for more faces in the tree line while listening to her soft breathing. We'd been attacked, and I wasn't taking chances tonight. I wanted nothing to catch us unaware while we were both sleeping, so I planned to stay awake as long as possible.

The idea that her brothers would come after me if she was hurt was strange to me, but I didn't doubt it for an instant. Leifur and Sindri adored Elva, and despite our unfortunate first meeting, the more time I spent with her, the more I understood why they were so devoted to her. She was far braver and stronger than most people I knew, but she was also kind and protective. I'd never known there were different sirens, let alone that a warrior could also be a seductress, and it was fascinating. At least that was what I kept telling myself. That my inability to stop watching her, thinking of her, was purely curiosity and nothing more.

I spent the next day keeping a close eye on the surrounding forest in between caring for Elva. She woke up only briefly, long enough for me to get her to drink some tea and soup before she drifted off again. Her deep sleep worried me. Had the sorcerer taken more blood than I realized, or had he cast some spell to keep her under? Maybe both. Whatever the reason, Elva couldn't stay awake for more than a few minutes at a time. So I sat beside her, waiting for those precious minutes where I could verify she was alright and make sure she was getting nourishment.

The storm ended on the second day of Elva being unconscious, and I decided I should venture out to find something other than potatoes. I didn't wander far because I was worried about what she'd do if she woke up and I wasn't there. But then on the third day, she stirred, and by the morning of the fourth, she groaned loudly and sat up.

"Welcome back to the world of the living, my little Pearl," I said from the doorway, trying to sound light despite the relief flooding me.

Elva rubbed her head, wincing as if it hurt. She stopped to examine the bandage around her wrist. "What happened?" she asked groggily.

I joined her on the makeshift bed and told her everything that had transpired. But after all she'd endured, it was the number of days she'd been unconscious that scared her the most.

"So four? You're certain it was four?"

"Yes. But why is that so important?"

"I just want to know."

I stared at her, sensing she was hiding something, but I let it go. "I'll get you something to eat and drink. You must be famished." I'd put together a rabbit stew from the critter I'd caught earlier in the morning, when I'd felt comfortable leaving her for a short time.

Other than a small thank you when I handed her the food, Elva ate in silence. She was glancing all over the room, like a wild animal in a cage, and more than once I caught her staring at me. Her expression was unreadable. After the third bowl, she set it aside. "The storm's gone. We should leave now."

"You need to rest up before we leave."

"We've been here a week. I need to get to my brothers."

"It's already midday. We'll leave at first light tomorrow. It'll give us time to prepare some provisions."

Elva opened her mouth to argue, but then closed it and dropped back onto the pillow. "Fine."

She demanded to help, protesting about how much faster we'd be ready if I would let her pitch in. I relented and gave her our saddle bags and clothes so she could remain resting while packing our items. The glare she gave me told me all I needed to know about her feelings on the matter, but in the end, she packed the bags while I scrounged up every scrap of food in the place and nearby woods that I could find for us to take.

Despite wanting to get an early start, it was hard for us to fall asleep. Curled up under the blankets on the floor, I stared at the ceiling, listening to the fire crackle and Elva tossing and turning and sighing.

"If you lie still, we might get some rest," I said after what felt like the hundredth time of her rolling over.

She huffed in reply, but then sat up and snapped at me. "Unlike you, I have people I care about who are out there alone, and probably scared. So excuse me if I can't just lie down and fall asleep like you can."

I was going to tell her off, but she turned her back to me and lay back down before pulling the blanket over her head.

Chapter 30

Elva

After days of resting, I was up long before the sun. I crept from the makeshift bed, being careful not to wake Njall. He'd been adamant last night that neither of us go anywhere alone. I'd agreed, but only to silence him. Whether a sorcerer or something else, it had only gotten the better of me because of the storm. On a clear day, like today, it wouldn't happen again, no matter how paranoid Njall became. I smirked as I slipped outside to tend to the horses, hoping to hasten our departure from this cursed place. I also needed some space from my princely prisoner to breathe and figure out what he was up to. He could have abandoned me and headed back home, and no one would ever have known, and yet he stayed. Not only that, but he nursed my wound and took care of me. The only men who'd ever taken care of me were Leifur, Sindri, and the old siren males. After placing my trust in the wrong person, it almost destroyed me when I was younger. The idea that anyone outside our kind could show us genuine care ... well, I wouldn't have believed it, had it not been me receiving it.

Lost in thought, I watered and brushed both the horses,

preparing them for the journey ahead. I didn't know how long it would take us to sneak through the forest to Eldenwood, but we had to get there sooner rather than later. Half my cycle had already passed, and if I didn't get around other men soon, I might end up having to sleep with Njall again. Sleeping with him wouldn't be terrible; if anything, it would likely be amazing, but it would complicate things. Outside of Leifur, I'd never been with the same man more than once, and I wasn't sure how that would sit with me. But if I didn't, it could get so much worse. My siren might take over, and she was likely to hurt him.

Once I'd tended to the horses, I went back around the cabin. When I opened the door, I froze at the entrance. Njall was naked in the middle of the room, holding the clothes we'd brought from Tyndorf for him. His gaze met mine as I stood in the doorway, staring. I couldn't help it. Despite his gruff nature, his body was impeccable. It was chiseled like the statues that littered the Siren castle; from what I could only assume was physical training, possibly with a sword. His cock was one of the finest specimens I'd ever seen, and as a siren, I'd seen many. Heat flooded my core as I watched him step into his pants and pull them up. It took everything in me not to whimper when he fastened them around his waist.

"You've been busy," he said with a hint of amusement. As he slipped on his shirt, I quickly felt my cheeks. They were hot—I hadn't been as smooth as I'd hoped.

"Someone had to get the horses ready." I closed the door and crossed the room to gather the last of my things. But as I passed by Njall, his hand shot out and grabbed my arm, pulling me closer to him.

"I told you not to go outside alone."

All my arousal vanished in that instant. I wrenched my arm from him and snarled. "I am not afraid of some little beast in the woods. Sirens are among the most feared creatures in Torian."

"You should be afraid of whatever did that to you." His fingers grazed my arm and entwined my wrist. He held it up to me, his thumb moving over the tiny pin-pricks. They'd healed, thanks to his care, but they'd leave a scar.

"Another reminder of what happens when I'm not careful enough around men."

He tilted his head slightly, releasing my hand. "How do you know it was a male?"

"I just assume," I said. "Every bad thing that's happened to me has been at the hands of one."

Njall's gaze softened, and he stepped closer. "Does that include the marks on your back and thighs?"

The question caught me off guard. No one—no man I'd lain with had ever asked me about them. It had never occurred to me that any of them would notice. But this human prince was looking at me with an intensity that made my blood run cold. I felt a tug toward him, and I didn't like it. This wasn't the first time I felt a draw to him. I couldn't tell if it was my siren or selkie side that sensed something in him, but I'd had enough. Stepping back from him, I strengthened my resolve before replying in a husky voice. "The moment I was finished with you, my body stopped being your concern."

A small smirk spread across his lips, and I felt the urge to slap him. As if he'd read my mind, he simply shook his head. "Not a good idea."

That made me even angrier, and before I could stop myself, my palm flew toward his face. But it never made contact. Njall grabbed my wrist and, in two movements, slammed me into the wall separating the kitchen and living area. The heat of his body set mine on fire, as he pinned me there, holding my wrist above my head.

His green eyes sparkled as his gaze dropped to my lips. He leaned in close, his lips grazing my neck before teasing my ear.

"Do you ever do what you're told?" His voice rumbled low, and it sent a shiver of pleasure right to my core.

Stupid siren cycle. I swallowed hard, and he stared into my eyes again for an uncomfortably long time before I got the nerve to reply. "I do. But only when I think the other person is right."

He laughed—a deep, genuine sound that caught me completely off guard. When he finally released me, I was left breathless and annoyed.

"Then I will have to prove you wrong more often," he said with a smirk.

"I'm still waiting for the first time." I grabbed my bag to load the last items on the horses.

Leaving the cabin brought both relief and absolute terror. While I was thrilled we were finally back on the move and heading to find my brothers, it was here that I first imagined that I'd have a home of my own one day. As we retraced our path through the forest, a feeling of heaviness came over me, one I hadn't noticed when we arrived. Unsure if it stemmed from my anxiety or from the forest itself, I lost myself in thoughts of what my brothers and I would do with a cabin like this. Then, a sharp pain shot up my leg.

Njall was holding out a stick. "What was that for?" I snapped, rubbing my thigh.

"I was talking to you, and you were daydreaming."

"I was not daydreaming," I grumbled as I ripped the stick from his hand and threw it on the ground. My horse jostled under me. "Easy girl," I whispered as I patted our old girl, and she steadied.

"Then what were you doing?"

"Trying to find the correct path back so we can figure out where my brothers went. Obviously."

"Well, pardon me, m'lady."

I rolled my eyes and went back to watching the trail, hoping to see some evidence of my brothers having come through. Getting back on track was a lot harder than I'd expected. The canopy on this side of the Bloot River was only marginally thinner, and it still blocked out the sun, so it was difficult to determine our direction of travel. Njall's attempts to lighten the mood were grating on my nerves.

"I don't need you to condescend to me," I growled. "I can get us out of here if you'd just leave me alone so I can concentrate."

"I never said you couldn't."

I opened my mouth to strike back, but closed it when I realized he hadn't attacked me. Anytime Njall said something that wasn't nasty, I felt conflicted. "So what, you trust me now?"

"To get us out of here? Completely. To not slit my throat while I sleep? ... Mostly."

I wanted to bite back at that, but really, I couldn't since it was something I would do if necessary. Instead, I let myself chuckle.

Njall dramatically feigned offense, throwing his hands across his chest and forehead. "My word, m'lady. You'd dare to end the life of a prince while he slept? I thought you were braver than that."

"Bravery doesn't mean you have to do everything the hard way."

A branch snapped behind us, and Njall straightened instantly. I stiffened; he'd been faster than me. *Did he always have those reflexes? How did I not notice? Oh, right—he was starved.*

I choked up on the reins, ready to dash off in an instant if needed. The trees waved their branches as a gust of wind moved through the clearing. We stood stone still, but I heard nothing beyond my pounding heart.

Njall broke the silence with a sigh. "It would seem we're both jumpy," he said.

I dropped my reins and rubbed the back of my neck, avoiding his gaze. I could feel him watching me with a focus I could hardly stomach. Kicking my horse forward, I called over my shoulder, "Maybe you're jumpy, but I'm fine."

Njall caught up to me in the blink of an eye and pointed to the edge of the clearing. "Do you think one of us could climb that tree to see where we are going?"

I followed his slim finger and found the tree he was referring to. It was as if two trees had grown so close together that over time they'd merged, their branches intertwining. Admittedly, I was no expert in climbing trees, but this one looked easy to manage. "That might work."

"Great. Hold Acorn." Njall tossed me the reins and was off his horse before I could summon a protest. He gave me a boyish grin as he scurried toward the tree.

"Are you ... excited?" I asked, feeling completely out of sorts.

Njall hoisted himself onto the first branch that was large enough to hold his weight. "I used to climb trees for fun with my siblings, and it's been years since I had an excuse to do it."

I couldn't remember a time when Sindri or I had ever climbed a tree for fun, even as youngsters. Sirens were taught to climb them to escape dangerous predators, and sometimes people. My eyes were fixed on Njall and his toned body. His joy was foreign to me, yet endearing. As he reached a high branch, I couldn't help but wonder—what exactly was he? Not fully human, certainly, given his family's mixed heritage. And certainly not anything in the water, since he didn't swim. But what?

"There's good news and bad news," he jubilantly called from the top of the tree, pulling me back to our world.

"Start with the good news." I slipped off my mule and led both horses to the base of the tree.

"I know where we are and where we need to go."

"And the bad news?"

"We have been going the wrong way ... all day."

I groaned loudly. Two more days, plus however long it would take us to get to Eldenwood. By the time we'd get there, I would be at least three weeks into my cycle. I was cutting it far closer than I liked. "Do you see any other clearings?" I asked.

"I can't tell. It's just treetops up here."

"How far is the sun?" *Please don't be setting.*

"It's well into the afternoon. It'll be setting soon. We should probably camp here tonight."

"Ferflucs."

"Did you say something?" Njall was already most of the way down the tree.

"Nothing important," I muttered, though he'd heard me.

"We'll find your brothers." Njall leaped off down, from a bit higher than was needed, and landed beside me. After he wiped his hands on his pants, he grabbed Acorn and tied him to the lowest branch. I followed, silently hoping he was right. Sindri had a knack for getting into trouble. Leifur had a solid head on his shoulders, but it was usually me who got Sindri out of trouble.

As we set up camp, it hit me just how much stuff we'd left behind when we fled from the Huestur guards. We'd replaced some items from the cabin, but the tent was still gone. "Did you see any bad weather up there?"

"Nothing but clear skies."

I nodded and unloaded the horses. The sun had started to go down, and we'd need to hurry to get a fire going. Njall must have felt the same because he pointed at a flat spot I'd been eyeing for a fire pit and told me to build it up while he got the wood. It seemed our time alone in the cabin helped us figure each other out, because we got a fire going and set up the sleeping area even faster than I would have with my brothers, and with fewer complaints.

"Do you want to take the first watch or the second?" I asked once it had become completely dark, and we were settled beside the fire.

"Second."

I nodded and glanced around at the surrounding woods. With only the fire to illuminate them, their shadows cast terrifying images into the forest. Every swaying of a branch looked like a monster coming to get us both. I shook my head, trying to cast out those thoughts. If I was already nervous in these woods, I could only imagine what my brothers were feeling.

"Have you ever slept outdoors?" I asked.

"What?" Njall stopped poking the fire with his stick and turned to me.

"It's a question. You answer it."

"I understand that, but why did you even ask it?"

I wanted to smack him. *Did he always need to answer a question with another question?* Truthfully, I was feeling nervous and wanted a distraction, but would not tell him that.

"Forget it." I pushed myself off the ground to go grab more wood for the fire.

"We used to camp often."

I stopped and waited to see if he'd say more.

"My brothers and I, that is. When we got to be too much for our father, he'd send us out with his men on some excursion. We'd travel and live just like the knights. A few times, we were gone for weeks."

I handed him the wood, then dropped down beside him, closer than before. "How old were you?"

"Around ten."

"That's barbaric!"

"How old were you when you started traveling outside of the Siren Lands?"

"Eighteen. Sirens treasure their children. We just don't raise them ourselves. They're raised together in one home so that we see each other as sisters and family."

"And the boys?"

I glanced over at him, and he was watching me intently, clearly very interested in the subject. My kind liked our privacy, and few ever learned of how we did things. "The boys, too. We just have so few boys that we don't think to mention them with our sisters."

"How many is *few?*"

"Very few," I replied, recalling my lessons. "Only about one in twenty siren pregnancies result in boys, and of those, less than half take after the mother. Most boys end up as whatever species their father is."

"I see. So what happens to them? Those non-sirens born to sirens? Present party excluded, of course."

I hesitated, unsure what he was getting at. "When a boy is born who takes after the father, we have a siren or two responsible for bringing those children back to their father's kind."

"So you don't eat them?"

"Eat them?" I shouted the words without meaning to. "Why would we eat them?"

"That's what I was taught."

"That we practice infanticide?"

"No ... that you're monsters."

And there was the truth. It didn't matter how much my brothers and I did to show we cared, and to show we were better than our sisters. To him, to everyone else, we would always be monsters.

Njall's face had gone pale, and he stared at me for a long moment before clearing his throat. "I didn't mean that you're a monster—"

"Of course not. Just my kind." I stood and brushed my pants off.

"Elva—"

"It's fine. We need wood, and you wanted to take the second watch. So I'll go, then you can sleep."

Chapter 31

Njall

Never in my life had I met a woman as enticing and, at the same time, infuriating as Elva. She had bedded me, robbed me, and then bedded my brother. She had wanted to kill me after I turned her in to my father, then risked everything to save me. Yet now, because of one thoughtless remark, she refused even to speak with me. I knew complicated women before, but it was as if Elva had two people inside her.

Hesitant to say anything else that might get me in trouble, I stood beside Acorn in silence and watched Elva studying a cold firepit we'd found. She must have suspected it had been her brother's handiwork. From the looks of the regrowth around the site, I figured it was too old, but I would not argue with her.

Elva stood up, brushing her hands together before setting them on her hips. As if moving on their own accord, my eyes drifted to her delicious curves. Her linen pants were loose on her legs, and her tunic hung low on her collarbone, being pulled down ever so slightly by her dagger sheath. Her hair was down and so mixed that it looked turquoise in the light rather than individual parts of blue and green. Even with a frustrated scowl on her face, she was gorgeous.

I grew up as the unwanted prince, but that title still brought me women with little effort. With Elva, it was different. Winning her over would take all the effort I could muster, and possibly more. I wondered what Baldr did to win her over so easily. Likely, he was no more charming than I was at the bar, but then again, he hadn't had her arrested and almost turned into a sex slave by our father. That's going to take a lot to overcome, but I do enjoy a challenge.

Elva exhaled loudly enough that I heard it from several paces away. She whipped around and crossed her arms. "It's not this one."

"You're certain?"

Her scowl deepened as she stepped closer to me. "I am, and next time, don't let me waste my time if you see something I don't."

"I didn't think you'd believe me," I replied, patting Acorn and trying to decide how to handle this.

"If you saw something real, I would. Opinions are not facts."

"Clearly."

"What did you see?" she pressed.

I nodded toward a log near the fire pit.

"The log?" Elva kicked it, and the entire thing broke apart.

"If anyone had sat on it recently, it would have been a pile of splinters."

"They could have sat on the other one." Elva prodded the fragments with her boot.

"Too small," I replied, and she huffed.

"Fine. You're right. Let's go."

Elva took her mule's reins but stood there, scratching the animal behind the ears before glancing at me. Her expression was a battle of emotions, and I fought the urge to smile—it would only anger her. After a long minute, I put her out of her misery and ended the silence.

"Would you rather go east or south?"

She looked at the surrounding forest. "South, I think."

The rest of the day brought us to three more campsites, but none of them showed any sign of her brothers ever being there. One was too old, one was used by a much larger group, and one had been used by women, or some female creature, judging by the hairs we found. I couldn't be sure, but Elva's siren was.

By sundown, we set camp. With how distraught Elva was becoming, I left her to prepare food while I fetched the wood, water, and tended to the horses. When I'd joined her, she sat with knees drawn to her chin, staring into the flames as ash danced in the air.

Outside of my mother, when I was very young, I'd never lost anyone I cared about. Granted, I only cared about a precious few —Baldr, and maybe Hulda on a good day. I didn't know what to say or how to comfort her. *A joke? Words of support? Maybe I'll just make her something to eat.*

Elva shivered beside me, so I fetched our shared blanket. Without a word, I shuffled up to her and wrapped the blanket around us. She jerked and seemed to come out of a trance, and pulled away from me.

"Elva, you're freezing—"

"No, I'm not."

"You are." I put my hand on her arm and shivered.

"I don't feel it," she said, pulling away from me. "Sirens can tolerate the cold."

"Tolerate, maybe, but you're shivering." I returned the blanket to her shoulders. She rolled her eyes and went back to watching the fire, but left the blanket in its place.

"Thank you," she said so softly I almost didn't catch it.

After two days, we'd traveled south enough that we were nearing the Bloot River again as it curved away from the Crimson Mountains and turned toward the mermaid and siren territories. I'd spent time with my father's men hunting deer, boar, and other animals for food, but never had to track sirens across the wilderness. As we discovered more campsites and no sign of them, she was becoming short-tempered and snappy with me. While it got on my nerves, I bit back the urge to fight with her. The fear she was contending with was enough torture for her.

By mid-afternoon, we found ourselves on the edge of an unusual-looking part of the Zverm Forest. I couldn't tell if it was the Bloot River that gave this part an ominous feeling or the darker hue that all the plants here seemed to take on. I was so busy studying the strange colors of the plants that I didn't notice Elva vanish. Calling her name, I waited ages before she replied.

She'd discovered a narrow path, overgrown with vines and ivy, and it led through a patch of old-growth trees and bushes into a small clearing. A few large stumps, each large enough to seat two people, were set up around a fire pit. There was even a stack of wood off to the side. Whoever had been here must have left in a hurry. They wouldn't have gathered all that wood just for fun.

Elva sensed something that I didn't and leaped from her mule, running the instant her feet touched the ground. I secured our animals on a low tree branch before hurrying after her. When I caught up, she was standing in the middle of the camp, and her fingers were transformed—the nails extended out much longer than normal. Her breathing was loud enough that I could hear it from across the fire area; the earthy scent of the forest was overpowered by the sharp tang of copper and sea salt.

Is that blood? I didn't dare ask. Her breaths grew ragged as I cautiously approached her to find a large puddle of blood at her feet. She turned toward me, and her eyes had gone dark—another warning sign to tread lightly. But when I glanced ahead, I knew we were in trouble. Stepping over the blood, I found a large patch of dirt that had been disturbed and scattered, more recently than the storm. Lying at the end of the area was a piece of fabric that had belonged to one of my favorite shirts, one that Elva had stolen.

I turned toward her and held it out, expecting her to take it. But tears welled up in her eyes, and she shook her head at me.

"No," she muttered before her hands flew into her hair. I couldn't tell if she was trying to stop her shaking or pull her hair out, but either way, it looked painful. Her talons dug into her scalp, drawing blood that trickled down her cheek. Then came the wail. It was a sound unlike anything I'd ever heard in my life. The closest sound I could think of was the shriek of a fox we'd once caught in a trap.

My heart ached for her, but we didn't know if it was her brothers' blood or someone else's. Her cries were getting louder, and as they echoed through the surrounding trees, an icy chill ran down my spine. The forest seemed to watch us, and I realized just how vulnerable we were. Thanks to Ingvar, I was used to being watched and stalked by a werewolf, but this felt worse.

Without thinking, I grabbed Elva's arms and forced her to look at me. "Elva, you need to stop screaming." She hissed at me, and I repeated. "Be quiet."

That was not the right thing to say. Her black eyes locked onto mine, and a growl rumbled from her throat. I'd fought Ingvar mid-shift before, and I had no desire to do the same with Elva in the middle of the woods, far away from any sort of help. Still, I wouldn't let go.

Elva wrenched her wrists free and shoved me back. I stumbled back a step before I caught myself. Her anger was now fixed on me. She lunged, and before I could brace myself, we both crashed to the ground. All the air left my lungs as I hit the earth, and the angry siren landed on top of me, her talons barely missing piercing my shoulder. When she placed her palm against her forehead, I saw my chance and flipped her off me. I straddled her and pinned her wrists to the ground beside her head.

"Let me up," she screamed at me.

I closed my eyes and willed my patience to stay strong before I leaned down over her so our faces were close enough to share breath. "I'll let you up as soon as you calm down and stay quiet."

The siren hissed and snarled beneath me, but I must have positioned myself perfectly because despite all her kicking and bucking, she couldn't move me. Elva tried a few more times, even going so far as trying to twist her neck so she could bite the arm holding her down, but she couldn't reach. Sharp breaths escaped her between pants and frustrated screams until she finally settled and didn't move.

Thinking she'd finally surrendered, I loosened my grip, but I'd fallen for her plan as she twisted her wrist free and punched me in the face. I barely got my hand to my face when she knocked me off of her, reversing our positions. Now straddling me, she pinned my arms down beside my head.

It shouldn't have happened, but seeing her above me brought back the memory of our night together, and I felt myself grow hard. *This is not the time for that.* The siren noticed—of course she did—and a knowing smirk tugged at the corners of her lips. She leaned over me, her body grinding against me with a slowness that left no doubt of her intentions. A moan escaped me as she leaned down and kissed me.

Heat exploded through me as if I'd been tossed into a boiling pot. I couldn't tell if it was coming from me or the siren sitting atop me, but I wasn't going to question it. Her lips devoured mine as my hands slid up her waist to anchor her in place. I felt a sting of pain when she bit my bottom lip hard enough to draw blood.

A deep, guttural groan rumbled from my chest, and the siren laughed, a low, wicked sound that was unsettling. She released my lip and sat up to look down at me, her mouth smeared with my blood. She brushed her plump lips with her thumb, then glanced at her glistening thumb for just a second before flicking her tongue out to lick up my blood.

This woman will be the end of me.

Sitting up slightly, I moved to cup her face when a chuckle echoed from the trees behind us.

Chapter 32

Elva

My body switched from my playful and seductive siren to warrior in the blink of an eye. I sprang to my feet, yanking my daggers from my chest sheath. Njall was on his feet faster than I expected, and I tossed him two of my blades since he'd left his sword with the horse. The woods had gone silent—no chirping birds, no rustling leaves, no scurrying animals. I kicked myself. If I had been paying attention instead of trying to distract myself from my pain with Njall's body, I would have noticed.

He leaned in close and whispered, "Stay at my back. We'll see more of the woods that way."

"Obviously," I muttered. *Does he think I'm that clueless?*

Pressing our backs together, we scanned the surrounding area. A wind rushed past us and through the trees, sending leaves and branches rustling. I let my senses take over and listened for the slightest shift in the forest floor. A faint crunch came from the left. Both of us turned toward it, and that's when they struck from the right.

A group of Huestur guards charged from the trees. There

were eight that I could see, too many for me to control with my charms. We'd have to handle them the warrior way.

One man in an ornate tunic, clearly the leader, went straight for Njall. I smirked inwardly; he'd regret that choice when I carved his precious crest from his chest and made him eat it. Njall shoved me aside just as the blade nicked his shirt. He dropped low, grabbed a fistful of dirt, and flung it into our attacker's face.

A battle cry came from behind us, and I spun to see two more men come running from the woods. These men were not as graceful on their feet as the first group, so I tossed the two daggers I was holding, landing one in the first man's eye and the second in the other's throat. Both men went down solidly, their bodies crashing against a log and sending it rolling. Blood seeped out of the one man's neck, while the other had fallen on his face, blocking my dagger from sight.

"Elva, watch out!"

I turned in time to duck under the fist that came flying at my face. Grabbing another dagger from my sheath, I lunged for the man, but he was too quick, jumping out of reach before I could stab him. The others were closing in behind us, and I struggled to keep track of them all. A pained cry came from the man Njall was fighting—not the captain, but a younger man who'd snuck up behind him. My dagger protruded from his chest, and Njall was wielding the remaining dagger and a heavy stick against the leader.

The captain laughed mockingly before he barked an order in his native tongue. His men surged toward Njall like a pack of wolves. They surrounded him and seemed to be toying with him —knocking him around between them, before they shoved him to the ground, pinning him in place.

A giant of a man emerged from the trees, his arms as thick as branches, and he came at me with impossible speed. I hurled my last dagger at him, but he swatted it away like an insect. Instinct screamed at me to run, but I couldn't—not if these were the men who'd taken my brothers. I needed to know where they were, whatever the cost. And if I wanted to have the quiet future I envisioned, I needed Njall.

Njall fought as if his life depended on it, which, honestly, it might. He kicked his legs and tried to free his arms until three men sat on him. As much as I wanted to help him, I couldn't take my eyes off the giant stalking toward me. I darted sideways, aiming for the trees. He snagged my tunic with a meaty hand, yanking me toward his chest. I drove an elbow back into his gut. I kicked my leg up to try to hit him in the groin, but he clamped his legs together, trapping my ankle.

His grip tightened as I writhed against him. Across the clearing, Njall's grunts of pain grew more desperate. The captain's men had hauled him to his feet, two holding him while the third threw punch after brutal punch. I expected the man in charge to gloat, but instead he fixed on me with an unreadable expression.

"A siren. Interesting." He left his men to manage Njall and strolled over to me.

I refused to play into their prejudices of sirens, keeping my features neutral as he grabbed my chin, examining me with a mix of curiosity and disdain. He paid close attention to my siren traits —my one green and one blue eye, my multicolored hair, and my iridescent skin that shimmered faintly this time of day.

"I assumed sirens would be beautiful beyond measure, but you are merely a pretty face."

"Maybe because she isn't singing," the oaf holding me suggested

The captain lowered himself to my eye level, his breath hot against my face. "Is that it, little siren? Are you only pretty when you sing? Or only when you ride a man's cock?"

I had to bite my tongue to keep myself from trying to bite

him. I needed Njall and me to get out of this alive, and getting vicious wouldn't help. The captain smirked, clearly pleased with himself, before yanking my tunic down and exposing one of my breasts. "You do have great tits."

"I grew them myself," I replied, narrowing my eyes at him.

"I can see that," he muttered, before turning to his men. "Tie the prince up."

"Will we be taking him back to the castle?" One of the lower-ranked men asked. The captain glared at him as if he disgusted him.

"The king has grown bored with him. Whether to keep him alive is our choice. The same for our little siren here. We could just make her disappear, and no one would ever know."

An uncomfortable heat was coming off the man behind me. I knew exactly what the captain was implying.

"We could just slit the prince's throat and be done with it now," another man suggested, holding up the dagger they'd wrestled away from Njall.

"No!" I cried out before I could stop myself. All eyes turned to me.

"No?" The captain raised an eyebrow, glancing between me and Njall.

I knew what was coming. I'd known it the moment the words slipped from my lips. The price of his life would be my body. But it was a price I was willing to pay, as I'd used my body countless times before today. At least this time, it would be my choice.

"I think I could be persuaded," the captain said, "if you willingly spread your legs for me and my men. We'll take you regardless, but it would be ... pleasant to have you eager." He twirled a strand of my hair around his finger and looked down at me, his eyes clouded with lust. The stench of sweat and greed clung to him. I could tell he was the kind of man who took what he wanted, that he'd done it before and would do it again given the chance. The arrogant ones always thought they deserved first dibs on the siren. It's what made them so predictable, and so easy to kill.

"Tie him to the tree," the captain ordered, gesturing toward Njall. "Let him watch me teach his siren how a real man should feel."

The younger man dragged Njall away as the giant loosened his grip on me. The captain and this monstrous oaf would be my first victims. Once I cut off the serpent's head, the rest would fall.

Njall fought and cursed as they dragged him across the puddle of blood on the ground. When they started to tie him to a tree at the edge of the camp, he broke free long enough to punch one man's groin. *At least that one won't be enjoying himself.* Another of the guards joined the fray, and together they managed to yank his arms back and secure them to the trunk.

The captain turned his attention back to me, tilting my chin up so my eyes bore into his. "If you hope to save his life," he said, "you'd better make me and my men very happy, little siren."

With my arms free, I stepped away from the giant. There were still too many of them for me to use my siren charms effectively, so I relied on my other skills. I slipped my empty dagger sheath over my head and began unlacing the front of my tunic.

The captain licked his lips as I loosened my shirt and pulled it over my head, leaving my breasts on full display for him and his men. One of the younger men whistled, but I ignored him. Young men who had never seen tits before were not the ones I needed to worry about. The seasoned warriors at my front and back were the ones I needed to manage.

The giant's enormous hands engulfed my breasts from behind, pressed against my backside like a weapon. I could handle a lot, but even I would likely struggle to take him.

"Wait your turn, Helmut," the captain snapped, grabbing the front of my pants and wrenching me away. He spun me around to face his men, and I could see the erections forming in their tight pants, as the captain slid his hand into my underwear and stroked between my folds. I let out a little moan as his fingers grazed my clit on their way deeper.

"How wet is she, Captain?" one of the younger men asked excitedly.

The captain laughed. "You'd drown in her pussy, Rolf." He pulled my hair back and wrapped his fingers around my throat before shoving his fingers inside me. "That's a good little siren whore. Nice and wet for us." He squeezed my neck, making me gasp as he pulled my head to his mouth. "I'm going to take you in every hole you have, and when you're covered in my cum, my brother Helmut will do the same, and then we'll give you to the men. After we're through with you, if you've pleased us, we might let your prince live. Understood?"

His fingers tightened around my throat, making it impossible to speak, so I nodded.

"Good girl." He dragged me toward one of the larger logs and undid his pants without releasing my neck. His cock sprang out, already hard and waiting, but nothing remarkable.

"Like what you see, whore?" he grunted as he sat on the log with his legs spread wide, finally releasing his grip on my neck. I focused only on him, ignoring the others, as I slowly stepped out of my pants. Swinging my hips, I moved toward him, running my hands along his thighs. I felt him quiver with each soft squeeze. Finally, I wrapped my arms around his neck and straddled him. He moaned as I hovered over him for a moment, but his patience ran out, and he grabbed my hips and shoved me down on his cock.

I let out a little gasp noise I knew men expected, and he half moaned, half chuckled, as I rocked on his cock. Njall screamed with rage behind us, while the other men fell silent. I glanced back and saw most of them were too busy stroking their cocks to notice exactly what I was doing.

The captain held me down and thrust up into me, grunting like a pig eating slop. I rolled my eyes and focused on releasing my talons and my fangs slightly, subtle enough not to be noticed. I still needed the big oaf closer to set my plan in motion.

I let out another girlish gasp and made sure to let my ass bounce and jiggle as I rode the captain. As expected, his brother grew impatient, and I heard him unclasp his pants. The ground crunched as Helmut came up behind me and pressed his massive frame against my back. The captain dug his hands in my hair, pulling my mouth to his—and that was my moment.

I sank my fangs into his lip before he even knew I'd grown them out. My talons burst from my fingers, and I slashed them across his back, flaying him open and spilling blood and flesh in their wake. Twisting sharply, I thrust my hand up into Helmut's neck before he could put that giant dick anywhere near me. As his blood ran down my arm, I turned toward the younger men.

The two youngest fled into the woods, but I wasn't worried about them. They wouldn't be believed if they even made it back to the Huestur Kingdom. When I stood up, the captain's body tumbled backwards off the log. Helmut lay on the ground behind me, still gasping and gurgling uselessly as he bled out. I smirked as I stalked toward the remaining guards.

As they raised their weapons, I opened my mouth and sang.

Chapter 33

Njall

The melody that left Elva was nothing like the one she'd used in Tyndorf. The one with our guards had been ferocious, more of a roar than a song, but this one flowed like a soft lullaby. The men between us froze mid-step, their swords slipping from their hands. Elva's eyes fixed on mine as she continued to sing. I strained against the ropes that held me against the tree as I fought to get to her.

She carefully stepped over the dead soldiers and approached one of the men who stood entranced near me. Leaning in close, she whispered something in his ear, and to my surprise, he nodded slowly, as if in a trance. He raised his sword and came at me.

For one panicked second, I worried she might have changed her mind about getting me home, but then he started to hack at my ropes. When my hands were free, I staggered to my feet and grabbed the sword from his hand. He gave no resistance. I looked him over slowly, and it was unnerving how still he stood, his expression blank, more statue than man. I gave him a shove, and he didn't even flinch.

"This is incredible," I said.

Elva chuckled. "I can only handle a few men at once. Too many and I lose my grip on them."

She could handle men all right. The image of her riding the captain's cock was not something I would soon forget. Without a word, I marched across the camp toward where the captain's body lay, then drove my blade into his face. Then, as I was cutting off his fingers, Elva appeared beside me.

"What are you doing?" she asked. She was still naked and streaked with blood. It took all of my willpower to direct my gaze at her face. She had a playful glint in her eye and looked amused. When her eyes locked onto mine, I realized she truly didn't know why I needed to deface the captain's corpse.

"I'm removing the parts of his body that touched you without your permission," I explained.

Elva leaned so close to me that her breasts pressed against my biceps. "You missed one," she murmured, her gaze flicking to the captain's groin. Without hesitation, I did what she asked, though it made my stomach twist with revulsion. When the deed was done, the way she looked at me shifted somehow. Her eyes went black, and she tilted her head, studying me like a predator sizing up prey.

I swallowed hard. What I'd just done had brought out the siren. Elva was a warrior, fierce and capable, but the siren was a monster, and while I hated that word, in this case, it was fact. The man before me had been nearly flayed into two pieces by her talons, and yet those black eyes regarded me with a flicker of confusion.

"Why?" she asked, her tone raspy and guttural.

I still hadn't figured out Elva and the siren. If I told the siren something, would Elva know it? Were they two sides of the same coin, or was the siren an excuse for Elva to unleash her dark desires? "No one touches what's mine," I said, trying to hide the fear crawling up my spine.

Slowly, her lips parted, baring her fangs at me before she let out a soft, mocking laugh. "Oh, sweet boy," she purred, leaning closer until her breath brushed against my ear. "Have you not figured it out yet? It's you who belongs to me."

Her lips pressed into mine, and every nerve in my body flared to life. I dropped the sword and pulled her close, desperate to get as much of her body touching mine as I could. She grabbed my shirt and pulled it over my head before slamming her mouth back onto mine. Her breasts pressed against my chest, and the heat of them combined with knowing that another man had touched them was enough to make me feral. My fingers dug into her backside, lifting her so she could grind against me. Her legs wrapped around my waist, and she rocked her pelvis into me like a woman possessed.

I winced in pain as a coppery taste filled my mouth. The little siren had bitten me. I pulled back and looked at her, and when she licked my blood off her lips, I couldn't tell if it had been an accident or if she'd enjoyed the taste. But that sting was enough to snap me out of the moment. There were still two men standing off to the side, bewitched by her song, and bodies scattered around us on the ground. And then there was the memory of what had just happened. Another man had been inside her. It was too much for me, and I lowered her to the ground.

I went to grab my shirt and handed it to her to cover herself. The siren glared at me, but I caught her face in my hand and pulled her close. "Not like this," I said, and kissed her, pouring every ounce of frustration, fear, and love that I had into it.

I grabbed the sword and went to finish the men. Normally, I would never kill men who couldn't fight back, but these men would have raped Elva and then killed me, regardless of whatever deal Elva thought she was making. I rammed my sword into the first man's gut, slicing upwards until I met the resistance of his ribs. He dropped to the ground like a felled tree. The second was quicker. I simply slit his throat and watched as the blood ran from him, soaking into the ground. Maybe there was more of my father in me than I cared to admit. My selkie mother had taught me mercy, but when I looked at Elva, who was now wearing my shirt, scavenging what she could from the bodies, I knew I'd show no mercy to anyone who wronged her.

When I finished checking the other men for anything useful, I found she'd finally put some clothes on, though she'd kept my tunic rather than search for her own in the mess of blood and bodies on the ground. She'd also found her daggers and was cleaning the last one before returning it to her sheath. "Do you think they have horses or that there's a camp nearby?" she asked.

"I'm not sure." I glanced around the bodies and spotted something. "Elva, I'm sorry."

She frowned. "For what?"

I picked up the shirt we'd found when we'd got here, an eternity ago, and shook the dirt off it. Somehow, it had avoided the bloodshed. "I think any hints of when Sindri and Leifur were here are gone." I held it out to her, and she took it, clutching it far tighter than I expected.

"We'll find them," she said, her voice cracking before she turned toward the trees. "I'll prepare the horses."

"I'll look around to see if I can figure out where the guards came from."

I watched her go, fighting the instinct to follow and comfort her. She'd been through enough today, and I would not force myself into her space just to ease my guilt. While she readied our mounts, I scouted the camp for any clues about where the guards had come from. There were no horses, no hiding places, and no trail leading in or out of the clearing. It was as if they'd materialized from the forest itself. They were in leather armor, and not steel, so they could have walked a great distance, but to manage that without disturbing the forest would be a challenge.

When I returned to the clearing, Elva was stuffing the gold and weapons we'd pilfered from the guards into our satchels. She was struggling to get the half-broken latch on my bag to close. I stepped up behind her and slipped my arm around hers to hold it so she could fasten it.

"Thank you," she whispered, turning to face me. I hadn't lowered my arms, and for a moment, just stared at her. "Did you find anything in the forest?" she asked.

"No, which is strange enough on its own." I searched her face for any indication of how she was feeling after what had just happened.

She tilted her head slightly, her expression unreadable. "That *is* odd. I've heard of water or sky creatures creeping up undetected, but never land dwellers. Something should have been disturbed."

"Exactly. So I suspect they came on foot."

"So we should get out of this area then, unless ..." Her voice trailed off.

"Unless what?"

Her eyes locked onto mine. "Unless they found my brothers."

Chapter 34

Elva

Frustration filled me as I tossed my satchel on the ground. We'd spent the last three days searching what felt like half the forest, but there was no sign of where my brothers had ended up. Every other camp we'd found was abandoned or covered in debris from the storm, and the trails showed no signs that they'd passed this way. No secret hints left behind, no messages carved into logs. It all pointed to one grim possibility: they'd been taken against their will, unable to leave me even the faintest trail to follow. The last chance we had was to head toward Eldenwood and hope they would either be there or that we'd at least find some trace of where they'd been taken.

"You want to gather fire or start the food?" Njall asked as he joined me beside the crackling flames. The forest at night was eerie in its stillness and downright terrifying. His offer to let me choose was kind, but I was too angry to appreciate it.

"What does it matter what job I do?" I snapped at him. "It won't bring my brothers back."

"No," Njall said, more softly than I deserved. "But it will help you rest so we can start fresh tomorrow."

The man was as confusing as he was infuriating. He should be annoyed at the delay in getting him home. He should resent me for trying to use my siren spell on him during the rescue, even if it hadn't worked for some reason. He should be frustrated that I'd dragged him all over this cursed forest to find my brothers. But he wasn't any of those things.

Njall was nothing like the horrible, spoiled prince I'd expected to rescue. He acted with more courtesy than my brothers and was pleasant company. He caught his share of food, knew a lot about the different animals and kingdoms that I hadn't learned in my lessons, and had an excellent sense of direction. We'd spend our evenings by the fire, and he'd share stories of creatures I'd never heard of. He taught me about human anatomy beyond the reproductive details that had been drilled into me, and told me about their rich culture that went back for generations.

In return, I corrected his misunderstandings about sirens, selkies, and mermaids. Of all the creatures, he knew the most about selkies, even teaching me a few things. It turns out that selkie males can breed with anything, but selkie females rarely carry non-selkie babies to term. When they do, those children seldom survive for long. It was why so many selkies chose to mate for life. They wanted the best chance at healthy children.

Even though sirens weren't maternal, I felt for those mothers. They had high hopes for their young, only to lose them so soon. Njall seemed troubled by the idea of selkie females being treated poorly by their mates. But I reminded him that the females of our kind were not fragile the way human women were. We had fangs and talons, and in fact, ours were larger and deadlier than those of our male counterparts.

"I forgive you," I said, poking at the fire with a stick before holding the pheasant over the flames to char it a bit more.

"For what?" Njall asked, sitting down beside me. He held out his hand for the stick. Since our encounter with the guards, he'd stayed closer, though still keeping a small space between us. It was confusing. He wanted to be near me, but at the same time, he didn't want to touch me.

"For believing such horrible lies about me," I said. I leaned in closer and shoved his arm with my shoulder, and the tiniest smile flashed across his lips. "I can forgive your lack of knowledge, considering that humans couldn't survive long enough underwater to study us. Especially if most humans are like you and can't even swim."

"I *can* swim," Njall said.

I sat up and stared at him. "But back at the castle, you said you couldn't swim."

"No, I said I don't swim. There's a difference. I just don't like to."

"How can you not like swimming?" I grabbed his shoulder and shook it. "The underwater world is magical. The schools of fish that move as one, the colorful coral that covers the seafloor like flowers in a meadow. So much life in one place, and no sun to burn your skin!"

"While that may be true, I'm just not a fan."

"Well, that's ... appalling," I exclaimed. "I'll have to change your mind."

"I have a better idea," he said, pulling our dinner off the fire. "Instead of you trying and failing—"

"Says you."

"Instead of trying to get me into the water, why don't I promise to let you correct the books in the king's library? You could fix all the errors recorded about sirens, selkies, and other sea creatures."

"Your father wouldn't allow that," I said.

"We wouldn't tell him."

"Won't you be in trouble when you return?" I asked. He

looked confused, so I elaborated. "Because you and Baldr set us free?"

"I hadn't considered that," he answered. "Possibly. He is vindictive like that." Njall pulled the bird off the fire, used one of my daggers to cut it in half, and held the two pieces up for me to choose from. As I grabbed one piece, my gaze fixed on his pendant reflecting in the firelight. Njall noticed and slipped it off his neck to hand it to me. "It was my mother's. It's one of the few things I have left of her."

I set down my dinner, recalling the rumors I'd heard in Tyndorf. "She stayed longer than the others, didn't she?"

"Yes, unfortunately. Hulda and Baldr's mothers left after giving birth. Ingvar's died in childbirth. Mine stayed to care for me, and it caused her death."

"You mean your father did."

"If she hadn't stayed for me, she wouldn't have died."

That a mother would stay for her child was foreign to me, but it clearly hurt Njall to think of her. I didn't know what to say to make him feel better. I ran my thumb over the smooth pendant before handing it back to him and biting into my dinner.

"How far from Eldenwood do you think we are?" he asked, clearly wanting to change the subject.

"If you trust what we overheard from those farmers we encountered, not far."

"Country people are so helpful."

"That's because we hid from them," I said, taking another bite of my food. Somehow, Njall had devoured his entire portion already.

"I'm worried by what else they said. Those guards we killed aren't the only ones we need to be afraid of. There's a price on our heads. The people seem nice, but I wouldn't put it past them to turn us in to improve their lives."

"Doesn't it bother you?" I asked.

"That the guards get to the townspeople?"

"No," I said, smiling mischievously. "That I'm worth more."

Njall chuckled. "You *should* be worth a little more, but five times more? *Ferflucs!* I'm a prince, and I'm only worth a hundred coins to them."

"Well, I *did* break you out of the king's dungeon. And murdered quite a few palace guards."

"Tell me more about how sirens live," he said, changing the subject.

"Aren't you bored with that yet?" I tossed the bird bones into the woods.

"Hardly. I've traveled a lot, but never anywhere interesting. Just human villages, and they're all mostly the same. *You* have been everywhere." He pushed his shoulder against mine, making me sway slightly. My stomach fluttered, but not from the motion.

"Sirens live on an island as much as the sea," I explained. "We guard it fiercely because it has everything we need. We grow the vegetables we can't harvest from the sea and have chickens and goats, eggs, milk, cheese—"

"What about grains?"

"Unless we're traveling, we don't eat many."

"That's a shame. Tyndorf is known for its grain, and our bread is better there than anywhere else in Torian."

"Is that so?"

"You don't believe me?"

"I didn't say that."

"But you implied it." His smile was as playful as ever. I couldn't help but smile back. *What is it about this human? I've never lost my head so much over a man.*

"I've heard there's a kingdom far to the east, over the Crimson Mountains, known for its grains, too. It wouldn't be fair to rule them out without trying it for myself."

Njall gave me a look I recognized as the one he gave when he knew I was right and couldn't think of a way to argue with me. I've seen it often these past few days.

"Stop sulking about being a cheap criminal," I said. "Maybe if you were more entertaining company, you'd be of higher value." I couldn't help but grin at the annoyance that crossed his brows. They almost touched, like a giant caterpillar on his face.

"We haven't found anything in the woods. What's the plan if there's no sign of your brothers in Eldenwood either?" he asked, his lips curling into a slight smirk.

"We'll check in town, and if there's nothing, we'll come back to keep checking the forest. We have to find something to confirm whether they are in hiding or were taken."

"Maybe they left you to do the hard work of bringing me back."

"Never," I replied sweetly.

"How do you know?"

"Simple. My twin brother would never abandon me, and Leifur adores me. Besides, the bartender in Eldenwood liked Sindri. She gave us food, drinks, and a room for free. Sindri loves to get things for nothing. If there were any way he could get back there, he would."

"I'm sure she wanted something." Njall gestured to make his meaning clear.

"Unfortunately for her," I said, standing and brushing myself off before grabbing the bedrolls, "Sindri won't sleep with women. Leifur will, but I don't think she wanted him."

"He's married to your twin, yet he sleeps with women?"

"He used to. That's how they met." I set up our bed beside the fire and watched Njall to see if he'd figure it out for himself how I was connected to my brother's marriage.

"You ... slept with Leifur?"

"For six months." I lay down on the bed and waited for Njall to join me. "It isn't a big deal to us. The bigger deal was how angry the sirens were when he left. Leifur was one of their best producers."

"Producer?"

"You'd say father."

"How many children has he 'produced?'"

"I'm not sure of the exact number, but I'd wager a few dozen."

"A few dozen! I thought my father had a lot when he impregnated five women in a year."

"If you consider that a siren's entire goal is to reproduce, it isn't that many. Besides, our pregnancies are often shorter than yours."

"What do you mean by 'often'? Do they vary in length by the season?" He turned toward me, resting his head on his hand.

"No. Where would you get a ridiculous idea like that? They vary by paternity. All siren mothers pass their siren gifts onto their children, but the other half comes from the father, and that determines the length of the pregnancy."

"I should have known. Baldr's mother was pregnant several months longer than the rest of our mothers."

"I thought you were the youngest. How would you know that?"

Njall looked at me with a puzzled look on his face. "Now who's confused?" He grinned like a child who had found out a secret. "Our position in the family has nothing to do with age, but with our father's preference. I'm actually oldest by six months."

I was so taken aback that I dropped back on the ground so hard that my head almost bounced. "I knew your father was a monster, but he's so much worse than I thought." I covered my face with my hands.

"Try being raised by him. It's why we were always happy to go off with the knights."

"How did he ... decide?" I asked.

"Who was first?"

I nodded slowly.

"When we were twelve, he tested the four of us."

"Tested you? How?"

Njall rubbed his arm for a long moment. I was about to tell him to forget it when he sighed. "Physically. To find who was strongest, fastest, and most like him. Ingvar was first, then Hulda, Baldr, and me."

"That doesn't make sense. I know your sister has magic, so I can understand why she was picked, but how is Baldr—"

Njall laughed. "Baldr asks me that at least once a month. I don't think my father expected him to turn into the drinking, gambling, womanizer he became, but truthfully, that is more like my father than any of us."

I laughed at Njall's honest reply. I couldn't remember the last time I genuinely laughed at something another man said. Plenty of times, I'd smiled and giggled at something stupid a man said so I could get into his pants, but Njall was the first man, other than my brothers, who made me feel truly at ease.

Chapter 35

Njall

We were getting close enough to Eldenwood that we could occasionally see the town wall as the road snaked around the forest and mountain edge. Yesterday, we spent more time hiding to avoid being seen by the people during the day, so now we hurried through the evening to make up for it. As we neared the gate, Elva's grip on my arm tightened, pulling me to a stop.

"What?" I asked.

She motioned silently toward the woods. "Something's wrong," she whispered, once we were hidden among the trees.

I followed her gaze toward the gate, where the usual guards stood. "How can you tell?" I whispered.

"I can feel it in the air."

"Aren't you a sea creature?"

She glared at me in that endearing way she would when I'd annoyed her, then sighed. "I am, but that means I can feel shifts in the surrounding air as well as water, and this isn't right. There are too many men at the gate."

I pressed against her, more than was necessary, to peer

around the tree. Her scent, like the sea, salty and familiar, was intoxicating, and the heat from her body pressed against mine sent a rush of blood to my cock. I bit back a moan, nearly forgetting about the guards.

"You're right," I admitted when I finally pulled away. "There shouldn't be seven men at the one gate, especially at this hour."

Elva swallowed hard, and I could practically read her mind. She was worried for her brothers, that the knights had found them. I instinctively wrapped my arms around her, offering what comfort I could. Her breath steadied against me, and she leaned into my touch.

"We didn't hear any travelers mention prisoners," I said softly.

"Just because they aren't talking about it everywhere—"

"I know," I interrupted gently. "But if they are here, we'll find a way."

The forest was unnervingly quiet as I gathered wood for the fire. I hurried in the dwindling light to avoid the countless broken branches and rocks that were strewn about from the storm. I couldn't stop thinking back to our conversations on the road. Elva's genuine laugh had lit up her entire face in a way I'd never seen on her before. For a moment, it was as if all her walls melted away and I glimpsed the true woman she was—not the siren, or selkie, just her.

I had insisted she get some rest. Now, alone by the fire, I toyed with the beach glass pendant around my neck. Before she died, my mother had explained that it was from the beach where I was born, and her and her parents, and all the generations of my family. She told me to hold on to it until I found my person. For selkies, giving the pendant to another would give that person sway over them, so choosing the right one was incredibly important. My mother had given hers to my father, and it had been her demise.

Since the moment I was born, I took after my father. Only a few traits of my mother had taken root in me—the most obvious one being my green eyes. She'd hoped my resemblance to my father would make him love me more, but in truth, I believe it only made him hate me. Of all his children, he despised me the most, and I knew it was because my mother had been the one he truly loved. When she became pregnant with me, he realized he could sire a legion of children with monster women and ensure we protected Tyndorf. He sought other creatures to bear his offspring, and five half-human offspring survived. Of all the women he chose, he only ever loved my mother, but when he found others to carry his stronger, more useful children, he shattered her heart, and she died slowly, withering away to nothing.

He had always been cruel, but after her death, he became ruthless—and not just toward me. That was the guilt that I struggled to carry—that it was my mother's death and his hatred of me that made him lash out against my siblings. I'd always wondered if my mother had any family and imagined what my life would have been like had they raised me, in that place, far from Tyndorf, on the beach where my family had lived for generations. As a boy, I dreamed of that almost every night, but now ... now I knew it was nothing but a fantasy.

I dropped the necklace back inside my shirt and gazed at the sleeping siren beside me. Elva was a dream too, but unlike those of my childhood, she was flesh and blood. When she slept, she breathed so softly it was barely evident that she was alive. I first noticed it when she was unconscious at the cottage, and honestly, it was fascinating to watch. My brothers and my father's men would snore loudly, their chests moving like the tide along the kingdom and the Crimson Mountains, so being around someone who didn't make a sound was as perplexing as it was fascinating.

Having learned how much I'd been lied to about sirens, it made me wonder what else was a lie. I knew Ingvar could turn into a wolf because I'd seen it. The same was true for Hulda's ability to communicate with animals, and Baldr was as strong as an ox, thanks to his satyr blood. But what about the creatures we didn't see? The selkies might not be as simple as I'd been taught, the Minotaur not as violent, and maybe not all kelpies or harpies were completely vicious. Over the years, I'd grown to expect my father to lie when it benefited him, but I could not fathom how deceiving us about creatures we had never even encountered would serve him—or our kingdom.

The fire crackled, pulling me from my thoughts, and I realized it was getting low again. If we wanted to eat before creeping off toward the town, I'd need to grab some more wood. Standing carefully to avoid making noise, I folded my cloak neatly and placed it in my spot so that if Elva woke, she'd know I hadn't gone far. Then I headed into the nearby trees, scanning the ground for branches and pieces of wood to cook the quail I'd caught earlier.

After that terrible storm, finding wood on the ground was a straightforward job. The sunny, warm weather over the past few days had dried everything. I gathered as much as my arms could hold without tangling myself in the outstretched limbs and vines, then turned back toward the fire's glow. But as I stepped out of the trees, I froze — a cloaked figure was kneeling beside Elva. Their back was to me, obscuring what they were doing, but I doubted it was anything good. Fear surged through me. If I hesitated, they might hurt her.

I shifted my grip on the wood, grabbed one of the larger branches off the top of my pile, and hurled it at the intruder. The rest of the wood tumbled from my arms.

What happened next was a blur. Elva was on her feet before I could even grab another piece of wood, her arms outstretched, each gripping one of the daggers she rarely removed. I hadn't even seen her move until she was in her defensive stance. The figure stumbled backward from Elva's blades and collapsed beside the fire. Luckily for them, their cloak was thick enough that it smothered our small fire rather than igniting it.

I crossed the clearing, seized the intruder by the collar, and yanked them to their feet—away from Elva. "Who are you? What are you doing here?"

The intruder's hood fell to the side, revealing a head of blue hair. "Got another one obsessed with you, huh, Elva? How do you always manage that?"

The fire flared back to life, now that the cloak was removed, illuminating the siren's face. She was attractive enough, with a small nose and deep blue eyes that almost looked black, but the smirk that crossed her lips made me grip her collar tight enough that my knuckles turned white.

"Do you know this thing?" I asked Elva. Her daggers were gone, and her arms were crossed over her chest.

"Hello, Coral," she replied coolly.

"Mind having your toy let me go?" Coral shot back.

"What did you call me?" I snapped.

"He's not my toy," Elva replied, then stepped forward and hugged the siren the instant I released her.

"Does that mean he's fair game?" Coral laughed and patted Elva's back before turning back to me. "I'm Coral. I've known Elva and Sindri since we were all babes."

Hope flickered in Elva's eyes for the first time in days. "Have you seen my brothers?" she asked urgently.

"They were taken," Coral said. "A large group of Huestur men arrived a week ago and took over the entire town. Their main camp is hidden deep in the bush somewhere, but they have been keeping men around to look for you." She pointed her slim finger at me. Coral went into detail about how Sindri and Leifur arrived a few days ago and tried to make it into town to find shelter. "You're lucky I found them before the guards did. Since then,

I've been hiding out and waiting for you. I knew if Sindri was here, you'd be close behind."

I listened, but never took my eyes off her. Although she seemed to be an old friend of Elva's, something about her felt off. She was too chummy, only talked to Elva while barely acknowledging me, and was too excited to see Elva while her brothers were taken hostage. Listening carefully, I gathered they'd just seen each other when Elva was on her way to find me. I nodded at something Elva said without hearing her, and she pointed to me, making both sirens laugh.

"So, where are Sindri and Leifur?" I asked, wanting to move things along.

Elva shot me an annoyed look, with the same pursed lips and wrinkled nose she usually used on her brother. It was much less adorable when aimed at me, but I brushed it off and watched Coral. "Well?"

"They're staying in the woods on the other side of the town. There's a clearing I like to use when it's too dangerous to stay in Eldenwood. I'll take you to them in the morning. You can't be too careful in these woods."

"Why not now?" I asked, crossing my arms.

Coral fiddled with the worn threads of her cloak, then wrapped it in a bundle and dropped it on the ground. "As I already said, you have to be careful in these woods. There are many things here to be feared beyond *us*." She cocked her head toward Elva.

I narrowed my gaze at her, but Elva spoke up. "That's enough of your pissing match." She ran her hands through her thick hair before sitting down beside the fire to warm her hands. "You're both big, powerful warriors. You don't need to prove it to me."

"Oh, don't worry," Coral rasped with her sultry voice. "I know how big my dick is." She smiled, revealing a mouth full of razor-sharp teeth, and it took everything in me not to flinch. She sat beside Elva and whispered something to her, making the half-selkie roll her eyes and playfully shove her friend.

I stood there, waiting. I knew she'd crack.

"Fine. A compromise," Coral finally said. "We'll wait until it's first light and go. We'll arrive in time for breakfast."

Elva's chest rose quickly. I could tell she wanted to go now, but she wasn't willing to speak up against her friend. The ridiculousness of it wasn't lost on me. Elva would stand up to anyone with her daggers out, but not against this siren. Could this Coral be a former commander? Someone ranked above her that the warrior in Elva still felt the need to obey? I wanted to know more, but knew I wouldn't get any intel while she was sitting beside Elva. So I volunteered to fetch even more wood.

I fetched us wood three times throughout the night, while the sirens sat beside the fire wrapped in Elva's blanket. They ate the quail stew, chatted, reminisced, and debated which species of male made the best lover. Coral brought up the topic repeatedly, smirking at me every time she coaxed Elva into discussing her favorite partners. The siren was perceptive—she'd figured me out within minutes, while Elva either remained unaware of my feelings or ignored them.

Eventually, we settled on shifts for the night. I offered to take the first watch, but Elva, hesitant after already napping earlier, finally relented when Coral volunteered to stay up instead—a task I had no intention of letting her handle alone.

When Elva settled down to rest, I took the opposite side of the fire and got comfortable for my faux slumber. It only took minutes for Elva's chest movements to slow to a standstill. How she could sleep in the middle of the woods with a sort of prisoner and an old friend staring daggers at one another was beyond me. She must have been drained from her injury, yet she hid it well during the day. I closed my eyes and focused on my breathing to make it look like I was falling asleep. The challenge, now, was to remain awake. I couldn't move without giving myself away, so I tried to focus on the wind rushing through the branches and the night creatures coming out to investigate us. The more intently I focused, the duller my focus seemed to become.

A branch snapped near my head, sending me upright in an instant. Despite my efforts, I'd fallen asleep, but before I could focus on my failure, Coral's face was in front of mine.

"Rise and shine. Figured you could keep me company."

A sharp pain exploded from my side, and when I glanced down, Coral had one of Elva's daggers pressed into my stomach hard enough for the tip to have vanished in my shirt and flesh, and a small trickle of blood gathered on my shirt around it.

"If you scream or do anything to wake Elva," she whispered, "I'll bury the blade in her pretty little neck. Understood?"

I nodded as much as I dared, and she moved the dagger to a safer distance so I could slowly stand. I considered whether I had the speed and agility to overtake her. I was nearly a head taller, but I'd seen Elva's reflexes, and if Coral's were the same, I couldn't be certain of the outcome, especially in the pitch black woods surrounding me.

The siren stayed near me, focused on my face. "None of that," she said, shaking her head at me. Grinning with those horrible teeth, she brought her free hand up to show me her fingernails had grown as long as the dagger she held in her other hand. She waved one lethal fingertip close to my neck and whispered. "Don't even think of trying to run off, because I'll find you, and then I'll kill you, and I need you alive to collect the reward money. So be a good little boy and pick a branch from the fire to light our way."

I did as she asked. Pain shot through my entire back and chest again. Anytime I stepped on a branch, Coral pressed the dagger sharply into my side. She somehow expected me to be completely silent in an old-growth forest, never mind all the twigs and sticks from the storm. I clenched my teeth to hold back a wince of pain and trudged on. The burning stick I'd grabbed illuminated a few steps away from my feet, but not enough to be useful. Trying not to be obvious about it, I darted my eyes through the shadows, looking for any opening large enough for me to get away from this crazed siren. It was clear she didn't know where Elva's brothers were, and that she just wanted to hand me over for the gold. But with Elva's bounty being so much more, it didn't make sense—unless she'd made another deal.

She jabbed me again with the blade. "Don't get any ideas, Your Highness. You're worth more alive, but that doesn't mean I can't make money off you dead."

Without a word, I continued on, nearly stumbling as I shuffled my feet to avoid snapping any branches and the inevitable jabs into my flesh of her dagger.

"Finally." The siren muttered and pushed me from behind toward a flickering light ahead. I stumbled between two trees and found myself at a camp with a pair of sirens, but not the two I was expecting.

"River. Talia. Tie him up."

Wait until the time is right. I held my hands out, and the taller siren came over with some rope. Her hair and eyes were so dark, they were nearly navy blue. The cord was bristly, and she bound my hands tightly enough to pinch my skin.

The other siren looked me over and laughed. "This is the human we made a deal for?" She had cyan hair, and I later learned she was named River.

"Like most men, he's not much to look at," Coral replied.

Talia tugged on the waist of my trousers. "I wonder if he has it where it counts."

I stepped away from her and growled, baring my teeth at them.

The trio laughed before River shoved me to the ground and

tilted my chin up at her. "Now be a good boy while River and I play with you. Coral promised us."

"Just keep him quiet," Coral said. "We don't need the guards or villagers overhearing you."

River looked down at me like a wolf hungrily examining its prey. "No promises," she said, and before I could say anything, her mouth was on mine.

Chapter 36

Njall

River's legs straddled me while her mouth devoured mine. I tried to buck her off, to twist my head away, but my arms were bound behind me, and River's grip on my face held me in place. Talia crawled up behind me and sang softly into my ear. I closed my eyes and tried to drown her out, but the melody was alluring, and it weaved its way into my mind like a drug. In a minute, I felt a haze settle over me, as though I'd downed an entire flask of ale. River's lips moved to my neck, and Talia's hands roamed across my chest. A raw hunger stirred in me as I strained against the ropes, desperate to reach out, to touch.

As I struggled to free my hands, River bit down on my lip and pulled it away from my mouth. The sirens giggled. Sliding off my lap, River bent down to unclasp my trousers while Talia alternated between singing softly to me and nipping at my earlobe.

River's claws scratched my skin as she tugged my pants down, and I hissed. My cock sprang from my underwear as she pulled them off and tossed them aside.

"He certainly has it where it counts," Talia murmured, her breath hot against my neck.

"Yes, he does," River purred, her claws tracing my inner thighs, making my entire body buck in surprise. "Think he tastes as good as he looks?"

A voice in my head tried to protest, but Talia's song drowned it out. River lowered her mouth onto my cock. I moaned loudly as the siren's tongue ran up my shaft before she swirled it around the head. I wanted to let out a cry, but Talia turned my face toward her and stuck her tongue into my mouth. Her song echoed in my head until it felt like it was coming from inside me.

River released my cock from her mouth. Nothing I did would have stopped my body responding to them. Between their song and soft touches, I was lost. River's voice cut through the haze, something about needing it more, and the next thing I knew, Talia was lowering herself onto my rock-hard cock. River took up the song, her voice weaving in and out, while her friend gripped my shoulders.

The song grew louder, and it was as if they could read my mind. Every move and stroke felt like exactly what I needed, as if they could read my thoughts, anticipate every twitch of my body. My skin felt as if it were on fire, but there was a coldness spreading within me, a strange, unsettling contrast that I couldn't explain. It was as if they were stealing my heat from me, but that couldn't be.

Talia moved faster as she slammed into me one more time. The song crescendoed, and, unable to hold back any longer, I burst with a force that left me gasping. River stopped singing, and Talia let out a satisfied moan before pulling away.

"Good boy," she said, reaching out for River's hand to steady herself as she got off of me.

As the song's influence faded, I felt a wave of disgust and twisted to my side, retching. The sirens just laughed. Coral's sharp voice cut through the sound, ordering them to pack up if they were done with me.

After they'd dressed me again, the trio moved with the finesse and speed of an army that had trained together their whole lives. I watched in awe as they cleared away their belongings and stuffed them into their rucksacks, scattered sticks around where there were none, and even gathered a pile of leaves to soak the fire. They would leave no trace of what had happened.

While they worked, I looked for a way to free myself from the ropes that were cutting my flesh. I hadn't felt it during their siren song, but now my wrists felt raw. I cursed myself for not stealing one of Elva's daggers when we were at the cabin. The only sharp rock was by the fire. Before I could make a move, Talia grabbed two burning branches to use as makeshift torches, and River and Coral doused the fire with the leaves, plunging us into darkness.

"Get up," Talia ordered, and when I didn't move fast enough, Coral grabbed my bound shirt and yanked me forward. I stumbled as I struggled to regain my balance.

River slapped me across the face. "Idiot male," she growled, revealing a row of razor-sharp teeth. If I tried to run, and they caught me, it wouldn't end well.

I nodded, and then the tall siren turned her back to me and walked across the clearing toward the darkest part of the forest. I was forced to follow, with my heart hammering in my chest. Goosebumps erupted along my arms from the chilly early morning air.

It was a half hour of walking until I dared speak. "Where are you taking me?" I asked.

"Back where you belong," Coral replied.

I had a feeling she didn't mean Tyndorf. Before I could ask, Talia clarified. "You'll be joining those useless male sirens back in Huestur. The guards were more than happy to pay us a small fortune if it meant not having to keep searching for you all. The king has offered an exceedingly generous reward to whatever group of knights brings you back."

"And a bonus if they provide the creatures who helped you escape," River added.

"What about Elva?" I asked, despite knowing the answer. "She is the one who released me. Isn't she worth more?"

"Turning her in is against the siren warrior code," Coral replied. "Her brother- and brother-in-law are fair game, but we fought alongside her, and many of us owe her a life debt."

"But you'll take away the one she loves."

River cackled. "You?"

"Sindri," I replied calmly. "I don't think she'll take kindly to you handing her brother over for a few gold coins."

"Try a thousand," Talia snapped. "Each."

And now I knew my price, and why Elva's was higher. The danger of taking a siren was significantly larger.

A large steel sword hung from a worn leather scabbard on Coral's hip. Talia wore a sheath for her daggers similar to Elva's, but hers was on her hip rather than across the chest. The jewels on the hilts of the daggers sparkled in the light from the torches. River had a dark leather whip hanging from her right hip, while on the other side was a quiver of arrows that had seen better days. Her bow looked almost new, gracefully slung over her back. These women were likely as dangerous as any group of my father's men; it was clear that capturing one would command a steep price. Knowing the prize the guards were offered made me wonder why they hadn't offered the peasants more, but likely they were being paid for information rather than apprehending us.

Lost in thought, I stumbled over a large tree root protruding from the ground and blocking our path. Coral swore under her breath and crossed the ground to pull me to my feet. Just as we turned around, we heard a crack behind us. Everyone froze, and

Coral's grip on my shoulder tightened painfully, but I bit back any sound.

A low growl echoed from the woods. The warriors quickly drew their weapons and formed a circle around me, brandishing them.

"Pay attention, ladies. We're not losing our cash cow to some wolves, got it?" Coral said.

"Understood," Talia and River replied in unison.

As we all scanned the tree line, I spotted a pair of glowing yellow eyes watching us from the darkness. "There." I pointed as best I could with my shoulder since my hands were bound behind me. River acted swiftly, and before I could even process what was happening, she'd fired an arrow toward those menacing orbs. A loud yelp echoed through the woods, followed by the sounds of snapping sticks as the creatures fled. For a moment, we dared to think the danger had passed.

Another snap broke the silence, and River's unease was palpable as she whipped her head around to inspect every angle of the forest. She grabbed Coral's arm and whispered urgently to her, but Coral pulled away, shaking her head. "Just stop it," she hissed. "The faster we move, the faster we'll lose her."

Chapter 37

Elva

I watched from the shadows as the traitors hurried away. Something had felt off; I noticed it when I had seen her in Tyndorf. She'd been louder and more boastful than usual, a feat I hadn't thought possible. When she found us again, I knew it wasn't a coincidence. Coral had always been a troublemaker in Konvern, even when we were children. She disliked authority, preferring to do things her way. It never even occurred to me she may have been exiled too, the same as I had, but now, seeing the dejection in her eyes and frustration on River and Talia's faces, I knew she had. Whether the others might have left with her willingly or had been cast out, I couldn't say for sure, but I knew they were driven by desperation. They were clearly in a worse situation than my brothers and me, otherwise they'd never have sold out a fellow siren, even if they disliked Leifur.

Njall's head swiveled nervously as Coral prodded him along the path. I knew I'd been discovered, but I wanted to see what they'd do next. Sirens had a particular way of moving when we traveled in groups—never more than three abreast, with our best seer leading and our best listener at the rear. Of all the casts, warrior sirens were the stealthiest, and Coral was indeed a very silent hiker. But I was better. They weaved around bushes, trees, and mounds of earth, trying to throw me off the scent, but Coral had made a crucial mistake—she'd touched what was mine. After years of sleeping side by side, I knew Sindri's scent. I'd smelled it on her at the camp, and I could still get a whiff of it now. Not only did I smell Sindri, I could also smell Leifur's blood on her, and Njall's arousal was mixed with Talia's.

No one touches what belongs to me.

I kept my distance and followed them.

After more than an hour of walking in circles and backtracking, all of which I presumed was a failed attempt to lose me, the group found their stride again and made some headway toward whomever it was that Coral was meeting. Despite everything, I was still undecided: should I reveal myself to the trio of sirens alone, or spare them and deal with the humans they planned to sell Njall to? In the end, the prince decided for me.

Njall stumbled and fell again, unable to keep up with the sirens' relentless pace with his hands bound behind him. His face slammed into the ground, making him cry out in shock and pain. Coral cursed and yanked him up by his collar. Blood streamed from his nose as he struggled to maintain composure, but he was suffering. River joined Coral in trying to hoist Njall to his feet, but he'd had enough and refused to cooperate. All three shouted at him, and Talia even kicked him in the hip, but he would not yield to them. Finally, Coral drew her sword and took a step toward Njall.

As tensions escalated, I seized my opportunity. My first dagger deftly sliced across Coral's knuckles, causing her to drop her weapon with a shrill cry. The next dagger soared through the air so quickly that by the time River pulled her bow from her back, the string was already severed. Talia unsheathed two of her daggers and took a fighting stance, though the tremble in her left hand and her heaving chest betrayed her fear.

"Elva? If you show yourself, I won't fight you."

Talia had always been the smart one in the group. I emerged from the shadows, daggers at the ready.

Her daggers thudded to the ground, and she retreated several steps. "I won't fight you. Take what you want."

I rolled my eyes. How she'd made it through training to be a warrior siren, I'd never know. Coral and River gathered behind Talia, and I eyed them both, knowing they couldn't be trusted.

"Untie him," I commanded, gesturing toward the battered and bound Njall. Talia obeyed me, but was interrupted as River lunged toward me with a sudden ferocity. I was caught off guard; I'd been expecting Coral's attack, not her's. I pivoted and slammed the heel of my hand into River's chin. She screamed, toppling into Talia, and they both crashed to the ground. Coral tried to capitalize on the chaos and moved for me, but Njall had gotten to his feet and lunged at her with all the force he could muster. With blood spurting from her nose, the siren clutched her face and let out a horrific wail.

I extended my claws and sliced through the rope binding Njall's wrists, then pushed one of my daggers into his hand. "Go," I ordered, but he hesitated, eyes darting between the wounded sirens and me.

"No," he replied.

"I don't have time to argue with you."

"Then don't."

He reeked of Talia, and I hated how much it bothered me. With a growl of frustration, I turned and stomped my boot down on Coral's hand as she reached for her fallen sword. "You have one chance."

"For what?" she spat through clenched teeth.

"Tell me the truth about what happened to my brothers ... before I decide you already hurt them and kill you."

"We sold them," Talia replied, voice trembling. "I'm sorry, Elva. We needed the money."

I glanced at River. She wouldn't meet my eyes, and I knew it was true.

"When?"

"Two days ago," Talia said, "to a group of guards." Coral tried to shush her, but Njall had picked up her blade and held it to her face, silencing her. Talia explained how they'd been discovered by the group of Huestur men who were hunting for me and Njall. Coral knew my brothers and that I had been responsible for freeing the prince. She'd been the one to rat us out. They took the gold in exchange for telling the men where my brothers were supposed to wait for me.

Their betrayal stung, but I understood why they'd done it. Unlike them, my brothers blend in and charm others into giving us what we need. Men didn't fear them; they didn't lose control in their presence. Mostly, guards would simply ignore us. Three female sirens traveling together would have none of those advantages. I didn't want to punish them for what they'd done to my brothers, but I needed to know they regretted their choice—that it had been a last resort.

"Where are you meeting them?" I demanded, narrowing my eyes as each siren averted her gaze from mine. Njall had to press the blade harder against Coral's cheek to get her to talk.

"How much?" I pressed on, arms crossed. "How much did they pay you to betray your kind?"

"Elva—" Coral began, but I threw a dagger at her. It whizzed past her cheek, slicing just enough to make her bleed. I knew it was deep enough to scar. Right now, I didn't care.

"A hundred gold pieces each. Not nearly enough," River finally answered.

"Liars," Njall spat. "They told me it was a thousand."

My hands clenched into tight fists when I heard that amount. At least they hadn't broken our code for some paltry sum, but a thousand gold pieces wouldn't last long, not with Talia and River's tastes. Anger seethed within me. I opened my hands, and my nails quickly sprouted into claws. It was already the end of my third week, and that meant my siren was hovering near the surface. If I lingered any longer, she'd wreak havoc on them all, and while I would love to see Coral on the ground, begging for mercy, my priority had to be getting my brothers back.

I turned and headed toward the dark woods.

"You're letting us go?" Talia asked, her voice laced with both relief and disbelief.

"Be grateful," I spat in reply, eyes blazing in a mixture of anger and sorrow. "I should kill you all for turning on your kind, but we lose enough of our kin to other species hating us. I will not add to that count unnecessarily."

"Thank you," Coral whispered.

I headed into the dark forest growth with Njall behind me. Neither of us said anything until we found a disintegrating log to sit on and let us catch our breath.

"I expected you to have run off," I said, breaking the long, awkward silence.

"I expected you to kill them. Guess we're both surprised."

I sighed and shrugged at him. "Killing my kind is harder than you'd expect. The pain lingers."

"Is that the only reason?"

I shook my head. "River is loud. She'd have screamed and brought the guards to us."

Njall regarded me solemnly and nodded, as if he understood all the conflicted feelings running through me. I could have asked him if he wanted them dead. It would have been the considerate thing to do, after what he had done to the captain for me, but my changing feelings for him were already getting me into trouble with my siren side, so I ignored it. But I should find out if he was okay.

"Are you alright? I mean, did they hurt you?"

He held his hands up, examining the damaged flesh on his wrists before looking at me. "I'll heal."

"Then let's go free my brothers."

Despite the dim morning light, we found our old camp, guided by the faint glow of dying embers. By the time we got there, the sun had risen. The knowledge that my brothers were being held by Huestur guards was infuriating and terrifying. Leifur would be fine. He knew how to keep his mouth shut, but if Sindri said something stupid, it would get them both into trouble. The idea sent me scrambling to pack our camp, shoving things randomly into bags without order or concern for what was mixed.

I startled when a gentle hand touched my shoulder, sending a shiver down my spine.

"Elva?"

"I'm fine," I snapped, wiping my tears with the back of my hand. I desperately tried to cram a small pot into the bag I was holding. When I failed, I broke, and my breathing became erratic. It was clear that I was in the last week of my cycle—always worse when I hadn't taken care of things by now. Frustrated, I threw the pot onto the ground only to realize the bag I was using was Njall's pants. I sank to the ground, tears streaming down my cheeks.

A comforting warmth enveloped me as Njall's arms wrapped around my shoulders. Affection from anyone other than my brothers wasn't something I usually sought, not since I'd been a teenager, but in that moment, I needed it more than I'd ever confess to anyone. So I let him hold me while I cried, releasing the fear for my brothers, the rage at my siren sisters' betrayal, and my hatred of how badly I'd botched what should have been a simple retrieval mission. As my violent sobs subsided, Njall shifted his position and pulled me close to him, stroking my hair and whispering it would be okay.

Exhaling contentedly, I nuzzled into Njall, letting him calm all the pain and rage churning inside me. When I turned to look at him, his face was right before mine, and he was watching me. I remembered what it felt like to kiss him, and how soft those lips were, but now, all I could smell was Talia. A jealousy I'd never known flared to life.

"We'll find them," Njall said softly, oblivious to the turmoil.

I pulled back sharply to escape the smell, grabbed the pot off the ground, and went to shove it into my bag. "I know," I replied solemnly. "And then I'll kill every man who dared to touch my brothers."

We worked in silence after that, gathering up the remaining items and loading up the horses. Their reins had loosened from the log we'd tied them to, but despite being left alone for hours, neither had gone anywhere. Either these were the most loyal horses ever to exist, or they were simply lazy, but I would not complain about it. I grabbed the mule's reins and scanned for the trail we'd used to sneak into the woods and hide from the road. Njall found it first, and soon enough, we were moving once more.

Despite the risk of being spotted, we stuck to the main road to make it to Coral's meeting point in time to save my brothers. The dew on the grass was completely gone by the time we found the narrow side road that Coral had described to me. I would have overlooked it, but a tree had fallen and covered the path near the road—a victim of the storm that hadn't yet been chopped into firewood. I dismounted to examine it. After I hacked off a large branch, I decided that the horses would have no issue going over it, and we were back to trot toward the meeting point.

As we rode, Njall broke the silence with a hushed query. "Elva?" He hesitated before continuing. "Do you have a plan for how we're going to get your brothers back?"

"Yes. I'll pretend to be working with Coral, and I'll convince them to take me to whoever is in charge so we can negotiate to give you to them, too. They won't be able to resist that. While I do that, you'll free them. It's the least you can do after you tried to get us arrested."

"You're going to throw that back in my face forever, aren't you?"

"Absolutely," I said with a sly smirk, pushing my horse forward.

A few minutes later, we heard shouts of laughter through the trees. "We should leave the horses here," Njall said. "If things go sour, we won't want to lose them."

I nodded and guided us toward a thicket near a towering oak tree that had many branches sticking out. I tied the horses to a low branch while Njall climbed up to scout the area.

"It's to the west," he said, jumping down and pointing through the trees. "They seem to be organized into three areas. If they're anything like my father's men, it'll be one for the highest ranks, another for standard forces, and the last for prisoners and waste."

"So we just have to figure out which one we each go to."

Njall nodded. I handed him my daggers and began rummaging through our supplies. His eyes flickered with curiosity as I pulled out my corseted top, but he said nothing. Without warning, I grabbed the bottom of my shirt and pulled it over my head, careful not to snag my hair. As I stuffed it into my pack, I realized he'd turned around to give me privacy. *Silly man.* I checked my wound, and it was still red along the scar, but the rest of my skin had reverted to its usual pale shade. Smiling to myself, I slipped into my corseted top and pulled the strings tightly along the front, sending my breasts spilling over the top enough to distract the guards.

I tapped Njall's shoulder. "Is this enough cleavage to seduce you?"

"I don't know how to answer that."

I rolled my eyes. "I travel with two gay sirens, I need a man who appreciates the female form to help me convince the guards that I'm a siren—the kind of siren *they* expect me to be."

Njall nodded, and I could feel his eyes rake over me. Finally, he beckoned me closer. He loosened the corset, so I didn't spill out as much, and pulled the straps from the top of my shoulder to the sides. "You should aim for *sultry*, not *easy*," he said. He also took my braid out, letting my wavy hair cascade across my bare shoulders. "Now the only thing you're missing is seaweed in your hair."

"Seaweed? Humans honestly think we walk around with seaweed in our hair?" I was incredulous. "You've obviously never come across week-old seaweed."

"Oh, I have," Njall said with a brief grin. "But I'm not all human males. Now go knock 'em dead."

"I will, if need be." I slid a dagger into each boot and slipped my small sheath into my waist so I could add one more. "Make sure you stay out of sight. I don't want to have to rescue three men today."

Njall smiled as he leaned against a tree. "I can handle myself."

"Take the ax," I said as I tiptoed out of our hiding spot toward the camp.

Chapter 38

Elva

Creeping through the woods wasn't as hard as I expected. The Huestur knights had found a huge clearing to set up their camp, so all I had to do was slink along the edge of it a few trees deep into the forest. The sprawling tents were a mix of dull khaki and muted greens. I'd stumbled upon the general population, not where I wanted to be. Men clad in green and brown weaved between the tents, carrying armloads of firewood back to the main area of the camp. Leaves crunched behind me, and I ducked just in time to hide from three men hauling a fallen tree back to the camp. As stealthily as possible, I hurried along the tree line.

The khaki colored tents gave way to green and browns, and then richer shades of green adorned with family crests—a telltale sign that I'd found the nobles' quarters. Standing up, I checked myself over and was happy to see nothing had snagged my shirt or pants while I was moving through the forest. I tousled my hair with my fingers and adjusted my shoulder straps to hang lower and push up the girls. Lifting my chin with all the confidence I could muster, I strutted into the camp as if I belonged there.

Giving myself a moment to take a deep breath, I pivoted and spotted another knight across the way. He had dark hair and was wearing leather rather than armor. It only took him a minute to spot me, so I glanced around the area quickly while he walked over to me. There were only about twenty tents of various sizes and shades, all centered on a huge fire pit. None looked large or extravagant enough to house the general or whoever was leading this manhunt, so I focused on the man coming for me. He looked younger than the other knights I'd come across, perhaps the son of one of the older, more experienced knights. I smiled coquettishly at him and playfully twirled a few strands of hair between my fingers.

"Are you a siren?" he asked, looking me up and down, before focusing on my breasts.

I let out the sweet giggle I'd been taught from a young age. "Of course I am, silly. Who else has such lovely blue hair?" I walked my fingers up his torso and batted my eyelashes at him. "I'm here to speak to your ..." I hesitated, unsure of the proper title.

"Captain?" he offered helpfully.

I smiled innocently. "How'd you know?"

"I'm trained to anticipate the needs of those around me," he said matter-of-factly, exuding confidence and pride.

"Are you now? That must come in handy." I slid my arm through the crook of his elbow and turned us away from the forest toward the firepit. As if by his own volition, he led me past the larger tents where we stumbled across more knights, until I saw the largest tent I'd ever seen. It sparkled in the morning light as if it had been made from spun gold, and it looked as if it contained at least five rooms. At the door stood two very tall and stoic guards, and unlike the young man who'd brought me here, they were dressed in full armor. Before he could say a word, I gave the young man a quick little kiss on the cheek and strode over to the guards.

To my surprise, they made no move to halt or question me. Instead, they dutifully pulled open the fabric door. "Captain Siegfried has been expecting you," one said.

"Thank you, boys," I crooned and sashayed into the tent.

The doors closed behind me, and my breath caught in my throat. The scale of the place left me breathless. Offshoots jutted out in multiple directions; two of which had curtain doors and three of which were just open. One area housed a dining table, while another had a desk covered in papers, and the final one boasted a few comfortable looking chairs. How they transported those, I didn't even want to know. Simple rugs covered the entire floor, while exquisite tapestries hung from the ceiling. A few scattered hall tables held pricey looking knick-knacks. As I reached out to touch a delicate mermaid statue, a deep voice rumbled behind me.

"So, Coral sent me a new pretty siren to deliver her bad news?"

I spun around, trying to look sweet but a little guilty from touching his things. The captain was a giant of a man. He stood nearly seven feet tall, with thick salt and pepper hair, several days of stubble, and a large scar across his cheek. My siren stirred within me, and I had to bite the inside of my cheek to silence her so I could focus on the mission at hand. If I had met him at any other place, I would have taken him right there.

"She thought you'd take it better from me than her," I replied with a coy smile, twirling my hair seductively.

The captain's eyes roamed over me appreciatively as he leaned against the pole that held up one doorway in his tent. "If you're my gift for being patient, I certainly can't complain."

In a sudden burst of motion, he grabbed me around the waist

and pressed his lips to mine. Bodies entwined, we stumbled toward the curtain, which he pushed aside to reveal the entrance to his sleeping quarters. His private sanctuary was smaller than the other rooms, and dominated by a large bedroll piled high with sumptuous furs.

Heat exploded through me as his rough hands groped at my breasts, and his mouth moved to kiss my neck. Not one to miss an opportunity, especially this late in my cycle, I slid my hand between us to stroke him through his pants while moaning in encouragement.

A deep guttural groan left him, and he spun me around to face him. I unfastened his belt and ripped it from his pants before opening the buttons and freeing his cock. His huge hands gripped my cheeks and pulled my mouth to his. The captain was skilled; his tongue slipped into my mouth while his hand moved down my body, grabbing my ass and pressing me against him so he could grind his cock against me. My hands roamed up his chest inside his loose-fitting tunic, and when he pulled his lips away, I immediately missed the contact.

Gripping the bottom of his shirt with one hand, I pulled it over his head and tossed it on the floor. He made light work of my corset by gripping both halves and ripping it down the middle, sending my breasts bouncing free. Palming one breast, he spun me around so my back was pressed against his chest and slid his hand down the front of my pants. I whimpered when his fingers found my core, and he shoved two deep inside me, making me dig my nails into his thigh for support.

"*Ferflucs*, I love how soaked sirens always are," he growled in my ear. "No foreplay needed with you." He pinched my nipple, and I let out a cry of pleasure as he removed his fingers from me. A wet sucking sound filled my ear before he ripped the front of my pants open and used his foot to push them down my legs.

"Now get on your knees and suck my cock, little siren. Earn my forgiveness for your captain's failure."

The idea of surrendering to him infuriated me, but I knew I had to keep him busy long enough for Njall to save my brothers. I lowered myself to the ground, intending to give him a show. But the captain was not a patient man. Fisting my hair, he shoved his cock into my mouth the moment I was on my knees. Needing to breathe, I pushed myself away from him and moved my hand to stroke his impressive length. The captain groaned and tightened his grip on my hair as I ran my tongue up along his shaft. I peeked up at him; as expected, he was staring down at me. Smiling sweetly, I licked the head of his cock before taking as much as I could down my throat.

This groan was twice as loud as the first one, and after a few more head bobs and swallows, he released my hair and pushed me forward onto my hands and knees. I slid forward, nearly falling on my face as he rammed his cock into me in a single thrust. Calloused hands groped my breasts and pulled me back as he slammed into me again and again. While his size had been impressive, his skills were mediocre, but I tried to make the best of the situation. If I could get him to finish, at least my siren would be silenced for another month. I sucked in a breath and let out the best moan I could muster under the circumstances. He bought it, and his grunts grew louder as his thrusts grew more vigorous.

"*Ferflucs!* You feel amazing," he moaned as he moved his hands to my hips and squeezed me so hard I knew I'd bruise. "And you take my cock so well! I might have to keep you and bring you back to Huestur with me."

Fat chance.

He slapped my ass, so I moaned again, giving him what I knew he wanted to hear. "Yeah, take my cock, you little siren whore. You love my enormous cock, don't you?"

Before I could reply, he slapped my ass again, this time hard enough to sting. But before I could react, a sickeningly sweet voice came from the main room.

Chapter 39

Njall

Ax in hand, I walked the opposite way Elva had gone, hoping that we'd picked the correct directions. I'd grabbed a strip of fabric from one bag, and every twenty steps, I tied a piece to the end of a branch. This would help us find our way back to the horses in a hurry, if we had to. Sticking close to the tree line, I couldn't hear much coming from the camp, which gave me hope I was in the right place.

As I walked, the scent of burning wood and roasting meat filled the air, accompanied by the rhythmic clang of hammer on steel; the telltale signs of a working camp. Stepping out of the trees, I found myself behind a group of small tents. I couldn't believe my luck; between the last two was a pile of uniform shirts. The putrid stench told me it was the laundry pile, but I couldn't let that stop me. I rummaged through it until I found a set in my size and slinked back into the trees to change.

This time, I emerged from the trees with a newfound confidence and an armful of wood. I barely made it into the open area past the tents when a knight barked at me to deliver the wood to the large firepit with the spit on it. I dropped my head and hurried along, depositing the wood where I'd been instructed before I glanced around quickly. With everyone preoccupied with their tasks, no one seemed to notice me, so I hooked my ax on my belt and set off to find the prisoners.

As I made my rounds, I overheard several guards talking about their plans.

"Do you think the sirens will find the prince?" A young soldier asked his older companion.

"Sirens can find anything if it has a dick," the older man replied. "The real question is whether the captain will share them with us after he gets what he wants."

The memory of Talia and River's hands and lips on me flooded my mind, but I held back the gag. I'd used women for sex before, and I'd been used to make other men jealous, but the idea of those sirens touching me again was revolting. There was only one siren I wanted, and while I understood their nature, that Elva would be with other men, even if it was to protect us, filled me with a rage I wasn't used to. I hurried on to the next group, where I found what I was looking for.

"Why do we always have to watch the captives?" a guard who looked maybe fifteen whined. "I want to go hunting too."

His friend chuckled. "It's going to be a while before they give you a bow again."

"Shooting the hunting dog keeper in the foot was an accident. I wouldn't do it again."

"Tell him that," his friend said, laughing even louder now.

I stalked the two as they made their way across the camp. We reached a large, windowless wagon parked beside a brown tent when they turned around and noticed me.

I held up my ax and rolled my eyes. "Anyone want to trade wood collecting for guard duty?"

The young men shook their heads. "Who'd you piss off?" The first one asked.

"Apparently, everyone," I replied nonchalantly and kept going.

Out of their line of sight, I crept behind the tent to eavesdrop. The current guards briefed the new ones, forbidding them from talking to the prisoners or engaging with them in any way. They were extremely dangerous, even if they didn't look it. The younger guards seemed only half-interested, having likely received this same warning every time they got stuck with this job.

After a few minutes of silence, I dared to glance around the tent wall and saw a pair of older guards emerge and walk toward the wagon. I watched them go up the stairs and fiddle with what could only be a lock before throwing open the door.

"Don't get any bright ideas, you mutts," the taller man bellowed.

"If you give those boys a hard time tonight, you'll deal with us in the morning," the second man chimed in before he slammed the door shut and they departed from the wagon. I wanted to run up the stairs and look just to be sure it was them, but I knew that would be stupid. Instead, I slipped back into the woods and took a quick walk around, seeing what else was in this part of the camp.

My lucky streak had ended. There was no armory, no food stores, and nothing else of excitement here. The only thing I found was the horses, and while not what I hoped for, I was glad to know they were here in case things went bad and I needed to make a quick getaway. On my way back to the wagon, I stumbled upon a lad sprawled out on the grass. Inspiration struck, and I snatched his bottle of ale before heading to the tent where the young guards were. I waited. The first time they left the tent to check the wagon, I managed to find a loose flap in the tent and slipped the bottle inside, far enough out of sight that they could have overlooked it, but easy enough to spot when they came back in.

My plan worked. In no time, the young guards were laughing and slurring their words, and I darted up the steps of the wagon. My ax made quick work of the lock, and I stepped inside.

The room was only as dark as the streets of Tyndorf when the last lanterns were still glowing, but the smell was worse than the brothel in the middle of summer. Everything stank of piss and rotten food. As my eyes adjusted to the dark, I could make out Leifur and Sindri on the ground. Their clothes were filthy, and both were sitting on the wooden floor. It was strewn with food, feces, and what looked like a dead rat. Massive chains tethered them by the ankles to the rear wall.

Leifur was the first to spot me and sat up as quickly as if he'd been stung. "Njall?"

"What?" Sindri joined him, and they were on their feet coming toward me until the chain stopped them a few paces away.

"What are you doing here?" Leifur asked, his voice filled with hope that made my heart ache.

Sindri cut in, his eyes searching for his twin. "Where's Elva?" he demanded.

"Your sister is busy creating a diversion while I free you."

Sindri sighed, and his shoulders dropped in clear relief, before Leifur patted them. "How are you planning to get us out of this?" Sindri asked, pulling on the chain.

I handed my ax to Leifur, who stared at me for a moment before glancing from the ax to the chains on the ground.

Any blacksmith should have been able to break the chain with that axe. "What do you need?" I asked.

"Can you help hold Sindri's chain?" He grabbed the part closest to the siren's ankle.

"I can, if you promise not to cut my hand off."

"If I found out you did anything to Elva while we were in here, I'll do more than that," he said, as I kneeled to pull the chain tight for him.

"Sorry, love," Leifur said to Sindri. "You'll have to live with the ankle bracelet for a little longer. This isn't the right tool for getting it off."

Sindri nodded, and Leifur swung the ax.

Elva

My ass stung from the captain's last slap, as he dug his fingers into my hips and pounded into me so hard it drove the breath from my lungs. Then, a horrible voice cut through the air, sickeningly sweet and melodic.

"Oh, Siegfried, I'm here to beg your forgiveness."

What is Coral doing here?

Knowing I was about to be found out, I closed my eyes and allowed just a sliver of my siren to surface, hoping I wouldn't need to give her full control. The captain continued his grunting behind me until the curtain was swept aside and Coral burst into view. Her jaw dropped in surprise. I smirked; now I had hope that Njall would be successful.

Coral looked at the man behind me, and he chuckled.

"Your payment for failing is amazing," Siegfried groaned, driving his nails painfully into my flesh.

Coral crossed her arms and turned her gaze to me. "He's terrible at that, isn't he?"

"What did you say, whore?" The captain shoved me off of him, and I slammed into the ground. I bit my lip so hard I tasted blood. By the time I got to my feet, he'd crossed the room and grabbed Coral by the neck. Her eyes darkened, and her claws burst from her fingers, but his arms were too long, and she was trapped.

It took me a second to adjust to the light as my eyes switched, and pain ripped through my gums as my teeth lengthened into razor-sharp fangs. My fingers were going to hurt tomorrow, but I stretched my hands out, and when the dagger's sharp talons appeared, I jammed them into the captain's back.

The scream he released sounded more like a dying cat mixed with a baby than a giant man, but he dropped Coral and spun to face me—his second mistake. The first had been trying to kill a siren in front of me. I hadn't extracted my claws from his body when he turned, so he ended up slicing his flesh open, sending blood spraying all over me.

"Ferflucsing whore," was all he could mutter as he started choking on his blood and spitting it out toward me before collapsing to his knees. Coral struggled to breathe on the ground, and I went to help her when I heard metal clanging outside.

"Help!" Coral screamed. "The siren killed the captain and tried to strangle me! Stop her."

I glared at her with contempt. "You always were spineless," I spat before slashing my claws across her neck, leaving her as a bloody heap on the ground just as the guards burst into the room. I swallowed back the acid rising from my stomach. Killing was one thing, but killing my kind sickened me, even if she had been terrible in life.

The curtain flew open, revealing four men. Standing there covered in their captain's blood, I only had one option: sing. These men had done business with Coral, so I wasn't sure how adept I'd be at keeping their attention for an extended period, so I needed to move. It certainly helped that I was naked. The men all froze, and while continuing to sing, I reached back to grab my clothes and stuffed them into a nearby satchel.

To save time, I donned the captain's shirt, and once my boots were on, I plunged my claws into the necks of the men until all four lay bleeding on the ground, gagging and coughing on their blood as it poured into and from the holes my claws left. Coral lay lifeless beside the captain as I grabbed the sword she had on her hip. Hearing more men outside, I snatched a dagger from one of the fallen guards and sprinted toward what looked like the back of the tent, slicing open the fabric to make my escape.

A group of about twelve guards was outside the tent.

"Ferflucs," I cursed. This was too many for me to sing into submission. My heart pounded in my chest, and my throat burned from all the dust I'd inhaled earlier. The only advantage I had was their lack of armor, but I was still severely outnumbered. I turned to run to the side, but three of the guards barricaded my path. I swallowed hard and opened my mouth to sing despite the odds. Then, one man at the back collapsed forward, followed by another a second later. Several of the guards turned to investigate their fallen comrades, only to be struck in the face by flying rocks. A rock nearly the size of a melon whizzed past me, and I could have wept for relief.

"Elva, go!" Leifur shouted, but before I could move, a guard seized me from behind. I struggled to scratch him with my claws without grazing myself, when he was forcefully ripped away. The abrupt release sent me stumbling backward, but I never hit the ground.

Njall's firm grip steadied me. As Leifur smashed another guard in the face with a rock, I spotted yet another charging toward us from the tent opening. Time seemed to slow, and without hesitation, I lashed at him, slicing his throat with my talons. Blood sprayed as he stumbled back, colliding with one of the tent's support beams. As the first beam went down, the force of it took the next one, and soon half the captain's tent crumpled to the ground.

In the chaos, I took down another guard while Leifur and Njall dispatched the rest. The ground was littered with bloodied bodies as shouts echoed through the clearing. Leifur took my bag, while Njall grasped my hand, somehow avoiding my still-extended claws. The three of us sprinted toward the woods.

"Where's Sindri?" I yelled as we darted into the tree line.

"With our horses," Njall shouted back, tugging me to the left.

"But Leifur—"

"Your brother is getting his horse from the other side," Njall said, pulling away before I could argue. "We're heading for the one we hid here."

"How can we possibly escape on one horse?"

Njall grinned. "Because your twin just freed all the other horses in the camp."

Clever. I followed him into a small clearing, and my eyes widened in awe. "That's the biggest horse I've ever seen."

"It's a destrier," Njall said. "Bred to charge into battle carrying armored knights."

As shouts rang out behind us, Njall hoisted himself onto the saddle and extended his hand. I gripped the saddle horn with one arm while he pulled me up by the other, settling me securely in front of him. He wrapped his arm securely around my waist, took hold of the reins, and urged the massive destrier forward.

"Hang on tight. This is going to be a rough ride."

Clinging to the saddle horn with one hand, and Njall's arm with the other, I braced myself as he spurred the horse and we took off.

Calling the ride bumpy was an understatement. I nearly tumbled off the oversized saddle more than once, but somehow Njall always gripped me tighter before I could fall. He took us through the woods back to the main road, where Sindri was waiting with Acorn. Not a minute later, Leifur emerged from the woods on another swift steed. As I moved to dismount, the prince tightened his hold on me.

"Not yet," he said. "Your mule is the slowest. She'll be faster with a lighter load."

Hearing the commotion in the woods behind us, I knew it was better not to argue and stayed put. Sindri had done a great job releasing all the horses. When we finally saw Huestur's men leaving the woods, they were all on foot. We exchanged broad grins and picked up the pace to get away from them.

We rode the horses as long as it was safe before I left Njall's horse and climbed back onto my mule. By the time we crossed the southern stretch of the Bloot River, the sun had dipped below the horizon. We followed the base of the Crimson Mountains, aiming to avoid small towns and settlements for the next week or two until we reached the Forest of Endilaus again. Njall and Sindri were doubtful, but Leifur and I were confident this was the best way to evade not only the Huestur men but also anyone else who might come looking for us to collect the bounty on our heads. Now that I'd killed both a captain of an army and a siren warrior, we'd have to be extra cautious. Even though Coral had been banished from Konvern, our kind did not take well to one of their own being slain.

We found a secluded mountain offshoot to set up camp and tended to the horses before seeking out a stream. All of us desperately needed a bath to scrub away the day's horrors. My travels with the sirens had taught me that certain parts of the Crimson Mountains contained hot springs, but that day we only found a cold one. Thankfully, I'd thought ahead and ordered everyone to bring extra clothes. Njall's and my clothes weren't in terrible shape, but Leifur and Sindri had been in the same ones since we left the beach, and those were beyond saving.

The spring we discovered was a haven: crystal clear and surrounded by towering trees, bushes, and wildflowers. The faint scent of peppermint and rose hung in the air. Never had I been more grateful to avoid a mountain runoff spring—washing off blood in a Bloot River stream would have been futile.

Sindri was the first of us to strip and leap into the water, tossing his stinky clothes at me with a grin. Leifur and Njall chuckled, but I quickly shed the oversized shirt I'd stolen from the captain, and after hurling it at Njall, leapt in after my twin. I moved swiftly to avoid any of them catching sight of the marks on my body after my failed tryst with the captain. Soon enough, Leifur and Njall joined us, and we spent what felt like an eternity soaking in the glorious water, allowing all the grime to wash away from our bodies.

"Elva, catch!" Sindri yelled as he lobbed the soap my way. I missed it and watched as it sank beneath the surface.

I shot him a narrowed look. "Whoever fetches it doesn't have to help with dinner," I called out and dove back into the water. The cool liquid enveloped me, washing away not just the dirt, but some of the tension that had been clinging to me all day. Having Leifur and Sindri back by my side, knowing we were all together and on our way to achieve the impossible, felt like a dream come true.

Ripples fanned out across the water as the others broke the surface to search for the soap to claim their prize. Holding my hair back, I scanned the floor of the spring for it while tiny flecks of dried blood floated away from my arms and chest. A flash of blue caught my eye as Leifur darted down to the muddy bottom. I hadn't seen any light colors there, so I turned my attention behind me, hoping the force of Sindri's throw had sent it that way.

I dove as quickly as I could and scanned the depths for the soap until I spotted a white shape nestled in some algae. Just as I reached for it, a hand shot out and snatched it before I could grasp it. Looking up, I expected to see Sindri, but found Njall's smirking face instead. He pushed off the bottom and disappeared into the depths, leaving me frustrated but amused.

When I resurfaced, the men were already arguing.

"Elva will be on wood and fire duty," Njall said. "You two cook and clean."

"I'm telling you now that just means Leifur will be doing all the cooking and cleaning," I said, swimming over to Njall and snatching the soap from his hand so I could wash my hair.

Leifur motioned for me to join him. I swam closer and handed him the soap, letting my brother-in-law lather my hair and scratch my scalp in a way that felt like pure bliss. When I opened my eyes, neither Sindri nor Njall was around. Both had climbed out of the water, leaving me alone with Leifur.

"Why'd they leave us?" I asked, as I used the soap to scrub the rest of the dried blood from my abdomen and breasts.

"Sindri was worried. How far along are you?"

"Twenty-two days, I think."

"We're cutting it close. Are you sure you can last a few more days?" His voice was gentle, and I knew what he was offering.

No. I won't let it come to that.

"I was close today, but it's just been a lot, and I can't reign her in like I usually do."

"That explains it," he said, tapping my temple gently. I dunked myself into the water, allowing him to work the soap from my hair. "I take it you were interrupted before he could finish."

I curled my legs up to my chest, wading with my arms to keep myself afloat. "Yes. *Ferflucsing* Coral was the cause."

"I hate her. When we see her next time, I'll—"

"There won't be a next time," I whispered, meeting his gaze, and hoping he wouldn't press further. He cocked his head and nodded briefly to let me know he understood.

Coral had been as much a rival as a friend, but being forced to kill her would haunt me more than any of the other times I'd killed. Finally reaching the edge of the spring, I pulled myself up, letting my hair fall wherever it wanted. Leifur followed, tossing the soap into the grass before climbing out and offering his hands to help me out.

"Elva?" he whispered, as I swung my arms in circles to dry myself off.

"Yes?"

"Thank you."

I turned back and gave Leifur a peck on the cheek. "And don't worry. I'll let you know if my urges are going to get me in trouble."

"I can see them hovering on the surface."

"Let's hope a hot meal and a good night's sleep will take the edge off."

Leifur grinned, holding his hands apart in an exaggerated gesture. "Or perhaps ... a certain *very* well-endowed prince." I turned to slap him, but he'd already darted away, cackling.

Chapter 41

Njall

As I laid out the bedrolls around the fire, I couldn't help but notice Sindri and Leifur whispering to each other. "What are you two talking about?" I asked.

"Nothing," Leifur said dismissively. But before I could press further, Sindri chimed in with a cheeky grin, "The size of your cock. Elva told us you were well endowed, but I didn't realize just how well."

"Thank you?" I was taken aback, unsure of how to handle a siren complimenting my dick. "She told you about our night?" I asked cautiously.

"She tells us about all her men," Sindri said, nonchalantly checking on the pot of stew on the fire before plopping down beside me. "It's one advantage of having an unattached sister when you're married."

"What did she say?"

Sindri grinned, but just as he was about to speak, Leifur interjected, "Don't tell him. She won't appreciate it, and you know how she gets this part of her cycle."

"She can't be worse than my sister," I said.

Sindri raised an eyebrow, a mischievous glint in his eye. "Oh, trust me she can. Female sirens have to mate every cycle, and if they don't, they go insane and kill people. Usually men."

"What?" I asked, horrified by the implications of this revelation.

Leifur stepped in, clearly trying to allay my fears. "As usual, my love made it sound weird. Female sirens have to mate with a male creature every cycle to continue our species," he explained. "If they don't manage to do that within four weeks, then the next day they find the closest male and mate him."

"Repeatedly," Sindri added matter-of-factly. "And then kill him."

"It didn't sound that bad until the killing part."

"Luckily, it hasn't come to that often for Elva," Sindri said. "Having Leifur around has helped us more than once."

I stared at him in disbelief. "Are you saying your sister ... has slept with your husband?"

Sindri shrugged. "Many times," he said. "That's how we met. Leifur was assigned to Elva."

"I know ... she told me that's how you met. I meant after you married."

"Oh," Leifur said, finally understanding. "Still yes, but only in desperate times."

"So you're a sultry siren too? Is that how you were so good at your job of helping female sirens?"

Leifur chuckled softly. "No. I'm a normal siren, but males are rare, and we have an easier time impregnating our females than other species do. My problem was that I fell in love with the female sirens, and then when they got pregnant and left, I was heartbroken."

Sindri smiled at his husband. "Until me," he breathed, as Leifur leaned down to kiss him.

I tried to process everything they were telling me and Elva's role in it all. "So if I understand correctly, Elva sleeps with a man every month to keep things normal?"

"Yes," Leifur confirmed.

"Is that why she slept with me when she came to town?"

Sindri shook his head slightly. "I can't remember exactly where she was in her cycle then," he admitted. "Leifur usually does that, but once we were in town, she had her pick of males, so don't think that she *only* slept with you for that reason."

"She found you very attractive," Leifur added. "And between us, she was very satisfied after her night with you."

A small smirk spread across my lips. *She was lying about it being forgettable. Not that it matters now.* But then another realization hit. "It's been a few weeks since we escaped the castle. Does that mean she's getting dangerous now? Is that how she could kill so many people today in the camp?"

"Yes and no," Leifur said, glancing nervously at Sindri before continuing. "The killing was because she's a warrior siren. She tried to take care of things with the captain while you rescued us, but Coral interrupted them, so she has less than a week to go."

"But no scales yet," Sindri added.

"Scales?" I asked.

"The day before her cycle ends, she'll get shimmering scales on her," Sindri explained. "It's a final warning of sorts."

Leifur nodded firmly, lifting the spoon to check the stew. "And that's when I step in."

I was still trying to wrap my head around everything they were telling me about sirens and their cycles. Some of it, Elva had already explained at the cabin, but the implications of it hadn't sunk in until now. "How is it you're a sultry siren, and she's a warrior?" I asked. "I mean, since you're twins, shouldn't you be the same type?"

Sindri looked away briefly. "We should have been," he admitted softly. "But Elva's siren was made."

"Made?" I repeated.

Sindri and Leifur looked around apprehensively before turning back to me. "Sirens are normally born as warriors, sultry or normal," Leifur said. "But in rare cases, a sultry or normal siren will become a warrior."

"How?" I asked.

Sindri and Leifur exchanged an uneasy glance before continuing their explanation. "Something terrible happens," Sindri whispered finally. "And it changes them."

"What happened to her?"

Leifur took a deep breath. "You know how selkies and sirens work, right?"

"More than you realize, now that Elva corrected all the mistakes I was taught."

"Sirens appear normal, but turn into bloodthirsty beasts to feed and mate," Leifur said.

I nodded in understanding and looked at the sirens expectantly.

"Fine," Sindri said, as Leifur tossed another log onto the fire and settled next to him. "From what I can tell, Elva and I are not exactly half selkie and siren. I'm more siren, and I believe she's more selkie."

I raised an eyebrow in disbelief. "What do you mean? She's the most blood thirsty siren of the three of you."

Leifur stepped in. "That's because her siren is buried so deeply within her. Warrior sirens are normally sirens through and through. Elva's only allowed out when she needs it, and the siren doesn't like that. It makes her extra ruthless. Whenever she lets the siren take control, it ends up very bloody."

Sindri continued where Leifur left off. "My sister was born a sultry siren like I am. When she was younger, she was even more gorgeous than she is now. Her skin glistened, and her blue and green hair was thicker and richer than any other siren in our entire kingdom ... and the other girls hated her for it." Sindri wiped his hands on his pants, and Leifur patted his back, taking over the story.

"Sindri is less selkie and more siren. So his selkie only comes out in water—he grows scales and gills, that's it. But Elva has a deeper connection to that heritage. Her abilities in water far outweigh any siren, but they are tied to a part of her ... and those wicked girls learned that."

"What part of her? You can't exactly remove a body part—" but the words left my mouth as I looked at her brother's shaved head. "It's her hair."

Sindri nodded. "The girls cut her hair in jealousy, and Elva became ill while it grew back. It only took a day, but the damage was done. The others knew that to weaken my sister, they only needed to cut her hair. They made a game of it to see who could cut the most before she would fight back."

"So, her fighting back was enough to make her a warrior?" I asked, still confused how something as simple as hair could have such a profound effect on Elva. But then I felt my pendant shift in my shirt. I moved my hand and grasped it through the fabric. I hated to be without it, and it felt like a piece of me was missing when I left it behind.

Sindri hesitated before continuing, in almost a whisper. "That was only the start. What happened the year we were to discover our types finished it." He stared into the fire, lost in thought.

"Sindri," Leifur cautioned. "I don't know if we should tell this story."

But Sindri was resolute. "He needs to know. Elva intends to settle down in Tyndorf or at least outside the kingdom walls. Njall deserves to know what can happen if you cross her."

"Then tell him that, not all of it," Leifur hissed.

I was going to ask them what could be so bad when a loud

pop erupted from the fire, and Elva appeared behind it, her arms laden with firewood. She glared at her brother with the same resentment my brother Ingvar would send my way anytime I did something better than him.

"Elva, you're back," Sindri said as he stood, trying to ease the tension, yet Elva's glare remained unchanged.

"And you're running your mouth again."

Leifur leaped to his feet and stepped between them, taking the wood from Elva. "Let's not start anything. We're all just tired and hungry. I'm sure a hot bowl of stew will soothe everything."

"We aren't tired enough," Elva retorted coldly. "All it takes for my brother to tell the world my business is for me to go gather wood."

"It's not the entire world." Sindri bristled defensively. "It's Njall—the prince you insisted we save."

In an instant, Elva leaped for him and gave him a shove, sending him reeling backward away from the fire. "My story is not yours to tell! Stop exploiting my trauma for your entertainment!"

"It's not entertainment," Sindri shouted back, scrambling to his feet. "It's an explanation."

Elva's eyes blazed with fury. "An explanation for what?" she screamed at him.

"For why you resent everyone and turn into such a vicious monster to protect yourself." Sindri blurted.

His words hung heavily in the air. Regret filled his face, and Elva's shoulders slumped. All of her rage was gone, replaced by an overwhelming pain.

"Elva, he didn't mean it," Leifur said, attempting to comfort her, but she recoiled from his touch.

"Perhaps that's the first honest thing to come out of his mouth." Elva turned and stormed around the fire. My heart clenched in my chest at the raw agony etched in her face, but before I could say anything, Elva trudged away from us back into the darkness of the woods. Sindri moved to follow, but Leifur grabbed him.

"No. We can't chase after her right now. She just needs space."

Sindri dropped back to the fire and wrapped his arms around himself. "I wouldn't have told it. I was just going to warn him."

"I know," Leifur said, rubbing his back while I watched Elva fade into the dark night.

Chapter 42

Njall

None of us got any sleep that night. Elva stormed off into the woods and didn't return until dawn broke. Even then, she refused to utter a word to anyone. Despite Leifur's warnings, Sindri tried to get her to talk, but all it got him was a swift right hook to the face and a black eye. After that, we all gave her a wide berth.

With tensions running high, we swiftly gathered our supplies and set off along the mountain base, hoping to slip past the last of the Huestur territory and make good time to the Forest of Endilaus. I knew once we arrived there, we'd find more of my father's men and allies to help us should we need it. Elva maintained her silence the entire day, which made the rest of us afraid to speak.

Watching her ferociously fight the Huestur guards had been a harrowing experience, more brutal than when General Magni had challenged the former general to take his title in Tyndorf. In my homeland, the king appointed generals, but required them to prove their mettle in combat by killing the current general—another one of my family's cruel traditions designed to control the population with fear rather than respect.

But after seeing Elva fight, I was sure she could best one of our generals, especially if her enchanting song were added to the mix.

The oppressive silence lasted for an entire day and another night. This time, she slept with us at camp, but she moved her bedroll as far away as possible, even foregoing the one blanket we had to share. It wasn't until we made camp on the third day that she finally spoke, though it was only to tell us she was going hunting.

"I'll come with you," Sindri said.

"No," was all Elva would say.

"Then take Leifur," he protested. "It's dangerous here."

Elva's glare would have scared any man in my father's army.

Sensing the tension between the siblings, I stepped in. "I have to collect wood. I'll stay close to her," I offered. A quick glance was her only reply before she vanished into the woods, leaving me to chase her.

We ventured deeper into the woods, sticks and leaves crunching beneath our boots. The late-daylight cast long shadows across the forest floor, making it difficult to track anything for dinner.

"I don't need a guard." Elva finally said after we'd gotten away from her brothers.

"I know you don't—"

"Good. Then you can collect your wood and go back."

"But Sindri is right. There are a lot of creatures here."

Elva rolled her eyes. "Which I'm not scared of," she retorted.

"No, but I am," I said sheepishly. I cocked my head to the side and grinned playfully. "Did you even stop to consider that I wanted you to protect me?"

Elva shook her head and turned to keep walking. I hurried after her, intending to bring up the conversation from the other night, but I wasn't sure how to.

"Njall?" Elva stopped between a pair of trees and looked back at me. "I'm sorry."

"For what?" I asked, taking a tentative step toward her.

"For not stepping in sooner ... when Coral and the sirens had you."

"You did."

"But not soon enough."

"You were there?" Realization dawned. "Wait, you were *there?*"

She nodded briefly. "Near the end."

I pictured Talia's face when she'd used me. River's song had been so different from Elva's—harsh, lacking the warmth that made Elva's voice feel like a balm to my soul. As much as the memory of Talia and River revolted me, it made me realize that what I'd felt with Elva had nothing to do with her being a siren. It was just *her.* Her laughter, her defiance, her quiet vulnerability. When I got home, Baldr would get a kick out of the story, after how many times I woke up in strange beds after drinking too much with him, but I could see the fear lingering in Elva's eyes, deeper and darker than she let on.

Her gaze lifted to meet mine, hollow and searching, as if waiting for something. What exactly, I wasn't sure. Did she want forgiveness for not stopping Talia, or something deeper? Our conversation from the other night resurfaced in my mind, and without thinking, I stepped closer, taking her hands in mine. They were cold and I expected her to pull away, but she didn't. Instead, she let me raise them to my mouth, where I blew warm air against her chilled fingers.

"You don't have to tell me," I said softly, "but if you want to share ... what it was that made you a warrior ... I'd like to know."

Her eyes grew wet with tears, and her lips twisted into a scowl. "Why? So you can be entertained? Hear what stupid things the young siren did?" She tried to pull her hands free, but I held them firm.

"No. So I can try to make it better for you."

She stared at me, her mouth parting slightly as if in shock. Her eyes locked onto mine, unblinking, searching.

"Some things you can't fix," she whispered, barely audible.

I stepped closer, my fingers tightening around hers. "I'd still like to try."

She swallowed hard and looked away from me for a long minute. "I was young and stupid," she murmured, as if speaking more to herself. "I loved a boy and ... I thought he loved me, but he just wanted to brag about bedding a siren. He brought his friends, and ... they ..." Her voice cracked, and she paused, her jaw clenched tightly as she fought to continue. "Afterward ... it was the elder male sirens who put me back together. And the warriors—they protected me. So I became one of them, so no one would ever make me feel weak again."

Her guilt for not stopping Talia and the others made sense now. So did her caution around men, her walls, her refusal to let anyone close. That she'd needed to use her body to save me from some guards made me want to retch, but then an even darker thought hit me. *What happened to them?*

Elva's expression had gone stoic just before she looked away into the near darkness, her eyes scanning the forest as if searching for something—anything—to distract her from the memories. Then, without warning, she sniffed the air sharply, her head jerking toward me. Her eyes widened in realization. "Do you smell that?"

"Smell what?" Her sudden change confused me.

"Rotten eggs." Her eyes lit up, and she took off into the brush, leaving me to scramble after her.

"Elva, slow down," I called after her. As we ran through the dense undergrowth, the stench of sulfur grew stronger. When I emerged from the trees, Elva was already leaning over the edge of a steaming hot spring, gliding her hand along the water with a big grin on her face.

I joined her, crouching to dip my hand into the warm, bubbling pool. "I've only ever read of natural hot springs," I said, longing to strip and experience the soothing waters for myself. "Is it safe?"

Elva nodded, her eyes shining with excitement. "The water's clear, and if it were too hot, it would have burned us by now."

I stood up and shook the water from my hand. "Should we get your brothers?"

Elva's fingers curled around her shirt, ready to strip, but she stopped and glared at me. "No."

I wanted to say something else, but as she pulled off her shirt and slid out of her pants, I found myself lost for words. My eyes followed her movements as she lowered her glistening legs into the water. As she turned, I caught sight of something glinting on her tailbone—a pair of scales, faint but unmistakable. *Ferflucs. She's running out of time.*

I stripped in seconds, leaving my clothes in a heap on the ground, and waded into the hot spring to join her. As I sank into the water, I couldn't help but moan. I couldn't remember the last time I'd had a warm bath, and the heat soothed my battered body, melting away the months of grime and abuse. I closed my eyes and sank below the surface, letting the heat envelop me until my lungs needed fresh air.

When I surfaced, Elva had moved closer. A shiver ran down my spine as she swam nearer, her eyes locked onto mine. "I'm not mad at you," she said, rising from the water. "I just don't want my twin telling people things I'm not ready to share."

"I'm not judging you, if that's what you're worried about."

Elva shook her head. "I didn't think you would. You have

your flaws, but you don't seem the type to judge me for that. The king and your werewolf brother? Absolutely. But you and Baldr are different."

"Can I ask one more thing?" I inched closer.

Her gaze never left me as her mouth vanished under the waterline. She seemed to consider it. "One thing."

I swallowed hard. "Were they punished?" I asked. "The ones who ... did that to you?"

Her expression shifted from shock to an unsettling grin. "Three of them were, yes. But the ring leader escaped with his parents. I never got to kill him, but one day I will."

"If he's hiding in Tyndorf, I'll make sure you get that chance," I said, my voice low.

"Now, can I ask you something?" She swam toward me, stopping just beyond my reach.

"It's only fair."

Her eyes darkened, and she studied my face carefully before lowering her gaze to the clear water between us. "Why did you follow me? Into the water, I mean?"

Inhaling deeply, I drew closer to her. "I wanted to offer my services for your little problem." My heart thumped wildly in my chest as her eyes widened in understanding.

"Ah," she said, pushing herself back into the water and moving away from me. "So you want a repeat of our night at the inn."

"No," I replied firmly. "I want a better one." With a sudden surge of boldness, I grasped her wrist and tugged her toward me. My mouth was on hers in an instant, and I gave her a moment to pull away, but when she didn't, I kissed her even more passionately, while reaching around to grab her ass. Our bodies entwined beneath the water's surface, and I let out a soft moan as I kicked my feet to keep us afloat.

Elva broke away for a moment to catch her breath before grinning wickedly at me. "Like that?" she teased.

"No," I murmured against her skin as I peppered kisses on her neck and chin. "I want so much more, but I won't push you."

"You don't scare me," she said, sliding her hands up my chest to squeeze my shoulders.

I nipped her neck before I stopped to gaze into her eyes. "Now tell me what exactly you need from me to keep things in check."

Elva's voice was barely above a whisper. "To cum."

I smirked. "All I have to do is make you cum? That's too easy,"

"No," she said, her fingers tracing patterns on my chest. "You have to cum ... inside me. Whether I do or not doesn't matter."

"That's it?"

She nodded, her eyes sparkling with mischief. "That's why it's easy for us—most men are happy to provide that service."

I fisted her hair and pulled her head back so she was forced to look at me. "I'll take care of that need," I said. "And make sure you cum more than I do."

"Is that a challenge?"

"No. It's a promise." I scanned the edge of the pool for a suitable spot and noticed a smooth patch of grass nearby. I slipped my arm around Elva's waist, letting my fingers brush against her little scales as I kicked softly with my legs. The scales were soft, with a sharp point on the end.

"What are you up to?"

"You'll see," I said, and gripped her hips and pushed her out of the water up onto the soft bank. She looked at me quizzically until I slowly pushed her thighs apart.

"Njall, you don't have—"

She sucked in her breath as I traced my thumb along her inner thigh, brushing against an X-shaped scar I was now sure was from the men who'd hurt her. Her hand moved to stop me, but I caught it and kissed her palm. Her chest rose and fell as I moved my lips from my hand to her thigh. When my lips pressed against her sensitive skin, she melted into me; her moans echoing through the clearing.

"Are sirens always this wet?" I asked.

"Yes," Elva murmured, her fingers tangling in my hair as I continued to explore her.

"Did you answer the question, or do you like what I'm doing?" I kissed the side of her clit, and she let out a strangled cry as I used my strength to hold her thighs in place, pinning them down with an intensity that surprised even me. As she struggled beneath my grasp, I couldn't resist pushing further, flicking my tongue along the seam of her pussy. The flesh around my fingers was white from trying to keep her from writhing around.

"Well?" I demanded as I released one of her thighs.

She gasped out a reply: "Both!"

"Good girl," I growled at her. The sound of her surrender sent shivers down my spine, and I reveled in the power coursing through me. With a satisfied grin, I released her other thigh, allowing me to move freely. I began flicking her clit with the tip of my tongue. When I finally wrapped my lips around it, I felt her hand close on the back of my head as she grabbed a fistful of my hair.

Chapter 43

Elva

Cool air surrounded my clit as Njall pulled his mouth away. I was about to protest, but he thrust two fingers inside me, curling them in the most wickedly delicious way. With only one hand supporting me, I bucked beneath him when his mouth returned to my clit; I cried out. It had been an eternity since I'd been with a man who cared about my pleasure as much as his own—outside of Leifur, likely not since I slept with Njall and then his brother, if I was being honest.

His grip on my thigh tightened, sending a jolt of pain through me before he inserted a third finger. The stretching sensation was exactly what I craved as he pumped his fingers in and out, all the while keeping his mouth fixed on my clit. Starved of pleasure for too long, I came embarrassingly quickly. As my body trembled, I heard the arrogant prince chuckle.

"Don't get cocky," I snapped.

He replied with an infuriating smirk I wanted to slap off his face. I lunged for him, but he caught my wrist and yanked it so forcefully that I slid from the grassy area and splashed into the steaming pool. Frustration surged through me as I threw my other arm to hit him, but he seized that one too, spinning me until my back was pressed against his chest, and his erection ground against my rear. This time, he moaned as he increased the pressure between us. I tried to squirm away from him, but his hold tightened and he pulled my arms tighter across my chest.

"Be nice, little pearl," he growled, "or I'll bend you over that grassy rock and make you behave."

The thought of him taking me forcefully was almost enough to send me over the edge again.

"Or maybe that's exactly what you want," he teased. His nose brushed against my neck, and he gently nipped at my shoulder. Instinctively, I tilted my head to grant him better access as I pressed my ass against him and rocked my hips. He groaned as I lifted myself just high enough for his cock to slip free and settle between my legs. Seizing the opportunity, he released my wrist and grabbed my hips, impaling me on his hard cock in one swift motion. My cry echoed through the clearing as he bottomed out inside me, pressing me against the wall. I clung to the ledge with all my might, which provided him with more leverage as he slid out before driving back into me.

A rough hand journeyed up my abdomen and captured my breast, kneading it firmly before rolling and pinching my nipple to the brink of pain. His other hand found my clit and gave it the same rough treatment that my nipple was getting.

"Harder," I moaned, leaning my head back into the crook of his neck. "Njall ... please."

"I know you like it rough," he whispered. Njall had an uncanny intuition when it came to my body; he seemed to know what I craved moments before I realized it myself. For a man who'd never met a siren before, he certainly knew how to handle one. As his thrusts grew more ferocious, and the pressure within me mounted, I climaxed once again, and he bit me hard enough that I knew my brothers would see it and tease me later.

The tingles were still coursing through me when he suddenly withdrew, spun me to face him, and pushed me back onto his cock. I grabbed his face, pulling him close to kiss him. Not a simple kiss that I'd give any man I bedded, but one with a deeper meaning behind it. I'd tried to ignore the feelings because of who and what he was, but this man was different—he'd tended to me when I was sick and he could have left, he'd cared for me and my brothers by providing food, and even now, he needed me to enjoy our encounter as much, if not more, than him.

Njall pinned me against the wall of the hot spring, filling me to the brim, and prolonging the waves of pleasure that had only just calmed. I wrapped my arms around his neck and held him close. The pressure was building up inside me again, and it felt as if I might burst and float away from the water.

Njall tightened his grip on me and quickened his thrusts. My body took over from me, preparing for the age-old ritual of taking all his seed, even though it wouldn't cause a new siren. He nipped at my neck with increasing ferocity until he bit me again, and I let out a sharp cry.

His roar drowned out all else as he started to cum, and I came again as my body locked him in place to take all he offered. For a moment his body went limp, but he grasped the ledge to keep us both steady.

As I let out a soft sigh, I could feel the siren within me silencing as a warmth surged up my core. The water now felt cool compared to the heat I was giving off.

Still panting, Njall leaned in close, his forehead pressed against mine. "Anytime you need help with this particular issue, I am at your service," he whispered.

I snorted at his corny line, but a new warmth blossomed

inside of me—one I hadn't known since I was young and naïve. "I will keep that in mind," I replied.

I dipped underwater to smooth my hair back, taking a moment to compose myself. Our time together since we'd left the castle had given me a great deal to think about.

Njall was waiting for me on the grassy edge of the spring. "Ready?" he asked.

"For what?" I asked, still reeling inside from our tender encounter.

"To head back," he said. "Dinner won't catch itself, and the fire won't survive without wood."

Groaning at the thought of leaving, I flopped onto my back, floating through the water. I heard a gentle splash, and a moment later, a pair of arms encircled my waist and pulled me under. His emerald eyes sparkled when we resurfaced, and I couldn't help but grin at his playfulness. I reached out and tickled his sides, laughing as he dove under again to get away.

When we broke the surface, both of us were laughing. I playfully splashed his face and growled as he batted the water away and dove for me. He went under again and locked onto my ankles, pulling me down once more. There, beneath the surface, in the water's stillness, I looked into his eyes as he caressed my cheeks. I was impressed that he could dive as much as he did without running out of breath. I grabbed his face and kissed him again, softly as we slowly rose to the surface.

The cool air made my skin bumpy after being in the hot water for so long, but it also helped to dry it quickly, and I made my way over to my clothes. I rubbed my lower back and sighed with relief that my scales had vanished again. I was set for another month. After Njall and I dressed, we silently ventured back into the woods to gather food and firewood.

When we arrived back at the camp, we found Leifur had

already collected enough wood to get the fire going, and Sindri had prepared spots for us to sleep. Njall dropped his bundle of wood next to my twin, who immediately whined about nearly being hit.

Leifur took the three brown squirrels I'd caught on the way back. "You look better," he said before turning away to prepare them.

Njall mentioned our discovery of a hot spring, piquing Sindri's interest. As I dropped my bag of supplies, I told him where to find it. Sindri glanced at his husband, and when he got a nod, he set off eagerly to find it.

"You're welcome to join him," Njall said. "We can prepare dinner."

Leifur looked at me for approval. I nodded, and he handed me a knife to clean the squirrels. With my brothers off getting cleaned up and enjoying a soak, Njall and I found ourselves alone. I tried to focus on the meal—boiling water, cutting the root vegetables, skinning the squirrels—but whenever I glanced up, his eyes were on me.

Could it be possible that he felt the same draw to me as I did to him? It seemed plausible; sirens had evolved to draw men in. Yet this reciprocal magnetism was unfamiliar territory for me. We stayed quiet and carried on with our work.

By the time my brothers returned refreshed and rejuvenated, dinner was ready. I was still angry with Sindri, so I sat next to Njall and avoided looking at him.

After eating yet another silent meal, Sindri finally snapped. "Are you ever going to talk to me again?"

I just grunted a reply, making Leifur and Njall shift uncomfortably.

"I said I was sorry," Sindri continued. "Why do you have to take everything so personally?"

My gaze locked onto my brother's face. "How could I not? I

shared the worst day of my life with Njall because you wanted to warn him why I was moody."

"You are," Sindri shot back, raising his voice.

"Were," Leifur calmly corrected him.

Sindri hesitated, glancing toward his husband before focusing on me and Njall. "Oh." A sardonic grin spread across his face. "Perhaps you should thank me."

"Your oversharing had nothing to do with what happened between us," Njall said. "While it answered a few questions I had about Elva, it doesn't change how I see her."

"It got you to take care of her siren for this cycle."

My mouth dropped open, and I stormed over to my brother and grabbed him by the shirt. "Did you tell him that so he'd feel sorry for me and sleep with me? What is wrong with you?"

"You were running out of time," Sindri protested.

"I still had days left."

"And with how cold and difficult you were, you'd never have won him over without your song, and I know you would have refused to use it."

I shoved my brother away and massaged my forehead in frustration.

"Elva, he means well." Leifur squeezed my shoulder, but I held up my hand, making it clear I didn't want to be touched, and he backed off.

"Sindri," I growled. "You don't always know what's best for me."

He opened his mouth to reply, but before he could, I unleashed my siren—my teeth sharpened into razors, and my fingers morphed into talons. He wisely leaped away from me, but I advanced on him. "You haven't gone through what I have, so do not assume you can speak for me, ever."

Trembling with fear, he nodded vigorously. As I turned from him, my eyes met Njall's; the smallest hint of fear was apparent, but the more dominating emotion was understanding. For the first time, maybe ever, I felt seen by a man. He was frightened, but not of me ... for me, and I wasn't entirely sure why I pushed between him and Leifur and stormed off into the woods to spend the night alone.

Chapter 44

Njall

My heart ached for Elva. I now knew the scars she bore and the burden she carried. As a brother, I could imagine what Sindri felt, knowing it happened and being unable to stop it. Had someone hurt Hulda like that, I would have killed him with my bare hands. I looked across the fire at her brothers; Sindri slumped to the ground and crossed his arms in frustration, but Leifur smacked him on the head.

"I told you to let her be," he scolded.

"She's my sister, not yours," Sindri retorted. "I should be allowed to speak my mind without her storming off."

"You're lucky she stormed off; otherwise, she might have torn you apart," Leifur said.

Determined to check on Elva, I stood up and brushed the dirt from my clothes,

"Don't bother," Sindri grumbled. "When she's in a mood like this, she won't come back tonight. Thought someone as educated as you would have figured that out by now."

"I've dealt with my share of monstrous royals," I replied, gathering our blankets into a satchel. "I can handle your sister and her siren."

Leifur handed me a large burning branch for light. Luckily for me, Elva did not leave gracefully. Her stomping away in rage had left deep indentations in the soft dirt, making her trail easy to follow.

As I walked through the underbrush, the forest's silence surrounded me. *Why am I hunting for this woman—this siren, selkie, or whatever else she might be?* It is the middle of the night, and the forest is dangerous. Recent experiences had taught me how easily sirens could ensnare men with their song. Yet none of my feelings for Elva felt forced. We'd shared a connection since our first night together, and I couldn't explain it away by mere enchantment. I'd seen what her song did to men, and having experienced a siren's lure myself, I knew that what I felt for her was all my feelings. I certainly wasn't attracted to her the night she saved me. I'd been furious that my father thought so little of me to not even try to send help for me, while my sister received the efforts of the entire army. My anger had been misdirected at her, and yet she hadn't wavered in keeping me safe.

As I walked, another thought occurred to me: was her affection for me genuine or merely part of the cycle she struggled against? The way her body reacted to my touch, and how hard she'd trembled in my arms when she came—I didn't believe she faked that, and there would be no reason for her to fake it, once she'd gotten what she needed from me. Still, it was hard not to question her motives. After all, she had saved me to get enough gold from Baldr to buy her home.

A branch snapped nearby, jolting me from my thoughts. I raised the torch, casting a circle of light around me. The forest was still, no eyes gleaming in the darkness. I held my breath and listened. When I heard another crack, I spun toward the sound.

"Elva?"

"Can't I just get some peace?"

I pushed aside the foliage and found her sitting on a fallen log, head hanging low with frustration and pain. I balanced the torch on some rocks, then pulled out her blanket, draped it over her shoulders, and took a seat beside her. Elva pulled the wool around her and looked at me with her beautiful blue and green eyes.

"Well?" she asked.

"Well, what?"

"Aren't you going to say something?"

"You wanted peace," I said carefully. Her siren had gone, and I didn't want to bring her back out.

"You're probably the only person to ever take that seriously."

"I know better than to push my sister when she's mad, so you deserve the same respect. I just didn't want to leave you alone out here."

Elva leaned her head on my shoulder, sending an electric heat coursing through me. After our tryst this afternoon, any touch from her sent my body into a frenzy. As she placed her hand on my thigh, I had to bite back a moan. I didn't want her to think I followed with ulterior motives.

"Njall?" Her whisper barely reached my ears, but the gentle kiss that followed was unmistakable. Desire coursed through me as I pulled her closer to me until her body was pressed against mine. A soft moan left her mouth, and my lips moved to kiss her neck. The next thing I knew, she was straddling me as we once again surrendered ourselves to one another beneath the stars of the forest.

I woke up on the cool forest floor, my body stiff after a night spent on the hard ground. I heard a soft sigh. Elva was sprawled across my chest, naked and asleep, her skin glistening in the morning light like dew on fresh grass. I eased my hand out to gently run it along her back and over her curves. I smiled, recalling that my dream was real—I had feasted on her before taking her against the felled tree where we now rested. When I kissed the top of her head, I smelled her sea scent, my potent musk, and a great deal of sex. As Elva stirred, she stretched and let out a long, sharp squeak.

"Good morning," I said as she sat up, rubbing the sleep from her eyes.

She blinked her eyes a few times. "Morning," she said as she stretched, emitting a melodious song's worth of cracks from her body. "How'd you sleep?"

I grinned, leaning in for a gentle kiss. "Amazing. You wore me out, so I slept like the dead."

Elva chuckled and returned my kiss with gusto. For the first time ever, the idea of only sleeping with one woman for the rest of my life made sense. If I had to tie myself to a single one, then only Elva would do.

The small fire we'd made from the torch had burned out hours ago, but the blankets and our bodies had kept us warm. I stood to follow her, suspecting she was looking for our clothes. I found them behind the log. Brushing away dirt and leaves, I handed Elva her garments and was rewarded with a grateful smile and a touch on my chest. She looked up at me, licking her lower lip.

"None of that," I chided playfully, moving out of her reach to put my pants on. "We need to go find your brothers and keep traveling. As fun as it is to take you in the woods, or a hot spring, I'd rather have a bed."

Elva pulled her shirt on and glanced down at her bruised and dirty knees. "Fair."

We returned to the camp where Sindri was just waking. As Leifur prepared breakfast, Elva hugged her brother. Feeling awkward, I left them to tend to the horses. By the time I returned, Elva was sitting next to her brother, and it seemed both siblings had made some efforts toward reconciliation. I counted it as a small victory.

Chapter 45

Elva

Now that it had become obvious that Njall and I were spending most of our alone time enjoying each other, my brothers teased him relentlessly. They left me alone, maybe because they knew better, or maybe because I was riding a prince and they couldn't think of any way to taunt me. I'd been with hundreds of men over the years, but Njall stood out. We had a connection I couldn't fathom—as if he could predict what I needed just before I knew it. He drove me crazy when he was arrogant, but his compassion toward me seemed to grow the more time we spent together. My biggest fear now was how we'd convince the king to let my brothers and me buy some land in Tyndorf to make a home for ourselves. If we stayed, I think Njall would become a good friend to us, and possibly more to me.

Without the need to track my cycle, I'd lost count of how many days or weeks we'd been riding, but I knew we were getting close to the Forest of Endilaus. Twice, we attempted to rest in nearby towns, only to encounter more soldiers searching for us or locals discussing their presence nearby. Our best option was to hug the crimson mountains until we reached the stream that ran from the mountains to the mermaid territory. While it didn't have a name, it marked the border between the Forest of Endilaus and the Tyndorf lands.

That night, when we'd cleaned up from dinner and settled around the campfire before bed, I asked how everyone was feeling about getting close to the forest and Tyndorf.

"I'm excited," Leifur said. "We rescued the prince and are bringing him home."

"In one piece, too!" Njall added, making my brothers chuckle.

Sindri was skeptical. "I don't know. I'm not sure how his father will react to his new obsession with a siren." He cast a mischievous glance in our direction.

Njall must have sensed my apprehension, because he tightened his arm around my waist and whispered, "You don't have to worry about that." After nipping my neck, he turned to my brother. "I have no intention of staying out of your sister's bed once we return home."

"That's not what I'm worried about," Sindri said.

"Well, if you didn't want to picture me railing your twin against a tree until she screams my name loud enough for the mermaids to hear, then you shouldn't have brought it up."

"I don't think it's that either," I said, but I couldn't control myself, and Leifur and I burst out laughing as Sindri rolled his eyes at us.

"Either way, you keep picturing that, while I go piss." Njall patted Sindri on the back on his way into the woods.

"Since when are you squeamish about my sexual conquests?" I asked Sindri, throwing a small stick at him once Njall was out of earshot.

"Since you started developing feelings," Sindri said. "Before you were a one-and-done siren. You'd bed them once, we'd get a fun story, and you'd never see them again, but Njall—I think he's going to stick around, and that's not as fun."

"I have developed nothing," I shot back. "Except maybe craving for his giant cock."

Leifur laughed so hard he snorted. "That, I can understand. He *is* incredibly well hung. But Sindri is right; you've changed."

I picked up a stick and idly drew patterns in the dirt.

"It's not a bad thing, Elva," Leifur said. "You deserve to be happy too."

"Catch your tongue," I hissed at them. "He'll hear."

Sindri raised an eyebrow. "Would it be so terrible if he did?"

I snapped the stick in my hand. "I can't say anything until I know he feels the same." Sindri and Leifur exchanged a silent smirk, and I threw the broken stick pieces at them. "Now drop it. Please."

Njall returned to the fire, looking bemused. "I leave for two minutes and you all start fighting again?" He sat down beside me and pulled me close. "How did you three travel together for so long without killing each other?"

"Well, there was less at stake," Leifur said. "Before we went to save you, we were just wandering around trying to find a place to settle down, and we knew that could take years."

"That, and my brother was the troublemaker back then," I added with a smirk.

"I was not," Sindri said indignantly.

Leifur and I shared a look before saying in unison, "He was."

"Sindri is quite good at charming women into giving him what he wants," I said, my smirk growing wider. "But he's terrible at picking the right ones to charm."

My brother rolled his eyes. "You pick the wrong widow *one* time—"

"Four times," Leifur said.

"Five now!" I corrected.

"Gah!" My brother crossed his arms and slumped down, turning his back to us.

I yawned and gave Njall a peck on the cheek before lying down to face the fire. The warmth of the flames bathed my face as Njall lay down beside me, wrapping his arm around my waist and pulling me against him. I'd never consistently slept next to a man, and was used to my space, but spending my nights with Njall was wonderful. His body was the perfect temperature at night to keep me warm, and I fit against him as if I was made for him. He'd gently stroke my hair, soothing me into a slumber. It was a comforting motion Sindri had done since we were children, but when Njall's hands were in my hair, the feelings ran deeper, as if he were trying to claim me. I had to be careful not to let him discover how giving him control over my hair could let him influence me—a trait from my selkie side.

A piercing roar shattered my peaceful sleep, and adrenaline surged through my veins. I grabbed my daggers from beside my head and held them defensively in front of me. Leifur and Njall sprang to their feet almost as quickly as I did, Leifur brandishing his hammer and ax while Sindri raised his hands to ward off whatever had made such a sound.

A second deafening roar echoed from behind my brothers. Leifur cautiously pivoted while Njall and I kept watch on the other sides of our camp.

"Elva," Sindri whispered, pointing toward the woods. I turned slightly and saw a set of horrifying, large red eyes glowing back at us from the shadows. My heart stopped as I sucked in a breath. Njall spun, shielding me with his body as a monstrous Minotaur emerged from the darkness.

The creature would have dwarfed even Baldr. It must have reached a height of eight feet, including the horns, which were at least the size of my thighs. I'd been taught that minotaurs only had a bull's head, but this one walked on powerful bull legs, too, with hooves as large as my head. Its chestnut brown fur was thick, matched by a muscular man's torso and a tail hanging between its hindquarters. Clinging to Njall, I peered at the creature as it sniffed the air and snorted before locking its piercing red eyes on us. Slowly, it turned its gaze from my brother to Leifur and Njall, finally stopping at me with a menacing growl.

"Sirens." The beast's voice rumbled several octaves deeper than any man I'd ever met.

"And selkies," another voice said from behind us. I was too scared to look.

"What do you want?" Sindri asked.

The two minotaurs growled back and forth at each other, seemingly in a conversation that we could not understand.

"Get out of our territory, or we'll kill you," one finally snarled.

"No!" Sindri protested.

The beasts bared their teeth and snarled at us. Acting on impulse, I stepped around Njall. "We'll go. Just give us a minute to grab our things."

"Now!" The larger beast roared at us, and my brothers scrambled to grab our things while the creature watched our every move. As we struggled to load our horses, the air grew heavier with each passing second. When everything was finally secured, Njall grabbed a few torches from the fire pit and distributed them among us.

"Leave, and never come back," the larger Minotaur warned. "If you return, we'll kill you."

"If you're lucky," the other Minotaur added venomously.

Leifur and Sindri led the way, with Njall and me following closely. We rode as quickly as we dared through the darkness of the dense woods. The torches we held meant we needed to navigate with only one hand on the reins. None of us said anything for a long while. I was afraid to speak and draw the attention of another one of those monsters. Eventually, my nerves settled with the rising sun.

"First wolves and now minotaurs," Sindri grumbled when we finally stopped to give the horses a break. "This is turning into a nightmare."

"I suppose you won't be complaining about kelpies or harpies anymore, eh?" Leifur teased, coaxing a giggle from me while my brother remained stone-faced.

Njall seemed genuinely curious. "Have you actually seen kelpies and harpies?"

"Yes," I replied. "And mermaids, sea dragons, unicorns, dire wolves ..."

"And you weren't scared?"

"Some of them scared us," Leifur said.

"Harpies and unicorns leave females alone," I said. "And the kelpie was harmless."

"I thought they tried to drown people," Njall said.

"Exactly," I replied. "Completely harmless."

"I've only seen sirens, selkies, werewolves, sorcerers, satyrs, and other humans," Njall said. "Oh, and I think a centaur."

"Considering half of those are in your family, I suppose you aren't too afraid of them," Sindri said.

Njall threw his head back and laughed. "That's because you've never seen Ingvar angry," he said.

Chapter 46

Njall

We'd been riding for so long that my legs felt numb. Yet, we were close to the Forest of Endilaus, and my father's men could appear at any moment, offering safety from lurking Minotaurs and the Huestur guards who'd been pursuing us. Elva rested her head on my chest, and my hand roamed around her waist to pull her closer. We'd slowed our pace over the last few days. Elva's mule had been hurt during our mad dash away from our camp, and the poor thing couldn't support Elva's weight and the bags. Her brothers had offered her their horses, but I insisted she ride with me. My massive warhorse wouldn't even notice the difference, or so I claimed. The truth was simpler: I wanted her pressed against me all day, every day.

Her gentle caresses and the whispers she shared ignited a desire within me. By the time we found a place to camp for the night, I practically dragged her into the woods. Once again, she came twice—first against my mouth, and then on my cock. I have no doubt her brothers heard her screams.

Today, we had to leave the safety of the Crimson mountains and venture to the only road that cut through the forest. The sun blazed high in the sky, and we were an easy target. As we rounded a bend, I had to yank hard on the reins, jerking my horse to a stop. Five knights blocked our path, clad in Huestur colors.

Leifur groaned, reining his horse in beside mine.

"There are only five," Sindri said. "Could we take them?"

Leifur and Elva exchanged incredulous looks. "I'd rather not risk one of us getting hurt," Elva said. She slid off our horse before I could stop her. "Get your ax and hammer ready, Leifur."

By the time we'd all dismounted, Elva had stripped off her shirt and was sauntering toward the knights, bouncing her breasts seductively. One of them threw a dagger, but she caught it in midair and wagged her finger at them. And then she sang.

The men stopped what they were doing and straightened for her, puffing out their chests as she strode up to them. One by one, she removed their helmets, tossing them on the ground behind her with a clatter. The last man was the oldest and likely in charge. When she whispered something to him, he snarled and grabbed her by the throat.

Leifur tossed me the ax, but before any of us could move, the man yanked Elva into a brutal kiss.

"What is she doing?" I asked through gritted teeth.

"She's seducing him," Sindri said. "Her song must not have worked too well on him, so now she has to try other things."

"Why? What *things*?" I demanded. Anger surged through me as the man groped her breasts, then shoved her to her knees. The thought that she'd use her body again to make our passage easier enraged me. When he started fumbling with his belt buckle, I could feel my blood begin to boil.

"She distracts them, so we can kill them," Leifur said, hefting his hammer. "Let's go."

I charged down the path toward Elva and the Huester men. By the time I reached her, the older knight was forcing himself into her mouth, and something inside me broke. I turned to the closest man and swung my ax with such force that it nearly split his head in half. I moved on to the second man, burying my ax in his neck so far that his head snapped back like a broken twig as he collapsed to the ground.

Leifur used his hammer to dispatch another one, taking out his knees before delivering a fatal blow to his head.

Then came a scream—a horrific, shrill cry that could have woken the dead. Leifur and I looked up to see Elva standing up as the older knight cradled his groin. A wicked grin spread across her lips, revealing her bloodstained siren teeth as she spat something into her hand.

"Show off," Leifur muttered, then turned back to the last remaining knight.

It took a moment to realize that Elva had bitten off the man's cock. I tightened my grip on the ax and approached him. He was sobbing, clutching himself as blood seeped through his fingers. "No one touches my siren," I growled at him before swinging the ax with both hands, hacking away at his neck until his head finally rolled off onto the dirt road and into the ditch.

Sindri appeared with a full waterskin and a rag, offering them to Elva so she could clean herself up. Once she was done, she pulled her shirt back on and rejoined me beside the bloodied body of the older knight. "What did you say to him?" I asked her, still reeling from the intensity of my rage.

"I asked him what he thought of sirens, and to show me."

"Why?"

A mischievous smirk graced Elva's beautiful lips as she stepped closer. She tugged at my shirt, pulling us together until our bodies touched. "I wanted to know if it would make you jealous. I never expected it to send you into a feral rage, though."

I grabbed her hair and twisted it around my fist. She let out a gasp as I crashed my mouth into hers. "You'll never kiss anyone but me like that again," I growled.

She pulled away from me and looked into my eyes, searching for something. "We'll see," she said, nodding softly in agreement, before nestling into my chest. I couldn't bring myself to admit to her that no man would ever kiss her in front of me and live—not yet. Once she had her land and was settled in my kingdom, then I'd tell her. Until then, I couldn't risk that she might leave and take a piece of me with her.

"Enough flirting," Leifur teased, breaking the spell between us. "Someone likely heard him screaming. We should grab whatever supplies we can from them and go."

By dusk, we'd reached the edge of the forest, barely a week's hike from Tyndorf. We set up camp just inside the forest to avoid any more unwanted attention. Sindri and Leifur quickly drifted off to sleep, but I could not rest. My mind was a ravenous storm of thoughts about Elva. She could use her body to protect herself and her brothers. She'd done it three times already on this trip—but how often? The question kept me awake.

A bolt of heat spread through me as Elva's hand glided up to my chest. "What's bothering you?" she asked softly.

"Nothing."

She kissed me gently on the chest before tracing lazy circles with her finger on my skin. "I know something is. Please tell me."

I sighed heavily. "It was so easy for you."

"Look, we don't relish killing humans—"

"The seduction."

"Oh." Elva paused so long, I thought she had dropped the subject. But then she continued, "All sirens are taught basic seduction techniques. For warriors like us, it's a tool, a weapon to prevent bloodshed. If we can end a fight before it starts, often the easiest way is to take off our clothes."

"Huh ... It did work."

"It always does." She rolled onto her side, pulling my arm

with her and placing my hand over her breast. "Don't worry—I promise not to use my powers against your men, unless I have to."

I hadn't even thought of that. The idea of her being near my father's men made me sick. I'd traveled with them enough to know how they treated women. The whores who traveled with them were paid well, but the men knew they could get away with things that were taboo at home. Most of the women ended up being discarded, pregnant after being passed around every night. The mere thought of Elva in that world ignited a ferocious protectiveness in me. As long as I breathed, I'd make sure none of my father's men ever laid a hand on her.

But that wasn't my deepest fear. It was the dread that gnawed at me, silent and persistent, that I might not be enough for her. That someday, she might seek more than what I could offer. And if that day came, I wasn't sure if I could let her go.

Our journey through the forest of Endilaus was the easiest I've ever experienced in my life. Traveling with sirens, it seemed, came with unexpected perks—no creature dared approach us. By the sixth day, we glimpsed the pale gray limestone walls that surrounded my kingdom. Elva had returned to her mule, and though I missed having her on my horse, I kept quiet to avoid more taunts from her brothers.

"You must be thrilled to get back home and not have to sleep on the ground," Sindri said.

"Oh, Sindri, not everyone is as obsessed with luxury as you are," Elva shot back.

"If anyone's going to be, it's a prince," Sindri replied. "Or have you forgotten that your new toy is royalty?"

Leifur snorted at that, but Elva was not amused. She guided her mule toward her brother, and he hurried his horse to my other side.

"We're in your kingdom now, Njall. It's your duty to protect me!" he pleaded.

"Not from your sister," I said, and picked up the pace so Elva could catch him. She swung at him hard enough that he almost fell off his horse.

As we neared the guards at the gate, I was grateful for the longer hair and beard that covered my face. I didn't want my father to learn of my return just yet. My plan was for us to stay in the Pirate's Booty for the night, so I could clean myself up and find out what happened while I was gone from Baldr.

"Do you have any coins?" I asked the other three.

Sindri eyed me suspiciously, tightly clutching his coin purse. "What for?"

"I'll pay you back once we're inside," I said. "I just want the guards to stay quiet about my arrival and track down my brother for us."

"Oh. The satyr, right? Baldr," Leifur wiggled his eyebrows at me.

"Yes, him."

"In that case, take it." Sindri tossed his coin purse to me. "I want to *properly* meet this satyr."

The gates were busy, and people were coming and going because of the markets. Chatter was all around us, but it was ordinary. Bread prices had dropped thanks to a bumper wheat crop, taxes were on the rise, and the other princes were up to their regular theatrics. Still, there was no word on either the missing princess or prince. Elva brought her mule up beside me and flashed me a smile, her vibrant green and blue hair hidden beneath a scarf. Leifur had used ashes from the fire this morning to darken his hair to an unassuming gray that was utterly convincing, so long as you didn't look at it for too long.

When it came our turn to enter the city gates, we didn't need any of Sindri's coins since none of them recognized me. It stung a little that my people didn't know their prince, but I pushed the feeling aside. This was, after all, the gate used by peasants to come in and trade their goods at the market, or by travelers who preferred not to draw attention. The grand gate to the east was reserved for armies, visiting dignitaries, the higher-ranked citizens of Tyndorf, and the royal family.

As we navigated the side roads, it was very clear we were in the less prosperous part of town. The buildings were weathered and worn. Paint peeled off doors and windows while shutters hung from rusted hinges. Nothing but dust adorned the window ledges. Sindri grimaced and made a noise I could only assume was disgust.

"Stop it," Elva hissed at him.

"It's alright," I said quietly. "This is why I stay in this part of town. To remind myself that not everyone lives in the same luxury as the area near the castle."

"I thought it was so people would leave you alone," Leifur said.

"That too."

We continued, passing boarded-up shops and abandoned buildings. It had always been a mess down here, but in the time I'd been gone, things had gotten much worse. The people here were in desperate need, and I'd have to make sure my father and brother were aware, not that they'd care.

After a few turns down narrow streets, we arrived at Pirate's Booty. I paid the stable boy to tend to our horses. Sindri left us to dash inside. He intended to sweet-talk the barmaid into free food, but I knew if Killian, the buxom redhead, was working, she'd have no time for his nonsense. Inside, Sindri had already claimed a barstool, and Killian was polishing a glass behind the bar while the other server delivered drinks to the full tables.

"Hello, love," I said, greeting my old friend.

"Glad to see the rumors are wrong."

"What did they say?" I asked, leaning in as we joined Sindri at the bar. The scent of ale and roasting meat filled the air.

"That you're dead." She set down her glass and reached behind her for a key and tossed it to me. "I locked your room when you didn't come back for a few days."

"I'll need the other suite too. For my friends."

She looked at Leifur and Elva the way she'd look at a plate of food found under a table a week later. Sindri caught her attention longer, and she winked at him. His charm had been working on her.

"One, or two?" She asked, looking back at Elva.

"She's bedding with me," I replied, and Killian nodded, handing over the key to the second room.

"Room's yours as long as you want it. And if you need anything else, let me know."

"Dinner would be amazing," Sindri said, flashing a charming smile at her.

"You got it, cutie," she said, and turned to shout an order at the cook in the kitchen. "You want to squeeze in here or have it brought upstairs?"

"To the room, please," I said. "And when things quiet down, could you have some hot water sent up?"

"You all look like you need it," she chuckled.

I slipped her a coin and asked her to have someone hunt down Baldr. Then we gave our thanks and headed upstairs to the suites.

Sindri was thrilled with his accommodations. He proclaimed the bed was one of the finest he'd had in years, and he went on about the luxuriously carved bedposts and silk curtains hanging on the large window. Leifur sank into the enormous couch, his eyes wandering over the unusual decor, such as extra sturdy chairs, and many ruffled pillows. Seeing how happy his husband was, I decided not to tell them they were in the newlywed suite.

Elva and I carried our bags to the end of the hall where my suite awaited. I unlocked the door and motioned for her to go in first. Killian had told the truth. Despite my being gone, everything was where I had left it months ago. I reached out to touch the ivy leaves carved into my bedposts while Elva leaped into the bed, letting herself sink into the satin duvet stuffed with swan feathers. I'd had the blanket custom-made for me, but it had never looked as good as it did now with Elva lying on it. She sat up and smiled at me before unwrapping her hair and giving her head a long scratch.

"My head gets so itchy when I have to tie up my hair," she said, her fingers tangling in the locks as she looked up at me with playful eyes.

I smirked and climbed into the bed, pausing above her. "Any other itches you have that I can help with?"

My siren fisted the shirt I was wearing and pulled me down to kiss her. "After dinner and a bath, I'll take you up on that."

The food arrived shortly, and the rabbit stew was among the best I've had in my life. Elva devoured three helpings, and Leifur, four, but Sindri just picked at his portion, complaining that he'd eaten too much stew on our travels. He insisted Leifur take him out to find something more appealing.

The hot water arrived before we finished eating, so we took turns cleaning ourselves off, and I took care of my bothersome facial hair. After I offered Sindri some nicer clothes from my closet to help him blend in, he set off with Leifur into the night, leaving Elva and me alone.

It would figure that just as Elva and I were taking care of that itch she had, someone knocked on my door. "Let me in, you lazy lout!" Baldr shouted as he banged on the door when I didn't answer right away.

Elva kissed me and slipped her shirt back on. I groaned under my breath as I answered the door.

"Welcome home, brother," Baldr said, slapping me on the shoulder before pulling me into a hug. "And thank you to our beautiful little vixen for bringing him home," he added, releasing me and moving toward Elva. As smoothly as I'd ever seen, he cupped her cheek with one hand and slid the other around her waist to her ass, before moving in to kiss her. My stomach clenched, but my little siren leaned into him and turned her face, letting him kiss her cheek before she winked at me.

Chapter 47

Elva

Baldr kept us up well into the night as we recounted our tale of returning from Huestur, and after he'd left, Njall and I were too tired to finish what we had started earlier. We'd planned to wake and have breakfast with my brothers, but now, in the early light, I was lying in bed with Njall's face between my legs. His arms were wrapped tightly around my thighs, holding them apart as he licked and sucked my clit. My moans became louder as Njall quickened his pace. As my first orgasm tore through me, I reached for him, and he climbed up my body to kiss my mouth.

I draped my arms loosely around his neck as he eased into me, inch by inch, until I arched up, taking him fully. Njall pressed his forehead to mine as he buried his cock deep. His lips traced my neck, then my breasts, before he rolled us over, positioning me atop him. His hands gripped my ass, and I clutched his shoulders for leverage as I rode him. Taking my nipple into his mouth, he nipped me, making me cry out.

A bang echoed from the wall we shared with my brothers. I froze, looking down at Njall, who grinned wickedly. Without missing a beat, he shuffled to the end of the bed and got to his knees, lifting me with him. I wrapped my legs around his waist and kept bouncing on his cock, as he pressed my back against the wall. One large hand pinned both my wrists above my head as he thrust into me relentlessly, each stroke so powerful it felt like I might split in two. I screamed out, tugging at my restrained hands, but he only gripped them harder.

Njall's teeth sank into my neck as he took me with a ferocity that left me breathless. Weakened from the intense orgasm he'd already given me, I only managed to wiggle my hands until he released them, his fingers shifting to dig into my ass instead. He drove into me, giving me more than I could endure, and yet I couldn't help but take it all. When I came again, I screamed so loud I thought I'd go hoarse. Njall roared with his release, his body shuddering against mine.

I pressed my forehead to his and waited for us both to catch our breath. Another bang echoed from the wall, and I couldn't help but giggle. Njall kissed my neck before moving to my mouth. When he pulled away, I stared into his beautiful green eyes. Something inside me felt alive in a way I couldn't explain when I was with him.

"Ready for me to go, so you can have your shopping spree with your brothers?" Njall asked, his lips brushing against my neck.

"In a minute," I murmured, then slammed my fists against the wall behind me and moaned loudly. A frustrated groan came from my brother's room, and I couldn't suppress my smirk.

Chapter 48

Njall

A pair of younger guards tried to escort us, but my brother and I refused, laughing them off. We walked along the same cramped entranceway we'd taken every time we went to see our father, and yet today it felt different.

"Do you have a plan?" I asked Baldr as we turned down the hall leading to our father's private library.

"I always have a plan."

I should have known. Glancing down, I realized Baldr's tail was wagging, a sure sign he was up to something.

"Care to expand on it?" I asked.

"Nope."

My heart pounded hard enough that I could feel it in my ears, but I focused my attention on the ugly teal tapestries my father adored and so hung on every wall. We rounded another corner and arrived at a large, elaborately carved walnut door. A guard was standing to the side of the door and moved to approach us, but Baldr growled and waved him off. The man slunk away, leaving the two of us alone at the door. It was adorned with an all too lifelike carving of our father's face.

"Ugh," I groaned as I leaned closer to the door.

Baldr looked at me and grinned like a boy for a moment before he threw it open. "Father!" He called loudly and stepped inside, holding the door open for me. "I have a surprise for you."

"Unless you have your sister behind you, I don't care," the king snapped. "I'm in a meeting."

"You were close," Baldr said and stepped aside to reveal me. My father's face fell into a scowl immediately, but it was then that I noticed the other lords present in the room. I glanced at my brother, but he had his perfect prince smile plastered on his face. "Look who just arrived home!" he announced

One of the older lords looked as if he might die from shock. Another, the one who owned the inn, Baldr, stayed in, stepped up, and slapped my brother's shoulder. "I knew you'd get him back," he said, reeking of the same whiskey Baldr favored. "What would you do without him to take the focus off you?" He turned to me and smacked me in the back. "Welcome home, Nial."

"Njall," my brother corrected.

"That's what I said." The lord replied, laughing loudly as he gestured for the servants to bring out the good ale. At least someone would celebrate my return.

"And how exactly did you find your way home, Njall?" Our father finally asked, after scrutinizing me for an uncomfortable length of time.

"The praise goes to Baldr," I said, patting him on the back. "He hired a group of skilled mercenaries who were able to retrieve me."

"And who's paying for that?" Father slammed his hands onto the table hard enough to rattle the drink glasses around him. The group of lords shifted uncomfortably, and I noticed the stack of finance books spread across the table. It seemed he was raising taxes again.

"I did," Baldr said, strolling toward our father, a mischievous glint in his eye. "Compared to what I spend on drink, I paid very little for it. But you can cover the cost of the celebration ball."

"Ball?" Father growled.

"Yes, a ball!" one of the younger lords chimed in. "It's been months since we had one."

Baldr clapped his hands together, grinning broadly. "Exactly! The last one was the day my siblings were taken. Now that one has returned, we must celebrate."

A vein in Father's forehead twitched. "Baldr, you know we can't afford to celebrate every stupid, triviality your brother does."

"I hardly consider coming home alive after being taken by the Huesturs, our greatest enemy, to be a trivial matter," Baldr shot back. The lords murmured in agreement, and Father's face shifted from annoyance to fury before settling into a regal mask. Only Hulda and Baldr could push him like that. Hulda had our father wrapped around her finger, and my brother was the people's favorite. If the king were to do anything to him, it might spark a rebellion.

"Fine. We'll have a small celebration—"

"Wonderful!" Baldr exclaimed, clearly prepared for this outcome. "I've already informed the kitchen, the maids, and the footman. Tonight's invitations are being delivered as we speak."

"Tonight?" I asked, shocked at my brother's ability to bring this together so quickly.

Baldr threw his head back and winked at me. "Of course. We need to earn the people's goodwill before they find out you're back themselves." He looked back at the table of nobility. "Bringing back a prince shows strength, and we must celebrate it properly. Plus, we should reward the mercenaries who saved his life."

"You said you paid them," my father snapped.

"I did, but I believe a bonus is in order. Say ... a small piece of land. Outside the gates, of course, near the forest. Mercenaries don't need the guards' protection." He chuckled, and the lords laughed along with him. He had them all eating out of the palm of his hand.

Father stood his back to the Lord and grabbed Baldr by the shirt.

"What are you doing?" he growled.

"I'm making sure your Lords are good and happy," Baldr said softly. "So when you drop that new tax on them, they'll be too busy telling their wives and daughters to get dressed up for a ball with the kingdom's three eligible princes to care."

The king released him with a scowl. "Fine. The old farmstead outside of town. It's been abandoned for decades."

"Exactly what I was thinking," Baldr said, pulling a piece of parchment out of his oversized pocket and handing it to our father. "Just sign here."

The older Lord smacked the table, laughing. "The boy knows you, Hilmir!"

"Nonsense," I said, stepping forward. "We merely know how busy our father is, and wouldn't want to come back and take up more of his time."

The king huffed, but grabbed a quill off the table and scribbled his signature on the land transfer papers. "Now get out. Go plan your *ferflucsing* party, while we do actual work."

Baldr and I bowed low to our father and walked backwards to the door, never turning our backs to the king. It was the ultimate sign of respect in Tyndorf, and one we rarely bothered with.

Once the door was closed, I turned to my brother in disbelief. "How did you pull that off?"

He smirked. "I've been overhearing a lot of arguing about money lately. Sending the entire army to Anginfill for months to bring back Hulda wasn't cheap, and he never expected it to drag on this long."

We walked down the hallway toward our wing. I was excited

to grab some of my favorite things to bring back to the inn. Despite Sindri teasing my royalness, I had no intention of staying in the castle if I could avoid it. Why would I stay here when there was a gorgeous siren waiting for me at the inn?

"So, about last night ..." Baldr said as we arrived at our wing.

My mind flashed to his attempt to put lips on Elva, and I balled my fists in annoyance. "What about it?" I asked, keeping my tone as calm as possible.

My brother saw right through it. "I didn't realize that you've taken to the siren so much. I will, of course, step back." He gave me his usual coy smile, but his eyes showed the sincerity that smile usually lacked.

"Thank you."

"Have you told her?" Baldr pushed open the door to my room. "You're not exactly one for grand declarations, are you? You shout your desires from the rooftops, but love ... that's different."

I rolled my eyes. "Just because you proclaim your feelings to every bedmate doesn't mean I have to broadcast mine the moment I feel them."

"What a pair we make," he chuckled. "Sorry about the mess. Father told the maids not to bother since you were gone, and when I sent your heroes after you, I needed to grab their supplies quickly."

Stepping into my room, it looked as if a war had been waged in here. That, or Ingvar threw a temper tantrum. "It's fine," I said, stepping over the piles of clothes strewn about. All I wanted was a few books and some decent outfits.

Baldr leaned against the doorframe. "After you've gathered your things, we'll need to take your sirens shopping."

"Shopping?" I asked, laying a shirt over my arm.

"For formal attire. I doubt they had clothing appropriate for a ball on the road."

"They're coming to the ball?"

Baldr laughed. "Of course they are," he said, enjoying my discomfort. "They saved you, and the ball is to celebrate your return—and their heroism. The more we praise them publicly, the harder it'll be for Father to reverse the land grant."

"But everyone will—"

He cut me off with a wave of his hand. "Know that they're sirens? Not yet. I've already got this covered, Njall. Every invitation that went out this morning explained that the ball is a masquerade, and the theme is the sea. So the ball will be full of sirens, mermaids, selkies ... all of it."

I stared at him in disbelief. "How?"

He shrugged. "You said it yourself. All I do is drink, gamble, and throw parties. Now come on—we need to get our new friends dressed for the occasion."

Chapter 49

Elva

Baldr had brought some, but not all of our gold with him when he'd arrived to fetch his brother. Sindri questioned him about it, but Baldr swore he was keeping it safe until we were in better accommodations. At this, Njall told his brother to stop being an ass. Baldr was furious at that comment because, apparently to a half-goat, the idea of being a donkey, was vulgar. I tucked that information away for another time.

With Njall and Baldr gone from the castle, I looped my arm through Leifur and strolled with my brothers through the market. Dressed in the nicer clothes Njall had in his room, and with my hair wrapped up in a silk scarf, we blended in without too much trouble. As expected, Leifur's blue hair drew a few quizzical looks, but people left him alone, since he wasn't a threat to any men. With a bag of the warm honey cheese buns we'd discovered on our first day here, we wandered in and out of various stores, finding some new clothes and replacement supplies for all we'd lost while traveling. I even allowed myself to look at some linens —though a not-so-small part of me worried I would curse myself later if Baldr and Njall couldn't get the king to allow us to stay.

Sindri demanded Leifur look at some shirts, so I wandered into a beautiful dress shop. I had worn dresses when I was younger; a properly fitted dress could be as much of a weapon for a siren as a blade. But after I was raped, I switched to pants and haven't worn a gown since. Still, in this shop, in a kingdom with a man who made me feel safe, I wondered if maybe it was time to let myself wear one again.

The shopkeeper kept a close eye on me but didn't stop me from perusing the dresses. I spotted one near the back that took my breath away. The skirt was a soft turquoise silk that flowed almost like a waterfall, paired with a bust adorned in small flowers carved from mother-of-pearl shells. I stood in awe of the gown for a long while before the shopkeeper appeared beside me.

"It would suit your eyes," she said. "You should try it on."

"I couldn't," I said, moving my hands awkwardly to my chest.

"You should." Njall's voice made me turn, and I couldn't help but smile. "She's right. It would make you sparkle." He took the gown off the stand and handed it to the shopkeeper. "Go on. She'll help you, and I'll wait."

A warmth spread through my chest. It wasn't the hot arousal or annoyance I was used to when men tried to woo me with material things, but something softer. Njall's smile made me feel as if he was excited to see me in it. I let the woman lead me to the back and help me into the gown. It was so lightweight it felt as if I was wearing nothing. The silk caressed my skin the same way Njall would when we'd lie together after making love. My heart stopped when I realized I no longer considered it just bedding him, but so much more. Terror gripped me at the thought that he might not feel the same. For all I knew, he bought a dress for every woman he bedded.

"You look gorgeous," Njall said as I forced my feet to leave the changing area.

I tried to smile, but fear and doubt had wormed their way into my gut, and I couldn't focus on the beautiful dress anymore.

"We'll take it," Njall said, nodding to the woman.

"Shall I send the gown and bill to the castle?"

"Send the bill to me, and we'll take the gown."

"Njall, it's fine. I don't need it." My nerves were beginning to get the better of me, but he stepped forward, cupped my cheek, and kissed me. His touch soothed all my nerves in an instant.

"But you need it," he said softly. "Baldr has arranged for a ball tonight to welcome me home and celebrate your triumph. Fighting leathers won't do."

I smoothed down the skirt and gazed up at him. "Well, in that case, you should probably let my brothers know too."

"Baldr's handling that."

We spent the afternoon finding the right clothes for Sindri and Leifur, along with masks and hair accessories for me. I was nervous about leaving my hair its natural blue and green, but after Baldr explained the theme and we spotted over a dozen women carrying all manner of wigs and hair color, I decided it should be fine. Njall tried to buy me jewelry to go with the dress, but I refused. While I believed I could manage the dress and the beautiful lace and pearl-beaded mask he bought, I wasn't comfortable wearing jewelry. Truthfully, I didn't trust myself not to pocket it at some point in the evening. Even Sindri was unable to sway my decision.

After we finished finding everything and were preparing to head back to the inn, a guard stopped us. "Your presence is demanded at the castle, Your Highnesses."

"What for?" Njall asked, moving ever so slightly between me and the guard. Both my brothers noticed and sent questioning looks my way.

The guard shook his head. "You've been summoned by the king. I am not privy to his reasons."

Clenching his jaw, Njall turned to me and grabbed my hand. "I'll see you at the ball tonight." He bowed down and kissed the top of my hand, forcing me to hold in a snort. Then he turned and handed my dress to my brother. "Guard this with your life." Sindri accepted the gown wrapped in a linen sack that was still prettier than most of my normal clothes.

Baldr pulled three pieces of paper out of his vest and handed them to Leifur. "Your invitations. Show them at the door, and you'll be allowed in."

"Thank you," I said as the guard led the princes down the road and toward the castle.

"What do you think that's about?" Leifur asked after they were out of earshot.

"Nothing good," Sindri replied, grabbing an invitation from his husband. "There'll be food and live music. This is going to be fun."

"We should get to the inn," Leifur said. "Someone is going to need a very long time to prepare, and no, I was not talking about you, Elva dear." I giggled as Sindri thrust his nose in the air and sauntered toward the inn.

Once we were inside, Killian brought us hot water and an assortment of fragrances and scented oils. It seems she missed nothing. Getting into my dress went smoother than I expected. Both my brothers were more than capable of doing up my corset for me and making sure everything was positioned where it should be. When I tried to add my thigh dagger, Sindri was appalled and insisted I leave it behind. Leifur agreed to bring his sword since we'd seen many men carrying them around the market.

The most complicated part of getting ready was figuring out what to do with my hair. In the end, Leifur fetched Killian and tipped her a gold coin to help us. She arrived carrying what looked like a piece of a spear. She warmed it in the fire, and when she wrapped my wavy hair around it, the locks fell off in elegant curls.

If she'd said it was sorcery, I would have believed her. But in the end, my usually wild hair had been turned into shiny, beautiful curls, each almost entirely one color. I would never admit it to my brothers, but I'd never felt more beautiful.

"A few important rules when you attend the ball tonight," Killian said as her magic wand cooled. "You must curtsy or bow to anyone of a higher rank, which for you all is everyone except the help. While you call them, Baldr and Njall here, in there, you must only call them Your Highness. Never turn your back on the king. It's considered disrespectful enough that he can have you arrested for it. The only exception is when you are dancing."

We listened intently. Many of the rules were things I'd learned as a siren about etiquette already, but there were a few customs unique to Tyndorf. Both Leifur and I committed them to memory. After thanking Killian, we headed off on foot and soon found ourselves in the well-off part of town, where groups of people were milling about, making small adjustments to their masks and clothes before heading into the castle.

Seeing the number of people with colored hair made me feel much better about leaving mine as it was. Several women had colored theirs similarly to mine, even though I didn't know how they'd managed it. While I was a little nervous about getting in, the guard barely looked at us and only examined our invitations. Finding them genuine, he waved us in. Already, the sounds and smells of the event filled the yard.

I locked arms with my brothers and we ascended the marble stairs, following the other elegantly dressed guests into a gigantic hall. While nowhere near as majestic as the Siren Queen's halls, the room was decorated with tapestries and ribbons that reminded me of the sea—coral, waves, and schools of fish. Swaths of green fabric hung from the ceiling like seaweed, and the centerpieces were vases decorated with shimmering mother-of-pearl mosaics. I made a mental note to ask Baldr where he found them so I could get one for our home. Once we found one.

A man in a tailored suit wearing a mask that reminded me of a sandy beach approached us with a tray of drinks. We accepted, and he moved on to the next group.

"I'm impressed how quickly Baldr brought this together," Leifur said.

"And the little details! He's outdone himself," Sindri added. I merely smiled and sipped my wine.

"Welcome to my party," Baldr boomed from a few groups over, weaving through the crowd toward us. "I'm thrilled you made it." He placed a hand on Sindri's and my shoulders before leaning in. "My brother is hiding over by the food—his shirt matches your dress. And I have some people I'd like you two gentlemen to meet."

"Oh?" I asked.

"A dear friend is looking for a talented blacksmith, and I told him I could put him in touch with the best. Shall we?" Baldr smiled, steering my brothers into the crowd. I turned to search for Njall, but found almost every man here was wearing a turquoise tunic. Spotting another servant, I drank my glass and handed it off before pushing my way through the crowd toward the food tables.

I reached the table laden with stuffed buns just as someone stepped behind me. Assuming it was Njall, I grabbed a bun and turned, ready to greet him with a kiss. Instead, I met a pair of predatory gold eyes.

"So, you're my brother's new whore," Ingvar sneered. "I could smell him on you from across the room."

I pulled my lips back just enough to show off my elongated fangs and growled at the crown prince. "Nice mask," I taunted, nodding at the gray wolf covering his face. "Scared someone might forget what a monster you are?"

"Says the actual monster," he retorted, stepping closer. "You might fool the humans here, but I smell the sea on you, *siren*. Don't think you'll be getting anything from my idiot brothers, because my father and I will make sure—"

"What?" Njall interrupted, appearing beside us. "That no one will forget she's different ... like us? That she has gifts others don't? Who does that remind you of, wolf boy?"

He wore a mother-of-pearl mask that matched mine.

"Catch your tongue," Ingvar growled, glaring at us both. "You might be stupid enough to let a siren lure you to her bed, but I'm not."

"What makes you so sure I lured him?" I shot back as Njall slid his arms around my waist, pulling me away from his brother. "I was sent to rescue him in exchange for gold, nothing more. And if I need a man, I'm more than capable of attracting one."

Njall chuckled behind me, before leaning in to whisper, "Don't antagonize my brother. He has a temper and the power to make your life here miserable."

"What was that?" Ingvar snapped, narrowing his eyes at Njall.

"Just telling my siren to behave herself," Njall replied smoothly.

The way he said *my siren* sent a wave of heat through me.

"You should keep it on a leash," Ingvar snarled before pushing past me to grab a bun and stalking off.

"That could be fun," Njall whispered in my ear.

"Only if you wear it." I tugged him close by the front of his tunic, pressing a fierce kiss to his lips. "Aren't you supposed to ask me to dance? Isn't that what humans do at these things?"

"We could dance," he said, adjusting his shirt with a smirk. "Or I could take you somewhere more private."

"I'll take option two."

Chapter 50

Njall

I took Elva's hand and guided her away from the ballroom's noise and chaos. I'd already made my grand entrance with Baldr and Ingvar, and no one would care if I stayed. Right now, all I want is to spend every moment alone with Elva.

We'd known our father would be furious about Baldr manipulating him, but we didn't anticipate the extent of his retribution. Elva had to know, but I didn't know how to tell her.

Our fingers intertwined as we crept down the deserted halls leading to the wing I shared with my brothers. The servants were all occupied with the festivities, leaving the corridors eerily quiet, and even some of the torches hadn't been lit. It reminded me of sneaking out of the Huester castle with Elva. Maybe she was feeling the same.

Pausing, I cupped her cheeks and kissed her deeply. She responded eagerly, her arms wrapping around my neck, pulling me closer. Her body was warm as she pushed herself against me, trying to connect us in every way possible. When she pulled back, she gave me a little smirk and winked before she began untying my pants.

"What are you doing, little siren?" I asked, glancing up and down the hall to ensure we were alone.

"Having fun," Elva replied, her voice low as she freed my erection. The heat of her hand on my shaft sent a shiver through me, and I pressed my fist against the wall behind her for support. Her eyes never left mine as she teased me with her lips.

Her mouth enveloped me, and my moan echoed through the stone halls. My hand instinctively tangled in her hair, guiding her rhythm. With no encouragement, she rammed her mouth on my cock, taking more of it than any woman I'd ever been with. A gagging sound left her, and I held her hair tighter, letting her choke herself on my dick. Her tongue ran along the shaft as my tip hit the back of her throat hard enough that I worried I might cum and embarrass myself. As if sensing my concern, she pulled her mouth back enough to get a breath in, and I wrenched her head back so she had to turn her face toward me.

"Easy, Pearl," I whispered. The wicked creature merely smiled.

I tugged gently at her hair, forcing her off her knees. I released her long enough to lift her dress and grip her by the ass. "*Ferflucs,*" I growled when I found she'd worn nothing underneath. Grabbing her thighs firmly enough that I knew she'd have marks in the morning, I hoisted her up against the wall and teased her entrance with the tip of my cock. She wriggled in my grasp, but I held her firm.

"Tell me what you want, my little pearl," I whispered, nipping at her ear. She whimpered, and I nudged her entrance again. "Say it."

She turned her face to mine and locked eyes with me. "I want you to take me right here, in your hallway, so everyone can hear."

I kissed her mouth and thrust my cock into her hot, weeping cunt, making her cry out. "Don't worry," I groaned. "I'll make sure everyone knows who you belong to."

I pulled out just enough to slam back into her. Elva was as wet as I'd ever found her, and she cried out with each brutal thrust. I had no intention of being gentle with her. She hated when I was gentle. The rougher I took her, the louder she screamed, the more she begged for it.

Pain seared across my back as Elva's fingers turned to claws, scratching me as she came. "Gentle, Pearl," I whispered. "Your siren is trying to play." She whimpered, but focused long enough to retract her claws, and I kissed her to muffle her screams. Her body clamped around me like a vice, like it was trying to pull my dick off with the intensity of her orgasm.

Ready to move her to my room, I glanced up and spotted Ingvar further down the hall. He was leaning against the wall, staring at Elva with an expression that made my blood boil.

Since we were children, he'd made it his life's mission to take everything from me I cared about. The only thing he'd never been able to take was my mother's necklace, likely because I never took it off. And now, he'd never be able to take Elva, either. Unlike all the maidens who swooned and dropped me when the *crown* prince showed interest in them, Elva didn't care for titles or rank. I pulled her closer to me and snarled at my brother as I spun her toward my suite.

"I'm very sorry about your dress, Elva," I said as I closed the door behind us. "I promise to buy you another one."

"What's wrong with my dress?" she asked, smiling up at me from my arms.

"I'm about to rip it off your body." I tossed her onto my bed and pulled off my tunic, quickly inspecting the scratches across my back. Grabbing her ankle, I pulled her down the bed toward me. As promised, I grasped the bust of her dress and tore it down the middle, leaving her naked before me.

Before she could utter a word, I pulled her ass to the edge of the bed and buried my face between her legs. Elva moaned and fisted the blankets as I ran my tongue along her wet folds and nipped at her clit. It baffled me that any man would bring this gorgeous woman to his bed and not want to make her scream his name to the world. I sucked and nipped at her until her legs quivered and her moans became incoherent babbling. A large wet spot was quickly forming on the edge of my bed.

Kicking off my pants, I climbed above her and flipped her onto her belly. I kissed her from her ass up along her back to her neck. My cock nudged her ass cheek, and she immediately got to her knees, pushing herself back toward me. Sliding an arm around her chest, I pulled her up so her back pressed to my chest and lowered her onto my cock.

A moan left her as her hands grabbed my arm for support. She rocked back on my cock, pushing me closer to the edge. Gently, I kissed her neck and collarbone until a feral possessiveness came over me as I got closer to finishing. I bit her just above the collarbone. Elva cried out, and a strange warmth spread across my face, as her pussy again locked my cock inside her.

As her body convulsed around my dick, I stopped biting her and realized what the strange heat was. Little bioluminescent spots had appeared on her skin, glowing faintly from her temple down her neck, arms, and sides, all the way to her ankles. They were like the ones my mother had, though hers were always visible.

"You're glowing," I said, wrapping another arm around her to support her weight as I sat back on the bed. "Maybe I should call you my little selkie now."

Elva held out her arm, admiring the light with a soft chuckle. "I haven't done this since I was sixteen."

"Do you know what it is?"

"No," Elva said, her body finally releasing me as she gently pulled away. "No one else ever glowed. Not even Sindri."

I was exhausted and felt as if my balls had been sucked dry, but pressed a soft kiss to her shoulder, trying to touch as many of the glowing marks as possible. "It's your selkie side. Female selkies glow."

She turned her head and smirked at me. "Did you read that in one of your books?"

"No, my mother told me."

Her eyes widened in surprise, and she sat up, turning to face me as if seeing me again for the first time. "Was your mother a selkie?"

I nodded.

"So you're ... you're a selkie?"

"Half, anyway."

"But your hair isn't green," she said, puzzled.

I chuckled and took her hands in mine, bringing them to my lips for a soft kiss. "No. I take after my father, except for the eyes ... and the ability to breathe underwater. That's why I avoid swimming. It's hard to pretend when you don't know how long people can stay under."

"But why lie?"

I sighed deeply. "My father ordered me to. Only a few people know what my mother was. I inherited too much of him, and not enough of her. He deemed me weak ... unworthy."

"Njall," Elva whispered, her hand moving to my cheek. She caressed it gently before pulling me close for a tender kiss. "Tell me about her."

Chapter 51

Elva

Njall and Baldr stayed on the road, talking, while I followed Sindri and Leifur toward the old hunting cabin that rested on the lands Baldr had secured for us. It wasn't part of the kingdom, so we wouldn't be under the king's watchful eye all the time, yet it was close enough to the city, forest, and sea to offer comfort and the means to earn a living. The excitement on my brothers' faces was worth every moment we struggled to get here.

We walked along the overgrown path that ran alongside the rickety cottage. We'd need a lot of wood to fix it up, but we had the gold Baldr had paid us and all the time in the world to make it perfect. Sindri inspected the weed-infested garden, while Leifur kicked at the crumbling fence, causing a log to tumble loose.

"Careful," Baldr said. "No need to hurt yourself."

Sindri snickered. "My husband is a blacksmith. A little fence won't hurt him."

"A blacksmith?" Baldr said teasingly. Though he knew Leifur's trade well—having introduced him to nobles at the ball—

Leifur's cheeks flushed slightly, clearly enjoying the satyr's attention.

"Did you see the small building south of here?" Baldr asked, pointing. "It was once a workshop. I bet you could expand the fireplace and turn it into a proper forge."

"Where?" Leifur asked, turning to find it.

"I'll show you," Baldr offered. "I used to hide from Ingvar in there when we played as boys. The burned wood threw off his sense of smell." He led my brothers away, leaving me alone with Njall.

I was bent over the garden pulling out weeds and examining some peculiar-looking plants.

"Find anything interesting?" he asked, appearing behind me, pushing my hair aside and brushing a kiss on my neck.

"I did," I replied and held up a strange plant with a green stem and a thick blue root. He sniffed it and recoiled, dropping it quickly.

"Not a carrot," he said, holding back a gag from the putrid stench.

I stood, wiping my dirt-covered hands on my pants. The sun behind us made his green eyes sparkle like emeralds, and my heart skipped a beat. Every time I looked at him, I saw more selkie.

"I don't know what you did to get us this land, but I can never repay you." I stood on my tiptoes, offering a kiss. It wasn't needy like the ones I would give when our bodies were entangled, but it was soft and loving.

He stepped back, looking nervous.

Glancing back at the setting sun and our new home, I knew I had to be brave. "Njall ... I have something I need to tell you."

"Elva ..." He moved back, rubbing his neck. I could see a bead of sweat forming on his brow.

"What is it?" I asked.

"I have to go," he blurted.

My cheeks warmed. *He must know what I was going to say.* "Why? Did I say something?"

"No. I just mean. Gah." He threw up his arms in frustration. "Baldr and I are being sent to the front lines."

"Military service? I thought you did that already."

"Not according to our father."

"Was that the price?" I asked softly, as my fingers tried to tie themselves into knots. "The price for letting us go that day, and for forcing his hand with the land?"

Njall simply nodded.

"How long?"

"Two years."

I looked down at the ground and sighed. I didn't want to hurt him or make this harder for him than it already was. After weeks of wrestling with my feelings, I'd finally admitted to myself that this wasn't just about physical desire. I didn't just want him; I loved him, but now I'd have to wait to tell him. It wouldn't be fair to confess that and then send him away, knowing I'd have to bed other men while he was gone.

"Don't blame yourself," he said, taking my hands and pulling me closer. "We chose to free you, and I have never been more sure of a decision in all my life. And as for the land? He's not mad about the land, he's mad that Baldr embarrassed him in front of the Lords to get it."

"When do you leave?"

"Tomorrow."

His face looked pained, and as badly as I wanted to cry and scream about how unfair it was, I knew that would only add to his burden. "That soon?"

"He doesn't want me to get too comfortable," Njall said bitterly. "Months rotting in an enemy dungeon followed by months of traveling home wasn't enough."

"I'm sorry, Njall. I know that isn't the homecoming you hoped for."

"True, but my father is who he is, and I shall obey."

I stepped closer, tracing my fingers along my biceps. "Will I get to see you at all before you leave?"

"Of course," he said, a determined glint in his eye. "I intend to leave you with a night you'll never forget."

Chapter 52

Njall

Elva had been sound asleep when I'd left the inn to meet up with Baldr and board the warship bound for Angin-fill. The mission was to retrieve my sister and continue the war my father had declared after their attack on our kingdom. Neither Baldr nor I had served on any of Father's military vessels before—only the cavalry. He'd decided that if we were to be of any use to Ingvar when he took the throne, we needed to broaden our experience. So we gathered our supplies from the castle servants and set sail. The only good thing about this journey was the sea air, which reminded me of Elva.

Aboard the ship, Baldr and I were assigned to sleep with the lower-ranked crew in the cramped quarters below deck. We claimed our hammocks, stowed our meager belongings in the provided crates, and stripped off our shirts to keep them clean while we began our duties.

"Where's your mother's pendant?" Baldr asked as we reached the deck. The sun was coming up on the horizon, giving us enough light to start our task of climbing up the riggings to check the sails for damage.

"I left it behind," I replied, testing a rope before placing my foot on it to climb the mast.

"In your entire life, I've never seen you without it."

"I left it in the bed with Elva."

Baldr shook the rope, forcing me to clamp onto it and shout curses down at him. "Did you tell her?"

"I told her what my mother was. She knows."

"No, *ferflucs!* I mean, about the pendant. What it means."

"Of course not! I gave it to her, but I couldn't tell her it gives her power over me. Not until we come back."

"Idiot," he shot back and shook the rope again.

"Explain how killing me will do any good!"

Baldr finally stilled the rope and began climbing up after me. "Why didn't you tell her how you feel? Are you that afraid she might love you back?"

"No," I snapped. "I wouldn't have been fair to her."

"Explain, or I'll shove you into the sea!"

"We'll be gone two years, and her cycle lasts twenty-eight days."

Baldr's irritation faltered, replaced by understanding. "I forgot about the cycle."

"Two years would be twenty-six cycles. How could I tell her? What if it made her feel guilty for handling things? Or worse— what if she felt the same about me, and I had to live with knowing she'd be with other men while I was gone?"

"Isn't it worse not knowing?"

I shook my head, focusing on the rigging. "No, because she has no idea how I feel. She can live her life however she chooses. When I come back, if I feel the same, I'll tell her then."

"So you gave up two years of each of our lives—"

"You did it to yourself. I never forced you to help me free her, or pay her to get me back."

Baldr shoved my shoulder hard enough to nearly unbalance

me. "I wouldn't let you rot in the Huestur dungeon! Do you know how boring my life would be without you?"

"I'm glad I amuse you."

"Oh, you won't be," Baldr's voice carried a warning as he climbed higher to inspect the topsail. "For the next two years, I intend to remind you that you gave up years of your life for a siren you love but couldn't bother to tell her."

I groaned under my breath and watched him disappear into the rigging. It was going to be a long two years.

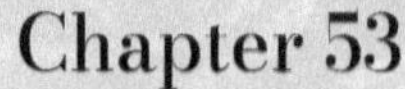

Chapter 53

Elva

I nuzzled into the pillow beneath me, inhaled deeply before I rolled over to look for Njall, but his side of the bed was cold. I pushed myself up and looked around, but the entire room was empty with only the fireplace to illuminate the place. Sitting up, I dropped my hand beside me and hit something hard. Lifting the blanket, I found a folded piece of paper and a box. Tossing the blanket aside, I slipped out of the bed and grabbed a shirt off the floor to keep myself warm before I made my way across the room to the fire. I tossed a log into it, sending the fire crackling before it grew larger and lit up the space better for me. Once the space was lit enough for me to see everything, I checked for any sign that Njall had just gone to grab something from Killian, but his satchel and boots were gone.

I sat back on the bed and grabbed the box and paper. Flipping open the paper, I held it toward the fire so I could read it.

Elva,

I'm sorry I had to leave you without saying goodbye, but I knew if I had to face you to do it, it would have made it impossible for me to leave.

Since I can't be with you to help you integrate into Tyndorf, I'm leaving you my most cherished possession to remember me by. Protect it for me while I'm away, and when I get back, I'll tell you why it's so valuable to me.

Until I return, take care of yourself and your brothers, always remember how precious you are to me, my little Pearl.

Njall

I read the note over three times before dropping it and picking up the box. Carefully, I lifted the lid and found Njall's pendant nestled inside. Pulling it out by the chain, it almost looked as if it glowed when I held it up to the fire. Exhaling sharply, I placed the rope around my neck and let the beach glass slide down my collarbone, finding a home between my breasts. Glancing around the room one more time, I grabbed the letter, Njall's pillow, and left the room to find my brothers'.

I adjusted my shirt and left the guard to compose himself in the alley behind the Pirate's Booty. Since the princes left two weeks ago, my brothers and I have moved into the cabin on our new piece of land. I had a room on the main floor at the back of the house, while my brothers took the larger bedroom upstairs. We even had a guest bedroom, though it wasn't much use, since we had no living relatives, no friends to speak of, but my brothers were thrilled to have all the space.

Leifur wasted no time setting up his workshop, and once it was ready, he began crafting everything we needed to fix up the house. Sindri focused his time on the inside of the house, making it *livable,* as he called it. He even furnished my bedroom for me, adding curtains, fresh bedding, a sturdy chair, and one of those mosaic vases Baldr had found for the ball. I appreciated his efforts, but it felt unnecessary. My days were spent outside, tending to our expanding garden and planting seeds for the future harvest. My nights, however, belonged to the Pirate's Booty, finding someone to fill the hole that had wormed its way into my heart that I refused to acknowledge.

Tonight, that hollow feeling returned faster than I wanted. Usually, I could manage an hour or two of relief after sending a man away, but this time it lasted all of two minutes—about as long as the guard had lasted. I traced the scabbed bite mark on my neck before I pulled the beach glass pendant Njall had left me out of my shirt and held it up to the lantern light. The way the light danced through it, scattering little rays around me, reminded me of Njall's smile.

I should have told him before he left. But it wasn't fair. How would I tell him I was falling in love with him, only for him to leave for years and know I had to be with other men while he was gone? Maybe he would have asked me to go with him. Would I have?

Tucking the glass back into my shirt, I decided to head home for the night rather than stay at the inn. I turned up the street and headed toward the city gate that would take me home. I'd made it halfway there when I heard footsteps behind me. Slipping my dagger from its sheath on my hip, I spun around, only to have Prince Ingvar grab my wrist and slam it into a wall, forcing me to drop the blade.

"Elva," he said. "We've been looking for you, dear."

I glared at the crown prince and his manservant, taking in their smug expressions before jerking my arm free. "I am not interested in anything you have to say."

"But we have a proposition for you," the manservant said in a deep but nasally voice.

Stooping to retrieve my dagger, I turned around to face them. "I want nothing from you."

"Good," Ingvar said. "Because I want something from you."

"And why would I give you anything?" I laughed incredulously.

"Because if you don't agree to give me a siren-werewolf heir," Ingvar growled, "my brothers will return from the front in coffins."

Blood of the Selkie coming April 2026

I know finishing the book on that cliffhanger was a bit mean (sorry not sorry), but rest assured I am hard at work on book 2, *Blood of the Selkie* and it will be released April 2026.

You can pre-order the ebook now on Amazon, or if you like to keep with bonus things, and spicy art, you can join my Patreon where I post the extra juicy bits.

Or if you simply NEED more of Torian, go read my debut fantasy romance series The Head, the Heart, and the Heir. The final book for this series will also release in mid-2026.

Blood of the Selkie Pre-order - https://a.co/d/aWo47Wp

Patreon - patreon.com/AliceHanov

The Head, the Heart, and the Heir - https://a.co/d/fMjaOM8

West Torian Species

Common coloring in various species. Depending on how pure they are these can vary.

Sirens - have blue hair and blue eyes

Selkies - have green hair and green eyes

Humans - have normal varied hair and eye color

Mermaids - have gray hair and varied eye color

Sorcerers - have normal varied hair and eye color

Satyrs - have brown, black, gray hair and varied eye color

Werewolves - have normal varied hair and eye color

Pronunciation Guide

Anginfill: An-gin-fill

Baldr: Balder

Elva: Ell-vah

Endilaus: End-i-laus

Huestur: Hue-ster

Hulda: Hull-duh

Ingvar: Ing-v-are

Konvern: Cawn-vern

Leifur: Lee-fur

Njall: Ne-gaul

Nordlic Sea: Nord-lick

Oreean Sea: Or-ian Sea

Sieden Sea: Sigh-den sea

Sigil: S-ij-ell

Sindri: Sin-dree

Torian: Tore-Ian

Tyndorf: Tin-door-f

Zverm: S-Ver-m

Acknowledgments

ALWAYS first. Thank you to my husband, Steve, and my children, Lillian, Katrina, and Zack. They believe in me, love my characters, and give up time with me to write my books.

To my mom, Elke, and stepdad, Al, thank you for supporting all my crazy dreams.

My amazing friend **Andrea** who is always there for me and gives me the best ideas and lets me ramble at her until I figure things out. I love you more than you know! And her cat is a lovely purrball.

To my amazeball friend **Brittany** you are AMAZING and I can't thank you enough for taking on my crazy.

To my amazing developmental editor **Killian** thank you for helping me figure out how to make this book shine, and pull out the story that it was meant to be!

Thank you to **Jasmine** my phenomenal line editor. You helped me know this story had worth and needed to be told. I'm so excited that you loved it as much as me. I can't wait to work on book 2 with you!

Thank you for your help catching all those missing commas and random words **Jahmayla**. It is so appreciated!

About the Author

Photo by Brittany Jean Photography

Alice Hanov was born in Germany and then raised on Pelee Island in the middle of one of the Great Lakes, spending her days imagining grand adventures in the woods around the island. She has never stopped writing and has a degree in rhetoric and professional writing from the University of Waterloo. Alice lives in Ontario with her hubby and three kids, various pets, and many, many books.

To learn more about her world and books you can visit her online at alicehanov.com.

www.ingramcontent.com/pod-product-compliance
Lightning Source LLC
Chambersburg PA
CBHW030751310726
48969CB00005B/1368